He's Amish...

He smiled at me triumphantly, making my heart melt into a puddle, and his thumb swirling in place on my hand sent goose bumps up my arm. Not trusting the feel of his hand over mine, I had to look down and see it with my eyes to make sure that I wasn't hallucinating the whole thing.

I couldn't deny the way Noah made my body feel, that was for sure, but my mind was still struggling with the whole Amish thing. Where on earth could this relationship go?

But then, I didn't care what the answer was. I just wanted to enjoy it while it lasted.

She's not...

In the back of my mind, I had hoped spending more time with Rose might dampen my interest in her. After all, it would be much easier if I fell for a pretty Amish girl. Only, it had the opposite effect on me. It would take all my strength to resist Rose now—if I even could.

I realized I couldn't say goodbye to her or make plans for a next meeting, with Jacob hovering around and Father marching toward us through the yard. But rebelliousness gripped my soul, and I stole a glance at Rose anyway. My heart raced when her eyes met mine.

In that instant, I knew she belonged with me.

But what is forbidden is not so easily forgotten.

temptation

Karen Ann Hopkins

HARLEQUIN®
entertain, enrich, inspire™

Recycling programs
for this product may
not exist in your area.

ISBN-13: 978-0-373-21054-1

TEMPTATION

This edition published by arrangement with Harlequin Books S.A.

For questions and comments about the quality of this book
please contact us at Customer_eCare@Harlequin.ca.

® and TM are trademarks of the publisher. Trademarks indicated with
® are registered in the United States Patent and Trademark Office,
the Canadian Trade Marks Office and in other countries.

www.HarlequinTEEN.com

Printed in U.S.A.

To my five amazing children;
Luke, Cole, Lily, Owen and Cora,
for walking beside me on this fantastic journey
and encouraging me to follow my dreams.

Also, to my mom, Marilyn, for believing in me from day one.

Rose ~ Preface

PRESSING MY HEAD TO HIS HEART, I LISTENED hard, straining to hear any gurgle or murmur of life. Hearing nothing, I felt the shock settle into my mind, slowing it down and then turning it off.

"Don't leave me, Noah. Please, don't go," I whispered into the darkness as the light spray of rain touched my face.

If only I could turn back time.

I would tell him yes.

1

Rose
Wide-Awake

HOLY CRAP. I WATCHED THE CHURNING WATER rush over the driveway and back into the swollen creek bed. I'd never seen anything like it before, and from the look of incredulity on Dad's face, neither had he.

Sam and Justin, on the other hand, were enjoying the bizarre scene, wading knee-deep into the current with their street clothes on, splashing each other like maniac dolphins. Actually, now that the storm had passed and the sun was peeking its way out from behind the fluffy clouds, it was beginning to feel like a sauna, and I was seriously thinking about joining my brothers.

"We shouldn't try to cross this with the truck yet. It's still pretty high," Dad said, almost to himself, his fingers playing with his mouth. He continued to survey the obstacle placed directly in the middle of the long, winding driveway leading to our new house.

New was definitely not the right word for the house. I guess "recently acquired historic relic" would be more appropriate for the three-story brick monstrosity on the other side of the raging creek that until a few days ago when we closed on the deal was no more than a lazy trickle.

My dad, who'd decided he wanted to raise his kids in the country, uprooting us from our comfortable suburban house in Cincinnati to move to middle-of-nowhere Ohio, was getting a good dose of country reality. I wondered if he was regretting it. Seeing the distressed look on his face right then, I think he was.

I sighed, wishing Mom were here with us. Then it would all be okay. But she was six feet under, buried in the cold, dark ground of Mount Hope Cemetery. If she were still alive, Dad would never have taken the stupid job as head of the E.R. in this forgotten place, and we wouldn't be standing here, trying to figure out a way to cross what looked like a small river to get to our house.

My life had been so blissfully ordinary before Mom had died. It was all gone now, just like the churning water rampaging over the driveway, disappearing into the abyss of overgrown grass and weeds on the other side. And there was nothing at all I could do about any of it, except watch it disappear—and maybe cry, which I'd been doing a lot of lately. Fortunately, I was getting used to that feeling of helplessness. I had no control over my life, and it seemed as if no one else did either. It was just an illusion, thinking that we could master our pathetic little worlds. The forces of nature, whether they were Mom's cancer or the flood rushing by my feet, were beyond my command, and they could steal all the happiness away in a heartbeat.

Up until now, I'd put on a pretty good poker face about everything, from this insane move to the boondocks, to Mom's five-month-long battle with the illness that changed and distorted her body before my very eyes. When the end came, there wasn't much left of her, except the brittle and weak shell of her former vibrant self.

It was strange how in that moment of tragedy, it had seemed so unreal, like an old-fashioned movie reel playing on a screen for my eyes only. The pain and broken heart were blocked off for a little while, leaving me numb with disbelief. *Shock* is what Dad called it. But after a while, the cruel reality started to seep into my tissues, and my body became a sponge, just sucking it all up until, finally, there was so much grief inside, I couldn't help feeling it.

That's how it happened for me. First, the numbness right after she died, next the agonizing pain and then the place I was at now—the land of perpetual depression. And to top it all off, I had to pee very badly. *How wonderful.* Staring at the rushing water wasn't helping the situation either. Crossing my legs over, I ground my teeth together in discomfort.

"I'm glad Jerry wasn't planning to bring your horse today. I just hope by tomorrow he can get the trailer through here," Dad said as he walked by me to the moving truck.

"You've got to be kidding—surely the water will be down by then?" I half questioned and half demanded of my father. About the only thing that made this stupid move bearable was that I was looking forward to having Lady, whom I'd boarded at the J & R Stables for the past two years, finally home with me. Even if home was in the flooded sticks. Geez, this is just unbelievable, I thought, watching Sam and Justin slapping the murky water back and forth at each other.

Dad appeared from the cab of the truck and held out a water bottle for me. I vigorously shook my head and said, "I need to go to the bathroom, Dad. I'm going to walk through the water and go to the house. Are you with me?"

"Yeah, here, let me hold your hand. Your brothers haven't been swept away, but they're bigger than you."

Dad grasped my hand and together we waded out into the

ice-cold water. It was pretty yucky, too, completely brown and thick with mud and debris. By midway across, it was past my knees, and the water was pushing on us. Not enough to drag us down or anything like that, but I still grasped Dad's hand tighter. Within a minute we dragged out of the water on the other side, soaking wet but one step closer to the bathroom. I hurriedly made my way up the driveway, leaving Dad behind.

I glanced back over my shoulder to see the barbarians, Sam and Justin, splash through the water like a pair of moose and hit the dry ground running. Of course, they passed by me with ease. How could they run in wet jeans like that? I gave it a quick try, and after two strides, and nearly falling on my face, decided to walk at a normal speed. I knew my limitations.

When I finally reached the rickety old front porch, I smiled smugly at the dorks who were both standing there without a way to open the door. Reaching into my pocket, I pulled out the key, dangling it in front of them. In an instant I was tackled to the ground by Sam, whom, being a year and half older than me and a football player, I was no match for. He jumped up, flicking his wrist with the keys inches above me. A smile of righteous triumph looked down at me from his face. A face that the arrogant jerk thought was good-looking, with his wide-set sky-blue eyes and Hollywood nose, topped off with a bushy head of unruly golden hair. At six foot two and well muscled, he was way too big for a seventeen-year-old. Sam never lacked for female attention.

It wasn't fair. Even my cute twelve-year-old brother, Justin, who could have been my masculine twin in coloring and facial features, was bigger than me now. I had no chance at all to win any physical matches with either of them anymore— just reinforcing my theory that the world sucked.

"Hurry up, Sam. I've got to go to the bathroom." I bounced

around in place while he fumbled with the key, finally getting the door unlocked. Instead of being able to just open the door like any normal house, it took all three of us to push the stubborn, solid piece of aged wood loose of its frame. When it finally swung open, scraping across the wooden-plank floor, I was through it in a flash, running to the back of the house where I remembered the only bathroom to be. I could just hear my dad complaining that he hadn't noticed a problem with the door before, when I turned in to the bathroom.

I felt much better when I stepped out into the foyer a few moments later. Until I saw Justin pulling the decades-old spinach-green wallpaper off the plaster as if he was unwrapping a Christmas present.

"What the heck are you doing?" I nearly shouted.

"Hey, look, it's just coming off. You hardly have to pull the stuff. Isn't it cool?" Justin said in an excited voice while he continued to strip a section of the wall off in spastic motions.

"Stop it, Justin! It looks even worse now," I yelled, grabbing his arm, which immediately turned into another wrestling match I would undoubtedly lose in the end.

"Quit it, both of you—now!" Dad appeared out of nowhere, attempting to push his body between us. I was more than willing to stop, but the little jerk had a clump of my long hair in his fist, and until he let go, I wasn't going to release his ear.

"I mean it…really, you're behaving like little brats." Dad had reached his boiling point. I could tell by the way he said *brats,* as if he was describing two small children who'd just knocked over his favorite vase.

Just as I was getting ready to free Justin's ear, I heard a loud clearing of a throat from the screen door. We all stopped moving, and simultaneously Justin and I both let go. The three of us turned to the doorway to see an Amish man, with a long, funky chestnut beard, standing there with a look of what could only be called wide-eyed bewilderment. He was wearing a dark blue button-up shirt with the sleeves rolled to the beginning of his well-defined muscles. The black suspenders were odd, as were the old-fashioned-looking pants he was wearing. Something about the man commanded attention, though, and I straightened up further as his eyes passed over me quickly.

"I am your neighbor, Amos Miller. I thought I would come by with my sons to offer you assistance getting settled in…if you need it." He said it in a relaxed and placid way, directing all his attention to my father, who briskly crossed the floor and opened the door for the visitors.

"Oh, how nice of you, Amos. Ah…I'm David Cameron and this is my daughter, Rose, and one of my sons, Justin." Dad stopped to look around and then went on, "My other son is Sam, and he's here somewhere. I'm not sure where at the moment."

Poor Dad—how embarrassing to be caught breaking up a fight between his kids the first time he meets his new neighbors, and Amish ones at that. Dad had already informed me that we would have interesting and eccentric neighbors here in Meadow View, but this was the first time I'd been so close to any Amish people. My heart started to drum faster when my eyes met and locked on the gaze of the boy standing a little behind and to the side of Amos.

Well, he wasn't a boy; more like a young man. Amazingly, he was as tall as Sam and as well built—probably the same age, too. His hair was wavy and dark, poised on his head like on one of those European statues of the men with hardly any clothes on. You know, a little on the wild side, but still looking totally perfect. A bit of bronze streaks gave the locks a brindle effect that shone in the soft spray of late-afternoon sunlight coming through the screen door. The hair matched his warm, almond-colored eyes perfectly.

And for the first moment in a very long time, the world didn't appear entirely in the muted, hazy color of doom. As a matter of fact, it seemed to have brightened considerably in the foyer when it sunk into my hardened brain that he was really cute—like Abercrombie & Fitch poster-guy cute—with his full, curving lips and sculpted nose and cheekbones.

I suddenly became conscious of the fact that I was standing in front of him soaking wet, muddy, with my hair in wild disarray. I could even feel a large portion of the strands sticking out from my head where Justin had pulled them. Figures, I finally meet a guy who makes my heart skip a beat, and I look like the Bride of Frankenstein.

He was appraising me from head to toe with interest in his eyes, subtle, but interested. I wasn't surprised by his examination of me. I was used to guys checking me out. I discovered three years ago, when I turned thirteen and started to develop little bumps on my chest, that the opposite sex found me attractive. I had been blessed with a slender, athletic body and curves in all the right places. I'd let my thick, acorn-brown hair grow long enough to reach the top of my butt, which guys seemed to appreciate. And on more than one occasion, some member of the male species would tell me how pretty my light blue eyes were. I found it all pretty embarrassing, especially since every time I looked in a mirror, I still saw the same skinny girl with a mouthful of braces that I used to be.

The thing I wasn't used to, though, was the way this Amish guy looking at me was affecting *my* body. As if it had just come out of a deep hibernation—all the fluttering and tingling vibrations that were now popping up in the center of my belly were spreading out, letting me know that I really was alive, after all the troubles of the past year.

Hmm...maybe this place wouldn't be so bad after all.

"It's a pleasure to meet you, David." Amos extended his hand and Dad grasped it in a friendly way, which was usual for my dad. "These are my sons Jacob and Noah." He nodded in turn toward the two young men with him. I hadn't even noticed the other one, probably because he stood directly behind his father with his eyes lowered, not looking at me at all. Almost rudely, I thought at first, but then it occurred to me that maybe his brother Noah was the rude one. He was still staring at me as if he'd never seen a girl before, only now a slight smirk touched his mouth. I liked his eyes, but I didn't like the tilt of his lips, and I averted my gaze from his as Sam came bounding into the foyer covered in cobwebs.

"You should see how creepy the cellar is! There were actually some animal bones..." His voice trailing off, he was clearly surprised to see the Amish guys standing there.

"Well, we've found Sam. Sam, these are our new neighbors." Dad motioned over at the guests with an impatient sweep of his hand, and Sam went forward automatically to shake their hands like a well-trained doctor's son.

"It's nice to meet you," Sam said in the courteous voice he didn't use much and definitely *never* used with me.

"What kind of bones do you think they are?" Noah asked curiously. For the moment, he'd lost interest in me, sending a ripple of irritation through my body. But I had gotten to hear his voice, and it was deep and sexy.

"Don't know. Do you want to see 'em?"

Noah glanced at his father, who nodded once, and then he answered my brother. "Sure, let's go."

That's just great. Within two minutes, fun-loving, happy-go-lucky Sam had made a friend—a gorgeous friend whose eyes made my stomach do flips. And even though I was cold and uncomfortable in my wet clothes, I decided to follow the boys and see what the fuss was all about in the cellar. The opportunity to spend more time with my hot neighbor had nothing to do with the trip underground, I told myself as I hurried to catch up.

We started down the crumbling rock steps, and Sam hit the switch, lighting the only bulb I could see. It was one of those scary dangling bulbs that are in all the horror movies. A chill ran through me, and I didn't think it was just because of the wet clothes. It would be my luck that the house was haunted on top of everything else.

The last step was more like a two-foot drop, and Noah, who was right in front of me, stopped and looked back, offering his hand to help me down. Wow, this was a new experience for me, a guy actually being chivalrous. I spent way too much time with my Neanderthal brothers, I decided. Slipping my hand into his warm, strong grip, I made my way down the last step.

When I reached the floor, he held my hand captive for a few seconds longer than was necessary, sending major goose bumps along my arm. I glanced up at him, and when my eyes met his, he let go. As quickly as he had given his full attention to me, he shifted it back to Sam, following my brother deeper into the sooty darkness.

The cellar could have just as well been a New York sewer, as damp and murky as it was. I wrapped my arms around my chest, trying to warm myself in the nasty environment while I lightly stepped over the hard-packed dirt floor. The one little lightbulb only illuminated the area right below it, and the farther reaches of the room—and it was big—were inky black, except for a few shards of light slicing through the darkness from cracks in the rock foundation. I wasn't an expert, but the cracks were probably not a good thing. Another part of the house Dad must have missed.

The light, sticky touch of something on my neck and face made me shriek, and I grabbed at it, swatting it away with my fingers in a panicked motion. Realizing it was a giant spiderweb, I wondered where Charlotte was—probably crawling around in my hair. Frantically, I plucked the rest of it off me, shaking my head vigorously.

"You okay?" It was Noah and he crossed the few feet back to me. I was happy that he was focused on me again, but I felt pretty stupid reacting like that to a cobweb.

"Fine. I'm fine. It's just that I can hardly see anything down here and—ugh, spiderwebs are just nasty." I looked up at his shadowed, almost-obscured face. I felt the flutter in my stomach again.

"Come on, Rose, don't be such a—girl!" Sam admonished me, and for once I kind of had to agree with him.

There was a minute of silence while Sam searched the ground, using his cell phone's dim light before he kneeled down on the dirt floor and announced, "Here they are, in the corner."

Noah went to join Sam at the skeleton. With my hands out in front of me, trying to catch any more of the webs before they touched my face, I moved up behind them and peeked over their shoulders. As far as I could see, which wasn't much in the limited light, Sam had made a big deal out of nothing. It was just a small animal. But then I hoped there weren't any critters lurking around upstairs that I'd have to deal with in the middle of the night.

"Looks like an opossum to me," Noah said, picking the

skull up and holding it toward the lightbulb for a close in-spection. "It's pretty old, though. I don't think you have to worry about it."

"Ahhhhhhh!" came a nerve-shattering scream behind us, and I nearly jumped out of my wet skin. Even Noah and Sam bolted up, whirling around to see Justin doubled over, laugh-ing hard.

He was so full of himself, he could barely speak, but he managed to spit out, "That was too easy—you bunch of girls!"

As I breathed a sigh of relief, Sam, in a snakelike move-ment, grabbed Justin and put him into a choke hold in two seconds flat—nothing new there.

"You little shit—just wait till the next time you're alone," Sam threatened.

"Boy, you guys are really violent," Noah observed with humor in his voice.

My brothers and I must seem like the equivalent of a rerun of *Jersey Shore* to this gentle guy, I thought, wanting to step back into the darkness and hide from embarrassment.

"Hey, you all come up here." It was my dad, and follow-ing the sound of his call, I briskly walked toward the stairway, all too happy to get out of the dark and bony cellar and away from the ridiculous behavior of my brothers.

As I led the way, Noah was close behind me, and I was extremely aware of his proximity. It was as if my body's nerve endings were on fire or something. I was only slightly distracted from this feeling by the sound of Sam and Jus-tin scuffling behind us as we walked up into the outdated powder-blue kitchen.

Dad was standing there alone, fiddling with the faucet on the yellow-stained porcelain sink. Lifting his eyes, he said, "Mr. Miller was kind enough to invite us for dinner, kids.

I looked out the front window a minute ago. The water has receded some, but since it's getting late, we'll just grab a few things from the truck tonight and unload the rest in the morning."

"Sounds like a plan, Dad," Sam said, still holding Justin's neck in a vise grip, grinning broadly.

"Let go of him, Sam—and since you seem to have so much energy, why don't you wade back across the driveway and bring our suitcases to the house. Better yet, Justin, you go help him." His voice resembled a growl. Then, changing his tone back to "friendly doctor," he told Noah, "Your dad said for you to head back home right away to finish mowing."

I watched closely as Noah ever so slightly rolled his eyes and sighed. Suddenly, he seemed more like my brothers or any other teenage guy not wanting to do the yard chores. And that little bit of familiarity made me brave. "I guess cutting the grass is a lot of work for you?" I said, imagining Noah surrounded by tall green foliage and hacking away at it with an old-fashioned hand sickle.

Noah's eyes jumped back at me, startled, and I felt a twinge of worry that I shouldn't have spoken to him, but he regained his composure quickly and replied, "Actually, the large deck push mower I use is gas powered and makes the job fairly easy. It's just boring as all get-out, though." He said it to all of us, but his eyes lingered on me for a few long seconds, his mouth twitching slightly, as if he was holding back a smile.

I was shy again and muttered, "Oh," not knowing what else to say.

"I'll see you later," Noah said in a rush, before he turned and followed Sam and Justin out the door.

The second the door closed, I ran to the front window and watched as my brothers strolled leisurely toward the truck.

But I wasn't really paying attention to them at all. Instead, the image of my new neighbor played over and over in my head.

Nibbling on my pinkie nail, I couldn't help saying a silent prayer—God, please let the shower work.

2

Noah
Feelings

I MADE MY WAY LEISURELY ACROSS THE HAY field, images of the English girl playing over and over in my head. Never in my life had I seen a girl in such a messy state. Amish girls always had their hair neatly pulled up in buns, covered with caps. And their dresses were orderly, unless they were in the garden or helping with the barn chores. This girl actually had mud in her hair and dirt smudging her face. And if that wasn't incredible enough, she was soaking wet. I had to admit, the soaking-wet part was the most intriguing of all— the way her jeans clung to her legs. And even though the girl had been a complete disaster, she was still amazingly beautiful. Definitely the prettiest girl I'd ever encountered, with her big blue eyes, pouting lips and shapely body. I imagined that if her hair were clean and brushed, it would be soft and shiny, too.

I sure was surprised at the way she'd stared back at me. Those robin's-egg eyes looked boldly at me, inspecting me openly in front of Father and Jacob. I could only pray they hadn't noticed her doing it. That was another thing an Amish girl wouldn't be caught dead doing—staring at a boy in such an inviting manner.

Friends had told me that girls from the outside were very

forward, but up until that moment when I came face-to-face with that particular girl, I'd never experienced it personally. I hadn't been around many before. In fact, the only one I could think of was that silly girl, Summer, whose mom drove us to town sometimes. But she ignored me for the most part and certainly didn't count. And although she was attractive, she wasn't as pretty as my new neighbor.

Thinking that I had a beautiful girl living close by brought a smile to my lips. I would be seeing a lot of her, and my parents couldn't say much about it. After all, how could you avoid your neighbor?

Come to think about it, it was strange that Father had invited the English family over for dinner at all after the way they were behaving when we first walked up to the porch. Father had lifted an eyebrow in surprise at the yelling coming from inside the house before he took a deep breath, rubbed his beard down in a tight motion with one hand and rapped on the screen door with his other.

I was just as shocked as he was to see the fetching girl fighting with her brother like a wildcat. So physically, with no care about who might see or what anyone would think. Amish girls just didn't do things like that. And although I knew some with tempers, like my sister Rachel, I had never seen one so openly angry before. It was shocking and yet, also refreshing.

The English girl had a liveliness about her that was like the push of wind just before a summer storm arrived. And even though I hated the idea of it, I had to admit, at least to myself, that she had wakened something deep inside me. I shook the prickling sensation away, not enjoying the feeling at all.

When the house came into sight, I could see that even though the grass was soaked from the rain, Peter was already mowing the side yard. That left the front yard for me, and all because church was being held at our place on Sunday and the entire farm had to be in perfect condition for the occasion.

I glanced around in irritation, wondering what kind of mischief the little boys were getting into. One of them could have started on the yard, but as usual, they had run off when a job needed to be done.

I should talk to Mother about it but knew that I wouldn't. It wasn't that long ago that I, too, was sneaking off with my friends to listen to an old radio in the woods behind the house or to have a puff off a cigarette that one of the drivers had sold to us for an exaggeratedly high price. I remembered those days all too well and understood my brothers' need to occasionally escape farm duties and commit acts of rebellion. It was just a part of growing up.

I sighed before sprinting over the spongy grass to the equipment shed. I wanted to get the mowing over quickly so I'd have time to get myself cleaned up for the company. I knew that some of the girls had crushes on me—at least that's what my sisters said—but this particular female was in a totally different league. For the first time in my life, I wanted to make a good impression on a girl.

Then again, what was I thinking? Even if she did find me attractive, what good would it do? Father and Mother would never allow me to court an English girl, and I felt the heat spread from my face down my neck for even considering it. What kind of trouble was I inviting into my life by even allowing such thoughts into my head?

Ever since I turned eighteen back in April, Mother had been hounding me incessantly about every available Amish girl in the community. She had informed me which girls were from the best families, which ones were the most robust, and on and on. The talk had been annoying the tar out of me.

The funny thing was, up until the moment I'd laid eyes on the pretty outsider, I had begun to come to terms with my inevitable destiny. I would pick a girl, start the courting process and eventually settle down in marriage with her. And I was *almost* looking forward to the idea of courting. The thought of finally being allowed to be around a female other than my sisters was beginning to appeal to me. But, when I hung out with the guys, talking about the prospects, I just wasn't able to get excited about any of the girls the way my friends did. There were a couple of them I thought had sweet dispositions and attractive faces, but now they just paled in comparison to the lively English girl.

The main problem was that no one in the community had struck my fancy yet. They were all boring. And they acted so shy around me, never speaking up the way my new neighbor did in her kitchen. At first, her question, and in front of her father and brothers, had stopped my heart, but then I realized with a quick scan of my eyes that her family didn't take her forwardness as wrong behavior. If one of my sisters had spoken so directly to a boy in my father's presence, he would have immediately taken her aside and chastised her for openly flirting.

As I unscrewed the cap on the gas tank of the mower, my mind raced. Even though I tried to block the curiosity from spilling over, I started to wonder about the girl. How old was she? What did she like to do?

Did she have a boyfriend?

The last question made me pause, and suddenly I felt unreasonably jealous—a foreign emotion to me. Why should I be jealous when I only just met the girl, and she was English besides? I knew the English kids began courting really young. I reckoned she was probably around sixteen, which was just old enough to begin courting in the community. But for an English girl, she might already have had several boyfriends.

That was a troubling thought.

"What did you think of our new neighbors?" Jacob asked quietly enough but still busting into my thoughts as he managed to sneak up on me. He stopped for a moment, his bright brown eyes waiting, with the harness over his shoulder.

I shrugged, not wanting him to know about my infatuation with an outsider. "They seem like nice people."

"I noticed the way you looked at that girl. I admit she was pretty, but don't be developing any ideas, Noah. It'll only get you into a whole heap of trouble with Father and Mother—and the church," he said sternly.

"Why did Father even invite them over for dinner if the elders are so adamant about us not interacting with the English, especially the ones our age? It makes no sense," I retorted, irritated that my almost-twenty-year-old brother was already giving me a rough time about the girl, and I'd only just met her. Why did everything have to be so difficult?

"Mr. Cameron is a doctor and he's going to be working at the hospital in town. Father feels that he's an important English man to know. But, and let me stress this to you, little brother, that doesn't include his wild daughter." With that, Jacob headed for the barn.

"Where are you going?" I asked, cross that he would threaten me and then walk away like that. Maybe the English kids had the right of it. Perhaps I should just beat the tar out of him for being so condescending to me. I was confident I could whip him in a fair fight.

"I'm going to pick up Katie. She's coming for dinner, too." He answered without turning to me and then disappeared into the barn.

Pity quickly replaced anger. Katie was Jacob's betrothed. They were marrying in November, and ever since he began courting her, he had completely changed. He'd become one of *them*—the strict "follow the rules of our church's Ordnung and never have any fun" adults in the community. The transformation had happened almost overnight once Father and Mother had agreed to the courtship. Jacob began spending every Sunday evening at Katie's house, arriving home after midnight with a goofy smile on his face. It was astonishing what a little bit of kissing could do to a fellow's brain. It was like a disease or something, and once a man caught it, he was doomed to never have any fun again.

And although it seemed like a distant memory now, it was only a couple of years ago that Jacob had insisted, in secret, of course, that he'd leave the Amish and go English when he reached eighteen. Unlike me, he hadn't taken to the farmwork as readily, and with his sharp mind, he'd been all too interested in the many gadgets that the outsiders had in abundance.

I was never tempted by such things. They were just…*things,* and confusing at that. But Jacob had been different. From the time he was small, his mind had been overactive. Unable to fight his urges, he had filled his curiosity in many ways; by studying the engine in the driver's truck or playing with the computers and games that were on display at the local stores— all to our parents' chagrin.

Believing that he was a brother lost to me, I was surprised when he did a full turnaround after choosing to court Katie. Now everything had changed—Jacob was one of the most dedicated young Amish men in the community

The same fate would catch me someday, too. It was inevitable. I'd watched all the older boys go through the same process, and many of them had been so adamant about leaving the community and going English. 'Course, they never did. It was easy to talk about it—and maybe even yearn for it—but to actually do it was a whole 'nother story. Surviving in the outside world was not an easy thing, especially for someone who'd been raised Amish. But it seemed that all desires to go outside the community and experience the English lifestyle were extinguished when a pretty girl came along.

Unlike the others, there'd never been a time in my life when I wanted to leave my world. The ties I had with my family and the members of the church were very important to me. I loved working the farm and driving the horses—I wouldn't trade those things for any of the comforts and entertainment of the English people.

Their way was definitely not my way.

Hurrying, I pushed the heavy mower to the house and started it up. While I pushed it through the short grass, barely needing any cutting at all, I decided that I wasn't going to waste my time pining away over a girl that I could never have—and one who wasn't a part of the life that I had been born into.

But even though I tried to block her from my mind, focusing on everything else under the sun, I couldn't stop wondering about what it would be like to kiss such a girl. Those thoughts made the time spent mowing go quickly. With more energy than I'd felt in a while, I finished the yard in fifteen minutes and raced to the house to get ready.

Mother, Sarah and Rachel were flitting around the kitchen like busy hummingbirds when I came through the door in a rush. I couldn't help noticing in just a glance that Mother looked stressed, having to stretch the meal unexpectedly for the guests.

To my surprise, even my littlest brothers, Daniel and Isaac, each had a broom in hand and were sweeping the wooden floor. Mother must have been desperate, to hunt the rowdy boys down and ask them for help.

"I'm taking a shower, Mother," I said, hurrying through the kitchen. I had spoken to her in English, but as usual with the older Amish, she answered me in Pennsylvania Dutch.

"Noah, tell me what they were like. Father said little except that they were coming for dinner." She had actually stopped working on the pork chops to stare at me with intense curiosity. My sisters looked about the same, waiting for my answer.

"Well, there are three kids," I offered, wanting to just get out of the kitchen.

"Are there any girls?" Sarah asked with wide-eyed excitement.

"One—her name is Rose and she's about your age, and the older boy, Sam, is probably my age, and then there's a younger brother. I think his name is Justin." I answered her in a very matter-of-fact way, especially trying not to give anything away when I mentioned Rose's name. Women were pretty intuitive about stuff like that, and I worried that just a few words and they'd see right through me.

"Rose... That is a pretty name." I couldn't help agreeing with her. Not that I'd admit it out loud.

She drilled on with the interrogation, asking, "How were they dressed—are they modest people?"

Here we go. The image of the dirty, wet and aggressive kids rose up in my mind. I was at a loss for words, but I recovered quickly and lied. "They were very modest and nice English people, Mother. Now, I stink, and I need to take a shower before they arrive." I impatiently waited for her to excuse me.

"Do you believe they're Christians?" Mother asked with a sharper-than-usual voice.

What was I going to say to that one? Father had already witnessed the young ones fighting like riled-up roosters, and I was sure he'd be filling her in on the details when they were alone in their bed after dark. I'd be surprised if they even went to a church. "I don't know, Mother. We only talked for a few minutes. Please, can I go take a shower?"

"Yes, of course. I want you all looking your best. Mr. Cameron is a doctor after all."

Thank God, she turned back to the chops and forgot about me.

I didn't miss Sarah's scrutinizing look before I spun and leaped up the stairs two steps at a time. My sister could be a real pain in the butt. No doubt she'd be grilling me later.

When I stepped out of the shower, I pulled on one of my ironed blue shirts, leaving the top button undone and hoping Mother didn't notice. Normally, she wouldn't care if it was just the family for dinner, but having company would make a difference. As I was clipping on the black suspenders, I wondered if the English boys thought I looked stupid with them on. After all, suspenders were the one thing that I hadn't seen any English men wearing.

But what was more on my mind than my own appearance was what the English kids would show up looking like. I certainly hoped they cleaned themselves before they came over. I mean, surely they wouldn't arrive for dinner in the state they were in when I saw them earlier. That would be absolutely terrible. Mother would never allow me to hang around with them if they made a bad impression tonight.

And even though I'd already decided that I would do my best to erase any romantic thoughts about Rose, I had also promised myself that I wasn't going to miss the opportunity to get to know her better either.

There wasn't a mirror to check out how I looked, but I was confident I was presentable enough when I walked back down the stairs at a lazy pace. I was ready now; no need to hurry. The smells in the kitchen wafted through the house. My mouth watered slightly at the pleasant aroma of cooking meat and seasoned potatoes.

Mother and Sarah had changed into their church dresses and were in the process of pouring glasses of water when I entered the kitchen. Rachel was at the window, with a rag, vigorously wiping fingerprints off it. She, too, was wearing her navy blue Sunday best.

"Where's Father?" I asked, scanning the immaculate kitchen. I had to admit I was a tad proud of the way the house looked and figured the new neighbors would be impressed—especially Rose.

"He's on the front porch with Naomi. She finally woke from her nap."

Mother was still very busy, and this time, she didn't even glance in my direction when she answered.

I stepped out onto the porch, pulling the rocker closest to Father beneath me. He was dressed in his finest black jacket and pants, sipping lemonade from a large glass. Three-year-old Naomi was perched on one of his knees, munching on an apple. Seeing me sit down, she abandoned Father, coming over to climb up onto my lap. In Dutch, she asked me if the new neighbors were nice. Funny, how females became nosy at a very young age. I proceeded to tell her that they were very nice indeed.

It was a perfect June evening, with a cool breeze blowing, the air crisp and clean after the rainstorm. I relaxed, listening to the wind chimes softly clanging their song through the air, until Father's voice shattered the moment.

"Noah, there's a matter I want to discuss with you," Father said, staring straight ahead, without meeting my eyes.

I sighed, knowing what was coming—and dreading it.

"Since that old house was vacant for so long, we have become used to not having outsiders living so close by. I am sure it will take some adjusting to. Also, the English children will want to make friends—which creates a very difficult situation for us. Their father is a doctor and a man of importance in the outer society, so we don't want to offend him. But neither will I have my children spending much time with the English, being influenced and corrupted by them."

He drew a deep breath, clearly immensely bothered by the idea. "They are wild, undisciplined children, and the less time you spend around them the better. Our Ordnung does not allow Rumspringa for a reason, Noah. We decided a long time ago that discipline for the young people of our church is the right path to God. You are at a point in your life when you will be taking on a woman and starting a family soon, and you mustn't do anything to tarnish your reputation in the community—such things may be forgiven, but they are not easily forgotten. Don't forget what I'm saying, son." He aimed a steady look at me, narrowing his eyes.

He *had* noticed my attraction to Rose.

I glanced away from him and stared ahead, silently fuming. It wasn't fair that I should finally meet a girl that I found captivating, and she had to be English. And my father was already telling me to stay away from her.

Damn, he was right, though, and I already knew it in my heart.

But then, why did it pierce my insides like a knife wound?

"Well?" Father pressed. He wanted me to tell him that I would never disobey him on this, but I would be lying. There was a war raging within me about this girl, but my fighting spirit had been roused by Father's words. I wanted to see more of Rose and I was sure that I'd take every opportunity presented to do just that.

Before Father could badger me some more, Isaac ran around the side of the house, telling us the English had arrived. Luckily he spoke in our language and the neighbors wouldn't understand. I wasn't sure they would like being called *English*.

Father rose up and marched down the front steps, with me closely on his heels. As we rounded the corner of the house, the Cameron family was walking past the barn with Peter and Daniel escorting them. I could hear the clip-clop of shod hooves on the road and without looking knew that Jacob was returning with Katie.

My eyes immediately settled on Rose as she stepped along with a spring in her stride, close beside Sam. With relief, I noted that she wore dry jeans and a loose-fitting T-shirt that had a picture of a horse on it. Not only did she look about as modest as an English girl could, it appeared she liked horses, and that meant we had something in common. My heart skipped at the discovery.

And by the clothes that Rose had chosen, Mother couldn't say anything negative about her either. I had secretly hoped that she would wear something that wasn't too revealing—I wanted my family to approve of her, and that wouldn't have happened if Rose had worn tight, inappropriate clothing.

As they approached, she lifted her eyes shyly at me. Odd that she was now acting a bit demure, I thought. But I was too distracted to dwell on the change by the long, wavy hair that was gently swirling around her face from the breeze, loose and free. She cleaned up very nicely, and looking at her made a rolling heat develop in the pit of my stomach. Feeling the growing discomfort in my body, I averted my eyes from her. Surely anyone observing me would see it plainly on my face.

I was not at all happy with myself for the reaction that this outsider whom I barely knew stirred within me, but when her eyes met mine briefly and then darted away like a rabbit spotted by the dog in the yard, I knew that I was truly smitten. Even though Rose had the spirit of a bear, there was something soft and vulnerable about her. My soul was tugged toward the English girl as if it knew that she needed me.

The realization was settling over me like a warm blanket just as Mother came out the back door with Sarah and Rachel. They moved to stand beside Father while tiny Naomi walked up to the neighbors, staring at them as if they were on exhibit at a zoo. Silence hung uncomfortably in the air for a second, until Dr. Cameron spoke up first.

"Thank you so much for inviting us over for dinner. It's been a long, tiring day, and a home-cooked meal sounds wonderful." He said it in a friendly manner, and I waited as Father introduced the rest of our family. When Jacob pulled alongside with the buggy, he presented Katie, as well.

I risked a glance at Rose and noticed she was staring at the buggy, her eyes wide with interest. I bet she'd enjoy riding in a buggy. Just how I was going to arrange something like that, I didn't know. But I promised myself that I would take her for a drive eventually.

Up to that point, Rose hadn't said a thing, except "hello" to my mother and sisters, and I suddenly realized that the English family was probably as nervous about this encounter as we all were. I couldn't talk directly to her in front of my parents, but I was trying to think of something to say to Sam to break the tension, when Peter did it for me.

"Do you want to see our new puppies?" He directed the

question mostly at Justin, who quickly nodded his head. The two broke from the group, running toward the barn.

Interestingly enough, Rose touched Sam's arm and she turned to follow the boys, with Sam joining her. How odd that an hour ago in the cellar they were behaving as if they couldn't stand each other and now in unfamiliar territory they seemed close.

I hurried to catch up to them, worried about what Mother must be thinking, seeing a girl go off with the boys. If Rose had been Amish, she would have joined my sisters. The fact that she had just chosen the boys worried me.

That was the problem with English girls—they did what they wanted.

But then again, maybe that was one of the things that made Rose so intriguing…and dangerous to me.

3

Rose
A New World

AS WE CROSSED THE QUAINT LITTLE STONE-AND-white-fenced bridge, I worried about the way I was dressed. Lazy Sam had refused to go back and get my suitcase and instead had brought my duffel bag to the house, the only contents being the T-shirt and shorts I slept in, spare panties, flip-flops and an extra pair of jeans.

Dad was impatient to be on our way to the neighbors', and even though I was willing to trek back across the water myself, he wouldn't allow it. He had insisted I just go take a shower and put on whatever I had in the bag.

Men could be so brainless about stuff like that. I wanted to make a good impression. After all, we were going to have dinner at a place where the women all wore dresses, and here I was in my sleep shirt and faded jeans, wearing flip-flops. The day held a strange hazy quality that made me feel as if I were dreaming. The fact that I'd walked through a hay field to have dinner at our new neighbors' house certainly added to the surreal feeling for me.

In slight consolation, at least I had been able to take a shower and wash the mud out of my hair. The bathtub had been gross, with the remains of a lot of dried-up bugs in it, and I'd taken a few minutes to wash them all down the drain before I could even get started. But amazingly, the water pressure was strong and the temperature was almost scalding hot—just the way I liked it.

Taking a breath, I paused to watch a gray-furred rabbit zig-zag in front of us, finally disappearing into a clump of thick grass. I wished that I had as much energy as the little creature, admitting that I was a little winded from the trek across the thirty-acre field that separated our houses to reach the creek running behind the Millers' barns.

Following the creek toward the bridge, I watched as the water flowed swiftly over smooth stones that jutted out here and there. It all looked calm and quaint now, but I could see where the rushing water had overflowed, flattening the grass on both sides well up the banks from the storm.

Once across the bridge, I focused my attention on the farm around us. It was absolutely immaculate. Everything about it was orderly and tidy. The grass was mowed to perfection, and there were several large flower beds overflowing with brightly colored petunias, gardenias and begonias. Dainty butterflies danced above the blooms in hectic motion. The huge vegetable garden we passed contained every kind of plant imaginable, the rows straight and freshly tilled. Not a weed in sight either. To our left was a massive barn and beside it was a large three-sided equipment shed. Both buildings were covered in bright white siding, with black roofs and trim, matching the house.

Four-board white vinyl fencing surrounded the pasture and barnyard, and I shielded my eyes from the lowering sun to search out the horses in the lush field. I quickly counted nine: a couple of huge Belgians, four buggy-type horses and three cute pinto ponies. My senses were on overload, trying to take everything in, when three little boys ran out of the barn toward us.

I gauged the age of the oldest boy to be eleven or twelve and the two smaller ones six and eight. They were so adorable in their light blue short-sleeved dress shirts and black suspenders. All three had thick, dark brown hair laced with golden highlights, just like Noah's. I was guessing they were his little brothers.

Funny, how when I'd met Noah earlier, I didn't even notice what he was wearing. I guess I was too focused on his striking face and steamy eyes. Would he look as good to me the second time I saw him? I was willing to bet he would. Just the thought that I found a guy that attractive was unnerving to me. I didn't really like the mushy, strange feelings I was experiencing, nearly popping with arousal at the mere idea of seeing him again.

One of the little boys left the others, running to the two-story, neat-as-a-button farmhouse. The remaining two fell in walking with us, peeking up bashfully from time to time.

"Hello, boys. Beautiful evening, isn't it?" Dad said to them.

"Yes, sir, it's a fine evening," the older boy answered.

So far the Amish I'd met sounded pretty normal. Just a hint of an accent, or maybe it was their vocabulary, very proper. Anyway, they weren't too different after all. Well, besides the beards, dresses and no electricity. If these boys walking with us were wearing normal clothes, they'd look like any other kids.

But then I heard the littlest boy shouting in a language I had never heard before. I glanced over to Dad questioningly. He answered, "They speak a form of German."

"It's called Pennsylvania Dutch," the younger boy corrected Dad. He seemed pleased with himself for being able to tell us something that we didn't know. He sniffed, walking on a little straighter.

I had to smile at that. He looked like such a little man with his clothes and manner. When I looked back up, my heart bounced at seeing Noah approaching with his father. He was actually a little taller than his dad, and this time I did notice what he was wearing—the same blue dress shirt and black suspenders that the little boys had on.

Most guys wouldn't be caught dead dressing exactly like their brothers, but hey, it seemed to be expected with these people. I also observed for the first time that the pants the boys were all wearing were extremely dark navy blue and homemade. They all had matching haircuts, too, with their hair left full on top and trimmed neatly at the ears and neck. I decided that these boys were good-looking enough to pull the hairdo off very well.

Noah's eyes met mine, and the way he was gazing at me made me glance away quickly. It was almost as if we already had a thing going on. He sort of looked at me in a possessive way, making me blush. I definitely didn't want him to see that. But maybe he liked me, too. At least that's what his eyes were saying. I could only hope, I thought, not willing to acknowledge just yet that I actually had a crush on him.

While I was getting all hot and bothered by Noah's eyes, a woman and two teenage girls came out of the house. They were all wearing blue dresses, in varying shades. The mother was in navy and the girls a lighter sky-blue. They also wore identical stiff white caps on their heads, with dangling narrow ribbons on each side, and black old-fashioned tennis shoes on their feet. What I could see of their hidden hair, the girls had lighter brown locks than the boys. I could tell nothing at all about their personalities from their outfits, and their faces were emotionless. Without having made a quick mental note about their slightly differing facial features and the freckles dotting the taller one's nose, I would have been hard-pressed to tell the two sisters apart.

After inspecting them from head to toe, I decided that it must be extremely uncomfortable to dress like that all the time. Being a dancer, I was accustomed to having my hair in a tight bun, with a dozen bobby pins holding my wild mane in place—and I *hated* wearing my hair up on performance days. The bun always gave me a headache, and these poor girls had to endure that pain every day.

As I gazed at the women, noticing that they wore no makeup at all and that the clothes concealed their figures completely, I felt a strong sense of pity for them. It seemed they weren't allowed any individuality at all.

It was then that I caught the tiny girl staring up at us. Her cap was jet-black and her dress a tiny replica of her mom's. She was without a doubt the cutest child I'd ever seen. I gathered that she didn't have many non-Amish people visit often by the way she was gawking at us with her mouth wide open.

There were so many kids. Surely they weren't all Noah's siblings. I counted eight, including Jacob, who was now coming up the driveway in an open buggy being pulled by a trotting, high-headed bay horse. Sitting next to him was a young Amish woman dressed in lavender. When they parked, I saw that she had a very pretty round face with a rosy complexion. She greeted me with a friendly smile.

My eyes were quickly drawn to the horse and buggy. How cool it would be to ride in one. That was the best part about being Amish, I imagined, riding around in the buggies. But I would definitely hate never being able to drive a car. I had my permit now and couldn't wait to get my license. The very idea that none of these people would ever drive a car was mind-boggling to me.

Dad's voice, thanking the Amish for the invitation to dinner, interrupted my thoughts, and then Mr. Miller proceeded to introduce his wife and all the kids. I tried to pay careful attention to each name, desperately attempting to quickly imprint to memory their faces and names. In the end, I knew I'd never be able to remember them all, especially when they looked so similar in dress and physical features. I couldn't believe such a little woman gave birth to all those kids. Didn't they use any birth control? I mean, who'd want to have that many children anyway?

An uncomfortable silence descended upon the gathering when the introductions were finished until one of the boys—Peter, I think, but I wouldn't bet on it—offered to show us some puppies. It sounded like a great idea to me. A way to escape from the intense scrutiny I was beginning to feel.

I wanted Sam to come, too, and poked his arm. Thankfully, he turned and walked with me, following the boys, who had pulled away from us in their mad dash to the barn. He must have been feeling the heebie-jeebies also, or he probably wouldn't have come.

In a whisper, Sam bent down to me and said, "That was awkward."

Before I could answer, Noah fell in beside Sam. A quiet happiness spread through me and all because he was coming with us. How pitiful of me. Surely it was impossible to become love struck in a few hours? I had to control my facial expressions, I warned myself. I didn't want *him* knowing.

Momentarily distracting my brain were the little puppy noises, whining and grunting, as we entered the open, airy hallway of the barn. The inside was as well kept as the outside, with a swept aisle and halters hung neatly on the pegs outside each black stall door. The smell of freshly baled alfalfa hit my senses immediately and I breathed the lush leafiness of it in deeply. Out of the corner of my eye I saw Noah look in my direction when I made the noise, with a quizzical look on his face.

"This is a great barn." I dared to look right at him, and he smiled slightly.

"Thank you" was all he said, but he continued to watch me intently, with that same appraising manner he'd had when we first met in the foyer. I wondered what was going through his brain, when Justin called out to me.

"Rose, you've got to come here and see—there's ten of 'em." His voice was thrilled, and I reluctantly tore my gaze away from Noah to join Justin in the box stall.

I caught my breath, seeing that they were Australian shepherds. What a coincidence. I plopped down on the thickly straw-covered floor, picking one of the squirming little things up and holding her to my face. She was a blue merle, with a smoky-colored coat and sapphire eyes—a puppy-size twin of our Aussie, Misty. She had passed away from old age about the same time Mom had died of cancer, making the days surrounding Mom's death even darker.

The dear little pup started to whine and wiggle, so I soothed her against my neck, smelling in the wonderful puppy smell.

"Do you think Dad will let us get one?" Justin asked me while petting two of the pups, a red one and a blue one, on his lap.

"Maybe… It's been a while since Misty died, and he did say that we could get another dog eventually." I looked over at Sam, who was sitting next to the mama dog, scratching her head.

"The only way he's going to go for it is if you beg him, Rose, with that teary-eyed thing you do." Sam quickly added, speaking to Noah, "Dad spoils her rotten. Anything she wants, she gets."

Anger flaring in me, I countered, "That's not true, Sam," giving him a withering look.

"It is so true, Rose. That's why you have to ask him!" Justin begged.

I rolled my eyes and sighed at the same time Noah sat down in the straw next to me. He picked up a puppy, distractedly rubbing its fur while he turned to me, saying, "So you have your father wrapped around your finger?"

I was glad he was talking to me, but I didn't feel like defending my uncanny ability to get my dad to agree to almost anything. It really wasn't any of his business, I decided, slightly bugged.

Shrugging my shoulders, I changed the subject. "What grade is Sarah in?" I asked him instead of answering his question.

He raised an eyebrow slightly, and I wasn't sure if it was because of the question I asked or the one I didn't answer.

"Ah…she's done with school." He said it slowly, as if he was talking to a stupid child.

"Why? How old is she?" I had guessed she was my age, and I was kind of hoping that we could be friends. Maybe she was older than I thought.

"She's sixteen," Noah replied as he changed out the puppy he was petting for a different one.

I looked around at the other three boys and noticed that they were all staring at me, again in that scrutinizing way. It was definitely less intimidating coming from the cute little boys but still irritating.

Noah's words about his sister's age suddenly sunk in.

"How long do you go to school for?" I asked Noah somewhat harshly and regretted the edge to my voice when his eyes widened in surprise.

"Eighth grade," he said simply, holding my gaze.

"Sweet—if I were Amish, I'd be done with school next year!" Justin exclaimed, like any normal thirteen-year-old boy would at the thought of being finished with school at that age.

Then Sam got into the conversation. "Don't you guys ever go to college?" he asked in amazement.

"No."

After waiting a few seconds, and realizing he wasn't going to elaborate on his answer, I asked, "What does your sister do every day, then?"

This time, instead of Noah answering, Peter beat him to the punch, saying in a matter-of-fact way, "She does the laundry and cleans the house, of course."

Sam and Justin, in unison, started rolling with laughter. I, on the other hand, with my feminist side rearing up in anger, said, "You've got to be kidding." I glanced at Noah, the mild shoulder shrug and expression on his face confirming what Peter had said.

"What's so funny?" the middle boy asked quizzically as he watched my brothers make fools of themselves while they laughed in the straw.

"Sam, Justin—stop it!" I ordered.

When they finally quieted, Justin looked at me sheepishly and said, "Gee, Rose, maybe you can come over here and get some laundry and cleaning lessons from their sisters. They can even teach you how to cook!"

Sam started laughing all over again, and the look I directed at Justin caused him to quickly press closer to the three boys who sat farther away from me. If those boys hadn't been staring bug-eyed at me, I would have jumped on Justin, pulled his hair out and then killed him. For him to say something like that in front of Noah—I was too angry to say anything, fearing I'd probably cuss Justin out, and that was the last thing those boys needed to hear.

The only sounds were the puppy noises and Sam clearing his throat when he finally recovered from his hysterics. What he said next surprised me and made me suddenly love him. "Oh, Justin, Rose has done a good job taking care of us since Mom died." Sam said it quietly. The mention of Mom made Justin lower his eyes and stare at the puppies in his lap.

"How long ago did your mom die?" Noah asked Sam in a surprised voice. He turned his head and was watching me when Sam answered him.

"I guess it's been about nine...or ten months now," Sam murmured thoughtfully, glancing in my direction. Actually, it had been exactly ten months and one week. I didn't want to keep track of it, but somehow my mind would add on the days subconsciously.

"I'm sorry about that," he told Sam, but his eyes seemed to change to a deeper brown, like chocolate, and they were looking into mine with compassion. The trance was broken by the sound of a loud ringing bell. The three boys jumped up, placing their puppies next to the mama's nipples and hurrying out of the stalls. Peter lingered, pressing his face against the black bars on the stall—watching.

"Dinner bell," Noah confirmed with amusement, twitching his lips. The boys' actions worked perfectly to lighten the mood, and I reached over to put my puppy back with her mother.

Before I had a chance to stand, Noah was already up, offering his hand to me, which I immediately took. He was strong and pulled me up easily. There was an electric current flowing between us, and I didn't want to let go, but I felt him start to release, so I followed suit. When we broke contact, the feeling vanished, to be replaced by a strange emptiness in me.

What was even stranger was when I caught the way Peter glanced from me back to Noah, with brown eyes wide with alarm. The look sent a prickling down the back of my neck, and abruptly I understood that my infatuation with Noah would probably not be welcomed by his family. Noah didn't seem to notice his brother staring, and when Sam and Justin went through the doorway, I shot a quick smile of thanks up at him and followed them out.

Inwardly, my mind shook the tickling sensation of foreboding away as we made our way out of the barnyard. Before we even reached the steps to the house, the delicious fragrance of food was coming out the open windows, settling into the summertime air. Trying to be subtle, I sniffed in the wonderful smells and picked up my pace a bit, discovering how hungry I was. Noah jumped in front of me right as I reached the door, grabbing it before it swung shut in my face after Justin let it go.

"Thanks," I said softly, dropping my eyes.

Noah shrugged and averted his eyes as if he was shy again. Or maybe he was just embarrassed by how rude my brother was.

I stopped a few feet inside the doorway, right next to Sam. Noah continued by us, walking over to stand beside Jacob. As I scanned the room, I first saw that the dining room and kitchen were combined into a gigantic space with an equally giant-size rectangular wooden table in the center of it. Okay, I've seen big tables before, but this one was ridiculous, with long benches on each side of it and chairs on the ends. It would have been the right scale for the giant's castle in "Jack and the Beanstalk."

The next thing I noticed was the long beige countertop running down one side of the room, flanked by a refrigerator and a stove on each side. There was a large ceramic sink in the center of the wall, with an open window directly above it. Momma could definitely serve a crowd in this kitchen.

Then I became aware of something really crazy, and I had to swiftly cross the room again with my eyes to verify what I was seeing. All the men and boys were on one side of the room and the women were on the other. My dad was standing with Mr. Miller, and Justin had gone over with the other boys without even thinking. So that left Sam and me standing in the no-man zone.

Just as I thought that, Sam sauntered across the room to join the other masculine beings, leaving me all alone. Luckily, in the blink of an eye, Sarah came over and silently stood next to me.

It must be an Amish thing, I decided. I wondered what everyone was waiting for until Mr. Miller bowed his head and said, "Let us have a moment of silent grace before our meal."

Everyone in the room followed suit, and so did I, cheating a little bit when I glanced up with my eyes, without raising my head much, to spy on Noah. I quickly put my head back down after seeing he was staring at me with his eyes wide open and his head only partially bowed. I could have sworn, before I looked away, that he had grinned at me. The second of eye contact had caused all those bizarre feelings to stir up inside me again. I made sure to keep my eyes cemented to the floor for the rest of the prayer.

After a long minute, which seemed more like an hour to

my grumbling belly, the family started moving about, indicating that prayer time was over. Mrs. Miller had the food laid out on the long counter and there was a glass of water at each place setting. Just as I was rocking on the balls of my feet, ready to head over to fill a plate, Sarah lightly grasped my arm. I gave her a confused look, which she returned with a friendly smile and a slight shake of her head.

Okay, now what was going on? I stopped, glancing around the room again. The men and boys were in line, from the oldest to the youngest, and the women—even the little toddler—were standing back, patiently waiting for the men to get their food first.

You've *got* to be kidding me.

This is like the Dark Ages, I grumbled inwardly, while my stomach growled. My blood began to boil when Sam bowed his blond, bushy head in a quick, silent laugh and winked at me with an evil grin on his face. I could see he and Justin were enjoying this backward thinking immensely. Dad, of course, was just going with the flow. Being an E.R. doctor, he was rarely fazed by anything, and ever since Mom had died, he just enjoyed doing things that kept his mind distracted—which this whole scene was doing perfectly.

Glancing back over at Sarah, I forced a smile.

"Thanks," I whispered.

She nodded once and then faced forward again. I was envious of how calm she seemed. She wasn't fidgeting or swaying or anything, just standing straight as a board, waiting as if she had no interest in the food at all. Maybe she had already eaten? I mean, how else could the women put up with this at every meal unless they snacked in the kitchen before the men arrived? I'd have to remember to ask her about it later.

I decided at that moment that Sarah and I were going to

be good friends. It was nice of her to warn me before I made a fool of myself. She could have just as easily let me walk up in front of all the men and commit a major faux pas, but she didn't. She warned me, making her best-friend material for sure in my book.

I breathed in and tried to look as casual as she was. It wasn't working, though. I couldn't keep my body from swaying back and forth from toes to heels, and my fingers wouldn't stay still either. I watched Mrs. Miller, Katie, Rachel and even little Naomi stand like statues, wondering how the heck they were accomplishing it.

Once most of the guys were through the line, Mrs. Miller moved forward with Naomi, and I was allowed to get a dish with the other girls. Noah walked by me but didn't even look in my direction—as if I didn't exist. That irked me, but I wasn't going to let it show.

I was starving by this time and resolved that I wasn't going to be shy about eating. After a minute of being forced to lei- surely stroll to the counter behind the other girls, I finally reached the source of the delightful smells. Wasting no time, I heaped two pork chops, mashed potatoes and creamy corn onto my plate. I also picked up two pieces of the thick, home- made bread and, to top it all off, a slice of cherry pie. Care- fully, I turned and made my way to the table, pausing to see where I should sit.

Just as I expected, the men and boys sat on one side of the long table, and the women were seating themselves on the other side. Dad took the chair to the left of Mr. Miller, who sat farther down the table. I ended up taking the chair across from Noah.

Believe it or not, it wasn't planned; just happened to con- veniently work out that way. Or maybe it was a sign from the universe that the two of us were meant to get together. Either way, I was a happy little camper in my spot.

With so many people at the table, you'd think it would have been quite boisterous, but it wasn't. The only sounds were the clinking of silverware on ceramic and the voices of Mr. Miller and Dad taking about all manner of things. The conversation started with the topic of the remodeling that our house needed. Mr. Miller offered to meet with Dad the following week to go through our lovely falling-apart home to give him an estimate for the work.

It turned out the Miller family had a building business, and I was secretly about to explode with excitement to hear the possibility that Noah might be spending a lot of time at our house this summer. Of course, he'd be working, but at least I'd get to see him, and that was better than nothing.

I tried to make eye contact with him during the meal, but he kept avoiding my gaze. He'd look over my head, out the window, down the table, but not at me. I was starting to wonder if I'd offended him earlier. I mulled that over while I took each delicious bite. The bread was especially yummy, and I was deliberating whether to get up in front of everyone and go for another piece, when I heard my name mentioned.

"Yes, they do keep very busy. Sam plays football, Justin soccer and Rose dances. As a matter of fact, Rose has been accepted to dance in the Cincinnati ballet youth program," Dad said proudly.

Finally, Noah looked up at me, only for a second, before staring back at the food on his plate. I could have sworn he had a troubled frown on his face at that instant. He seemed to be listening closely to the conversation, though, pushing the mashed potatoes around with his fork, without bringing any of it to his lips.

"Dancing? How long have you done that, Rose?" Mrs. Miller asked in a slightly weird, clipped way, causing my face to flush with heat before I answered. I instinctually knew that what I was about to say wasn't going to please her.

"For about seven years now." I tried to change the subject. "But I also spend a lot of time riding my horse."

This time Noah's eyes shot directly at me, but I had picked up on the vibe that I shouldn't be caught looking at him in front of his parents, so I didn't. Instead, I just reveled in the fact that he was looking at me, making me feel both satisfied and disgusted with myself at the same time.

"Do you boys ride also?" Mr. Miller directed the question to my brothers, and Sam answered.

"No. Rose is the equestrian in our family," he said politely and then went back to shoveling food into his mouth.

"Actually, Rose's trainer is hauling Lady, her horse, to our place in the morning. I hope the creek is off the driveway by then," Dad said, voicing his concern.

"Oh, no worries on that. I am sure it will be fine. It is a rare occasion that the creek swells that big. I think it's been a few years since I last saw it go over your driveway."

"That's a relief," Dad commented before asking Mr. Miller about the lights and the hot water that were powered by natural gas. As I glanced up, I realized that there was a queer odor in the house, and it turned out the smell was coming from the lights over the table.

Interestingly, I wouldn't even have noticed them except for the smell. They gave off a similar light to an electric bulb. Actually, the house was very comfortable looking. Not at all how I'd imagined people who didn't use electricity or drive cars would live. The inside was immaculately clean with pristine white walls. The open windows were letting in the dim evening light and allowing a gentle breeze to flutter through the house. I even caught a glimpse of overstuffed burgundy sofas in the adjoining room.

Still, as pleasant as the picture was, the quiet, reserved behavior of all the kids was unsettling. If Sam and Justin hadn't been starving to death, I was sure they'd have been talking up a storm. But then as I watched my brothers, the thought occurred to me that maybe for once they had the sense, or fear enough, to follow the old saying "When in Rome, do as the Romans do."

For the rest of the dinner, Mr. Miller, Dad and Jacob did most of the talking, with creepy Mrs. Miller occasionally asking one of us a probing question like "Who is going to stay with you when your father is at the hospital?"

"No one," I answered. "We can take care of ourselves." Then I sneaked a peek at Noah, who was staring at his plate with quivering lips on his handsome mouth. I guess I had managed to amuse him.

Mrs. Miller responded with a "hmm," and I gathered she thought my answer was not appropriate by the inflection in her voice. But after all, Sam and I would be in college in a couple of years, and Justin wasn't a little kid. Why would she care? The willies crept into my bones, and I avoided looking in her direction the rest of the meal. But I felt her eyes on me.

Following dinner, I helped clear the table with the women while the guys went out to the front porch. No surprise there. I was at least proud that my brothers and father picked up their own dishes and brought them over to the sink. The other men and boys left theirs on the table. These Amish guys liked to be waited on, that's for sure, but the women didn't seem to mind at all. In fact, Katie hadn't stopped smiling through the entire meal.

I didn't care how gorgeous Noah was. If I ever somehow managed to get together with him, I would have to completely retrain him, sort of like working with a horse. But then, my horse probably wasn't as stubborn as the Amish boy.

Why on earth had such a thought even come into my mind?

I'd been thinking about all kinds of irrational and strange things since I'd first seen my handsome new neighbor standing in the foyer. It would all be well and good if Noah were a normal guy. *But he was Amish.* There was no way the two of us would be hooking up—he'd never be interested in someone like me. And even if he were, would I be able to deal with the bizarre world he lived in?

Silently, I worked alongside Katie, scraping the leftover food from the plates into a black bucket and handing them to Sarah, who then washed them in the sudsy water. The kitchen was quiet except for the clinking of the dishes against one another as they were stacked.

My mind drifted, and I couldn't stop myself from thinking about Mom. Maybe it was the home-cooked meal, I didn't know, but the sadness pushed softly against me once again.

Before, I had missed her because she was my mom and she was gone, but as I glanced over at Mrs. Miller bustling around the table, I realized what I had really lost when she died—her wisdom. I needed her guidance now more than ever.

I figured Mom would have liked Noah well enough, although I couldn't help wondering how she would have felt about him being Amish.

Deep down I knew the answer—but I wasn't ready to acknowledge it yet.

4

Noah
The Beginning

DIM MORNING LIGHT SPILLED THROUGH THE open window, along with a trace of chilly air. I quickly sat up, wide-awake and eager for the day ahead, in spite of the fact that I hadn't gotten much rest the night before. I'd tossed around in bed for hours, it seemed, before finally settling down. It was the first night in a very long time that I could recall not being able to fall asleep straightaway. Usually by the time my head hit the pillow, I'd be unconscious from exhaustion. My days were filled with so much backbreaking work that sleep had never been a problem before. This was hay-baling season after all, and my body was definitely tired. Not my brain, though.

After supper the night before, when I glanced through the window and saw Rose standing with Sarah and Katie at the sink, an unexpected feeling of contentment washed over me. Besides her English clothing, she looked completely natural there with the other girls, behaving like one of our women.

Now that the sun was rising, the conflicting thoughts of the night before faded, and I wondered why I even cared about this girl that could never be mine. After all, Rose was just another pretty girl, right? No. She was the most beautiful girl I'd ever seen. Who could blame me for admiring that beauty?

But it was more than her face that had caught hold of me— her lively spirit had connected with me, and that was the scariest part of all. I shook my head trying to erase Rose from it. I reasoned that within a day or two I'd be over the infatuation with the girl—probably the next time I saw her I'd look upon her with just as much boredom as I did the other girls in the community.

But still, I couldn't keep my insides calm. Today, I would see her again.

Quickly I changed into my work shirt and pants and jogged down the stairs to the dimly lit kitchen, attaching the suspenders as I went. Mother already had a plate of scrambled eggs, sausage patties and hash browns put out for me. I sat and waited for Father and Jacob, who entered the room yawning and stretching. After a brief moment of silence for prayer, I began wolfing the food down.

I didn't even really taste anything, eating so fast that Mother exclaimed, "What's the big hurry, son?"

Then I realized the mistake I'd made, and I slowed myself down deliberately. Avoiding Mother's searching eyes, I said, "I'm just hungry today, that's all."

She seemed satisfied with the answer and continued to dish out Father's and Jacob's plates.

Of course, the real cause for my hurry was that Father had told Mr. Cameron that we'd be over first thing in the morning to help unload the moving truck. But Mother could never know that.

I had hoped that the English family would have stayed longer after dinner the night before. But when Rose finally stepped onto the front porch with the other girls, her father stood up and thanked us again, saying that he was exhausted and needed a good night's rest.

I'd caught Rose's eyes regarding me during dinner, and then when she came out on the porch afterward. That was something a girl shouldn't do, unless she was already officially courting, and even then she'd be modest about it. But Rose didn't know any better. And even though I wanted nothing more than to gaze back into her clear blue eyes, Mother was watching me, so I controlled myself and avoided looking at her altogether.

And even though the morning light had made me realize how foolish I'd been for even considering that I could become involved with a girl from the outside world, I still wanted to be Rose's friend. The only way that could happen was if I made her understand the way things were with my folks so she didn't get me into trouble with her outgoing ways. The last thing I needed was for Father and Mother to think I liked her. And unless I was reading Rose all wrong, she definitely seemed interested in me. But then again, maybe that was just her normal behavior, being an English girl and all.

Hearing the roar of a diesel engine signaled that our driver had arrived with the work truck. The sound sent a pounding sense of anticipation through me. But I was careful not to let it show, continuing to sit at the table, waiting for Father and Jacob to finish eating.

The touch of the cool morning air invigorated my senses as I stepped out the door. I lifted my eyes to the overcast sky, taking note of the slices in the clouds where the sun sprayed through, convinced that the day would clear up to be a fine one. Stepping lightly over the gravel, I was filled with a sense of excitement that felt downright good.

It was almost seven o'clock when we climbed into Mr.

Denton's faded blue pickup truck. He was about as old looking as the truck was, but I liked him a lot. He was a nice man,
playing country music on the radio while we were driving
to work sites. Father hated the music but really couldn't say
much about it since the man was dependable.

I squeezed into the little backseat of the extended cab, next
to Matthew Weaver, who was seventeen and worked on the
crew with us. Matt was a good buddy of mine, but I knew
that I couldn't tell him about my attraction to the English girl.
He wasn't bright enough to keep his mouth shut about it, and
if any of the adults found out, they'd tell my folks for sure.

I could already picture myself standing alone in front of the
entire church congregation, repenting my sins the way poor
Jacob had to do a few years back when he shot those paintballs
at the Troyers' buggy. It was all in fun. Jacob didn't mean anything by it, *and* Elijah *had* shot at Jacob first. But the Troyer
boys seemed to always get out of punishment. It was benefi-
cial when your grandfather was the bishop.

Matt's suntanned, freckled face grinned broadly at me,
and he asked how my weekend was as Jacob squeezed in on
my other side. The expression on his chubby baby face indicated something was up, and I answered suspiciously. "Fine…
Why?"

Rolling his eyes, he snickered. "I heard you had the new
English family over for dinner and that the girl is very pretty.
At least that's what Katie told Ella. And she wasn't happy to
hear it neither."

Amazing how fast news traveled in the community, even
without home telephones and computers. Twisting around, I
checked to see how close Father was to the truck when he'd
said it. Only Matthew Weaver could get away with saying

something like that about a girl. He was such a clown that no one paid him much attention—up until now anyway.

Directing a threatening look at him, I hissed, "Shut up about it, all right?" The last thing I needed was his lack of common sense getting Father onto me.

After a few seconds of shock, he recovered from my anger and replied in a dejected voice, "Sure...whatever."

The two-minute drive over to Rose's house was free of conversation, with only the drone of country music playing softly against the rumbling of the truck's engine. Pulling in, I was glad to see that the creek was moving high and swift through the culvert under the driveway, but above it was dry and relatively clear. Only the mud clumps were any indication that water had flooded over the previous day.

The ryder truck was already backed up to the house, and I immediately spotted Sam and Justin carrying a mattress in through the side door. My eyes searched for Rose, but she was nowhere in sight.

"Work quickly, boys, so we aren't too late arriving at the Schrocks' place," Dad ordered, stepping out of the truck.

"We're really going to help the English unload their belongings?" Matthew asked in cheerful amazement.

"Yes, Matthew, try to calm yourself—you don't want to scare them with your enthusiasm," I mumbled, shooting him a disapproving glance.

This time he came close to my ear and whispered, "Do you think they have a game system?"

Ever since we had worked on that English house last year where Matthew had had the chance to sneak in a video game with the teenage boy who lived there, he'd been obsessed with getting another chance to play. I playfully cuffed him on the head, moaning to myself as we climbed into the yellow trailer.

Mr. Cameron was inside, surrounded by towers of cardboard boxes. When he saw us, he stopped and said with obvious relief, "Oh, good, I'm glad you were able to make it. There's quite a lot to unload here."

"It shouldn't take too long with all of us chipping in," I said after quickly introducing Matthew to Sam and Justin, who'd just entered the shaded compartment. I picked up the closest manageable box and headed eagerly for the house.

Sam caught my arm and pointed to the large black *R* written on the side, saying, "That goes to Rose's room, up the stairs, second door on the right. Just leave it outside her door in the hallway." Then he went back into the trailer.

Funny how that worked out. I smiled crookedly walking up the stairs to the second floor. When I got to the door, I stopped, hesitating. I'd never been in a girl's room before. Well, besides my sisters'—and that certainly didn't count. The eagerness I felt earlier suddenly turned to apprehension as I peeked in through the crack where the door was ajar.

After a quick check over my shoulder to see that the stairway was still clear, I rapped softly on the door. I waited a few breaths, but nothing happened. The upstairs was dead silent; the only sounds reaching my ears were those of the others bringing in the boxes below. Impatience gripped me, stealing my sound mind, and I carefully pushed the door open wider.

My heart thumped faster in my chest when I saw her lying there, asleep on the wooden floor. She was curled up in a ball, with a pillow under her head. She had no blankets or cushioning, and she was wearing the same clothes she had worn to dinner the night before. Her hair was spread out around her in a wild halo like what I imagined an angel would look like.

Seeing her on the cold, hard floor, I felt my nervousness quickly disappear. A punch of anger flared within me. A girl shouldn't have to sleep in this condition, I thought with indignation. My mother could have invited her to spend the night in our guest room—on a soft, comfortable mattress—until her family got her own bed set up.

Rose especially needed the help since she didn't have a mother of her own to show her how to set up a new household. And as I gazed down at the sleeping angel, the fact that she didn't have a mother opened my heart even more to her.

If my own mother had understood what Rose's sleeping arrangements were going to be, she would have been more charitable—I was sure of it. But the abruptness of the dinner invitation the night before had her in a fluster and I couldn't blame her for the lack of hospitality that she normally showed to those in need.

As I watched the soft rise and fall of the beautiful girl's breathing, my mind began to change directions and I wondered how she could even sleep like that at all. A second of craziness touched me and I shrewdly looked around to be certain that I was still alone at the doorway.

What I really wanted to do was talk to Rose—so much so that I became brave and took one step into the room.

She was sleeping so soundly I doubted she'd wake up anytime soon, unless she was helped along a little with the process. Glancing back toward the door and seeing it clear, I debated for a fraction of a second and then dropped the box hard onto the floor, hoping, too late, that there wasn't anything breakable in it.

Her reaction to the noise surprised me, as she yawned big and then mumbled without opening her eyes, "Go away, Justin, you little creep, and let me sleep."

I had to smile at that. She had a temper even when she was sleeping. And at that moment of staring down at her, the feeling of complete familiarity washed over me, and I was abruptly filled with the desire to be closer to her. All rational thought must have left me, because I carefully crept down to her sleeping body and whispered loud enough for her to hear me, but hopefully not loud enough for anyone else to, "Rose—are you awake?"

Her eyes popped open wide, and she bolted upright with a confused look on her flushed face.

"What are you doing here—in my room—Noah?" she squealed, and I brought my finger to my lips, shushing her.

Whispering, I said, "I was helping unload the truck and… well…you just looked so uncomfortable." I paused, finishing with, "I thought I was doing you a favor waking you up."

The emotions playing on her face went from surprise to agitation, and finally, while I unconsciously held my breath, her plump pink lips broke into a wide smile.

"Oh, really, well, thank you so much for rescuing me from a deep and dangerous sleep." Her voice was smooth, holding a hint of amusement, and I breathed in relief when I realized she was teasing me.

She pulled her legs up to her chin and clasped her hands around them. Looking at me boldly, she asked, "What are you doing today after everything is off the truck?"

At the same time I wanted to be closer to her, I also felt nervous kneeling on the floor only a foot away from her. I stood up and walked to the door again, peering out. When I was confident the coast was clear, I went back and sat down next to her.

At first I was afraid to look directly at her, an action I'd avoided doing with girls my entire life, so I simply stared at the ugly wallpaper. But that was unsatisfying, to say the least, so with all the confidence I could muster, I turned to look directly into her eyes. It was nice when she didn't turn away.

"I have to go to work. We're building a house up the road for a new Amish family who moved here from Indiana."

"Oh," she murmured softly, appearing to be lost in thought.

The sound of footsteps on the stairs brought me briskly to a standing position. I quickly crossed the room and was in the process of hurrying through the doorway when Sam walked in. He stopped, and after glancing from me to Rose, and seeing what I'm sure appeared to be a guilty look on my face, scrunched up his eyebrows and said in a menacing tone, "Hey, bro, what have you been doing in here with my sister?"

For a second there was dead silence, and I searched my mind for the safest way to respond without causing a scene that would bring Father up the stairs. I didn't have to worry about it long though when the room was abruptly filled with the sound of Sam's laughter. He reached out and punched me in the arm. It seemed like a friendly gesture, but damn, he had a solid swing, and I couldn't help worrying that maybe he was feeling angry behind those laughing eyes.

Winking at me, he said, "Just kidding, Noah. But, man, the look on your face was classic. Come on, I need your help with the couch."

Glancing over my shoulder as I followed Sam out of the room, I saw that Rose had a wide smile on her face. I couldn't help shaking my head in wonder at their strange sense of humor.

The next time I saw Rose was in the kitchen about a half hour later. She was still wearing the same clothes and was perched on the only seat in the room, a tall stool. I was happy to see her thoroughly enjoying one of the cinnamon rolls Mother had sent over with us. When she looked up at me, she was licking the sugar off her lips. I wasn't even sure if she knew what she was doing or how it was affecting me, but I paused for a second, staring at her with all kinds of mischief in my mind.

"This is…awesome," she said, popping the last bite into her mouth and then reaching for another one. "You have to thank your mom for me, okay?"

"Of course" was all I could manage to say as I watched her begin eating another roll. How on earth she could fit two of those things into her little body was beyond me. She ate more like a boy than a girl. It must be the dancing and riding, I figured.

"So when does your horse arrive?" Finding an opening for conversation, I grasped it.

Her eyes lit up. "Any minute now. Jerry called me a little while ago and said he was almost here." She went on, talking between bites. "I'm so excited. I've always boarded Lady. This'll be the first time I really get to take care of her on my own. And I can just go out the door and ride her whenever I want."

At her words, an idea began sprouting in my mind, but before I had the opportunity to say anything, Matt stumbled into the kitchen carrying a microwave. Rose jumped up and showed him where to put it on the counter. I could tell he was trying to be good and not gawk at Rose's beauty, but he couldn't help staring at her like a puppy dog.

His dumb-faced attraction to her caused a tightening in the pit of my stomach and I said more briskly than I wanted, "Rose, this is my friend Matthew." And then to Matt I said, "Would you please wipe that silly look off your face."

Matt didn't get the chance because a horn beeped, causing Rose to slip by me. To my astonishment, and right in front of

Matt, she did the most irrational, stupid and wonderful thing ever, grabbing my hand with her little one and tugging me along, saying, "Come on, it's my horse!"

Matt's mouth dropped open, and his eyes followed me as I was being pulled away by the English girl, who was half my size. Before Father or Jacob had the chance to see, I tugged my hand away from her. When she looked up, her eyes were wide and her cheeks were an attractive pink hue. I was astonished that she hadn't realized that touching my hand in front of Matt, let alone Father or Jacob, could have gotten me into a mess of trouble.

She lowered her eyes and mumbled an apology before flinging the screen door open. She ran out to the driveway, where an extremely large, fancy aluminum horse trailer was parked behind an equally impressive shiny red pickup.

Even though we weren't allowed to drive, that didn't mean we didn't appreciate nice vehicles when we saw them. For a minute I admired the truck, before being distracted by Rose excitedly hugging the man and woman who were getting out of the truck. She displayed her emotions so forcefully, whether she was snarling at one of her brothers, hugging her friends or just talking to me with her velvet voice. She did everything with such intense feeling that I imagined she must get exhausted from it. Like a flash of lightning, I understood why she'd grabbed my hand in the kitchen—she simply couldn't control herself.

I continued to watch her as she went to the back of the trailer and disappeared for a minute, only to reappear leading a leggy dapple-gray mare who moved with an arched neck and raised tail. The horse had an exquisite head and I guessed she was an Arabian.

After another minute of enthusiastic chatter, the couple left to talk to Mr. Cameron, leaving Rose alone. I took the opportunity I was given and swiftly walked to her. Catching her arm for a second to stop her, I immediately let go, glancing around for spies. I was standing inappropriately close to her, so close that I could actually feel her without even touching her. It was as if there was a tingling substance in the air between us, and I breathed deeply, collecting myself before I spoke.

"You know, Rose, right across the road is a farm that we're allowed to ride on. There are fields and woods." Quickly I scanned the area again to make sure no one had noticed us. I rushed the words out, fearing I wouldn't get another chance. "Do you want to meet me over there this evening and go for a ride together?"

I held my breath for her answer.

"That sounds great!" she replied with an impish smile.

By the exuberant way she answered, I realized that she didn't understand that we needed to be very careful about what we were beginning to do. I mean, this was serious business—making plans for a secret meeting with an English girl. After another sweep of my eyes for an audience, I whispered, "We need to keep this a secret, Rose. My parents wouldn't allow me to be out riding with you. You need to be extra careful that no one sees us together or guesses that we've become friends. *No one* in the community can be trusted about this—even Sarah. They wouldn't understand. Okay?"

When she nodded her head surely, her eyes glinting with serious concentration, I knew she would keep her lips sealed on the matter. I continued, "You'll see a green metal gate. Just go about sixty feet past it, up the hill, and you'll find a break in the fence. There's a worn hoof path in the trees at the opening. Once through it, follow the dirt lane straight. Don't make any turns, and I'll meet up with you around seven o'clock."

"Noah, come on, we're leaving," Jacob's voice called out from near the house. It was just dumb luck that he hadn't looked back this way and seen me standing close enough to Rose to kiss her. That would not have been good, and I felt the unease of that realization spread through me as I took a step back from her. After a quick search of her eyes, I knew she'd do what I'd asked, so I gave her a smile and a nod, before I turned and leaped into a run toward the work truck.

As we were backing around, I shifted in the seat to look out the window. Rose was leading the frisky horse, which was prancing alongside her, back to the old barn behind the house.

If everything worked out as planned, I'd finally get the chance to be completely alone with Rose. Taking a deep breath, I stared out the window, my heart thumping in my chest as I felt the worry settle over me.

What had I gotten myself into?

5

Rose
Flame

THE DAY TRUDGED ON, GOING NOWHERE, IT seemed. And even though I had a million things to do to occupy my time, I continued to glance at my phone every few minutes, hoping that the magic time of six o'clock would suddenly appear—the time when I felt it would be reasonable to head out to the barn and get Lady ready for the ride.

The ride—just thinking about it stirred shivers of excitement through me. Still, a tingling doubt ran through my mind. Why was it such a secret anyway? We were just going riding together—not a big deal at all. Were Noah's parents always so strict with him? And why would his community care about it? Maybe I'd get some answers this evening. Right now I would go with my instincts, which were telling me that I had to get to know my handsome neighbor better—even though the whole cloak-and-dagger thing was kind of weird.

After a minute of searching through the clothes in the box, I became impatient that I wasn't finding what I was looking for and dumped the contents unceremoniously on the floor.

Distracted for a split second, I contemplated turning over a new leaf regarding my clean-room policy, which was basically never having one. But then, surveying the clothes scattered around the floor, I decided I liked having my room like this. It was sort of homey, and it drew attention away from the eighty-year-old peeling wallpaper, with the faded pictures of George Washington look-alikes dancing and playing instruments. That was definitely a good thing.

I thought about just tearing the chaotic paper off the walls the way Justin had in the foyer, but then I'd have to clean it all up, and I didn't want to deal with that at the moment. Again I looked at my cell, groaning that only a whopping two minutes had passed since I'd last checked.

Leaving the walls as is for the time being, I hopped over the piles of clothes to lean out the window. It was strange not having a screen in it. I was sure birds would be flying around my room in no time, but the alternative was closing the window and dying of heatstroke, which wasn't really an option. I had to remember to add the window to Dad's ever-growing list of repairs for Miller's Construction. That made my mouth spread into a little smile, thinking that the longer the list, the more I'd be seeing Noah, which suited me just fine.

Closing my eyes, I held my face up to the sun, relishing the heat as it absorbed into my skin. The day had grown almost unbearably humid, but I was glad for the hot temperature. It gave me the opportunity to wear one of my cute summer tank tops this evening.

After several minutes I grew bored with the facial tanning and instead checked out the view from the bedroom window. I'd picked this room for two reasons. First, I could see the field Lady was in, and right now she was peacefully munching grass under a big oak tree. And second, I could see the Miller farm. I never would have told anyone about the second reason.

Spinning away from the window, I dropped to the mattress on the floor. Lying on my belly on top of the cozy comforter, I pressed my face into one of the mushy pillows that now adorned my temporary sleeping arrangements, all too happy that I'd have a soft place to sleep that night.

I still couldn't believe that I'd woken to see Noah peering down at me with a look of extreme irritation on his face. What a shocker that was. Never in a million years had I expected to see him in my room. But what really got me was that he seemed genuinely concerned about me sleeping on the floor. I was used to guys paying attention to me, but this was the first time one actually gave a crap about me personally. His concern touched a deep place in me that had never been fooled with before.

Quite frankly, I was so exhausted by the time I went to sleep the night before that I was like a zombie and couldn't have cared less where I slept, as long as I had the chance to close my eyes. When we'd returned after dinner, the water was down enough that an invigorated dad drove the ryder truck up to the house and Sam followed with his big dually truck, also fully loaded with boxes. After spending the following four hours unloading Sam's truck and unpacking some basic necessities, I nearly passed out in the kitchen. That's when Dad directed us all to find some clear floor space somewhere and go to sleep.

I had to admit that I was a little stiff this morning, and my lower back was tight, but hopefully my body would loosen up during the ride. Again I looked at my cell and was pleased to see that ten more minutes had passed since my last check.

Getting ever closer...

I rolled onto my back and frowned, remembering what Noah had said about his parents not being happy if he was with me. I wasn't stunned at the revelation. I'd sensed that at dinner, but it still bugged me. Everyone always loved me— my friends' parents, my teachers, my dance coaches. Noah's family had no right to form opinions about me when they didn't even know me. The idea that they would find him being with me offensive just wasn't right, and it was going to create a lot of problems. You could only sneak around for so long before something had to give, and I didn't get the feeling that Amish people gave in much. I mean, after all, they lived their lives as if they were stuck in a rerun of *Little House on the Prairie* and they did it *forever*. Never doing so many things I automatically took for granted, like driving, going to movies or listening to music.

While we'd been unpacking, Sam, Justin and I attacked Dad with questions about our new neighbors, and although he admitted he was no expert, he did tell us a bunch of interesting things. I was looking forward to asking Noah more about his life tonight.

Sleepily I closed my eyes, listening to the shuffling and thuds of the guys moving furniture around downstairs. I hoped they all left me alone so I could take a little catnap. Within a few minutes I was drifting away, an image of a black buggy with Noah at the reins the last thing in my mind.

"Rose, wake up. Rose. Rose!" I heard Justin but ignored him, all too warm and comfortable curled up in the plushy comforter. The afternoon sunlight was down far enough to leave the room in a dull, dreamlike haze and I burrowed deeper into the softness, close to falling back asleep. Then the little twerp had the nerve to grasp my shoulders and start shaking me violently. That woke me up.

With all my weight I hurled myself onto him, knocking him off the mattress. Satisfaction filled me as I observed Justin lying on his back on the floor. But the feeling was short-lived, replaced with a panic attack when it suddenly occurred to me how late it was. Swiftly I slid across the mattress, frantically searching for the phone.

Once my hand grasped it under the sheet, I said a silent prayer and peeked at it. Yes! I danced in my head when I saw that it was five o'clock, early enough to leisurely start getting ready, but late enough to be almost ready to go. *Perfect.* I bounced up, grabbing the clothes I'd set aside for the occasion.

"Gee, Rose, you didn't have to do that," Justin said, rubbing his head.

I figured I had five seconds to spare, so I rounded on him and hissed, "What do you want?"

"I was going to invite you to go with Sam and me to the movies in town tonight. Dad went to the hospital to get his office in order, so we thought we'd eat dinner out and go see the *Transformers* movie."

"You've already seen it twice. Isn't there something else playing?" I suggested impatiently.

"We like that movie. It has everything—robots, explosions and a hot babe." Justin smiled slyly.

"You're too young to be interested in *hot babes,*" I informed him with my nose wrinkled in disgust. "But I'm not going, so I don't really care what you guys waste your money on. Now get out of my room so I can change."

"What are you going to do?" he asked keenly. Maybe he was growing a brain.

That would be dangerous.

"Not that it's any of your business, but if it gets you out of my room faster, I'm going for a ride."

With that I pushed Justin out the door and locked it behind him. A few minutes later I was dressed, and hearing Sam's truck engine revving up, I leaned out the window to watch him drive away—perfect timing again.

Turning to the big round mirror attached to my retro-style dresser, I studied my reflection. I left my long, wavy hair down, with a few stray curls around my face. I decided to put a little blush on my cheeks and some gloss over my lips. Less was definitely more with Amish guys, I determined. Besides, I didn't wear much makeup anyway.

Standing back, I admired myself in the mirror. I looked pretty good. Hmm, except the top. Maybe it was just a bit too formfitting. Turning sideways, I was impressed to see how I was filling the shirt out this year. I certainly didn't remember looking so…developed in it last year. Yeah, probably the wrong shirt for a guy who was used to seeing women dressed in smocklike dresses. I took it off and rummaged through the closest pile on the floor.

I finally decided on a cute light blue top that had a little lace along the collar. His family seemed to like blue, and it hugged my chest just enough, without being trampy. And the lace made it feminine—just right.

Stopping in the kitchen briefly, I spread mayonnaise on two slices of bread and stuck a thick piece of cheese between them, proceeding to eat quickly. Justin's comment about my cooking popped into my head, and I was doubly glad I had body slammed him. I was in too good of a mood to dwell on it, though, and let my obnoxious brother slip from my mind, to be replaced with thoughts of Noah.

Catching, grooming and saddling Lady didn't take much time, and when I did the final time check, it was six-thirty. The exact time I wanted to be heading up the road.

Easily, I found the opening Noah had told me about, and once on the other side, I was delighted to see the fields went on as far as I could see. There were pockets of woods dappling the scenery, separating one hay field or crop from another.

The picture was breathtaking enough to have been plucked from an art-gallery wall. And the property was isolated by a thick row of trees along the road, making it a superb place for a secret meeting. The lane was wide and level, spotted intermittently with grass and dirt. After a few minutes of getting used to the new surroundings, I squeezed Lady into a canter, reveling in the exhilaration of her muscles moving beneath me as we sped up, the wind whipping my hair back.

I was so into the joy of the ride that I failed to hear another horse moving up behind me fast. Almost too late, I caught sight of Noah from the corner of my eye, just in time to urge Lady faster before he passed us.

Glancing sideways, I saw him grin wickedly at me, and I knew the game was on. Leaning lower over my horse, I moved with her, pushing with my lower legs, asking for still more speed. We were going so fast tears were developing at the corners of my eyes—still I urged her on.

He was right alongside us, and if Lady swayed at all in his direction, we'd brush legs hard. I didn't care, though. I wanted to win. I saw the challenge in his eyes, and I knew Lady was fast. Faster than the tall bay buggy horse he was riding. And even if she wasn't, I was sure my Arabian could keep the race close.

But before either of us won, we ran out of running space as the path narrowed and I could see a sharp turn ahead leading into a stand of trees. Noah held out his hand, indicating for me to slow down, and I responded in unison with him and his horse, reining down to a walk right before the turn.

Sitting up and patting Lady vigorously on the neck, I exclaimed, "That was awesome! I would have beaten you if we'd had more room." I exhaled loudly, still filled with the powerful adrenaline rush.

"Your horse is really fast," Noah commented, catching his breath. He studied her for a moment and then brought his eyes up to me with the same admiring look on his face.

Blushing, I glanced away, feeling butterflies spreading out in my stomach. It was a strange feeling, being both pleasant in one way and totally unsatisfying in another. When I got the nerve to turn back to him, he was still silently watching me, this time with an unreadable expression.

"Wow," I breathed. "Do you do that often?"

"No. That's the first real race I've run in several years," he answered thoughtfully.

"Why?" I asked him, relaxing in the saddle, swaying with the movement of the horse.

Pausing to answer, he said, "Well, since I've been done with school and working full-time, I just don't have much time for joyrides. Then when I do, it's difficult to make plans with my friends. There's always so much to do around the farm." He scowled and I suddenly felt sorry for him. He was too young to have to work all the time.

I was miffed and without thinking I blurted out, "Do you like being Amish?"

He sighed, scanning the trail ahead, brooding over my question for an amount of time that I was becoming uncomfortable with, when he finally answered, "Yes, I like being Amish—for the most part." He glanced over at me with a slight tilt to his mouth and then continued, "I enjoy the simple way of life we have, the sense of community and the closeness of our families."

After considering what he said for a minute, I asked with astonishment, "But don't you want to be able to drive a car or watch TV?"

He laughed at that, shooting me a look of amusement. "Do

you think those things are so important?" His grin spread into a full-blown smile. "I can get to most places I want to go in my buggy, and if I need to go farther away, I hire a driver. And you know...there are more enjoyable things to do at night besides watch TV."

He eyed me speculatively. When comprehension dawned on me, my eyes widened and a blush heated my face, causing him to chuckle.

Okay, I wasn't even going there, so instead I swallowed my embarrassment and asked him, "What's your horse's name."

He laughed again, obviously entertained by my squirming discomfort at the last topic of conversation. While his tanned face attempted to be serious, he patted the horse's neck and said, "This is Rumor."

"That's a cool name," I said, looking closer at the gelding beside me, glad for the distraction.

"You're probably right. I don't think Rumor could have beaten your horse," he said complacently, as if the fact didn't bother him in the least.

"Yeah, but I bet Rumor's got a lot more sense than Lady here," I pointed out as I ran my fingers through her long mane.

"Why do you say that?" he asked with curious eyes.

"Well, she's usually pretty spooky about things. You know, freaking out at mailboxes, the wind, even birds."

After running his eyes over her again, he commented, "She's doing fine now."

"Probably because she has a big, strong gelding like Rumor to protect her," I joked with a little laugh.

Noah just nodded his head, a whisper of a smile playing on his lips.

The path narrowed. Really more suited for single-file riding, but we continued side by side, with our knees now rubbing, and with each touch a jolt of hot energy coursed through me. I wondered if he was feeling it, too. I glanced over at him and he was looking straight ahead, focused on some imaginary object in the distance.

We were moving between two fields of corn, and the stalks were beginning to press in on us, being as tall as the horses. I became aware that we were very much alone, sheltered and hidden from the rest of the world. And that realization sent my heart thumping unnaturally hard. Loud enough that I feared he'd be able to hear it. He was definitely close enough to hear it, at a proximity that I was sure his parents wouldn't have approved of. Close enough to kiss even—with a little stretching. I dismissed that thought quickly and twisted in the saddle to stare at the corn plants, feeling the still, warm air that was emitting from them.

After a few minutes of silence, the only sound coming from the horses' breathing and hooves touching the ground, out of the blue he asked, "Do you really like to dance?" His voice was different, raspier than before. That was random. Turning back to him, I saw conflict on his face.

"I love to dance. I do both ballet and jazz, but it's going to be difficult now."

"Why?" he probed.

"Well, for one thing, my dance company is in Cincinnati, and that means I'll have a two-hour-long drive each way if I continue, which would be near impossible with my dad's schedule at the hospital. And there aren't any studios of the caliber that I'm at around here," I said, spreading my arms wide at the stalks around us.

Just saying the words out loud dampened my mood—how I'd miss dancing.

"What do you wear when you dance?" he asked with a scary intensity, his eyes never leaving my face.

With that question, I was starting to get the gist of his troubled look, but I decided to answer honestly anyway. "I wear leotards, stretch shorts and tights to practice in and dance costumes for the performances." I looked right at him, daring him to say something bad about it.

"Are you comfortable being in front of all those people with so few clothes on?" He asked it in a guarded way, as if he was trying to be as polite as possible.

With a soft laugh, I said, "Everything important is covered up, and yes, I'm very comfortable with it. I've always been a bit of an extrovert, and dance is a form of artistry, Noah. People aren't looking at my body. They're watching me dance."

"Yeah, I bet they are," he said sarcastically.

I squeezed my lips together tightly, trying to control the anger that was rising in me. With a small breath and an attempt to keep the sound of my voice level, I said, "What's that supposed to mean?"

"Did you know that the Amish don't dance?" When I lifted my eyebrows at his interruption, he continued, "The elders believe dancing is very sensual and that it gives young people ideas about...things." He waited for my reply with his eyes slightly narrowed, obviously expecting an argument.

I was going to control myself, though. I'd already decided hours ago that I wasn't going to be too judgmental about his way of life. It would be hard, though.

"Well, that's too bad for you all. Dancing is wonderful. It's a way to express myself and be athletic. And the music..." After a pause, I added, "The music really is the heart of it all. Is it true you don't listen to any music?"

"We're not supposed to, but sometimes we do." He shrugged.

"Usually when we ride in a car, we listen to what the English driver has on the radio."

Our legs were still rubbing as we walked down the lane, and the bothersome fluttering in my stomach and beating of my heart were causing my brain to turn to mush under the physical bombardment. But still I managed to find the brain function to know that I didn't comprehend the last part of what he'd said.

Confused, I asked, "What do you mean *English?*"

With a quick glance back at me, as if he was disclosing an embarrassing secret, he said in an even tone, "Just not Amish."

"You mean that I'm considered *English* to you?" I asked, incredulous.

"Yep—it doesn't matter where you're from or what color your skin is. If you're not Amish, you're English." He said it with a surety that I found slightly disturbing.

Looking squarely back at him, I sighed. "Now, let me get this straight. You don't dance and you aren't allowed to listen to music, but sometimes you do, and the entire population on the earth is English to you?"

"That's a bit simplified," he muttered with an edge to his voice I hadn't heard yet. I watched him deal with his agitation by running his hand absently through his thick hair, leaving it wonderfully ruffled.

At the second I was admiring his hair, a couple of birds, quail, I think, flew up noisily in front of us with their feathered wings pumping hard to get airborne.

Lady, being true to her spooky nature, shied right into Rumor—hard. Noah reacted quickly, reaching out with his free hand and grasping my arm to steady me on my horse. Not that I really needed the help, but it was a chivalrous thing to do. I certainly didn't mind the physical contact either.

For a few seconds we just stood there with his hand gripping my arm and Lady trembling beneath me, almost on top of Rumor. Glancing down at his fingers, I bit the corner of my mouth and looked up at his face, which wasn't very far from mine. Both our legs were being mashed between the horses. I could only speak for myself, but I assumed he was feeling the same pain I was.

Still holding on to to me but with a looser grasp, thank goodness, he asked, "Are you all right, Rose?"

His voice was anxious, and I felt his warm breath touch me when he spoke. I was actually a little faint, and it certainly wasn't because my stupid horse was afraid of a ten-ounce bird. My breathing quickened, and I waited for him to lean in and kiss me. This was the perfect time and place. Well, besides the fact that our legs were being crushed.

I waited—but nothing. He didn't do it. Instead, when I couldn't get my lips to answer him because they were too busy getting ready for a kiss, he released my arm and moved Rumor out a little in front of us with a nettled expression written on his face.

I must have been mistaken about his attraction for me. Feeling suddenly and completely disappointed, I inadvertently sighed too loud, squeezing Lady into a walk.

But before my emotions could play too much havoc with me, he stopped Rumor and waited for me to walk up alongside him. And again our legs were lightly brushing together— a truly wonderful feeling—and I was happy once more. Talk about mood swings.

"Do you have a boyfriend?" He stared straight at me with smoldering eyes, and his voice was low and serious.

That question meant I still had a chance with him, I assumed. I admitted in an equally low and serious voice, "No."

Watching him closely, I noticed he breathed a little easier, but he still had something on his mind.

Not looking at me this time, he asked tentatively, "Have you ever had...a boyfriend?"

So he wasn't just worried about a current guy in my life; he was going to obsess about any previous boyfriends, too. That was interesting. Was he the jealous type? I spied at him from the corner of my eye and saw that he was a statue of stone, hardly breathing at all, waiting for my answer.

"No—I've never had a boyfriend. You know, too busy with my horse and the dancing..." I trailed off, fidgeting with the laces on my saddle, feeling suddenly awkward explaining to this gorgeous guy why I was sixteen and always single.

The curiosity got to me, though, and I took a little gulp of air and bravely asked, "What about you—do you have a girlfriend?"

Instantly, he relaxed in his saddle and turned to me with a brilliant smile. "No, up until now I hadn't met the right girl yet."

My eyes must have bugged out, because he laughed at my expression. Was he insinuating that I was the right girl? His confidence was beginning to irritate me. What made him think that I was automatically available?

Somehow I managed to recover my composure enough to again change the subject to safer territory. "So how did you manage to get away tonight to go riding?" I asked in the calmest, most disinterested voice I could summon from my mouth.

It was so infuriating how a part of me wanted Noah's lips pressed against mine and the other part was scared to death of what he was doing to my poor body. I kind of had a clue as to which of the battling sides would ultimately win when I glanced back at him, suddenly thinking of Mom's favorite

Western movie. He was sitting straight in the saddle but still relaxed, just like Captain Call from *Lonesome Dove*. At ease, but ready for a gunfight. There was something very cool about him. Unfortunately, I think he knew it, with the little bit of arrogance he carried around with him. He was looking at me now with a lazy curiosity that was so mesmerizing I couldn't turn away.

"I try to go for an evening ride occasionally when my work schedule permits. So it wasn't shocking to Father that I went out tonight." He removed the flirty look from his face when he said it, but his eyes still seemed to be twinkling.

"Do you normally come out here by yourself?" I had a bunch of good reasons to ask that question, but I hoped he wouldn't pick up on the main one—that I had turned into a jealous vamp the moment I laid eyes on him. Now I was wondering how many Amish girls he met out here in the cozy cornfields for his joyrides.

The amused smile erupted again on his lips and he made sure to hold my gaze with a steady stare while he answered. "Usually I'm very much alone, but occasionally—" his smile widened to keep me in suspense "—one of my little brothers comes riding with me," he finished, flashing me his teeth.

I wondered at that second if my face and voice were so transparent that he'd understood why I'd asked that particular question. He certainly seemed to have a clue. The thought that he could read me that well was unsettling. So, even though his answer was a good one and gave me a warm, fuzzy feeling, I still felt insecure in his presence, worried that he'd already figured out that I had a major crush on him.

We rode along quietly for a minute or two, until we finally reached the end of the cornfields. In front of us rose a thick wood that the lane meandered into, disappearing within the dark shade of the trees. It was a fairy wood, full of secrets, and just then, as the sun dipped down in the western sky, a beautiful pinkish-red sunset spread out on the horizon, causing a magical creamy light to settle over the corn.

The air was turning chilly. I shivered once, looking deeper into the trees.

Noah must have seen my uncontrollable shake, and with a resolute voice of authority, he said, "I better get you home. It's getting late, and it'll be dark soon."

I nodded, totally disappointed to be leaving the magical forest behind. We reined the horses around, entering the cornfields once again. And even more disappointing was that he didn't seem to have any plans to kiss me that night. At least he certainly wasn't taking advantage of being out here in the middle of nowhere, without a soul to see us. Maybe he's being gentlemanly, I considered. Or maybe I should take the lead. But then, I'd never kissed anyone, and I'd probably mess it up.

All my friends had been initiated into the world of kissing as preteens, but I'd been different. At the age most girls were learning the dating secrets, I had been more interested in kissing my horse's velvety nose than swapping spit with a boy. I was also cursed with an overly protective brother, who had regularly threatened to beat up any of the guys who showed an interest in me.

Noah said he hadn't met the right girl yet. Did that mean he hadn't kissed before either? For guys that statement could mean any number of things. I found it hard to believe that an eighteen-year-old guy as handsome as Noah hadn't done a lot of kissing already. Maybe he wasn't making out with girls in the fields, but he could be sneaking off somewhere else for that sort of thing. The thought bothered me a lot more than I cared to admit, and I was starting to think my brain's unhealthy obsession with my neighbor was bordering on a fatal attraction.

"So, what are you going to do tonight?" he asked in an upbeat manner, giving the impression of a person without a care in the world.

"Well, my dad is at the hospital and my brothers are seeing a movie, so I'll probably continue unpacking and organizing stuff," I said sullenly, still thinking about him and a bunch of imaginary girls.

"Won't you be afraid in that big old house all by yourself?" he asked playfully.

"No." I hesitated, wondering how much of my inner soul I should share with him. Feeling an odd comfortableness with him, I decided to be honest and said, "Mom dying was the scariest thing I've ever faced. Staying alone in a spooky old house really pales in comparison to that." I shifted in the saddle to smile ruefully at him.

There was really nothing he could have said to make me feel better. He seemed to know that, and instead he reached out instinctively and took my hand softly in his. His touch caused a warm feeling to spread through my body, leaving me perfectly content and totally shocked at the unexpected gesture.

He smiled at me triumphantly, making my heart melt into a puddle, and his thumb swirling in place on my hand sent goose bumps up my arm. This was a monumental achievement in my life—my first real hand-holding experience. Not trusting the feel of his hand over mine, I had to look down and see it with my eyes to make sure that I wasn't having a hallucination. Nope—I wasn't dreaming. I was really holding hands with this Greek god look-alike who wore suspenders and didn't drive a car.

Maybe now that we'd gotten to this stage of the relationship, I could begin to relax a little, I reasoned with myself. But then the tugging of worry harassed me. *What am I doing?* There was little chance that Noah and I could work through the obstacles in our way. The fact that I didn't wear dresses and a bonnet and that he probably had never heard of my favorite bands before, and even if he had, he wasn't allowed to listen to them, were just the first things that had popped into my mind. There were so many issues we'd have to deal with. How could a relationship possibly work?

We continued to ride holding hands, in silence, with only the sound of birds calling to each other in the air around us as they settled in for the night. I could tell that Noah's mind was filled with as many thoughts as my own by the way he stared out into the corn with his lips pressed tightly together. But the warm press of his hand calmed the voices in my head and I relaxed, savoring the moment—until my cell phone rang.

My rock-song ringtone raised his eyebrows, and he was suddenly alert, glancing around in quick movements. I assumed that he was checking to see if anyone had sneaked up on us or if the loud noise had given us away.

I pushed Noah's startled look from my mind and glanced at the phone. It was Sam and I answered with irritation, "What do you want, Sam? Yeah, I'm fine—I'll see you later. Bye."

He looked at me questioningly while I shoved the phone back into my pocket. "Just my big brother checking up on me," I told him, wondering if he'd try to hold hands again.

"Sam is very intuitive to be calling you."

"Should he be worried?" I teased.

"Most definitely," he said brightly, holding his hand back out.

Without hesitation, I quickly gave him my hand.

"So, what are you doing tomorrow?" I asked lightly.

"If Jacob can find a driver, we're going to a horse sale in Sugar Creek. He wants to trade his older Belgians for a younger team."

"Really, that sounds like fun." Plans were already forming in my mind.

"Yeah, but our driver has a wedding to go to, so unless Jacob can find someone to pull our trailer for us, we won't be going." He was looking down at my hand when he said it, pulling Lady and myself even closer to him and Rumor, so that my leg was wedged in behind his—making my body go crazy all over again.

But my mind was still working, and I suggested, "Maybe Sam could do it." He looked up in surprise, and I continued hurriedly, "I mean, he has a big truck with a gooseneck hitch, and he's hauled my horse to shows for me before. He's actually better at pulling the trailer than my dad is. Jerry and Rita just hauled Lady here to save us a trip and to see the new place."

His face scrunched up in concentration, and slowly a smile spread onto it. "Maybe my father will allow it—but I don't know if he'll let me go." He looked up suddenly and squeezed my hand. "Will you go with your brother?"

"Of course. I wouldn't miss a horse sale, but why wouldn't your dad let you come with us?" I said, somewhat disgruntled. The whole reason I came up with the idea was to be with him.

Sighing, he said, "Father will not allow me to go if you're going. Boys and girls our age are not allowed to be around each other without an adult chaperone. But my uncle might be going along also, and then my father would consent," he said, thinking.

Glancing back at me with concentration lining his face, he said, "We'll pay him well for the service, but are you sure your brother will do it?"

"He has nothing else to do tomorrow, and if he can make a few bucks, I'm sure he'll be up to it. I'll ask him tonight. How will we get in contact—you don't have a phone, right?"

He laughed at that, shaking my hand with enthusiasm. "Yes, we have a phone—it's not in our house, though. It's in the shed."

"That's not very convenient. How can you hear it when it rings?" I asked, thinking about all the calls they must miss.

"It has a very loud ringer, so we can usually hear it from the house." He said it as if it was obvious.

Oh. I felt a bit stupid. But it was difficult to wrap my mind around the idea that some people chose to not have things like telephones conveniently located within their homes. Glancing again at Noah, I had to admit that other than the clothes and his extreme good looks, he seemed like any other guy at the moment. Maybe that's what made me forget that he wasn't ordinary at all.

Reluctantly, I let go of his hand and pulled the phone from my pocket, handing it to him. "Go ahead and put your number in, and I'll call you tonight after I talk to Sam."

He held the cell in his hand as if it was a hot grenade, staring down at it with extreme thought.

Shoot, I did it again. He wouldn't know how to work my smartphone. "Oh, sorry, I forgot. This is a little complicated if you aren't used to one. So, what's your number?" I said, taking the phone back as casually as possible.

As he recited it, I entered the number and then put the phone away. Once my hand was free, he reached for it again.

"It's nice holding your hand," he said. Then in a fluid motion he brought my hand to his lips and lightly kissed my palm, causing a tingling that spread from my hand upward. Anticipation filled me. *This is it—he's going to kiss me now.* I wanted him to so badly at the moment it was hurting my insides, and I looked up with hooded eyes, waiting—waiting to get another first out of the way.

He swayed closer to me, but then cussing "damn" under his breath, he lowered my hand and exhaled loudly.

Exasperated, he said, "You're going to drive me crazy, Rose."

I started to pull my hand away, but he held it firm, going on to explain, "Look, we're almost to the road. Someone might see us—and that can't happen." He spoke harsher and looked grave as he continued, "If we want to spend time together, we have to be very careful about it, always looking out and thinking ahead. Do you understand?"

I nodded.

He sighed, saying, "And have your brother call tonight—not you. It's not proper for Amish girls to call boys on the phone."

"But I'm not Amish," I pointed out.

"But I am, and if we're going to be able to see each other, you're going to have to start acting a little more like an Amish girl." As an afterthought, he said, "Just pretend, Rose. Make it a game."

He said it as if he was talking to a small child, ticking me off a little bit. I couldn't keep the huff from escaping my lips in agitation.

Annoyingly, he just laughed and asked, "Want to race back to the road?"

The irritation that had rippled through my insides slipped away, to be replaced with a sudden jolt to my heart. "You bet," I answered, giving Lady a bump with my heels and grabbing her mane as she took off.

I almost reached the road first, but every time I glanced back, it didn't seem as though he was trying very hard. I was

starting to think he was going to let me win, which wasn't
the way that I wanted to beat him at all. I began pulling on
my reins at the same instant that Noah's horse had a burst of
speed. Doing a totally unsafe guy thing, he passed by me,
swerving hard before he nearly hit the wire mesh that ran
parallel to the tree line.

"Crap!" I muttered as I pulled alongside him, our horses
bumping each other again. I was starting to get the feeling that
Lady had as much of a thing for Rumor as I had for his rider.

"Gotcha!" He grinned, reaching out for my hand.

Only this time I ignored it, trotting ahead of him. When I
arrived at the gap in the fence, he wasn't with me. Instead, he
was standing behind a copse of trees about a hundred feet back.

Darn, I didn't mean to make him mad. I was just aggravated
with his daredevil riding. Whirling Lady around, I squeezed
her with my heels and quickly closed the distance back to him.

"What's up?" I asked, pulling up close to Rumor.

"You have to go home first, Rose. That's what I mean about
being careful. We can't just ride up the road together. Someone might see us, and that would be a disaster. Just please trust
me on this," he implored.

"But how long are you going to wait, then?" The fact that
there would be dire consequences if we were caught together
or if I even called him on the phone was triggering little bells
to go off in my head, but I chose to ignore them. My girlfriends back in Cincinnati would be locked up in jail for sure
under these rules.

"I'll hang out here for about fifteen minutes and then head
home. Now, Rose, you ride straight home, and if any cars slow
down for you, just gallop that mare as fast as I know she'll go
until you reach your driveway. Hopefully, everything will
work out and I'll see you tomorrow."

The urgency in his voice finally got me moving, and I turned, cantering toward the gap. Once on the road, I trotted the rest of the way home, the darkness quickly descending around me. Goose bumps spread up my arms when the light vanished and I squeezed Lady back into a canter once I reached the driveway.

I couldn't deny the way Noah made my body feel, that was for sure, but my mind was still struggling with the whole Amish thing. Where on earth could this relationship go?

But then, I didn't care what the answer was. I just wanted to enjoy it while it lasted.

6

Noah
Walking the Amish Line

IT WAS GOING TO BE DIFFICULT TO GET AWAY with it, I thought as I passed through the gap in the fence and rode onto the road. Rose was absolutely naive about what we were up against. And she certainly didn't hide her emotions well either.

Whenever she looked at me with those lovely eyes, there was no doubt about her feelings. She wanted me as badly as I wanted her. And as much as I liked having those eyes directed at me in that way, she'd have to learn to control them or she'd get us in a whole heap of trouble. Secretly meeting up with an English girl was the type of thing that could get me sent off to a community in Pennsylvania. And I wouldn't be able to come home until the bishop there felt I was truly rehabilitated.

Nathaniel Yoder barely missed making the trip out of state when his father caught him with a cell phone last year. Lucky for him, the worst punishment he received was being forced to smash the phone with a hammer.

Of course, I didn't think Rose even worried about getting in trouble. It seemed she was allowed to do pretty much anything she wanted, and even if she did break a rule in her house, she'd probably be able to talk her way out of it with her father. She was very compelling. I certainly hadn't planned to touch her hand, but when she talked about her mother and then looked at me with her sad eyes, I just couldn't resist. And her hand had fit perfectly into mine. I really wanted to kiss her there in the cornfield, and had almost done just that, except somehow I'd been able to rein myself in before I got carried away.

It was just too soon for that. We weren't even courting, and although I realized that the chance of doing so was slim at best, I still needed to try to make it happen. Somehow, in just a few short hours, I had developed feelings for Rose—strong feelings. And the thought of her being mine was intoxicating.

I'd never reacted to a girl this way before. My body was on fire when I was around Rose, and when I wasn't with her, all I did was think about her. Today had been the longest day of my life, dragging on forever until it was finally time to go meet her in the field.

I was planning to sneak up on her, but when I saw her start to canter ahead of me, I was impressed by what a good rider she was, and impulsively kicked Rumor into a gallop to race her. If the field had been a little longer, she would have definitely whipped me. Rumor was carrying a lot more weight and beginning to labor. I was happy that we were even able to stay with the gray horse for as long as we did.

Not being able to keep the smile from stretching my mouth, I decided that the evening had been the most fun I'd had in a very long time—maybe ever. She was the perfect girl for me, I reckoned—except for not being Amish. But I didn't care that she was English. My ideas about the people of the outside world had changed overnight—at least about one of them anyway. I knew that my feelings weren't rational and that my behavior was dangerous, but I wasn't willing to walk away at this point. I was driven now to see it through.

Cantering up the driveway, I quickly unsaddled Rumor and put him out in the pasture. I finished cleaning the stalls and then hurried to the house. The sky was coal-black by the time I entered the mudroom and pulled my boots off.

Seeing Jacob and Father sitting at the kitchen table under the dim light of the gas lamp with a pile of papers strewn out around them, I wasted no time asking, "Jacob, have you found a driver for tomorrow yet?"

Without raising his head, he replied, "No, I called several people, but they're all busy."

His voice held a hint of disappointment, and I seized the opportunity. "I found a driver for you." Both Father and Jacob looked up at me speculatively and I continued, "While I was out riding, I met Sam on the road and he was in a dually truck with an extended cab." I took a second to breathe. "I asked him if he would be interested in driving us to a horse sale tomorrow with our trailer, and he said he would—but he'd have to check with his father first."

It was strange how easily the lie came to me. I was willing to do just about anything to see Rose again. Obviously the time spent with the beautiful girl was already corrupting me.

Studying their expressions, I saw Jacob's face brighten at the news and Father purse his lips, thinking for a few seconds before answering. "That sounds like a possibility. This is the biggest sale of the season, and I'd hate to miss the chance to trade those two horses in for the quality of team you could find there, Jacob." He paused, meeting my eyes directly before asking, "Will the girl be going?"

"I don't know, Father." I said it with no emotion, hoping my face showed none either.

Father thought for a minute or so longer, absently scratching his beard, before saying, "Well, I suppose it will be all right. After all, your uncle Reuben will be going with you boys. But..." He paused to look at me, unsmiling. "If the girl does go, I'll not have you talking to her *at all,* Noah. Do you understand?"

"Yes, Father, I do," I said tonelessly, but inwardly my heart was beginning to race. *I'd say anything you want me to say, Father.*

The phone in the shed rang at that moment and I knew it was Sam. "That's probably Sam. Do you want me to go talk to him?"

"Yes, you can make the arrangements. I think I'll be turning in now—morning will be here before we know it."

I put my hand on his shoulder as I passed by him and said, "Good night, Father."

Stepping out into the cool night air, I knew that sleep would be a long time coming for me. I was so stirred up with the knowledge that I'd be spending the entire day with Rose that I'd probably be up all night.

When I saw Sam's truck coming up the driveway, all feelings of sleepiness left me. I could make out that Rose was in the passenger seat, and my heart skipped a beat. I quickly turned away and continued currying old Buttercup's tawny fur, being careful not to let my eyes stray back to the truck.

I finished Buttercup and moved over to Sally. Starting on her, I could hear Sam backing up to the trailer behind me. I was nervous that Rose would walk over and begin talking to me. She was so forward that it wouldn't surprise me at all if she ignored my warnings.

Instead, when I spied over my shoulder with a glance, she was standing behind the truck, directing her brother to the hitch. Not something a girl would usually be doing, but at least she wasn't talking to me, and that was a good thing at the moment.

Resuming Sally's brushing, I registered that Rose's long hair was pulled up in a ponytail, and she was wearing faded blue jeans and a blue T-shirt. She looked good in blue. It matched her eyes. I had thought the same thing the night before, but that shirt had been different than this one, prettier in a way. Then again, she was beautiful in anything.

Once the trailer was hitched up, Jacob and I loaded the horses and climbed into the backseat of the truck. Jacob explained to Sam that we were picking Uncle Reuben up on the way.

As Sam pulled carefully out of the driveway, I couldn't help wondering what Rose was thinking at that moment. She had been silent, not even a nod in my direction. I was beginning to think either she was a very good actor or she didn't like me anymore. How irrational to think that. She was doing exactly what I had told her to do, but now I was aggravated with how well she was doing it. It made no sense at all, but then, all my common sense went out the window when I was around her.

It was still early morning and the cloudy, overcast gray sky had not opened up to the sun yet. The air was warm, though, and I figured it would be a hot day later on.

Pockets of wispy fog covered the roadway, and Sam slowed down accordingly.

Rock music was blaring from the radio, and I wasn't surprised when Jacob, speaking loudly to be heard over the noise, said, "You probably shouldn't play the radio when my uncle gets in." He said it in a friendly but uptight way.

"Sure thing, bro," Sam replied amicably as Rose reached for the knob and turned the music off.

It took just a few minutes to reach Uncle Reuben's house, where he was waiting by the roadway for us. When the truck stopped, Rose jumped out of the front seat, offering it to my uncle, who tipped his hat and thanked her. Then she did the unthinkable—pushing the front seat forward and climbing in the backseat, right next to me.

While I was worriedly trying not to let my long leg touch hers in the cramped space, Uncle Reuben turned and said, "Good morning, boys."

I froze.

"Good morning, Uncle. It looks like we'll have a nice day for the sale," Jacob answered in his best adult voice, thankfully getting Uncle's attention away from me.

Uncle Reuben then looked over at Sam and said, "I don't think I've met you, young man."

"I'm Sam Cameron, sir, and that's my sister, Rose," Sam said, not taking his eyes off the road.

"It's a pleasure to meet you, Sam," Uncle responded without acknowledging Rose. Usually I didn't pay much mind to how the other men ignored the young, unmarried women of the community, but at the moment I felt the heat of embarrassment wash over me at my uncle's rudeness. Wondering what Rose thought of it, I shifted just my eyes over to her. She sat perfectly still, looking out the window away from me, so I couldn't tell what was going on in her pretty head.

It was uncomfortably tight in the backseat with very little legroom for two men over six foot. I continued to be careful not to lean my leg onto Rose's, instead holding it awkwardly away from her.

As I tried to listen to Jacob and Uncle speak about crops and workhorses, the closeness of her body distracted me. I wanted to hold her hand and relax my leg onto hers. The scent coming from her was tantalizing my nostrils, a subtle, warm smell of lavender. I knew that smell well, for Mother had the plants growing in her garden.

I tried not to think about her scent, her body or her face, and just stared straight ahead for the hour-long journey through the countryside. It was damn near impossible, though, with her sitting just inches away.

When we finally arrived at the stockyard, I was happy to get out of the truck and stretch my legs. I needed to get my body away from the object of all its discomfort. Sitting so close to Rose without being able to touch her was like having an itch that I couldn't reach to scratch. It bordered on torture. Careful not to look in her direction, I went to the back of the trailer with Jacob and unloaded the horses.

Uncle Reuben waited with me while Jacob went into the building to get the horses' numbers. The place was filled to bursting, and we had to park in the neighboring field just to get a spot.

There was a festive atmosphere surrounding us with the murmuring of so many conversations popping from the crowd, mixed in with the neighing of horses in the air. The scent of grilling hamburgers floated on the breeze and my mouth watered even though I wasn't actually hungry. Once Buttercup and Sally were tied to the trailer, I risked peeking at Rose and saw her staring intensely at the workhorses.

Then she turned to my uncle and asked, "How old are they?"

He seemed a little surprised that she had spoken to him, but he recovered and answered, "I believe they are eighteen and nineteen."

"That's not very old. There was a lesson horse at the barn

I boarded at that was twenty-nine." She spoke with a sharp voice, and I braced myself for what she'd say next.

Uncle took her statement in stride. "Well, I've heard of riding horses being usable to that age, but truly, the type of strenuous work these horses must do on a farm is too much for them when they get on near twenty."

"But what's going to happen to them now that they're too old to work?" she asked Uncle pointedly. Then she turned her frown on me.

Uncle didn't seem to notice her worry since he was barely paying any mind to her at all. Instead, he was inspecting the pair of black horses that were being unloaded off the trailer beside us.

"Oh, don't worry about those drafts, missy. Some English will buy them for a small hobby farm or recreation," Uncle said as he walked away to greet Simon Troyer and his four teenage sons, who were coming up from the sale barns.

Timothy, who was the oldest, broke from the group and strode over to stand with me. Surveying the stockyard in the near distance, I could see several other Amish families I didn't recognize, and realized that Amish from communities all over this part of Ohio would be in attendance—making it virtually impossible for me to talk to Rose. We'd be seen for sure, I thought, chancing another glance at her.

What? To my surprise she was walking away from us, by herself, toward the sale barns. My mind raced. She shouldn't be alone in a public place like this. It wasn't safe or appropriate with all the men around here.

I urgently rounded on Sam, who was leaning against his truck doing something with his cell phone. Forgetting my code of silence about Rose in front of the others, I snapped,

"Sam?" He didn't hear me and I spoke a little louder, "Sam—your sister is walking away, *alone*."

"Huh?" He looked up at me, confused, and then toward Rose, who was almost out of sight. "So—what about it?"

With an exasperated sigh, I informed him, "There are a lot of people here, and some of them look unsavory." I nodded toward two cowboys with tattoos running down their arms, ambling a little ways from us.

Sam's gaze followed them for an instant, and then he looked back at me with the same look of bewilderment. "Those guys? Rose can take care of herself. Besides, she has her phone on her. She'll call me if there's a problem. Noah, don't worry about it." And then he went back to whatever he was doing, dismissing me entirely.

I was too maddened with him to say any more. If I did, my emotions would show, and someone would notice. My behavior would raise questions, so I silently fumed, waiting for Jacob to return.

After what seemed like forever, he finally showed up with the numbers, and I quickly put them on the horses and followed Jacob to the sale barns with Timmy still in tow, chattering about something unimportant. I scanned the crowd looking for Rose, but she was nowhere to be seen. Unease spread through me like a wildfire as we entered the barn and my eyes quickly adjusted to the shade. Dismayed, I saw that the building was immense on the inside, with several other barns interconnecting to accommodate the hundreds of pens filling the place. There were so many people milling around, and horses of every breed and color choked the aisleways, making it difficult to even move toward the pen that our horses were assigned to, let alone locate an English girl in the crowd.

The fact that Rose had just left me and gone off by herself

really exasperated me. Not only was it dangerous, it wasn't the way a girl should behave. Rose thought she could take care of herself, but I knew that kind of thinking could get a girl into a bad situation. And fast.

Amish girls, on the other hand, were raised from a young age to be obedient and dependent on the men in their lives. The men cherished their women and the women loved them for it.

But I was already in over my head with Rose, and now I had to deal with her wild behavior. Somehow I'd have to curb her impulses and make her listen to me. But it was for her good—I'd heard all kinds of stories about what happened to women out there among the English.

I grunted to myself, pondering the difficulty of getting Rose to change her ways. And I didn't think she'd be receptive to being told what to do directly. I'd have to be subtle about it and make her think she was doing what she wanted. What a challenge that would be. But I was up for it. If we were destined to be together, then Rose would come around.

As we squeezed through the crowd, I impatiently greeted several people from our own community and nodded to several more I didn't know. When running into other Amish people at an event like this, even if you didn't recognize them, there was a good chance you had some connection—either being related to them directly or through the community. I had to keep up the pleasantries.

After we got the horses in the pen and I had latched the gate, Jacob said, "I'm going to have a look around. Are you coming?"

I was uncertain whether it was a question, indicating I had a choice in the matter, when I glanced at Timmy and took a chance. "I thought I'd walk with Timmy... Is that okay, big brother?" I was friendly, hoping he'd give me some space. Jacob nodded, pivoting away and slipping into the crowd. Okay, one less obstacle to worry about.

I turned the opposite direction my brother had gone and strode forward, looking left and right for Rose without paying attention to Timmy, who was struggling to keep up with me in the press of people.

"Was that pretty English girl you were talking about at the truck your new neighbor?" Timmy whispered loudly, trying to match my stride.

So Timmy had noticed she was pretty and wasn't too shy to say it. I glanced at him, perturbed, but figured he'd probably not report me to the elders. He sneaked around enough that I had a few incidents I could hold against him, and decided that it was safe to give him a small amount of information.

I stopped and focused on Timmy's dark complexion and eyes and said, "Look, I'm a little worried about the English girl. Her mom died last year, and she just doesn't seem stable enough to be wandering around a place like this alone." Again the partial lie came too easy. Pausing, I saw curiosity on his face and continued, "So I'm going to try to find her and talk her into staying with her brother. I can do that quicker without you." I started to back away from him and said, "I'll catch up with you in a little while. Just don't say anything to anyone."

I was about to leave, when he grabbed my shoulder and asked in astonishment, "You talked to her?"

"Yes, and if you say anything about this to anyone, I'll make sure the elders know about your driver buying you that beer last month," I threatened.

His eyes became enormous, and racing the words together, he said, "Don't worry, Noah. I wasn't going to tell anyone." He stopped and scanned the crowd with a quick motion before going on. "But you better be careful. You'll be in more trouble running around with an English girl than I will for drinking some beer." What he said hung in the air for a few seconds before he left me to check out the horses in the nearest pen.

The entire conversation worried me, but then, I had more pressing things on my mind—like finding Rose. Spotting a stairway to the catwalks above the pens, I sprinted up them sideways, avoiding the people I passed. Once on the walkway, I leaned over the railing searching the building.

Amazingly, as if the two of us were linked together invisibly, it only took a few seconds for me to spot her from the vantage point I had. She was standing alone, looking into a pen with a few ponies in it. I made a mental note of her location and quickly went back down the dust-covered stairs to her. By the time I reached her, an English man I guessed to be in his twenties was talking to her. He had a square jaw, roughened with short stubble. He was wearing a black cowboy hat on his head and a big silver belt buckle above his groin. His physical closeness to her riled me and I sped up. As I neared, I could instantly tell by Rose's body posture that she was uncomfortable in the presence of the man. She was leaning away from him and looking straight into the pen.

Rose seemed to sense my approach. Turning her head suddenly toward me, her eyes caught mine and immediately she relaxed, a bright smile spreading across her face.

The man bent near her and asked, "Are you here alone?"

Before she could say a thing, I was by her side, answering for her. "She's with me." I shot a hostile look at him, bringing a snort and a crooked smile from his lips at the same time. He tipped his hat in an exaggerated way to Rose and walked away.

Before I risked talking, I surveyed the people around us. Finding none of my kind nearby, I leaned in close to her, only inches from her face, to whisper darkly, the tumult I was feeling clearly in my voice, "What do you think you're doing, Rose?"

She looked up at me, puzzled. "What are you talking about?"

Sighing, I stated the obvious. "You shouldn't be wandering around here by yourself. Imagine what could have happened with that cowboy if I hadn't found you when I did. You should have stayed with your brother," I said forcefully, realizing that I didn't have any authority over her. That really troubled me more than I cared to admit.

"I was just trying to do what you said and stay away from you in front of your people," she said sulkily, pouting out her lower lip in defiance.

The expression brought a smile to my lips, even though I tried to stop it. And in a milder tone, I said, "I know, you're doing a good job at ignoring me—almost too good, in fact." I took another quick look around. "But I didn't mean for you to go off by yourself. It's not safe."

She lifted her eyebrows and smiled tightly. "You're kidding…right?" Seeing my smile disappear, she said in a quiet voice that held a hint of threat in it, "Really, I can take care of myself."

"That's what your brother said," I answered coolly.

I watched the expression change on her face from annoyed, squinting eyes, to softer, flirting ones. I wondered at the change until she said, "What do you want me to do, Noah?" For a second I was at a loss for words. Was she sincere? That this beautiful girl was willing to ask what I wanted, and hopefully listen to me, sent a tingle through my body, and I chose to take her at her word, realizing how important she was to me now. Maybe she would be more receptive to our ways than I originally thought. Quickly, I came up with a plan.

"I'm going to follow behind you, close enough to keep an eye on you, but far enough that we won't look like we're together. Then when we find Sam, you should stay with him for the rest of the day," I told her. I was shocked when after several seconds of staring at me, she lowered her eyes and nodded her head in agreement.

That was almost too easy, I thought, watching her stroll away very leisurely. It soon became apparent to me that she may not have objected, but she wasn't in a hurry to find her brother either. She was very clever. The worst part was that she obviously had a lot of practice getting her way. That she was able to make my brain fizzle with a sultry look was not going to help me take charge of her either.

After she stopped for several minutes, staring into the same pen, I impatiently ventured up behind her to whisper, "You really need to go faster, Rose, so I can get back to Jacob and my uncle."

"Isn't he pretty?" She ignored what I said, squeezing her hand through the gate. She began petting a nicely built black-and-white paint colt, murmuring soft words to him as she did so.

"Yes, he is," I agreed, still slightly upset with her but more so with our circumstances. What I really wished for at the moment was that the two of us could walk around the sale together, looking at all the horses, and actually have fun. We could if we were officially courting. And she was Amish. Then I wouldn't have to boss her around and risk making her angry with me.

"I wish I could buy him," she said, gazing up at me with the look I imagined she used on her father when she wanted something. Then she said worriedly, "What if someone bad gets him?"

I sighed. "Would your father let you keep him?"

"I doubt it," she admitted.

While I was considering the colt, and checking to see if there were any of my people around, I spotted Sam a few pens down. To my amusement, he was leaning up against the wall talking to two cowgirls. Each had bleach-blond hair, and they were almost identical to each other, from the tight jeans they wore, to their tan straw hats.

"Found your brother." I pointed at him for Rose to see. When she did, she rolled her eyes at his companions with extreme flourish.

"Oh, great, now I'm stuck hanging around for the rest of the day with the bimbos Sam picks up. Thanks a lot, Noah." She met my eyes with a seething look and began to stalk away toward her brother.

The worry of someone catching us momentarily forgotten, I reached out and snatched her arm, pulling her back to me. "I'm sorry, Rose. This is just the way it has to be for now," I said in a whisper, but firmly, hoping she'd get over her anger with me quickly.

Holding my gaze, she muttered, "It's okay, I'll probably survive." Then she lowered her eyes to my hand still clutching her arm. I let go. She pressed her lips together, giving me a half smile before leaving.

I made sure she met up with her brother and his *friends,* silently wishing that Sam had chosen nicer girls to hang out with. But at least I wouldn't have to worry about her safety now.

Turning, I joined the mass of people and horses, in search of Jacob and Uncle Reuben. Finally, after a few minutes of wandering the stock pens, I found them, along with several other men from our community. As I made my way toward the group, I felt suddenly weary from the stress of looking for Rose and the lack of sleep the night before. All the sneaking around was tiring. I wondered how long I could keep it up before faltering and getting caught.

The sale ring was smoke filled and crowded, with barely an empty seat. The cigarette fumes were stinging my eyes, and dust clung to my pants, having rubbed off from the dirty seat I was sitting on. Actually, every object in the room was covered with the thick, dusty substance, dulling the red color of the seats to pink and even causing me to sneeze a couple times. I'd been sitting midway up the bleachers for the past several hours, all the time scanning the room hoping to catch sight of Rose.

Where could she be? Why hadn't she come in to watch the horses selling? Maybe she didn't like the smoggy dirtiness of the room. I would completely understand that, but interest in the sale would surely have brought her in here by now, I reckoned.

I was beginning to worry, and was just about to tell Jacob that I was going to grab a bite to eat as an excuse to see where she was, when I caught sight of Sam's big body pushing through the crowd near the sale ring. The two cowgirls were closely shadowing him. Rose, wearing a frown, was following farther behind.

I waved my hand at Sam, who saw me and headed up the narrow steps to the few vacant seats beside me. Rose sulked up the stairs behind them. Probably for the better, Sam sat next to me, with Rose finally settling into the chair four seats down. I would have liked her closer, but at least I knew where she was now. If she were sitting next to me, it would be too much of a temptation to talk to her. And with practically the entire Meadow View community in the seats around us, we'd be caught for sure.

The frisky black-and-white colt, entering the ring, caught my eye and swiftly I made a decision, probably a dumb one, but I only considered Rose's happiness. Leaning over, I whispered to Jacob my intentions and he responded, "Are you sure, Noah?"

"Yes—definitely," I replied firmly.

"We'll see how it goes, then," Jacob said and, listening to the auctioneer, held up his bidding number.

The spotter in the ring noticed and his hand shot up. "Yep!"

With a sideways glance, I saw Rose bounce forward and gawk in my direction, openmouthed. Her expression sent a jolt to my senses, exhilarating me. That one look was worth the money I'd spend on the colt.

There were a couple of other hands shooting up as the auctioneer raised the price by fifty-dollar increments. Jacob anxiously looked my way, and with my nod, he raised his card up and another "Yep!" was shouted from the ring.

The colt was spirited, and the yells from the ring were inciting him to pull against the green lead rope that bound him to a skinny little man who resembled a weasel wearing a cowboy hat. The cowboy was having a real time with the colt, being mowed over at one point and ending up on his backside in the soiled shavings littering the ring floor.

I had to smirk when the man was dragged back to his feet as the colt burst across the thirty-foot ring in a mad dash to escape. When it reached the metal fence, it stopped and stood motionless, except for a slight quiver, regarding its handler with a look of annoyance. The now-red-faced cowboy gave the colt some room while he brushed the pieces of wood chips from his fancy Western shirt. I liked the colt's spunk. It made me think of Rose.

The bidding slowed and then stopped at five hundred and seventy-five dollars. The auctioneer said, "Going once, twice...sold to number 1029." That was our number. I'd just bought a wild paint colt I really didn't need but, twisting subtly to see Rose was immediately thrilled with my purchase when she rewarded me with a dazzling smile. That smile was irresistible. Flashing a grin back at her, I straightened up and continued to give the illusion of watching the horse sale.

Two more hours passed and it was dark outside. The team of Belgians Jacob was interested in were just coming up now. Buttercup and Sally had already sold to an elderly English man for a decent price. I'd been pleased that the man seemed like a nice fellow, especially with the amount of interest Rose had showed in the workhorses. I had watched her stand up to get a better view of the buyer and then sit down appeased by what she'd seen.

Sam's *friends* had left a while ago, and right now Rose was leaning against him with her head on his shoulder, apparently asleep. *I wish I could trade places with him.* I spent the next few minutes staring at the action in the ring but not really seeing the horses. I was fantasizing about Rose. Sometimes the images heated my face, until Jacob finally bought his new team and we were loading them up in the trailer, along with my spunky colt.

The drive back home was very interesting. With the truck engine rumbling, Jacob immediately fell asleep, leaving me without a chaperone in the shadowy light of the backseat. Unable to resist the temptation, and careful not to startle Rose, I slipped my hand over and took hers between both of mine.

She tensed at first and then relaxed when I started trailing my finger over the inside of her wrist softly.

Just touching her like that, with my brother and uncle only inches away, gave me a quiet thrill. She responded to my hands by sliding closer to me until our sides were pressing into each other from shoulder to foot. It felt incredibly right, sitting beside her, touching her skin and feeling her softness. And the fact that she was English didn't matter at all right then. I was beginning to think that she already belonged to me.

While I sat there in the dark, my body was getting fired up, keeping me fully awake the entire drive. Rose let me know she wasn't sleepy either when she took her free hand and began touching my arm in the same way I was touching her. That sent a bolt of pleasure rippling through me. My brain started to cloud over with recklessness and I boldly leaned deeper into her, not caring about Jacob or Uncle. I guessed she was feeling the same desire that was igniting my body when her warm fingers caressed my arm lightly at first, then started to press harder—nearly pushing me over the edge. We touched each other like that, secretly in the darkness for the entire trip, until I felt certain that I knew her hands and arms as well as my own.

I was so wrapped up in the pleasurable sensations coming to life inside me that I completely lost track of time. All too soon, the trip ended and I had to release her and sit back up, pulling my body away from her. The places where she had been tucked against me were warm and relaxed. When we separated, my body responded as if it were losing a part of itself, becoming chilled.

In the back of my mind, I had hoped spending more time with Rose might dampen my interest for her. Only it had the opposite effect on me. After all, it would be much easier if I fell for a pretty Amish girl. I figured God was playing a cruel joke on me for bringing such a lovely temptation into my life. Because I knew it would take all my strength to resist Rose now—if I even could.

With disgust, I realized I couldn't even say goodbye to her or make plans for a next meeting while Jacob hovered around. And with Father marching toward us through the yard, I had to avoid even looking in her direction.

But rebelliousness gripped my soul, and I stole a glance at Rose anyway. My heart raced when her eyes met mine.

In that instant, I knew she belonged with me.

7

Rose
Amish Grace

THE *CLIP-CLOP, CLIP-CLOP* WOKE ME FROM A dreamless sleep. After stretching, I crawled along the floor to the open window. Propping my arms up on the windowsill and feeling as if I was in a time warp, I watched the line of buggies go down the road.

Two, three, five…they just kept coming. The solid-black covered buggies with large narrow wheels, all being pulled by bay or black horses, moved along the road with speed, looking like a bizarre funeral parade from the 1800s. *Clip-clop, clip-clop.* The sound was mesmerizing, pulling at some deeply hidden subconscious part of my brain that remembered back to the days when it was the only form of travel.

Stranger yet was the car passing the buggy parade—what a juxtaposition that was. I wished I could go and see what it was all about. But that was probably not allowed. The Amish people had so many rules. I could hardly believe they could keep up with them all.

Reluctantly leaving the window, I dressed in my most comfortable hanging-around-the-house gray sweats and oversize T-shirt, and headed down to the kitchen, where Dad was already scrambling some eggs.

"Do you have your room unpacked, Rosie?"

Only Dad called me that, and I cringed at the sound of it. I'd just about had him trained to only call me Rose. Sometimes he slipped up, though.

"Yeah, I'm almost done," I replied, pouring two glasses of orange juice.

"Did you have fun at the horse sale yesterday?" he asked, dropping bread in the toaster.

"It was interesting," I said tentatively.

"Why, what happened, honey?" He actually stopped his chef duties and looked at me.

"Well, the Amish people are so strict. I mean, Noah can't even talk to me or he'll get in big trouble, not only with his parents but his whole community." I took a sip of the juice, swallowed hard and said with force, "Can you believe that?"

He went back to stirring the eggs with the hint of a smile on his mouth. Dad was a handsome guy, I had to admit, even though he was my dad.

"And…do you like Noah?" He got right to the point. It was a doctor thing.

Without hesitation I answered, "Yeah, Dad, I like him. But why bother? We could never date. Heck, he says he can't even look at me." I was disgruntled and it showed.

"So you've actually discussed this with him? We've only lived here a few days. How'd you manage that?" he asked pleasantly.

He was a cool dad, not the type to get uptight about me liking a boy. In fact, he'd even tried to get me to go to the spring dance with Sam's friend Tyler. Tyler was cute, but I knew if I went to a dance with him, we'd be hooked up, and I wasn't that into him.

"We went riding together on Friday. He told me all sorts

of things about being Amish." Dad handed me a plate of eggs and after a big bite I told him, "And, you know what? I don't think I'd be very good at being one of 'em. I would hate having a group of people telling me what to do all the time," I grumbled.

"I'm really glad to hear that. I was beginning to worry that you'd convert and run away with the handsome neighbor boy." He laughed.

"Oh, don't worry about that, Dad…but do you really think he's handsome?" I teased.

Throwing the dish towel at my head, he said, "Not as handsome as me."

After breakfast we went and sat on the front porch together while the vampire boys slept in. Dad read his newspaper and I stared at the road waiting for more buggies to pass. But no more came. The road was very quiet now, almost eerily so.

"Dad…"

"Hmm?"

"Did you see all those buggies go by this morning?"

"Ah, a few of them. It was pretty neat, wasn't it?" Dad said, half-distracted with whatever he was reading.

"I was wondering…do regular people ever get to go to Amish church?"

He looked up then, abruptly, fully focused on our conversation, replying, "I don't really know about that, but from what Mr. Miller told me, the morning service lasts several hours, and then they all have lunch together and fellowship throughout the afternoon until the evening supper." He took a breath and went on, "After supper, the youth sing hymns, and following that, they play games like volleyball or basketball into the night."

"Whoa—that's crazy! Do they do that every Sunday?" I pushed for more information.

"I think they may take a Sunday off each month. But that reminds me, Mr. Miller invited us over to join the evening youth supper and singing tonight." The way he said it, all nonchalantly, I was sure he knew how excited I'd be about it.

"For real, tonight?" I was nearly jumping out of my skin.

"He said the food would be served at six o'clock and the singing would start at seven."

I started to think it was too good to be true and suspiciously grilled Dad. "Why would he want us to come over? From everything I've seen, they don't seem to like outsiders around."

"That's simple enough to figure out. I think Mr. Miller wants to introduce the new doctor in town to his community. It's a reasonable assumption anyway," he said humbly.

Excitement rising again, I asked the big question. "Are we going?"

"I think it would be rude not to, but I'm on call tonight, so I may have to leave early."

In a swift motion I jumped up, kissed him on the forehead and flung the screen door open.

"Where are you going?" he asked, looking startled.

"To wake up the barbarians and tell them about tonight."

Here I was again, walking through the mowed green field under the buttery sunshine of late evening, contemplating if I'd worn the right thing. I had been extremely conflicted. Should I wear my comfortable khakis or do I go all out and wear a dress? I even stooped to the level of taking a vote from the three men in the house. Not that they cared that much about what I wore, but they played along anyway. In the end, it was two to one, with Dad and Sam in favor of the dress, and Justin going for the pants.

Then I had to decide on the dress; obviously, not a short one. It came down to a long, flowing brown one or a sort of long black party dress. In the end, I put on the sleeveless brown one and judged that it had a beachy-tropical look, which I liked, and it was almost to my ankles, ultimately giving it the win.

I left most of my hair down, with just a few strands from the sides pulled back lightly with a leather barrette. On my feet I wore simple mocha-colored sandals, trimmed with turquoise.

The only jewelry I had on was a tiny golden cross that had belonged to Mom, and it rested in the center of my chest.

Overall, I felt extremely girlish. I usually didn't wear dresses unless forced to for some function or event that required it, but I was surprised that I felt pretty comfortable in this one at the moment.

Glancing at my guys, I had to admit they looked pretty good, too. Dad was wearing his usual casual dress clothes, totally expected and not shocking at all. But Sam and Justin both had on tan Dockers and button-up dress shirts that made them look like youth models for the JCPenny catalog.

Even before we crossed the bridge, I could see Amish people everywhere. Babies, toddlers, little kids, big kids, teenagers, adults, elderly—every age group was represented. As we approached, I noticed a group of little girls playing on the supersize swing set. Their pretty dresses were in varying subdued colors, flapping in the breeze, reminding me of Easter eggs. And their bright white caps fit their heads so snugly that they didn't budge at all with the motion of the swinging, as if they were extensions of the girls' bodies.

Close to the swings was a larger group of preteen girls

standing together quietly. They appeared to be watching the littler girls, and they were wearing mostly the same colors as them, although a few sported dark maroon and hunter-green dresses.

Groups of little boys, pretty much identical in appearance from their haircuts to the perfect little-man clothes they all wore, were scattered about chasing each other. I thought I might have seen one of Noah's brothers run by but certainly wouldn't bet any money on it. With this group, I wouldn't have been able to pick one out in a police lineup.

My eyes finally wandered to the gang of about fourteen teenage boys who were hanging out near the barn, trying to look cool, idly leaning against the white boards. Some wore that bland blue that dress shirts usually sported, while others had on sand-colored ones. The shirts were all long sleeved and every one of the guys had on matching black vests. Studying them, I decided they all had a sort of self-important quality about them that vexed me—until I saw him.

My pulse quickening, I spotted Noah easily. He was one of the tallest boys in the group and he was lounging like the rest of them, with one leg propped up on the barn. He hadn't noticed me yet, so I had a few seconds of privacy to drool over him. He was one of the guys wearing a sand-colored shirt, and it complemented his dark ruffled hair in a very hot way.

I fretted over whether he would be happy to see me here, as my sight strayed to where the teenage girls were gathered near the house. They were standing neatly in a long line, as if they were waiting for something to happen. The dresses and caps they wore mimicked the younger girls', but that's where the resemblance ended. The littlest girls were playing and having some fun. The preteen girls were standing in a group, talking a bit, but definitely starting to take on a more disciplined approach to life. In contrast, the girls my age exhibited no personalities whatsoever. They were standing silently and without expression, unnaturally so. It was difficult to tell them apart at a glance, but a few were taller or shorter, bringing my eyes to settle on them for an instant longer.

Continuing to roam my eyes around the quaint setting intently, I tried to commit the unusual sight to memory. My initial assumption had been that the main differences between Amish culture and the rest of the world were the obvious ones, the way they dressed, not using electricity or driving cars, things like that. But the cultural divide was much deeper than that. As I absorbed and scrutinized what I was witnessing, it became apparent that the subtle differences were the ones that separated our worlds the most. There was a lack of sound you wouldn't expect from a gathering this size; no yelling, calling out or loud laughing. The totally pent-up emotions of everyone over eight was creepy. But what bugged me the most was the division between the sexes. Don't these women know that we fought for and won equality?

While I was inwardly ranting, something else caught my attention, causing me to scan everyone in the crowd twice before I realized I must have entered another dimension or alternate reality. Most of the little boys and almost every girl, from toddler to teenager, were barefoot! The girls' perfectly clean, pressed and tailored appearance ended at their feet. And they weren't discriminating about where they walked either—barn dirt mixed with horse manure, gravel, hot pavement, none of it seemed to bother their rhino-hide feet at all. I could barely walk across a driveway without wincing the entire time.

Seeing the enormous number of children, and the teenage girls lined up with their modest dresses and bare feet, invited a slight grimace to my mouth, thinking that these women took the whole barefoot-and-pregnant thing seriously. And then I did see a very pregnant woman, holding a toddler on her hip, and yep, she was very barefoot. I had to cover my mouth to hide the uncomfortable giggle.

That was the exhilarating and terrifying moment when all the Amish seemed to notice us—including Noah, whose stunned eyes traveled over me from head to toe and back up again, with a swift examination. For an instant his mouth dropped open slightly and then, regaining his composure, he averted his eyes. But all the other boys certainly didn't, and neither did the girls or even the adults scattered in among the young people. They were all staring at us wide-eyed as we walked past the barn and toward the house. If I thought it was quiet before, now you could have heard a pin drop.

I suddenly felt completely and ridiculously out of place. But then I caught Sarah's attention, and without hesitation, she came forward, took my hand and pulled me toward the waiting girls. I inclined my head to watch Sam sauntering toward Noah's group. Justin met up with Peter and Daniel and they darted off together to join a bunch of boys in the shed. Dad had completely disappeared.

I abruptly realized I was abandoned. If Noah had been with me, I would have been fine, but surrounded by all this strangeness, I felt alone and self-conscious as I forced a smile at the waiting girls.

"This is Rose, our new neighbor," Sarah told the group, and the orderly wall line folded in around me. Sarah was pretty perky now, and with enthusiasm she began telling me all the girls' names. If I were tested on them, I would have failed miserably for sure.

A few of the girls' names and faces did register with me, though. Maretta was a short, pudgy brunette who beamed at me with a huge smile. Suzanna had the palest blue eyes I'd ever seen, with a few wisps of white-blond hair escaping from her cap. She had a devilish grin on her face, making me think that some of these girls might not always be as reserved as they first appeared to be.

Then there was Ella. A feeling of instant dislike struck me when I was introduced to her. She was Katie's younger sister, and while she wasn't quite as pretty as Katie, with her doelike hazel eyes, she was close. Unlike her sister, she had a meanness about her that I immediately picked up on—almost as if she hated me, even though she didn't know me. She put on a friendly show for the others, but something about the way her eyes narrowed and her brows knit together for a fraction of a second told me that she was undeniably no friend of mine.

For the next few minutes, I answered a variety of questions from the curious girls. How old are you? Where did you used to live? How old is your brother (meaning Sam)? Do you drive a car? All of which I responded to simply, keeping my answers short and sweet.

Saving me from the interrogation was a middle-aged woman, also barefoot, ordering the girls to come in and get the tables ready for supper. Sarah tugged on my arm and I joined the succession of girls into the house and down the steps to a vast, fully finished basement.

I had to admit I was impressed, surveying the dozen extra-long tables set up in neat rows and bordered by long, simple wooden benches. The tables were covered with white plastic cloths and the smells floating around the space triggered me to lick my lips.

The girls made their way to a fully appointed kitchen in the corner of the room. Like a very well-oiled assembly line, they began their task. It started with a couple of girls putting ice into the cups, several more pouring the water and then the remaining girls carrying the cups out to the tables, setting them at perfect two-foot intervals.

The women were also working seamlessly together, carrying trays and large pots of food to the buffet-style table at the near side of the room. The sight of about fifteen pies on the end of the table dropped my jaw—chocolate, cherry, apple, cream, to name just a few, were waiting to be cut into.

Yes...I had some issues with Amish society, but the food wasn't one of them. These ladies knew how to cook and bake. I was anxious to sit down and begin, until I recalled the dining experience with Noah's family. I breathed heavily, suddenly deflated. Sarah heard me as she walked by and, slowing, she questioned me with her eyes. I smiled slightly and shrugged, following her into the kitchen area where the other girls were lining up neatly, along with the women and little girls.

Silently and working hard to stay motionless, I stood between Sarah and Suzanna, observing the procession of men and boys stroll into the food line. In front were the older ones and Dad was among them, conversing with a long-bearded gentleman I hadn't seen before. The younger guys were crowded in at the back with some structure but not the organization that the girls exhibited.

Again, I didn't have to look hard to see Noah. He towered over the other boys. Well, 'cept for Sam, but he was a freak and didn't count. When Noah walked into the basement, I saw him carefully scan the room, until his eyes met mine. After gracing me with a sly grin, he quickly glanced away. My body heated up at his look, and I willed the blush to stop spreading across my face. At the same time, the pleasurable feeling that Noah had started in me was tantalizing my senses, a trace of the hair on my neck went up, and I was compelled to search down the line of girls, finally meeting Ella's face. She was staring at me with pure loathing.

Bingo. Now I got it. Ella had a thing for Noah, and she'd seen the looks he'd been giving me. Unease settled into my bones while I dissected the information. The Amish got married relatively young, and Ella was probably two years older than me, making her all too ready to tie the knot with the best-looking Amish guy in the community, especially with Katie marrying Noah's brother.

The way she regarded me was bordering on sinister, finally giving me the first taste of what Noah and I were up against. His parents had already given Jacob the green light to marry into that particular family, so they must approve of them. That meant they'd support Katie's younger sister hooking up with Noah, and probably even push for it if they knew Ella was interested.

So how could Noah possibly pick me? How could a relationship of any kind work at all? Why was I even wasting my time with all these goofy romantic feelings for a guy I was doomed to never be with? But then, my eyes made their way back to him and he was closer now, having moved up in the line, while I'd been distracted. He was joking with Sam about something and they were both laughing. How unfair that was! Sam got to talk to him and stand next to him and look at him, while I was stuck here like a Grecian statue, starving and receiving nasty looks from one of Noah's admirers.

As if Sam could read my mind, he glanced over at me, and immediately an obnoxious twist appeared on his mouth. Then the jerk had the nerve to raise his hand and wave. I breathed deeply in fury and was close to marching over there and smacking him, when my peripheral sight caught Noah's eyes, thick with warning. He actually tilted his head a tad and set his jaw—as if he was commanding me to behave.

Before I could act on the violent rage developing in the pit of my being, Sarah took my hand, guiding me along with the other girls to the end of the line. As much as I detested not responding to Sam's rude display, I did just that, reluctantly being pulled along by Sarah.

After filling my plate, I drifted over to the teenage-girl table, noting that I had more food piled on my plate than any of the other girls. Oh, well, until I started gaining weight, I was going to enjoy all the good cooking I could eat. After all, it was about the only thing these girls were allowed to do.

Funny, the young men's table was right beside ours, and without even wasting a glance in that direction, I had walked by, feeling not only Noah's eyes on me, but several other pairs of eyes also. Now sitting with my back to the guy table, I could still sense the penetrating look coming from Noah. To test my supernatural powers of observation, I eyed over my shoulder, subtly as I could manage, and then briskly straightened again after seeing that I was right. Noah was staring at me, sending a shiver through my limbs and a jolt to my heart.

"Do you have a boyfriend, Rose?" It was Suzanna with the same sparkle in her eyes I had seen earlier, bringing me back to my senses.

"Nope—and I don't want one either," I said, hoping Noah had heard. I was still miffed that he could control me with a menacing look.

"I've heard English girls have multiple boyfriends at once," Ella commented sarcastically without tearing her attention away from her fried chicken.

"Gee, I have a lot of *English* friends and none of them attempt to juggle more than one boyfriend at a time," I shot back without thinking. I stared hard at her, hoping she'd raise her face. But she didn't—lucky for her.

Several of the girls giggled, letting their quiet and reserved demeanor drop for a second.

"Is it true that you dance?" Maretta asked in a hushed voice, as if she feared she'd be overheard. I was happy for the change of subject, though.

Before I answered, the girls all leaned in to me to hear better, paying close attention. I had a flashback to when I was fourteen, and Olivia Hemmer had gone into great detail about her first sexual encounter with her boyfriend to a group of us at a slumber party. This was so bizarre. I was only going to talk about dancing, but these girls were focused on what I was about to say with the same intensity that my friends and I'd had listening to Olivia.

Not wanting to disappoint the crowd, and fighting a grin, I said in a mysterious voice, "Yes, it is true, I've been dancing since I was nine."

"What kind of dancing?" a girl, one whose name I couldn't remember, asked.

"Oh, mostly ballet and jazz, and I used to be on a dance team. We would travel all around the country competing and winning," I answered, finishing the last bite of the delicious, creamy peanut-butter pie, which I couldn't resist eating before the main meal.

This time it was Sarah's question, again in a whisper. "Is it true that you wear a bikini for the performances?"

Maybe it was the way she asked it or the question itself, but I burst out laughing, causing the loudest noise in the crowded room. Seeing several adult men and women whirl around to locate the source of the noise, I promptly pulled it back in, covering my mouth with my hand.

Clearing my throat, I replied in the calmest voice I could muster, "No, I don't wear a bikini when I dance. I wear costumes that allow me to move freely."

"Which translates to something skimpy," Ella informed the group with mockery.

I really hated her—the way I hated poison ivy or waking up to discover I'd gotten my period. At that moment I wanted to slap the smug grin off her snobby face, and I was pretty close to doing it, but the tiny sensible part of my brain yelled, "Don't do it, that's what she wants, to get a reaction from you, so you look bad in front of Noah and all the other Amish." I could control myself, and I wasn't going to stoop to this snake's level.

Ignoring her comment, I said to the others as amicably as possible, "Maybe sometime you all could come to a performance in Cincinnati to see for yourselves."

"Oh, I don't think we'd be allowed to do that," Maretta said quietly.

No surprise there. "Don't you ever have dances with boys?" Seeing their shocked faces and remembering what Noah had said, I modified the question quickly. "I mean, when you're all...older?" I fumbled.

"The bishop and the ministers would never allow us to dance with the boys," Suzanna said with a thick coat of resentment in her voice.

"And who are the bishop and the ministers?" I figured this was a good opportunity to fish for more information about Noah's life.

"The bishop is the leader of our church and we have three ministers who are right below him. Together they make the rules and decide the punishment if the rules are broken," Sarah said in a hushed voice after she glanced around first.

The way Sarah anxiously scanned the room put my nerves on edge, but I plowed on with my reconnaissance mission anyway. "If your elders are so strict, how do you go about dating someone?"

Sarah, who I was beginning to see was the Amish teenage-girl equivalent to the president, answered, "When we turn sixteen, we're old enough to join the church youth group and go to all its functions. When we decide we really like some-one—" here she paused and smiled "—enough to marry, we tell our parents. Then the couple has to go before the church with their intentions. Once they officially join the church, then they're allowed to begin courting." Speaking about the matter had given her face a healthy pink blush.

That's complicated, I pondered. Then something occurred to me, prompting me to ask, "Do you mean...that you're not allowed to date someone unless you want to marry that person and then you're forced to join the church first?" The entire premise was distorted and sounded more like sexual bribery to me.

"Yes, that's the way it works," Sarah said smoothly.

I concentrated on what she said for over for a minute. After sipping some water, I ventured another question. "What are you allowed to do when you're courting—I mean, do you get to ever be alone and, you know...make out?"

All the girls, except the wicked Ella, giggled and blushed deeply, including Sarah, whose skin was a darker shade of pink now, almost red, poor thing. She answered, "Well, we see each other at the youth functions and family activities... and...every Sunday, when a couple are courting, the boy goes to the girl's house in the evening." She paused and swiftly glanced around again before lowering her body over the table. I had to lean in close to hear her whisper, "And then the parents go to bed around ten or eleven o'clock and the couple gets some alone time. 'Cept our community has a *hands-off* policy for courting."

Seeing the confusion that must have showed on my face and the way my lips were pursed to question her, she said quickly, "Oh, that means that the boys and girls aren't supposed to touch each other at all during courting. But some of the kids get around the rules," she whispered, a frown developing on her mouth and her eyes darting toward Suzanna and back to me again.

I ran the information around in my head for a few seconds and then blurted out, probably louder than the girls would have liked, "Do you mean that you girls aren't allowed to kiss your boyfriends—or even hold hands?" Good grief, Noah was already breaking the rules.

Before any of the shocked girls could attempt a reply, Dad's cell phone went off. I saw him fluidly answer it and walk through the basement door to the outside. I was used to that; he always had someone calling him. But many of the Amish watched him depart and my brain switched gears wondering if they thought he was rude or whether they understood that the call might be important since he was a doctor.

The girls were now quietly finishing the last of their meals or sipping their water to avoid any more talk of kissing boys. One good thing that had come from the conversation, though—obviously Noah hadn't gotten the chance to kiss any of these girls. I felt better already.

The hand on my shoulder gave me a start, until Dad leaned down close to my ear and whispered, "I'm heading to the hospital. You and your brothers can stay until nine o'clock, but then I want you guys home, packing for your trip to Cincinnati tomorrow. Remember…you have to leave the house by

6:00 a.m. to make it there in time for dance camp." He stood back up and hesitated, saying, "If I don't see you tonight, you have a good time and be careful." Then he bent down and pecked the top of my head with his lips before walking away.

"See ya on Saturday," I called out before he got too far away.

Turning, he smiled and said, "Say hi to your aunt and uncle for me."

Glancing at my watch, I saw that it was almost seven o'clock, and in a sudden swirl of activity the girls were getting up and clearing the tables. Several of the men began to move the tables and set the benches up like church pews. Very efficiently and systematically the room transitioned from a dining hall to a church building. A long table was left in front of the make-shift pews and I wondered about it.

I also wondered what it would be like not seeing Noah for a whole week. Boldly glancing around as I rose from the table, I saw him in a serious conversation with Sam. At one point he glanced over at me and so did Sam. It was weird, but then maybe Noah had overheard Dad talking to me about the trip and was asking Sam about it.

Personally, I hadn't even thought about dance camp the past few days. I guess I'd been way too preoccupied with Noah. A week ago, I'd been immensely looking forward to the trip back to Cincinnati, getting to hang out with my friends and spend a week dancing.

Now, I sort of…kind of had a boyfriend. Well, at least I had someone to occasionally hold hands with and sometimes make eye contact with. So that made all the difference in the world. I could only imagine how the week would drag on now. All bummed out, I trailed along behind the girls to the kitchen for the "female" duties.

Doing the dishes and putting the leftover food away went

faster than I would have imagined with all the well-trained girls working in sync. And even I had to admit it wasn't so bad doing the work when everyone did it together. I was somewhat entranced watching the girls flutter around me. They took the work seriously, remaining relatively silent the entire time, having specific jobs that they did with smooth precision. I, on the other hand, was completely out of my element. I had to constantly ask Sarah, Katie or one of the other girls where to put this or what to do with that. But, to give myself credit, I was at least trying to be helpful.

When the girls finished, they immediately went to the long table in the front I had wondered about earlier and began sitting down—all on one side, of course. Sarah guided me to the bench closest to the table and motioned for me to sit down. The girls' backs were to me, and I had a pretty good idea about where the guys were going to sit when they started filing in and taking their places. I instantly wondered if there was any significance to whom they sat across from, but when I saw that Katie wasn't directly in front of Jacob, I gathered it must be random.

Sam sat down on the bench next to me. I whispered into his thick blond hair, "What's going on?"

"Singing time," he said with a piratical smile.

I swiveled in my seat to see where Justin was. I spied him in the very back, sitting in the middle of a long line of barely pubescent boys. He'd clearly been accepted into their pack. The rest of the benches were filling up, and an ancient grayhaired woman sat close beside me. She handed me a hymnal with a toothless smile.

After a quick glance through the book, I elbowed Sam and shoved the book into his hands, pointing to the German words. He rolled his eyes and began to flip through it as if he were going to learn a new language in the next minute.

Up to this point I had purposely not looked for Noah, but the anxiety was gnawing at me, and I couldn't wait any longer, so I succumbed and surveyed the table. I was inwardly and blissfully aware that he'd taken a seat almost across from where I was sitting *and nowhere near Ella.*

As a matter of fact, he was going to have a difficult time avoiding my face, and while I stared at him, I could see his cheeks flush slightly and his lips twitch. His eyes lowered to the table and he was desperately fighting a smile that I somehow knew would be directed at me if unleashed.

Then his eyes lifted again for a brief second, causing my blood to rush through my veins, and now I was the one with the red face. I focused on the hymnal, deciding to try to learn German with Sam—definitely easier than looking at Noah.

An old man, very tall and distinguished looking, with a long gray beard stood up stiffly and began speaking in his language to the crowd. Of course, I had no idea what he was saying, but studying his Abraham Lincoln features, I guessed he must be the bishop. He did look rather grumpy. I could understand why the Amish kids would be scared to provoke him. Seeing the young people in front of me with their heads bowed, I suddenly realized they were praying, and I quickly lowered my head.

There was a long, boring pause after the prayer, until one of the boys sitting at the table said something and everyone started searching through their hymnals. Sam looked at me and I shrugged with ignorance until the nice old lady next to me showed us her open hymnal. Sam quickly found the page.

The boy who had called out the number began singing the song, and after a few words, the rest of them joined in.

No instruments were used, and the song was the most somber tune I'd ever heard. The voices harmonized well, but the singers lacked any enthusiasm at all. They could have benefited greatly from a Southern gospel choir showing them how it was done. Listening to the music drone on, I came to the conclusion that not being able to understand any of it didn't help the song's appeal either.

Poor Sam tried a few of the words and then gave up, handing the book to me. Holding the hymnal out in front of me and making an effort of participation, or at least the appearance of it, I let my my thoughts stray to the youth sitting at the table. They must all be courting age, I surmised. This whole singing event was a way to play matchmaker. My eyes were pulled back to Noah. I couldn't help watching his full lips barely move while he sang the words. Watching his mouth sent an electric current through my veins, and I had to look away, chewing my own lip to avoid the irritating feeling.

When the song finished, there was another long and silent break before the next number was called out. This time it was a girl's voice. She started the lyrics out and soon everyone joined her. It sounded exactly like the other song. Hardly any change in tempo or rhythm. Actually, the song didn't really have any rhythm that I could tap my foot to.

This went on for almost an hour, and I started to think how torturous it was. My butt was sore from the hard benches and my back was killing me from sitting up straight for so long. The air in the basement was warm and still, making me feel sleepy. I fought the urge to close my eyes and took a deep breath. Out of curiosity and boredom, I scanned the room to see how everyone else was handling the discomfort. To my chagrin, they all seemed perfectly fine—hardly any slouching. The only thing I could imagine was that doing this for hours and hours every Sunday since birth had configured their bodies for the harsh treatment. Or I was really sitting among a bunch of bodies that had been taken over by aliens. Either way, it was very unsettling.

At last we seemed to be nearing the end when everyone started shifting around in their seats. I was filled with happiness, the tired cloud suddenly lifting from my mind, until I saw that different books were being passed down the line. *No freak'n way.* I didn't think I could take much more of this. When I eyed Sam, I saw that the weakling had fallen asleep! With a sharp jab of my elbow in his ribs, he bolted awake and gave me a dirty look, which I ignored, handing him the new book.

Seeing the book was in English, my interest was aroused. Well, this was more like it. At least I could sing along now. That should improve the torment slightly.

Hearing the next number called out, my head snapped up. It was Noah's voice. Quickly thumbing to the page, I was immediately delighted. It was one of my favorites, "Amazing Grace." Noah started the song off in the same fashion the others had, and surprisingly, his voice was nice—level and masculine. I joined in enthusiastically this time, and even Sam sang along. The version was not like any I'd sung before, very reserved and slow, but it was obvious everyone liked it.

When the song was over, the pointy-faced bishop stood and recited another very long prayer in Dutch. When the prayer ended, there was a sudden frenzy of movement, startling me, when everyone jumped up and began passing the books back down to women waiting to collect them. In a blur, the boys rushed out of the basement single file and the girls followed them. Watching the mass exodus, I was a little at a loss of what to do, so instead of hurrying to join the Amish kids, I stood and leisurely stretched my arms over my head. I cringed at the sound of all my joints popping.

Noah was heading for the door with the others at a much slower pace, and before crossing the threshold he paused and glanced back at us. When he saw that we weren't running to join them, he hesitated at the door and then abruptly turned and strode back to us. Well, actually, he walked straight to Sam, without even breathing in my direction.

He asked Sam, "You both are coming outside to play volleyball, aren't you?" His voice had an anxious, almost pleading sound to it, causing me to smile just a little.

Sam turned to me. "What time did Dad say we should head home?"

"About nine," I answered placidly.

Sam shrugged and said, "You bet. Let's go."

As we were walking out of the basement, Noah held a position a step behind Sam so he was closer to me, but he still gave no acknowledgment that I existed. As annoying as it was to be ignored, I was beginning to get used to the weird behavior. I silently trekked behind him through the grassy yard and over to the volleyball nets.

There were four extremely battered nets, and they were set up in a long line across the thick green carpet. The teenagers were spreading out, claiming sides already. And of course, the girls had their own nets and the boys had theirs. No potential battle of the sexes here. And no surprises with this group, I thought as I wandered over to the closest "girl" net and took up a position near Suzanna, who honored me with an exaggeratedly elated smile that clued me in that she was happy I was on her team.

I noticed Noah had joined the boy team closest to me and had settled on the side of the net right beside where I was standing. I caught his gaze for a second when he dared to look my way. An almost smile rose on his lips and I smiled back big. I was personally getting tired of all the avoidance. What I really wanted to do more that anything was walk over to him and in front of everyone, take his hand and lead him out to the barn where we could get that kiss out of the way.

I blushed at the idea and then chuckled at my slinky imagination, dropping my head. Such daydreams weren't doing me a bit of good. Noah might be flirting around with me, but in reality, he was unreachable. I needed to get it through my thick skull before I made a complete fool of myself—or worse yet, got my heart broke.

The air suddenly became cooler as the sun dipped low enough to shade the yard, clearing my gloomy thoughts. I looked down, considering my dress. *How the heck was I going to play volleyball with this on?* At least all the girls had the same disadvantage, but it was still mildly ridiculous. With a sigh, I kicked off my sandals and joined the barefoot movement.

I was athletic and had played volleyball in gym class too many times to count, so it wasn't a surprise that within a minute I had given our team a point. Suzanna high-fived me with a smack that left my palm stinging red, and I finally got the first peek into how these kids released some of their pent-up energy. A few of the girls were really sporty, and although I didn't see any of them crash into the ground the way I did a couple of times, they were running around with abandon, seriously trying to get the ball.

Sarah was on our team, too, and she commented, "You're really good at this, Rose. You have to always be on our team!"

Her saying that made me wonder if I'd be invited to these events every Sunday or if this was a one-shot deal. It would be a bore to sit through the singing again, but the volleyball part was more than okay.

The last time I hit the ground saving the ball, I managed to smear grass clippings all over the front of my dress, and while I was attempting to brush them off, the ball from Noah's game flew into my chest hard, bumping me back a step. It happened so quickly I barely knew what hit me.

Within a split second Noah was beside me, asking if I was all right with an edgy voice. Even Sam was walking with purpose from the other side of the net. The girls had gathered around me, and as if I didn't feel idiotic enough, the boy who'd spiked the ball was there in front of me, pleading for my forgiveness.

I would've spoken right away, but when I tried, the air wouldn't come and within seconds Sam was with me, holding my arms over my head and patting my back. Finally, with his help, I caught my breath and took a big gulp of air.

The intense worry on Noah's features hadn't escaped my notice. Luckily for him, everyone was looking at me as if I was on exhibit in a freak show, and not paying attention to him at all.

"I'm…fine…really… Just lost my…breath for a…minute," I stammered, breathing slowly in and out of my mouth.

"I didn't mean to hit you. I'm so, so sorry," the dark-haired boy repeated.

"Don't worry about it," I said. My words came out easier and I could fill my lungs up fully again.

He continued to hover over me until Noah pulled him back and ordered him with a tight voice, "Give her some space, Timmy. She doesn't need you in her face." Then he said to me, "Are you really okay, Rose?"

My eyes locked on his and my heart slowed. Time seemed

to have stopped altogether and for a brief instant Noah and I were completely alone. His dark eyes stared into mine and I knew right then that he really did have feelings for me. The realization shocked me and a cool sweat prickled along the skin of my neck and arms.

Maybe we had a chance…

The trance was broken by Sarah's dove coo of a voice beside my ear and her hand going around my waist. "Come on, Rose. You come into the house with me for a while to rest."

I looked into her kind eyes and mumbled, "Yeah, that would be good. Thank you."

As we walked up the gentle slope leading to the house, I stared at the grass, not looking back toward the other kids…or Noah. My mind was swimming with uncertainty and my legs were still wobbly, but Sarah's strong arm gripped me tightly as we walked, giving a sense of realness to the moment.

She shuffled me in the side door and up the stairs quickly, which I was grateful for. I could hear the buzzing sound of women's voices coming from the kitchen, and I was all too happy to avoid their questions and concern. Again, I took notice that Sarah was a quick-thinking kind of girl. And even though we were as different as night and day on the outside, there was still a strange kind of connection we shared that made me feel as if I'd known her forever.

She guided me around a corner and into a dusty-pink-hued room with maroon curtains. Lightly she pushed me onto one of the two twin beds in the room and muttered something about a glass of water and then she went back through the doorway with a swish of her dress.

The trek from the nets to her bedroom was hazy to me, but now that I was sitting on the bedspread, the sharp smell of roses hit my nostrils, fully rousing me. I looked around for the source and immediately located a vase with white flowers on the dresser by the window.

Sarah must share the picture-perfect room with Rachel, I thought, noticing that although the bed on the opposite wall had the same blanket on it, it was mostly covered up by a quilt that sported royal-blue-and-white designs. There were also wooden letters above the other bed spelling out Rachel's name.

The room was amazingly clean and free of stuff for two teenage girls to be sharing, and for an instant I wished that my room was so organized. Then I reconsidered. My posters, photos, trophies, clothes and shoes scattered about my own sleeping space made it *my* room. I wouldn't want all those things hidden away—I wanted to see them each and every day.

Either Sarah and Rachel had no interests, or they weren't allowed to display them. But as Sarah stepped back into the room and softly closed the door behind her, I decided that it didn't even matter that she was a neat freak and I was a slob—we were still going to be close friends.

Handing me a glass filled with water, she sat down on the bed beside me and began rubbing my back.

I said, "Thanks," closing my eyes and enjoying the peaceful moment.

"That ball hit you pretty hard, Rose. Are you sure you're all right?" Sarah asked kindly.

I opened my eyes and met her brown ones. "I'm fine, really." I paused and said, "I feel kind of stupid causing such a ruckus, though."

Sarah shook her head and smoothed out the crinkles in her dress, saying, "Oh, don't feel like that. It's not your fault that some of the boys have such rotten aim."

The corners of her mouth twitched, and a second later she began laughing wholeheartedly, giving me a slap on the back that surprised me. At first, the big snort and barking laughter had me staring at her, but her mirth was contagious, and all too quickly I was laughing right along with her.

When we finally calmed and she was patting the wetness from her eyes with her sleeve, I took a breath and asked her, "Do you like any of the boys, Sarah?"

Her eyes widened, followed by a quick shake of her head, which slowed and then a blush darkened her cheeks. "Well, maybe one, but I don't think that he knows I exist."

She was a pretty girl, with the same wide-spaced eyes and full lips that her brother had, but the sprinkling of freckles over her nose made her look girlish, even younger than me. Her deep blush and downcast eyes showed how shy she was when it came to the boys, and I figured that was probably the reason that her crush was ignoring her.

I couldn't help reaching over and squeezing her knee when I said, "I bet he's noticed you. You're too pretty for him not to have. He's probably just afraid to approach you since you aren't very outgoing. Maybe if you start flirting a little bit, he'll be more confident."

Her eyes went as round as her mouth for an instant before she said, "Do you really think that he's *afraid* to ask me to court?"

Feeling a twinge of worry stir my insides, I swallowed and hoped that I was guessing right. After all, I didn't know a thing about this boy—he might have his sights on another girl altogether. But seeing the bright hopefulness suddenly light up Sarah's face, I decided that I couldn't be wrong. The best thing in the world for my new friend would be for her to gain some of her own self-confidence. She spent too much time with her eyes down and her shoulders slumped.

"Yeah, I think a lot of guys are as afraid of us as we are of them. The only way they begin to open up is when they know for sure that the girl they like is into them, too."

As I talked to her, I thought about how quickly things had progressed between me and Noah. I had no doubt that he liked me now, and the knowledge made me want to jump up and squeal, but at the same time I had the urge to cover my head with Sarah's pillow and cry. Why did I have to be falling for a guy that I could never have?

"But what can I do to let him know that I like him without being...well, you know, too forward." Sarah leaned in closer, speaking in a whisper even though the door was solidly shut.

I tried to keep the smile from spreading my lips. She was very serious and I didn't want her to think that I was mocking her, but the thought that this girl sitting next to me had no idea how to flirt was amazing.

Remembering back to all the guy tips that I received from my friends Amanda and Britney when I was younger, I said, "Eye contact. The best way to let him know that you like him is to keep your eyes locked on his for a couple of seconds the next time he looks your way."

Of course, I wasn't totally sure that it would work with an Amish guy, but I didn't think that it would hurt anything either.

Hesitantly, she asked, "Is it really true that you don't have a special boy in your life, Rose?"

The question startled me until I saw that her face lacked the look of knowing—thank God.

Shaking my head, I lied, "Nope, not a one."

Even lower, she said, "Do you miss your old home and your friends there?"

I glanced away toward the window, thinking. I'd been too

busy pining over her brother to miss anyone, but I certainly couldn't tell her that.

"Oh, I'm okay so far. I've got Dad and my brothers...and now I have you."

Sarah's eyes were misty when they glanced up quickly and looked away, saying, "I could never leave my community. It would be awful." Then her eyes met mine and stayed locked. "And I'm so sorry about your mother. I don't know how I'd cope if I ever lost mine."

I had no words and the tears were threatening to spill. It was obvious that Sarah was as emotional as I was, and the last thing I needed was a giant cryfest—lucky for me that's when Sam's voice boomed out from down the stairs.

"Hey, Rose, are you up there?"

I quickly bounced off the bed, hating the sound of my brother yelling for me in front of everyone like a barbarian.

Pulling the door open, I said, "I'll be right out!"

"Thanks for taking care of me, Sarah. That's another one I owe you for."

She looked at me with raised brows. "I don't understand—"

I interrupted her with a quick hug. "I'm just happy that you've taken me under your wing, that's all."

Before she could say another word, I was out of the room and jogging down the stairs.

"We need to get going, Rose. We've got to be up early tomorrow, and you're so hard to wake, even on the weekends." Sam wasn't teasing. That was the truth.

We managed to exit the house with only a few nods and waves to the ladies peering around the corner at us and again I was extremely grateful for the side door.

Once outside in the faded dusky light, depression began to descend over me. It was sinking in that I wouldn't see Noah for an entire week. And even though a part of me rationalized that it might be for the best, the bigger part was silently mourning the fact.

Sam called out to Justin, who was near the barn with the rowdy boy group playing with, of all things, a pellet gun. The boys were target shooting some cans on the white board fence, with not an adult in sight to supervise them. Momentarily tearing myself away from my self-induced moodiness, I decided that I'd have a discussion with Dad about it—or at the very least, threaten Justin with death if he ever did it again.

I didn't feel like getting into it with my kid brother when he joined us at the corner of the barn, though. For a change, I wasn't in the mood for battle.

As we passed the last building and came into the open field, the sound of the birds calling to each other while they settled in for the night filled the air, along with the soft swooshing sound of the tall grass bending in the breeze. On the horizon, the sun was about to disappear, and I watched in fascination as the sky to the west blazed with the reds and pinks of the sunset.

What a wondrous evening it could have been, I thought to myself, if Noah and I'd been allowed to hang out and watch the sun go down together. As I trailed along behind my brothers, picking the seed heads off the top of the blades and rubbing them between my fingers, I began to review in my head every glance, smile and facial expression Noah had directed at me. Especially his dramatic display when my chest had stopped the ball. I'd probably have an enormous bruise. I absently rubbed the place the ball had smashed, thinking it was well worth it to have Noah's full attention in that moment.

"You have an admirer, Rose," Sam said in a slightly testy way.

I narrowed my eyes and demanded, "Who?"

Justin came to full attention and was waiting expectantly beside me when Sam finally responded with tight lips, "Noah asked for my permission to call you sometime. It was so old-fashioned, just like that dude in the *Little Women* movie…and he became quite distressed when he heard that you'd be in Cincinnati for a *whole* week." He stressed the word *whole* way more than necessary.

It took a long second for the information to sink in. Holding my breath, I begged, "What did you tell him?"

He looked at me sheepishly and said, "I gave him your cell number. You'll have to be gentle letting the guy down, but I think it's better to do it sooner than later." Then with a more serious look he asked, "You okay with that?"

My head was spinning. Noah might actually call me on the phone like a normal guy? I could hardly contain the bubbles from multiplying in my belly. I gave Sam my most brilliant smile before saying, "It's perfectly okay with me."

Sam must have understood the excitement that I was sure was shining on my face when he said, his words thick with agitation, "You've got be kidding me, Rose. I mean, I like the guy all right, but he's Amish, for God's sake! How would that ever work out?"

Weakly, I suggested, "Maybe he'll change someday."

"Oh, brother—don't hold your breath on that one. He's really close to his family, and if he did *change* he'd risk his relationship with all his relatives and friends. I really doubt he'll be willing to do that just for a pretty girl," Sam said, his voice leaning toward sympathy, but the words still stung me. It was as if there were little needles pricking at my heart.

I hardly knew Noah, and yet he had become such an important part of my life. And astonishingly, it seemed he felt the same way about me. Sam could be all doom and gloom if he wanted—it didn't matter to me. Noah liked me for real, and that's all my mind was filled with as I walked beside Justin with a springy step and a fluttering heart toward our new home.

8

Noah
Easy Choice

THIS WAS THE THIRD TRIP I'D MADE DOWN THE ladder and back up again for something I'd forgotten. This time it was the box of roofing nails, last time it was my hammer and before that, my work belt. What was wrong with my brain today?

I had a pretty good sense what was going on—my lovely neighbor was driving me nuts. Rose was a constant visitor in my mind, distracting me to the point of obsession. It was unhealthy, and I wondered if Jacob had it this bad over Katie. He certainly didn't seem to—at least I hadn't noticed him making extra trips up the ladder since he started courting her.

But maybe that was the problem with me. I wasn't really courting Rose. I sure wanted to be, though. All day I'd been thinking about how to make it happen, with no sudden ideas or schemes appearing in my worn-out mind. And then, other thoughts had been trickling into my head as well, like: How did she feel from the volleyball hit? What did she think about the youth service? Did she like the Amish girls? What was she doing right then…and with whom?

That last question got to me the most. If Rose were Amish, it wouldn't be a question at all. She'd be strictly disciplined in what she could do and diligently watched over by the entire community. But instead, she was off dancing in some big city and probably staying out late with her friends. That image caused my breath to come harder and my blood to simmer. I felt so possessive of her, and no matter how my brain tried to rationalize that I shouldn't feel such emotions for an English girl I hardly knew, I couldn't rein them in.

I sighed heavily, gazing out over the gently rolling hay fields in the direction of my farm, just a half mile away. Katie's family was throwing a twentieth-birthday party for Jacob that evening, and most of the community had been invited. Father and Jacob had already left the work site for home a while back, leaving me alone with my worries. I was in no hurry to go to the big event and had offered to stay behind to finish up the corner of the roof. An easy choice; I liked working without my family's prying eyes, especially with all the mistakes I'd been making.

Nailing the last shingle on, I gathered my tools and climbed down the ladder. Hopefully, for the last time today.

Mr. Denton drove me home in relative silence, except for the softly playing Johnny Cash song. He was a nice old guy, always telling me the names of the singers or bands playing, as if the information would benefit me in some way I hadn't figured out yet.

Reaching the house, I jumped out, waved goodbye and made my way to the back door. I walked slowly, with no energy to my steps. The knowledge that today was only Monday and I wouldn't see Rose until the weekend, and then only if I was lucky, irked me. And having to go to the Weavers' and pretend to not have a care in the world would be near impossible. But I'd have to put on a show or suspicions would be roused. I certainly didn't need that.

After kicking off my work boots in the mudroom just as unenthusiastically as I'd walked across the yard, I entered the kitchen to the frightening scene of Mother and Father both sitting at the table, dressed to go to the party but obviously not in a hurry to get there.

Before they said a thing, unease swept through my body and I strained to listen for other voices in the house—*nothing*. Now I was even more disturbed. The house being utterly silent was the worst sign of all.

"So how was your workday, son?" Father spoke in Dutch, asking in a friendly manner, keeping the real reason they were sitting alone at the table, waiting for me, hidden at the moment.

"It went well, Father…but why aren't you at the Weavers'?" I inquired of him, while my eyes searched Mother's face for hostility. Not seeing any, I breathed a little easier, continuing to stand before them, shifting between my feet.

"There is a matter that Mother and I want to discuss with you before we leave for the party. Please have a seat," Father said, pushing the chair closest to him out for me with the toe of his boot.

I stared at the chair, a dozen thoughts flashing through my mind. If Father had any inkling at all about Rose, he wouldn't be so calm. But then again, emptying the house for a secret meeting definitely meant something was up. Trying to slow my heart, I crossed the room and sat beside him, waiting with resolve for whatever was to come.

"Noah, have you taken notice of the way Ella Weaver looks at you?" Father asked quietly with a tilt to his head, smoothing his beard beneath his fingers as he talked.

That was not what I was expecting. I thought for sure someone had spied my reaction when Rose was hit by the ball the night before, and told my parents. Now I was torn between relief that they didn't suspect my relationship with Rose and sudden dread at the direction the conversation was moving.

Mother informed me with hardly controlled enthusiasm, "Bessie Weaver approached me last night, Noah, and she informed me that Ella would be interested in a courtship with you."

When I didn't immediately answer, she arched her brows and piped, "Aren't you happy? She's one of the loveliest girls in the community."

So this was it—the beginning of the end. I was in trouble no matter what I said. If I told my parents I wasn't interested in Ella, they'd wonder why, and if I couldn't give them a good reason, they'd continue to harass me about her until I gave in or picked another girl. If I dared to tell them I'd fallen for an English girl, they'd each have a heart attack and send me away. But at that moment they were staring at me with intense eyes. I had to say something. "Wow...I didn't know Ella liked me. I mean, I guess I've been too busy lately to notice."

Impatiently, Mother asked, "But what do you think about the news, Noah? Will you ask to court Ella Weaver?"

Both Mother and Father waited, not breathing, for my answer. I needed to stall for time—time to think and plan. "I don't believe Ella and I would be a good match, Mother. We don't have anything in common." Seeing her face drop in disappointment, I quickly added, "Seriously, I've been observing a few of the girls lately and I haven't made up my mind yet—so if you can just let me take my time, I'm sure I'll be able to make a decision soon," I said as convincingly as I could manage.

"You seem restless of late, son, and I know that once you've settled on a girl, you'll feel peace in your life. It's a very important decision for you to make, and your mother and I want you to be happy. We believe that married life will suit you well." Then winking, he said with a grin, "There are many advantages to having your own wife to welcome you home after a long workday."

Yes, Father, I've already been envisioning what it would be like, but with Rose Cameron, not Ella Weaver, or any other girl. I wanted to shout it out, but I didn't. Instead, I drew in a long breath and said, "It will happen in time. Just give me a little space to make a decision."

"Noah, it's not that we're trying to rush you, but you're eighteen now and there are many boys your age this year. We're concerned that you'll miss an opportunity with one of the better girls in the community if you wait too long." As Mother said it, she reached across the table and placed her hand on mine, smiling worriedly.

At that moment, I wished I could tell her the truth about my feelings for Rose, and I almost blurted it out, being drawn into her kind expression. But luckily I caught myself before I made *that* mistake.

"Mother, I'll pick a girl eventually. I promise."

"You need to pray to God about it, Noah. Ask his guidance on your choice. He is always with you," Mother said softly.

"*Uffgevva,* my son. You must give yourself up to God's will in this matter," Father directed. And then, his voice growing harder, he said thoughtfully, "You must not let the devil mislead your heart. Conflict and indecision are brought from his evilness. Listen to God's word in Romans 12:2—'Be not conformed to this world, but be transformed by the renewing of your mind that ye may prove what is that good and acceptable and perfect will of God.'"

I lowered my eyes to the table, focusing on the grains, swirls and imperfections of the well-used wood. I sat at this table several times every day and I never bothered to see them before. Yet they were there, plain to any eyes that took the time to look at the wood and *see*. Could Mother and Father not see Rose—really see what a perfect match she was for me? How could the feelings I had for her be evil? I wouldn't accept that God felt that way. He wouldn't have opened my heart up to her if I weren't meant to be with her. Somehow I had to convince Mother and Father that it was God's will that I spend my life with Rose—*an English girl*.

Finally, raising my head, I met my parents' eyes bravely and told them in a firm voice, "I do believe in God's providence and I am willing to open myself up to it."

That seemed to please Mother and Father, and they visibly relaxed, breathing easier.

With an encouraging smile, Father said, "We have a party to attend. Shall we go?"

I took that as my cue to exit the kitchen and head upstairs, where I quickly and unceremoniously took a shower, brushed my unruly hair and dressed in finer clothes for the occasion. My head was still swirling with the conversation when I harnessed Rumor and hitched up the buggy. I wondered how much time they'd actually give me—and then there was the whole uncomfortable business with Ella. She would have been aware of our mothers' discussion, and she would inevitably expect a courtship invitation from me any day now. She had always thought quite highly of herself, and ever since we were kids she'd made it clear that she was interested. Oh, she was subtle about it, all right; always nearby, lurking like a tunnel-web spider, ready to strike with the shy fluttering of her lashes and the flirty half smiles.

I couldn't help the snort of laughter that erupted from my

lips at the thought of prissy Ella with eight dangling legs. But quickly, my mood blackened. The thought of spending my life with Ella created a cold tightening in my stomach. She was pretty enough, but she didn't have the warm and inviting nature that Rose had. I feared that even if Rose wouldn't have me, I'd never feel the same attraction for another girl the way I had for her.

When I finally pulled into the driveway, it was late enough that most of the guests were already in the gathering building, with just a few of the smaller children playing in the expansive yard. The Weavers' place was pristine. The flower beds along the driveway overflowed with the bright purples, pinks and whites of perfectly tended flowers.

Glancing around, I realized, as if for the first time, that the Weaver farm was one of the more impressive homesteads in the community. The ten children worked diligently to keep it in pristine condition, and with Mark Weaver being one of the three ministers in the church, he had to set an example to the other members, which he did in an exemplary way.

It was the same in our household, since Father was also a minister. My parents fretted as much as the Weavers about appearances. That was what made the situation with Ella Weaver even more delicate. The Weavers would be offended if I wouldn't have their daughter, and if I chose an English girl over Ella, it would cause serious problems between the families, becoming a church matter.

Rubbing my face from the stress of it all, I entered the dining hall and made my way to the buffet table, only lightly filling my plate. I didn't have much of an appetite, and the food I did place on my plate was more for show than anything else. I was oblivious if any eyes followed me as I walked to the table, sliding in between Matthew and Timmy.

"Hey, buddy, why are you so late?" Matthew asked with his mouth full of chicken casserole.

Taking a fork in hand, I pushed the food around on my plate, not really wanting to be social but answering anyway, "Oh, Mother and Father harassed me for a while, that's all."

"I bet I know what they were bugging you about," Matthew stated simply, continuing to shovel food into his mouth.

I'm sure he did know, too, I thought distractedly. Ella was, after all, his sister, and although he wasn't close to her, he would have heard things being discussed in the house about a possible match.

Matthew went on somberly, "If I were you, I'd run screaming, Noah."

The mental picture brought an unwanted smile to my lips.

The light feeling only lasted a second, when I was snapped back into the real world by Timmy's question. "Was the English girl really all right, Noah? I mean, that ball hit her hard. She didn't seem to be mad at me, but I still feel bad about it and all."

Before I even had a chance to respond, Levi Zook said quietly, definitely not wanting to be overheard by any adults, "Damn, she was gorgeous. I'd like to get a piece of that."

The fury swelled so sudden and unexpected in me that I had to grip the bench with my free hand to keep from smashing Levi's head into the table right then and there. I became even angrier when several of the other boys, including Matthew, murmured agreement with Levi. Only Timmy sat silent, staring at me with wide eyes. He had the inkling about my interest in Rose. His face now showed worry about how I'd react to Levi's lewd comment.

Struggling to compose myself, I narrowed my eyes and leveled a piercing look at Levi. A little louder than a whisper, I threatened, "You shouldn't talk that way about her."

At first, Levi was obviously taken aback. His face showed the surprise of someone not expecting my reaction. The surprise slowly turned to understanding. Then a wicked smile spread across his mouth. *He knew.*

"Maybe Noah here has a thing for the sexy English girl and he wants to keep her all to himself." He smirked nastily and his friend Nathaniel Yoder huffed agreement with him. The other boys were as silent as Timmy now, glancing between Levi and myself, feeling the tension that had sprung into the air.

I had never liked Levi, from the time we were kids up until today. He'd always been difficult, stirring up trouble and running to narc on anyone who upset him or made him look like a fool, which wasn't hard to do. He was gangly and uncoordinated, with bright red hair and strange dark eyes, almost black. Those eyes were out of place on his pallid face.

The quiet sounds of eating and conversation around the room faded away, leaving me alone with Levi and my rage. With an outer calmness that I wasn't feeling internally, I spoke to him from across the table. "Maybe we should go outside to discuss this in private," I invited him.

"Bring it on, Noah. I'm not afraid of you," he said with pure hatred.

As we both rose from the benches, Jacob appeared like a wraith at my side. A quick glance to his face proved that he was aware there was a problem, and I exhaled in irritation, knowing that I wasn't going to have the opportunity to beat the crap out of Levi after all.

"Can I have a word with you, Noah?" Jacob asked calmly enough. It was his birthday, so I couldn't refuse. Nodding, I followed him out of the building. Glancing back once, I shot a look at Levi that promised I wouldn't forget what he'd said.

The fresh air smacking into my face felt good. I breathed easier, seeing that we were relatively alone, besides the old white dog lying in the grass under the shade of the maple tree. I didn't think he was going to judge me.

"What was going on in there, Noah?" Jacob asked in a harsh whisper. When I only shrugged, he went on with his quiet tirade. "Is this about a girl?"

My eyes met his and whatever he saw in them confirmed his suspicions. "Listen, Noah, Ella wants to be with you—Katie's told me that. You don't have to worry about any of the other guys. But you should make it official as soon as possible, to get the other hounds off her scent," he said with a calmer voice, now only mildly annoyed with what he thought was my stupidity.

So, Jacob, and probably everyone else, thought I was interested in Ella. Astonishment spread through me like a rainstorm dousing the anger I'd felt a minute before. That Jacob didn't realize all my turmoil was because of Rose was unbelievable to me. And he thought *I* was the stupid one. The only thing I could do was play along. I certainly couldn't think of a better alternative at the moment.

"Yeah, maybe you're right, Jacob, but I feel like I need more time to think about it, and I never have a chance to be alone with my thoughts. Would you mind if I went home and missed your party?" I asked quietly, hoping he'd fall for it.

"No, that's all right with me. I understand, Noah. It's scary to make a decision about the woman that you're going to spend the rest of your life with." He paused and with a knowing smile said, "But trust me, when you begin courting, you'll forget about all the worry you have now. Time alone with a woman can make you forget all manner of things." Jacob was grinning suggestively and I looked away, embarrassed. God, I didn't need Jacob's advice about women just then. Silently I thought, you don't need to tell me about it, Jacob. I already know.

"I'll inform Mother and Father discreetly that you've gone home for some quiet reflection time," he said as he patted me on the back, with a warning look clouding his face. "And, Noah, make good use of the time."

"Sure thing," I retorted. A few minutes later I was in my buggy, and with a snap of the reins had Rumor moving out, trotting down the long, winding driveway. Fifteen minutes later when I reached the barn, I hurriedly unhitched the horse. After rubbing him down and putting him into the pasture at lightning speed, I ran full blast to the shed.

It was about seven-thirty, I guessed by the low light in the sky, and an involuntary shudder went through me while I stared at the telephone. I could do this. I pulled the piece of napkin with Rose's number on it out of my pocket and picked up the phone.

I hesitated. What if she was busy and didn't want to talk to me? It would be better to know that now rather than later, I reckoned. I dialed the number and then waited, listening to the rings, leaning impatiently against the stack of hay bales and willing Rose to answer the phone. I couldn't control the thumping of my heart, and I realized how desperately I wanted to hear her voice.

"Hello?" My heart stopped when her timid voice reached my ear. For a second I was speechless.

But for just a second, hearing the background noise raised all the questions I'd had earlier on the roof and I found my voice. "Hey, Rose, it's Noah."

"Oh. Hi." There was a muffled sound while she spoke to someone with her, and then she said, "Hold on a minute, I have to get to a quieter place."

I waited for what seemed like eternity, but it was probably less than a minute when she was back. "Noah, can you hear me okay?"

Her voice sounded loud, clear and…sweet, very sweet. "Yeah, I can hear you just fine. Where are you anyway?" I hoped I didn't sound as jealous as I felt.

"I'm at the movies with some friends."

"Am I bothering you?"

"No, no. The movie hasn't even started yet, just the previews. And it's probably going to be dumb anyway."

"How does your chest feel today?"

She laughed a little and said, "Oh, it's fine, except I have a pretty big bruise right above my…" She stammered and said, "Well, on my chest. But it's no big deal."

"Are you having fun there?" I asked, trying to erase the picture of Rose's body from my mind.

In a quiet voice she answered, "It's okay, but I missed seeing you today."

Hearing her say that caused my heart to skip a beat. Then I relaxed, sitting down on the nearest bale of hay, feeling more at ease and confident than I had when I dialed her number.

"I miss you, too—today's been a tough day for me."

"Really, why?" she questioned with a twinge of worry in her voice.

I wondered how much I should tell her. I wanted to tell her everything. She was the only person in the world I felt I could talk to. But would she understand at all what I was dealing with? Her world was so different from mine. The whole thing might be beyond her comprehension.

But I chanced it anyway. "My parents are trying to arrange a courtship for me."

There was silence for a second and then she said, "With whom?"

The way she said it made me smile. She was the one who sounded jealous now. "Ella Weaver." But I quickly went on to tell her, "I don't have any interest in Ella at all, Rose. You have to believe me."

"Oh, I believe you. She's a rotten egg in my book." I chuckled at that and when I had finished, she asked, "You don't have to do it—do you?"

Her velvet voice sounded strange, upset, and that was all I needed to make me brave enough to say what I said next. "I thought I was already taken. Am I right about that?" My heart seemed to stop beating altogether as I waited for her answer.

A pause of silence and then I could almost see the grin on her face when she said, "You're definitely taken."

"That's all I needed to hear from you, Rose."

"What do we do now?"

"I don't know, but I'll figure something out. Don't worry about it."

"Of course I'm going to worry about it! As insane as it sounds, you might be forced into a marriage before I even get back this week." The edge to her voice was real, and I knew then that she did understand what I was dealing with.

"They won't do that, Rose. The choice is mine. There are just so many factors we have to take into consideration before we go public with our relationship."

"Like what?"

"Well, there are the obvious difficulties we're going to face with my family and the church. But what about your family? How are they going to feel about all this?"

"They won't care."

"You don't think they'll have a problem if you marry an Amish man?"

The silence on the other end of the line went on uncomfortably long. When I was sure she wasn't there anymore I asked, "Rose, are you still there?"

Softly she said, "Yes, I'm here."

"What's wrong—did I say something to upset you?" I didn't get it. She told me herself I was definitely hers. Had the word *marry* bothered her?

"Um, I was just not thinking quite that far ahead, Noah. You know, I'm only sixteen."

At least she was talking again. "When's your birthday?"

"November thirtieth—why?"

"That's only five months away. Courtships usually last that long anyway and often longer than that."

"Oh" was all she said in a tiny voice.

Maybe I was moving too fast for her. She was young, and she wasn't accustomed to our ways. It would take her some time to adjust.

Hearing hoofbeats on the pavement in the distance, and seeing the sun had been replaced by the grayness of twilight, I abruptly realized how late it was. My family would be arriving home soon, and I didn't waste any time before asking her, "When will you be coming home?"

"Saturday afternoon, I think."

"That's good. We'll meet in the fields again on Saturday, at five o'clock this time. Will that work for you?"

"I'll be there."

"I don't know if I'll get another chance to call you, Rose, so you be careful. And, Rose...?"

"Yes?"

"Remember that I'm here waiting for you."

"I know. I won't forget that."

"Enjoy the movie."

"Like I'm going to be able to focus on the movie after this conversation." The prickle in her voice made me laugh again.

Then she added in a sultry voice that made my blood pulse harder, "Good night, Noah. Sleep well."

"Good night, Blue Eyes." Hanging up the phone reluctantly, I laughed, realizing she'd purposely used that warm-honey voice on me to keep me up all night thinking about her—the same way I hoped she'd be thinking about me.

9

Rose
The Thrill of It All

I SHOULD BE HAPPY, LYING ON THE SOFT blanket, surrounded by my friends with the warm late-afternoon sun soaking into my skin—but nope. I scanned the crowd gathered on the village green, listening to the local rock band do a decent imitation of Kevin Rudolf's "Let It Rock." No, I certainly wasn't happy. I was totally miserable.

Where I really wanted to be was in the cornfield with Noah. But I'd have to wait until tomorrow for that, unfortunately. In the meantime I needed to put on a good act for my friends, who'd dealt with my moodiness the entire visit.

I thought the week would take forever, but actually, my busy schedule had kept the days flying by. Now I was so exhausted that I could seriously go to sleep right here in front of everyone. That was something Sam would do—not me. But here I was with my eyes closed, on the verge of entering dreamland. Worried I'd actually do it, I slowly pulled up into a sitting position, rubbing my eyes. I needed some major caffeine.

Each day had started out at six-thirty in the morning when Aunt Debbie woke me for a long day of dance camp. When I danced I usually forgot everything else, but it had been a struggle for me to stay focused that week. Ms. Lily had taken me aside on Tuesday and, without beating around the bush, asked me what was wrong. I managed to talk my way out of it, telling her the move had taken its toll and that I was missing Mom.

I felt some serious guilt after I said the last part since I hadn't thought about Mom as much as I probably should have lately. It was a relief not to have all those emotional waves rolling through me at the mere vision of her face in my mind. Letting go of all the negative thoughts was like blowing out a giant gulp of air that I'd been holding in for what seemed like eternity.

For the first time in a long while I felt truly alive again. But the tickling of guilt was there, just below the surface, because feeling good meant not thinking about Mom. And I also felt crappy about lying to Ms. Lily. But I rationalized that it was better to lie to my instructor than to tell her the real problem was just a boy. How lame would that have sounded?

After dance camp each day, my evenings had been filled with dinners at Skyline Chili, movies and the mall, keeping me distracted for the most part. Amanda and Britney had been like masterful activity directors, planning something for every minute I wasn't dancing. Amanda would arrive promptly at my aunt's house at five every afternoon to chauffeur Britney and me to our nightly excursions. I should have been having a great time, but I just couldn't get into it. My mind was always wandering to Noah, and I sure didn't want to tell my friends about him. They would think I had gone loony and probably try to discourage me from a relationship with an Amish guy.

The quiet, dark nights when I lay awake in bed for hours was the most difficult time of all. That's when I'd replay every conversation, look and touch I experienced from my short time knowing Noah. It was beginning to wear me down physically to get up early in the morning and dance my butt off each day while my stupid brain wouldn't allow me to sleep at night. Ugh, I was like one of the walking dead from the lack of shut-eye.

And the thoughts that plagued me at night were harassing me now. What the heck had Noah meant about how my family would feel if I married an Amish man? *Was he serious?* He sure didn't sound as if he was joking around. After all, his people got married young, and he was eighteen, ripe and ready for a wife. My face flushed with that thought, and I hurriedly covered it with my hands before someone noticed.

The crazy thing, the absolute insane and ridiculous thing, was that each night that I tossed and turned, I fantasized about what it would be like to be married to Noah. And a part of my brain, a large part of it, in fact, was enjoying the make-believe way too much. Ideas about college and vet school, or owning my own dance studio, began to fade away smaller and smaller, until the life I'd always dreamed about for myself was beginning to seem like a distant memory. I wanted to be with Noah more than anything else at the moment, but I was scared to death of what that meant for my future.

Absently, I chewed on my pinkie nail while I checked my phone. I was so bummed out that Noah hadn't called again. I knew he would have, if given the chance, but it still irritated me. It was pretty hilarious that he was talking about marriage and he couldn't even call me on the phone. Even worse—we hadn't even kissed yet.

With that thought, my eyes traveled over my friends. Amanda was snuggled up to Heath, sitting between his legs with her back and golden head resting against his chest. Britney was up swaying to the music, and Erin, Sam's old girlfriend, was plastered to his side, whispering into his ear. Whatever she'd said made him laugh. For a long second I watched him brush the blond hair from her face and lightly kiss her cheek.

Feeling like a perverted voyeur, I quickly looked away, sighing. The Amish kids could never hang out like this, with boys and girls mixed together, touching and enjoying each other. They couldn't listen to the band and feel the music pumping through their veins, and they would never excitedly go to the DMV for their first driver's-license photo.

There were so many things that they would never get to do. But then there were other things, like the quiet evening rides or the nights alone together without the distractions of a TV or a computer.

That thought caused the heat to again spread under my skin, and the only thing I could do about it was reach over to the cooler, take out a soda and press it to my cheek. It only helped a little, though.

"Hey, how are you doing, Rose?" Tyler sat down unnecessarily close to me. Smiling at him, I had to admit that he was cute, with his curly brown hair and friendly green eyes. I might have even gone for him this summer if I hadn't met Noah. For so long the thought of having a boyfriend wasn't really on my mind, but maybe I was finally at the point in my life when I actually wanted one.

"Fine. How 'bout you?" I asked as I listened to the band doing another popular rock tune.

He leaned in close to my ear, and I shifted my head away as far as I could without actually moving my butt. He didn't seem to notice my attempt to escape. He said in a deep voice, "Do you want to go hang out after the concert?"

As usual, Sam picked the worst possible timing to do me a favor when his voice suddenly boomed out, "Hey, Tyler, leave Rose alone. She already *has* a boyfriend." I attempted to shoot a warning look at him, but it was too late—everyone had heard. Including Amanda, whose mouth hit the ground, her eyes popping with betrayal.

"What the hell do you mean Rose has a boyfriend? She hasn't said a word about it all week," she demanded of Sam. When he shrugged his shoulders and grinned, she rounded on me. "Do you really have a boyfriend?"

"I think *boyfriend* is a little too serious for our relationship. I mean…I've been spending a little time…hanging out…with this guy. That's all." I stumbled through, wishing I could just blow away with the wind that was now picking up.

"What's his name?" Amanda asked, dropping onto her knees directly inside my personal bubble. She was pressing me uncomfortably back toward Tyler, who hadn't moved yet. I'd caught a glimpse of his face an instant before Amanda attacked me. He wasn't pleased.

"Noah," I said softly.

"And he's *Amish.* Can you believe it?" Sam's voice cut the air again like a razor blade, followed by his chuckling. He put his arm around Erin and whispered something into her ear that caused her to look at me wide-eyed and interested.

"Sam, could you just shut the hell up for once in your miserable, good-for-nothing, useless life," I shouted as I stood in a lightning-speed movement that sent a rush of blood to my head. Without giving the big mouth a chance to respond, I stomped away with furious strides. Yeah, I was being pretty dramatic, I knew, but I felt totally justified—and I needed to get far away from the mophead and everyone else for that matter.

"Hey, Rose, wait up." It was Amanda. Britney was close behind her.

When she saw the tears welling up in my eyes, she grasped my hands and pulled me to a stop, asking, "Why are you so upset? I was just messing around with you. I mean, at first I was pissed off that you didn't say anything to me about your first boyfriend, but I understand why you'd feel weird talking about this particular guy—even to us," she said, glancing at Britney, whose brows were raised expectantly. "We're your best friends, though. You can talk to us about anything." She glanced away, pausing for a second before adding, "That is, unless you don't trust us."

"No, it's not you, Amanda. It's me. I'm just a stupid idiot, that's all," I said, feeling I was sinking to an all-new low.

"Let's go to the car and you can tell us all about it." She pulled me through the crowd forcefully, past the mobile ice-cream trailer and shops until we arrived at her sporty little red Camaro. An hour later Amanda and Britney knew everything. All the gory details about the sordid four-day-long relationship with an Amish boy that had already progressed into a possible marriage proposal. They had exhausted every possible question and in turn analyzed each of my answers to the point of mental exhaustion.

Looking at them now, their faces bright and thoughtful, I hoped the interrogation was over. Britney was twirling a section of her nearly black, shoulder-length hair absently through her fingers with intense concentration in her brown eyes. Amanda, who looked like a beach goddess from California, simply stared at the steering wheel before turning to me.

"I think you're being too serious about this, Rose. Just have fun and see where it leads" was all Amanda said. I nodded lamely at her in total surprise. Who would have thought she'd be so open-minded about it all.

"Yeah, and make sure you call us every day with updates," Britney demanded.

"I'll try. Do you mind taking me back to my aunt's now?" Amanda had compassion and granted my request.

For the first time in a week I immediately fell asleep when I hit the bed. I didn't know if my body had finally had enough, or if what Amanda had said gave me a more restful sleep. But I knew one thing for sure. I would try to have fun with Noah before it had to end.

The drive home was free of voices except those blasting through the radio in Sam's truck. He had enough sense not to say a thing to me. Justin was fast asleep in the backseat, having spent a similarly sleepless week with his friends, due to Xbox fatigue.

I'd woken Sam up extra early, whacking him in the head with his jeans to get him moving. That was a fringe benefit of going home early—making him suffer for his big mouth. He didn't argue with me about it, and here we were arriving home at nine in the morning. I hadn't seen any activity at Noah's when we drove past. I wondered if he was lucky enough to still be in bed or if he was out toiling in a field, until my thoughts shifted in another direction when I saw a silver BMW parked beside our house.

Forgetting that I hated him for a second, I looked questioningly at Sam, who shook his head in confusion. We parked and decided to leave Justin asleep in the truck. I rolled the windows down to make sure he didn't overheat and then walked to the house with Sam.

Intuitively, I knew something was up. I guess Sam did, too, the way he was hanging back with me, in no hurry to reach the house. I got an uneasy feeling as the door started to open before we reached it. We both stopped dead, and my jaw dropped in shock. An attractive middle-aged woman with shoulder-length dyed-blond hair, wearing a short black skirt and a button-up blouse, which wasn't tucked in, came out the door. Dad was right behind her and for a brief instant before he noticed us standing there, he had his hand on the middle of her back.

Oh, my God. This can't be happening. My heart stopped, my stomach rolled and I felt faint all at once. I actually started to sway, but Sam's hand gripped my arm, steadying me.

The look of agonizing guilt on Dad's face was the worst part of all. The screaming and cussing I wanted to inflict on him just caught in my throat. I couldn't say anything. All I could do was stand there, dumbly watching the woman mumble to Dad, "I'll see you tomorrow."

She cowardly slipped by us with a tight smile and went to her car. She drove with speed to the road, leaving just the three of us standing there in the new-morning air, waiting for a showdown.

Dad was the first to speak after he regained an ounce of his composure. "Where's Justin?" he asked with concern, but I figured he was also trying to divert attention from himself.

I still couldn't talk. I was too numb to move my mouth. Sam, on the other hand, didn't have that problem.

"He's asleep in the car. Who the hell was that woman, Dad? Some ho you picked up at a bar?" he said in a high-pitched voice, not holding any emotion back.

"Don't ever call her that again, Sam," he said angrily. I couldn't believe he had the audacity to be mad at us when he was the one having the affair.

"What do you want us to call her—*Mom?* 'Cause that ain't happening, I can tell you right now," Sam said with tempered wrath, somewhat keeping control. I was satisfied with the way he was dealing with the situation and decided to let him continue doing the talking.

With a heavy sigh, Dad slid a hand through his thick dark hair that showed only a touch of gray at the temples. He was in perfect physical condition, a man in his prime. For the first time, the thought occurred to me that maybe he missed Mom for reasons other than those Sam, Justin and I missed her. Well...I guess that's obvious now.

"Kids, I didn't mean for you to see that, really I didn't. I never dreamed that you'd be home so early on a Saturday morning." He breathed another deep sigh, and with great discomfort continued, "Her name is Tina Nolan. She's the director of personnel at the hospital. We had several dinners together this week while you guys were gone...and there's a mutual attraction between us.

"You two aren't little children anymore—you're old enough to realize that I'm not just your dad. I'm also a forty-five-year-old man. I don't want to be alone anymore."

He said it softly, yet with conviction. I finally found my voice.

"But you're not alone—you have us." I sniffed, staring at the flat rock I stood on.

With a soft laugh, Dad crossed the distance and forced my chin up with his hand. His eyes were troubled when he said, "You might not understand this fully now, honey, but as much as I love you and your brothers, and that love is stronger than I feel for anyone else in the world, I need to have someone with me again that will belong to me—someone that I can spend my life with while you kids go out and discover your own dreams."

We were silent.

"I am so sorry that you had to learn about it this way. I had every intention of sitting down with you all this week to discuss it as a family," he begged for our understanding softly.

"So, is this Tina woman the one you want to spend your life with?" Sam asked with a mixture of mockery and venom, causing me to look up through my teary, hot eyes expectantly for Dad's answer.

"It's not that serious yet, Sam. But I am very fond of her and want to spend more time with her. I think you kids will like her, too, if you give her a chance." He said it as if he believed it.

It was all too much for my brain to handle. The creepy feeling I got in my gut when I looked at Dad's face, knowing that he was having sex with a woman, made my skin go cold. And that we might even have a new stepmom sooner than later was pushing me way over the cliff of mental stability. Before I totally flipped out, I brushed past him into the house in a huff of tears and eye wiping.

"Where are you going? Rose, come back here. We need to talk more about this," Dad shouted, following me up the stairs.

I turned on him in a soul-rupturing rage. "Don't you dare tell me what I have to do! How could you betray Mom?" He was speechless and I rampaged on. "I don't have to do anything at all to make you feel better about your disgusting affair. You can deal with that on your own. I'm going to lie down now, and you had better just leave me alone!" I screamed at the top of my lungs, crossing the floor to my room and slamming the door shut in my dad's distraught face. Jumping onto my mattress, I sobbed uncontrollably for an hour, maybe it was longer, until I finally did cry myself to sleep.

When my eyes flicked open, they were sore from all the tears and I rubbed them vigorously before stretching and glancing at the clock. It was five and the significance of the time didn't immediately sink into my poor, disturbed brain, just a tickling of the suggestion that it was important to me. After a few fuzzy-headed seconds, the memory flooded back to me with the force of a tidal wave. I was supposed to meet Noah in the field. I bolted up, and feeling the chilly air blowing into my room from the window, I grabbed my pink hoodie and ran out of the room.

Sam and Justin were watching TV, and I passed by them without much of a glance. Sam was on his feet and overtook me in the kitchen. He grabbed my shoulder, spinning me around.

"Where are you going?" Sam was upset.

"Out for a ride—why do you care?"

"Meeting your boyfriend in some secluded woods someplace?" He smirked in a nasty way and before I could stop my hand, I slapped him, hard, across the face. Probably residual anger toward Dad caused me to do it, but I quickly stepped back, fearful that he'd toss my body into the table for retaliation. But instead he breathed carefully, rubbing the red place on his cheek. He stared at me with an unfathomable expression.

"Okay, maybe I deserved that." He looked suddenly uncomfortable about whatever he was getting ready to say. I held my breath waiting.

Without making eye contact, he said, "I know that with Mom gone, you don't have anyone to talk to about…girl stuff. Now that you have a boyfriend, I'm just a little concerned for you—that's all."

The direction this conversation was going was starting to freak me out. I wanted to leave but my feet were rooted to the kitchen floor, being held there by some sick curiosity within me. Sam's blue eyes stared at me and with a little pink rising in his cheeks he whispered, "You know—I don't get the feeling that these Amish guys are too worried about birth control…and I hope you're going to protect yourself. You know what I mean."

I wanted to die right then, be buried alongside my mom and be just a distant memory on the planet. That my big brother was talking about sex and birth control to me was my worst nightmare.

"I know that you've probably been doing it since you were fifteen, but it's not like that with me and Noah. So you don't have to worry your shaggy head about it," I said, completely embarrassed, looking at his chest, avoiding his eyes.

His overly loud sigh raised my eyes. Sam rolled his own eyes, and with an air of condescending superiority and a heated voice said, "Well, it won't be like that for long—so if you need a condom, let me know. And you probably should talk to Amanda or Erin about birth-control pills. That's really the better way to go."

That definitely was the last straw! I darted by him and out the back door toward the barn. But again the future running back for the Bengals caught me. Only, luckily, this time he didn't say anything else about sex.

"Leave me alone, Sam," I insisted, punching his big arm as hard as I could. *Crap.* That hurt.

"Hey, calm down, would you. I wanted to tell you that Justin doesn't know anything about the woman from this morning. So don't mention it to him," he told me in his bossy way.

"Don't you think he should know about it? Why should he go on idolizing Dad the way we did, when the truth is that he's just a…a…womanizer?" There were so many words to pick from to describe what Dad was, and that was the best I could come up with. How sad.

Sam was thoughtful for a minute before he said gently, a strange tone coming from him, "I know I'd rather not have seen it, and I'm sure deep down you feel the same. Why cause Justin that pain?"

I understood what he meant, and I nodded reluctantly.

"Where is Dad?" Just mentioning his name bugged me. It probably showed in the harsh voice I used.

"Went to the hospital. I'm going to get some pizza for Justin and myself. I'll save a few pieces for you." As an afterthought he asked, "You have your cell phone, right? If you need anything, call me. Okay?"

Again I nodded, not meeting his eyes, still too disturbed about the earlier advice from him. He must have sensed that because he did his funny little laugh as he strolled back in the house.

With the fastest saddling job I ever did, I was cantering up the road and through the gap in about ten minutes. It was after five-thirty and I anxiously looked around for Noah, hoping that he hadn't given up on me and gone home. I didn't need to worry. He rode out from the trees along the road, and without saying a word his face told me he would have waited there for me all night.

He trotted over to me, his face bright and cheerful. That was until he got close enough to see mine was puffy and tear streaked.

He blinked, and concern clouded his features. "What's the matter, Rose?"

When he was close enough, he immediately took my hand. It felt so good, so right, that all my walls came down. I began to cry. Damn it. I didn't want to do this in front of him.

His eyes were alarmed, and he guided Rumor in even closer to Lady and put his arm around my waist. His voice rang with worry when he impatiently asked, "What happened? Why are you crying, Rose? Please tell me," he begged.

"Let's just ride right now. I can't talk." Pulling away from him, I squeezed Lady into a slow canter. In a flash, he was beside me, watching me with a frown as we crossed the distance of the first field. Not racing this time, just comfortably cantering along the path. The cool air was waking me up, clearing my mind from the fog that had descended on me since I'd seen Dad's hand on that woman's back.

When we reached the curve, I slowed to a trot and continued through the small stand of trees. I finally reined to a walk when we entered the cornfields on the other side.

We walked in silence for a minute longer before I pivoted in my saddle. I was immediately met with Noah's intense dark eyes.

"I'm sorry about that. I've had a really bad day, and I needed some time to get myself together," I said, reaching out for his hand again.

He took it without hesitation. With an all-too-troubled expression, he inquired again, "What's going on, Rose? Will you tell me now?"

"Sam and I caught Dad with a woman today. They had spent the night together." Okay, I said it out loud. It sounded even worse than when I thought it.

Noah's eyes went wide with shock. Then his gaze wandered out over the corn and back to me again. "That's hard to believe. Are you sure there wasn't some kind of misunderstanding?" he suggested softly, clearly not wanting to believe that the nice doctor would do such a thing.

"He admitted it, Noah. He had the nerve to tell Sam and

me that he needed a woman to belong to him—or something like that. I almost threw up when he said it."

"I'm so sorry, Rose." He paused, his face serious with thought. "What's going to happen to your family now?" he asked with more than just a passing curiosity, almost as if he had something else on his mind.

Scrunching up my face in concentration, I responded, "I don't know. He'll probably date the woman for a while and then marry her. I'll have to deal with an evil stepmother."

Squeezing my hand, he said softly, "It can't be that much a surprise to you. I mean, your dad is still fairly young and the English are known to be promiscuous. That's one of the big problems with their society."

He said it as if he were talking about some foreign regime or something. But what startled me even more was the way he said *their,* as if he was not counting me among the "English."

"Excuse me?" Anger flared in me.

Catching his mistake, he grinned lightly, giving the impression he was talking to a child. "Did you know that Amish couples almost never get divorced?" he said proudly, starting the swirling thing with his thumb on my hand, causing the butterflies to flutter in my belly. But I ignored the sensations, focusing on his words.

I breathed, "No, I didn't know that."

"It's because we take it very seriously when we pick a wife. We know when we say our vows, it's for life." He stared deeply into my eyes, and his handsome face made the breath catch in my throat, and a little dizziness touched my head. I was tempted to drop the reins and touch his smooth face with my finger, but I didn't, the soft swell of agitation still coating my insides. Then something Amanda had asked popped into my head and right out my mouth.

"Why don't you have a beard?"

His brow furrowed slightly, followed by the explosion of a wide grin on his mouth. "I'll let my beard grow when I get married."

"Do you *have* to grow a beard?" I studied his face, trying to imagine it with a long, fuzzy beard, like his dad's.

"Yes—it's a rite of passage, and more important for the wife, the beard signifies that a man is married—and taken." He looked sideways at me with a twinkle in his eyes, and the small smile quickly turned into an intimate smirk.

The sunlight was hidden behind the thickening clouds, and the fitful air was charged with a raw energy that seeped into my skin, making me feel amazingly alive at that instant. The feeling prompted me to temporarily forget my dad, and the even crueler reality that Noah was Amish and I wasn't.

"Don't you like beards, Rose?" he teased.

"I hadn't really thought about it. It might be a little prickly when…kissing, to be honest." I smiled shyly, risking a glance at him.

He laughed at that and smiled radiantly back at me. In a fluid motion his hand let go of mine. Nearly freaking me out, his firm, callused fingers were suddenly at my face, gently touching it. I stifled a gasp as his fingers ever so softly traced my cheekbone and then down to my chin and finally over my mouth, which parted slightly on its own, to my chagrin. Sometime during his exploration of my face, the horses had stopped and I didn't even notice. A surge of pleasure traveled through my body, starting from where his fingers touched and spreading outward.

He lowered his hand, and I knew he was as affected as I was. He breathed out a rush of air and said, "Mmm-hmm, yeah, I could see how a beard might scratch an amazingly velvety face like yours."

He took my hand again and the horses began to walk freely, our knees rubbing wonderfully, as Lady's and Rumor's sides bumped along.

"Did you know that our women never cut their hair?" he asked cautiously.

"Is that a rule that has to be followed, too?"

"Yes, another rule, but a good one, I believe. You've let your hair grow really long, so that wouldn't be a difficult one for you to follow." His eyes journeyed over my hair, and he nodded as if he was agreeing with himself.

"But I've had my hair trimmed many times before," I contradicted.

"But you would never cut your hair short, would you?" His face was serious again and his voice sounded frustrated for some strange reason.

"I like to be able to wear it in a ponytail, so I suppose I wouldn't cut it short. But it's the idea of being able to make my own choices. I mean, whose business is it anyway if I wanted to chop all my hair off?" I said reproachfully, pursing my lips.

He let go of my hand and tentatively lifted his finger to a strand of hair resting near my elbow. Holding it between his fingers, he softly caressed it. Before I knew what he was going to do, he brought it to his face, touching his mouth to it, breathing it in. The gesture was incredibly sensual, and I could feel my blood rushing through my veins, almost achingly so, when he did it.

I had totally forgotten my little rant when he said, "Your husband's business." I sighed with disappointment when he let go of the hair, taking my hand again. *Is he ever going to kiss me?* I silently screamed.

"I think English women are too willing to make battles out of things they don't need to." He was hard-faced again.

"What do you mean?"

"Well, look at yourself, Rose. You have the most beautiful long, wavy hair that any girl could dream of, and you like it that way. And I love your hair and want to touch it and feel it, but..." He paused and with troubled eyes boring into me said, "But you'd go out and have it cut short to some hideous modern style just to prove the point that you could...and..." He obviously wanted to say more, but he had worked himself up into such a state that he just trailed off, shaking his head.

I really tried to hold it in, but seeing him so torn up about my hair, I made a loud snort, followed by a giggle. When his eyes shot back at me angrily, I bit my lower lip and promised him in a soft, inviting voice, "Don't worry, Noah, I'm not going to cut my hair. Well, I'll trim the ends to keep it healthy and all, but if it's that important to you, I'd leave it long." I had the dark feeling pushing against me that I had just promised more than keeping my hair long. What I said was more significant to him than it would be to a normal guy.

The tightness disappeared from his features. It was replaced with a warm smile and placidness in his eyes. I liked to see him happy, and would probably say about anything to see that smile on his face.

"Noah, why do your women wear caps all the time? Do they ever take them off?"

He sighed, sounding tired with my questions—or maybe he was worried that I wouldn't like his answers.

With a faint smile he said, "The women do remove their caps at night...for their husbands."

Seeing I was about to interrupt, he lifted his rein hand and motioned with a loose finger to his lips for me to shush. Then he went on to say, "A woman's hair is a very seductive thing, Rose. It invites unwanted attention from men—other than the woman's husband, especially hair like yours." He sighed heavily, staring at me.

"Can't you men control yourselves?" I asked sarcastically.

"It's not a matter of control, Rose. It's that a husband doesn't want other men looking at his wife, coveting her. A wife should reserve her beauty for her husband, and no one else." He instructed me as if I were mentally challenged, too igno- rant to understand the fundamentals of life—his way of life anyway.

"It's so much more comfortable having my hair down. Women shouldn't have to be tortured just so their husbands can have their wife's hair all to themselves. That's just…dumb," I argued. I was disappointed with myself for not coming up with a better word, but at the moment my annoyance with Noah was growing, distracting me.

He silently studied my hair for a moment before saying, "I can understand that. I love to see your hair blowing in the wind, but I also hated it when the other men noticed your beauty. Jealousy is a very frustrating emotion to deal with, I've learned lately."

Yeah, I definitely knew what he meant about that. I almost had a nuclear meltdown when he said that his parents wanted to fix him up with the witchy Ella Weaver. Glancing at him now, and seeing the bothered look on his face, I couldn't help being astonished that the gorgeous guy riding next to me liked me enough to get jealous about some other guys finding me attractive. I kept thinking that I would wake up any minute and discover that I'd dreamed Noah into existence just for my mind's personal entertainment.

We reached the dark fairy woods as a gust of wind rustled

the leaves of the trees, blowing the scents of the forest over the cornfield. I deeply inhaled the sharp pine smell that was mingled with the aroma of decaying leaves. Although an invisible force seemed to be pulling me to the path into the trees, I fought the impulse and began to rein Lady around at the place we had turned the last time.

Unexpectedly, Noah shook his head, and holding my hand firmly, he tugged me along with him and Rumor as they sped up to a trot, entering the quiet shade of the trees. Excitement bubbled up in me as a blast of cooler air from under the trees tickled my skin. I was immediately glad for my hoodie.

After a few minutes of hard trotting had forced me to start posting, Noah finally pulled up on his reins when we entered the sunshine of a small clearing in the middle of the forest. Several huge old trees were randomly littering the ground like a child's giant Lincoln Log set, creating an oasis of late-afternoon light from the dark shade of the imposing trees that surrounded the clearing. With our sudden arrival, several squirrels bounded up the fallen trees, and rabbits scampered off in the undergrowth, rattled by our appearance. The feeling that this was a magical forest entered my mind again, and a peaceful kind of happiness filled me that I was here in this special place. And especially that Noah was with me.

In a fluid action, Noah jumped off Rumor. While I watched him, he amazingly took off the horse's bridle, hanging it loosely on a broken branch of one of the felled trees.

"Are you going to just turn him loose like that?" I asked with concerned awe.

"Don't worry, Rose. He won't go anywhere." Half smiling to himself, with his lips slightly twitching, he took my reins and motioned me to dismount.

Which I did, but on the way down I informed him, "You

aren't turning Lady loose like that. I wouldn't trust her not to spook at something and bolt off into the trees. Then I'd never see her again."

Laughing, he pulled a halter and lead rope out of his saddlebag and, holding them up in front of me, said, "I figured you'd say that. I came prepared."

I let him take Lady, exchange the bridle for the halter and tie her to a tree, near where Rumor was standing. While he was doing that, I found a smooth section of one of the logs and sat down, watching Noah take care of my horse.

Normally, I would have done that myself, but for some strange reason I let him do it. As if I knew he wanted to take care of me—and a part of me wanted him to. That was mildly unnerving, I thought, admiring his tall, muscled body as he ambled over to me. Most guys his age weren't built like that. He was even bigger than Sam, and I envisioned him making a great football player. It must be all the farmwork and building houses he did, I guessed. He hopped onto the log beside me, sitting very close but not quite touching. Glancing over at him, I wondered why he was just staring ahead into the trees with a pensive look on his suntanned face. Impatience and frustration rolled together inside me as I watched him ignore me. What was he waiting for?

As if he could read my thoughts, a grin appeared on his face, and breathing deeply he turned to look at me. I waited expectantly for him to do or say something. I was way too chicken to move a muscle.

He licked his lips and said in a deep, smooth voice, "So you've never been kissed, and I've never kissed anyone."

Relief washed over me at his words—we'd both be each other's firsts. But even though I was bubbling with happiness that he wouldn't have a bunch of other girls to compare me to, I still could hardly breathe. My heart was pounding in my chest in a mad fury. When he leaned in closer, I swallowed hard, not knowing if I should keep my eyes open or close them. I was suddenly scared to death. I knew he knew it when he softly went, "Shh." Slowly he brought his face to mine, but instead of going for my mouth, he touched his moist lips to my neck, just below my jawline. The feeling sent a tickling spark that jolted every part of my body to attention, especially deep down in the pit of my belly.

His mouth trailed softly, slowly along my neck and behind my ear, then over my ear and to my face, leaving a warm tingling wherever his mouth went. He was moving so deliberately slow that it was driving me insane. I wanted him to kiss me, to press into me. I wanted him closer. I was becoming impatient, when he whispered close to my ear, his hot breath caressing me, "Are you all right?"

Gulping, "Uh-huh, it feels so…good," I breathed out in a whisper.

That's what he needed to hear. With more force than I expected, his mouth was on mine, parting my lips, his tongue entering hungrily. I stifled a gasp, matching his hunger with my own. His one hand was in my hair, gripping it tightly, and his other hand was lower on my back, pushing me harder into his chest, until my breasts were pressed against him firmly.

My own hands had gone around his neck and I was weaving his thick, wondrous hair into my fingers, stroking the skin beneath. He groaned loudly, pulling his mouth away from mine to bring it to my neck, where he kissed deeply, sucking firmly on my neck for an instant, until I felt faint and dizzy. Just when I thought I'd explode with feeling, he brought his mouth back to mine. This time my mouth was open and waiting. Our tongues were probing, experimenting in a primal dance that even though we'd never been taught, we knew instinctively. And it all felt so wonderful, so right. I shouldn't have worried about the kissing part. It came so naturally. I already felt like a pro and I'd only been doing it for a minute or so.

His hand slipped under my hoodie and the shirt beneath it to softly rub the bare skin of my back, while his mouth was still hot on mine. The feeling of his hands on my skin was wondrous, but then they began to travel higher, squeezing his fingers under my bra strap. The action caused me to tense, suddenly aware of what might happen if I didn't do anything to stop it. The slight tension in my body was enough for Noah, though. He wrenched himself from me, breathing heavily and rubbing his forehead vigorously. He stood and walked away a few steps, pausing for some seconds before returning to me. In an abrupt movement, he grasped my hands and pulled me off the log and up to him. Cradling my body against his, he hugged me gently, rubbing my back—now from the outside of the hoodie.

"I'm sorry, Rose. I got carried away." He took a shuddering breath. "I've never felt so out of control before. I almost—I mean, I was close to just…going all the way without stopping."

He moved his mouth down to the top of my head and kissed my hair. The shock of having him jump away from me had doused my flames a little, leaving just an uncomfortable longing behind. But now the pulsing sensations were springing to life once again. I tilted my head up, and pulling his head down with my hands, I met his mouth again, reveling in the feeling. For some seconds he was very much into the kiss, delving his tongue deeper and cupping my face between his hands. Then he was pulling away again. I tried to hold him close, not wanting him to let me go.

"Rose, stop it. We can't get carried away." His voice was

thick with emotion and I understood that he was trying to be a good guy, and I was acting like a tramp.

Tears started to flow and I let go of him, leaning back against the log. He was there hugging me again in an instant.

"Don't cry, Rose. It's okay—shhh," he soothed.

"I'm s-sorry. It's b-been…a…rough day for…me," I stuttered, letting him comfort me. I never wanted him to let go of me. I wanted to stay like that, in his arms, forever.

Smoothing my hair, he stepped back and looked down at me with tender eyes.

"There's nothing to be sorry for. Someday we won't have to stop. Just think how amazing that'll be." He said it all with such passion that the words were partially lost on me.

I just nodded and he laughed, hugging me again. His face pressed into the side of my neck, the heat of his breath warming my sensitive skin. I leaned into him, my body becoming jellylike. This was the best part—being held tightly in Noah's strong arms was even better than the kissing. I really did have a boyfriend now.

"Now, let's get you home before Sam comes looking for you," he said softly into my ear.

Noah bridled Lady up for me and helped me onto her back. I felt weak and didn't refuse when he took my reins and led me along as if I was an infant. I didn't know what the heck was wrong with me. I never acted so emotional and sappy. His mention of Sam brought back the conversation I'd had with my brother before I left on the ride.

Although I'd never tell the big jerk, he was right. I had been so caught up in the feelings raging through my body, I would have done about anything with Noah in the woods. And we didn't have any protection. I finally understood why girls got pregnant. I had always stuck my nose up in the air at those girls with the swollen bellies at school. Now I finally knew why.

We rode in relative silence the rest of the way back to the road, both of us lost in our own thoughts about what had happened in the secret meadow. My body still felt the traces of his touch, and although my heart had calmed down a bit, it still was slightly spastic, causing me to take a gulp of air now and then. When I would make my drowning noises, Noah would glance over with a knowing smile on his face and give my hand a tighter squeeze. He knew what I was feeling because he was feeling it, too, making me able to deal with my hormonal prison break a little easier.

When we were almost to the road, he guided our horses into the privacy of the hedgerow trees. He pulled me into such a tight embrace that it would have been uncomfortable if I hadn't wanted him to get even closer still.

"Rose, sweetheart, I'll see you on Monday," he mumbled into my hair.

I wrestled with his arms for a second, pulling back to look at his face. "Can't I come to the youth service tomorrow evening?" I hoped I didn't sound as if I was begging.

He sighed unhappily, releasing his hold on me. Then he reached up with both of his hands to run them deeply through his hair before answering, "I wish you could, Rose. More than anything, but church will be held at the Hershbergers' tomorrow, and my parents can't invite your family to another family's house. I'm sorry."

Seeing my disappointment, he added, "We'll have it at our house again sometime, and I'm sure Father will include your family then."

"That's okay. I understand." I said it, but didn't really mean it.

"Cheer up. We'll be seeing each other every day next week

while I'm fixing your house." He grinned, before swiftly and all too fleetingly bringing his lips to mine. "You better get going, Rose. It's almost dark. And be careful," he warned.

Funny, I didn't even notice that we were surrounded by the thick gray haze that settled in the air right before night hit. While I was in Noah's embrace, I felt warm, but now that he'd let go of me, the chilly night air was creeping through my clothes, causing me to shiver.

I was determined to show him that I wasn't a clingy emotional wreck. Pivoting Lady away smoothly, I squeezed her into a trot, leaving him alone in the darkness of the trees.

I turned back before I was out of sight and, stopping, blew him a kiss. "I'll see you on Monday, Noah." I couldn't resist adding, "And good luck with Ella tomorrow. Don't forget me." With that, I blushed and whirled Lady around again, cantering through the gap without another glance back.

It was only after I was riding down the driveway to my house alone that his comments about us someday not having to stop, and being together every night, came crashing into my thoughts. Was that truly possible for us? I *almost* believed it could happen as a cozy contentment fanned out in my body, while the memories of Noah's lips on mine came flooding back to me.

10

Noah
Dealing with Temptations

SITTING UP ABRUPTLY IN BED, I SEARCHED OUT the window. It was way too early to head downstairs yet. Darkness was just beginning to be pushed away by the muted light of morning. Even the birds were still silent. Sighing, I leaned back on the pillow, trying to control my anxiety for six o'clock to arrive. The time I'd be able to get ready to start the day.

And see Rose.

I shook my head slightly, exhaling softly in the dark room when I remembered her look of disappointment before we parted ways on Saturday night. I had told her that church would be held at the Hershbergers' and that she wouldn't be able to come. She didn't hide her emotions well. The dismay was plain on her face, even though she said she understood. That was one of the things that attracted me to her, though— all the emotions and feelings she had. With Rose, I never had to wonder what she was thinking for long; she'd just blurt it out, which was refreshing.

Of course, at some point she'd have to learn to rein in her outbursts. Well, at least around the others. I was certainly okay with her speaking her mind to me.

And then, right before she cantered away, she told me not to forget her. Was she kidding me? I couldn't stop my mouth from turning up into a smile when I thought about how she said it felt so good when I touched her. The way she had responded to me kissing her had made my blood run so hot that I thought I'd lose it. Even though I had no experience kissing a girl like that, it had come so naturally for me with her—as if she was meant to be in my arms. Somehow, I knew what to do, and I didn't want to stop at the kissing either.

A crazy recklessness had come over me, with Rose's warm and willing body against me. I didn't care about anything else in the world. I just wanted to touch her. I wanted her so badly that it nearly killed me. The only thing that had held me back was the feel of her body stiffen for that fraction of a second when I lifted her bra strap.

I couldn't do that to her. I wasn't like the English boys who'd chase after her if they had the chance. She would come to our wedding bed a virgin, even if it killed me. Frankly, the way she kissed me back, she wasn't going to make it easy on me.

All the intimate thoughts were making me uncomfortably warm, so I crossed the room to the open window and looked out toward Rose's house, letting the breeze cool my passion. Only a few hours now and I'd get to see her again. But it felt like an eternity, leaning on the windowsill, waiting.

I was in luck today. Mr. Denton had driven Father to a new work site to bid on a job after he had dropped Jacob, Matthew and me off at Rose's to begin the repairs. Jacob and Matthew were starting on the rotten boards of the front porch, and I was in the process of taking the new screen up to Rose's bedroom, which I had brilliantly volunteered to do. Jacob was so ignorant, he'd agreed to it without even thinking about whose window the screen was for. I gave a silent prayer of thanks for his stupidity as I climbed the stairs.

I certainly wasn't as nervous walking into Rose's bedroom this time as I'd been the first time. But even worse than the nerves, in a way, was the uncomfortable heat that was racing through me at the thought of seeing her again. I knocked lightly, and after a few seconds without sound, I rapped on the door even louder. Suddenly it occurred to me that she was probably still asleep. Following my gut, I gently turned the knob and pushed the door open softly. I ducked into the room, leaving the door halfway open, giving me a reason not to get carried away with her again.

She was lying on a large mattress this time, piled with pillows. Luckily for me, since she was sprawled on top of the blankets, she was well covered, wearing cotton jogging pants and an oversize T-shirt.

Setting the screen down against the wall, I silently crept closer to her, kneeling down on the mattress. I watched her sleep for a long minute. She looked so angelic, hugging her pillow, with her mouth slightly open and her eyes fluttering occasionally.

I couldn't take it any longer. I bent down and kissed her mouth tentatively, then sat back waiting. The corner of her mouth rose into a mischievous smile. Without opening her eyes, she reached up and somehow managed to wrap her hands around the back of my neck and pull me down to her. My lips found hers and I kissed her fiercely, all the thoughts and day-dreams of the past day taking control of my judgment now that I had her in my arms.

She moaned softly, encouraging me to move on top of her, which I all too readily did. The warmth of the bed from her body and the smell of her skin rammed into my senses, to the point that I didn't care if my brother was nearby. I pressed her into the mattress, not being able to get close enough, wanting more of her.

"Oh, God, could you at least shut the door so you don't traumatize your brothers," Sam said angrily, flinging the door wide open instead.

"Damn," I muttered under my breath, disengaging from Rose's arms and sprinting to the doorway. After watching Sam's head disappear around the corner as he stomped down the stairs, I turned back to Rose, who was sitting up, lounging on her pillows with a seductive smirk on her lips.

"Sam's right for once in his life—you should shut the door. Then we'd have more privacy," she said in a soft drawl.

"That's the last thing we need, Rose. You better be good while I put this screen in your window," I said, refusing to look down at her while I crossed the room. I knew that if I did, I'd be a goner.

Somehow I managed to get the screen in, even though she continued to make stretching and yawning noises that I knew were meant to entice me back to the mattress. I held firm and ignored her. For her own good, of course.

Before leaving the room, I blew her a kiss from the doorway, not wanting to get too close to her for fear of my body going nuts again. She pouted back at me, clearly disappointed, making me laugh.

After the encounter in the bedroom, I saw very little of her the rest of the day. The one time I did stop outside her door hoping to say a few words, she was on the floor stretching her body over her legs. I stood mesmerized for a minute while I watched her reach down to her toes, her belly flat against her legs. The soft music coming from her radio and the sight of the unusual exercises that she was doing affected me like a punch to the chest. That glimpse into her strange world caused all the doubts to again rise within me and I walked away without her even knowing that I had been watching her.

It was well into the afternoon and she was still wearing the same flimsy sleeping clothes that she'd awoken in. I didn't want Jacob and Matthew to see her dressed like that and I carried the anxiety around with me throughout the day.

Other thoughts crept in uninvited as I worked. Rose slept until an unreasonable hour and I wondered how she'd handle a more strict morning schedule at the farm. Probably not well. No matter how I tried, I couldn't imagine her waking up at the crack of dawn to make breakfast, start the laundry and work in the garden. Not to mention the cleaning and taking care of the babies. She just didn't seem to have the energy to do all those things.

But with each negative thought, my mind raced to fix it. I could break the rules a little in the house and help her out with her chores. After all, if she was sleepy in the morning because we'd been busy all night, that wasn't a bad thing at all.

Oh, Lord. I needed to sit down and talk to Mother and Father soon about all this. It would be bad at first, but surely I could convince them how much I loved Rose and that we were meant to be together. Yes, I could admit it now—I was in love with the English girl, and after holding her in my arms, no other girl would ever do.

By the end of the workday, while we were driving home, an idea started to take shape in my mind. Something that would make Rose very happy, and I looked forward to making it happen.

"Are you sure it'll be okay with Mr. Cameron?" Jacob asked, hooking the traces to the buggy.

Jacob didn't know about the little affair Mr. Cameron's children had discovered. But I did. I figured he'd be all too willing to give Rose anything she wanted at that point.

"I don't think it's going to be a problem, Jacob, and besides, you wanted to start getting rid of those puppies," I said, heading over to the barn. I remembered the little female pup that Rose had been snuggling with the first night she'd come over for dinner, and that's the one I picked. Holding it up, I said softly, "You're going to have a *very* affectionate new owner, pup." Tucking it under my arm, I walked quickly back to the carriage.

Of course, Jacob was coming with me. For a change, I didn't really mind. Being alone with Rose had become a very dangerous ordeal. I needed some more time to prepare for our next encounter. For right now, though, I was just excitedly anticipating her reaction to the squirming, fuzzy little gift she was about to receive. Come to think on it, this would be my first official present for her. And even though it might appear that the puppy was for the entire family, Rose would know that it was meant for her.

The Cameron family came out the side door as Jacob parked the buggy beside the stone walkway. Justin ran ahead, followed by Sam walking more leisurely with his father. At the back was Rose, her arms crossed over her chest, a pouty look on her face.

"Hello, Dr. Cameron. I heard that you were in the market for a guard dog," Jacob said humorously, reaching between us to pull the puppy from under the bench.

I didn't take my eyes off Rose. Her face brightened instantly when she saw the puppy wriggling in Jacob's hands.

Justin was the first one to the puppy. "Oh, man, how cool—one of the puppies!" He beamed, taking it from Jacob and hugging it with abandon. Sam and Rose crowded in next to Justin. Sam petted the pup's head, while Rose controlled her enthusiasm. She patiently stood by, waiting to hold the puppy. She glanced up, smiling a secret smile meant only for me. I hoped to God Jacob hadn't seen or he'd know for sure what was going on.

"Dad, can we keep her—please!" Justin exclaimed.

"Yeah, Dad, a puppy would be a nice…peace offering, for the whole…moving business." I noticed that Sam's words were dripping with hidden meaning. I watched Rose glance up at her father with her eyes narrowed, her jaw firmly set. The look made me realize that she could be formidable in an argument.

Dr. Cameron smoothed his hand through his hair, saying, "Why, I think it's a marvelous idea to have a new puppy. What do you want to call her, Rose?"

She turned her attention to the puppy, pulling it away from Justin. Searching its face for a minute, she looked up at Sam and said, "What do you think about Hope?"

"That's a good name," Sam agreed.

"Hope it is, then," Dr. Cameron said, reaching out to stroke the puppy's head. Rose snatched the puppy away from her father's hand, giving it to Sam, who rolled his eyes at his sister's action.

Dr. Cameron recovered nimbly from the rebuke and asked, "You boys want to stay for dinner?"

Rose's head shot up, her eyes looking expectantly at me.

"Thanks for the invitation, but our mother has dinner about ready at home. So we'll be going now," Jacob answered.

"Oh, what do I owe you for the puppy?" Dr. Cameron said, reaching for his wallet.

"No, really, it's a gift. But we'll be by first thing in the morning. We've probably got four more days of work here,"

Jacob answered before clucking to his horse, Strider, turning the buggy in a wide loop.

"Thank you, boys. See you in the morning." Dr. Cameron waved.

As we drove down the driveway, I glanced back once to see Rose take the puppy back from Sam. Walking slowly toward the house, she held the puppy up close to her face.

"One down, nine to go," Jacob said enthusiastically as he slapped me on the back.

I didn't feel the same enthusiasm as Jacob, though. When I faced forward, the chill of loneliness crept through me. I hated to be so near to her and not be able to speak to her. The smile Rose had given me was as if someone had turned on a bright light, chasing away all the shadows of doubt I felt about what I was doing. It was insane. And yet, I would do just about anything to have her grace me with such happiness again—and my mind was already imagining our next meeting.

The rest of the week at the Camerons' wasn't nearly as interesting as Monday morning had been. Father shadowed my every move in the house, and since Rose didn't even leave her room until noon, I'd only caught a few glimpses of her each day. I went home every night feeling disappointed.

I was starting to get paranoid. She seemed to be avoiding me altogether, and that left me confused and worried about our relationship. She was so moody. One minute she was all seductive with me, and the next she wouldn't even spare a glance in my direction. Maybe she was just being careful with my father around. I tried to convince myself of that, but by Friday I still hadn't spoken directly to her all week. Each evening I'd been too busy putting up hay or shoeing horses to make arrangements to meet her in the fields, so I decided to take matters into my own hands.

Late in the afternoon, while Father and the others were loading up the work truck, I took the opportunity to talk to Sam alone in the kitchen. He was making a ham-and-cheese sandwich that would've been big enough for two men. When he noticed me, he pushed the sandwich aside, looking at me curiously.

With cheerful sarcasm, he said, "What's up, bro? Is my sister being too much of a handful for you?"

Something about the tone of his voice pricked me. Clearing my throat, I ignored his question. "Do you think you could bring Rose by for the benefit dinner at the schoolhouse tomorrow?"

He thought for a second and shrugged. "It's pretty close. She could ride her bike. Or better yet, you could pick her up with your buggy."

"No, no, she can't come without you as a chaperone. It wouldn't be proper." After a big sigh I admitted, "There's no way I can take her. My family still doesn't know about our relationship and…it'll be difficult to explain it to them."

"What? Isn't my sister good enough for you Amish?" He said it with a bit of a sneer. I found it fascinating how he could allow a man to make out with his sister in her own bed and do nothing about it, yet he was definitely upset with me right now, sticking up for her worthiness.

"It's not that at all, Sam. Our men just don't get together with English women normally. It's unheard of, especially in this community. But I want you to know that I love Rose, and I'm going to find a way for us to be together. You have my word," I tried to convince him.

"Why don't you just become English? That would solve

the problem," he said straightforwardly, dropping a slice of cheese onto his monster sandwich.

"If it were only that easy." Looking into his clear blue eyes, which, strangely, were similar to Rose's, I tried to think quickly about what I could say that would make him understand my situation. "You see, when I get married, my parents will give me some acres. My community will help me build a house for my new wife and a barn for our livestock. I'll be a partner in my father's business, and we'll have a church to embrace us. It wouldn't make sense to leave all that and try to live an English life with Rose. I wouldn't have the means to provide for her in your world."

Shaking his head, he said, "It's ridiculous for you to expect Rose to give up her freedom so she can be with you. Dude. It ain't gonna work. I'm just warning you."

I didn't like what he said. I suddenly saw not only my family as an obstacle to a marriage with Rose but also her family, and especially her older brother. I had underestimated his interest in the matter. The beep of the horn alerted me that I had no more time to talk. "Please, just bring her, would you?" I said, hating to plead about anything, but here I was.

"Yeah, sure, I have nothing better to do on a Saturday night than hang out in a nineteenth-century schoolhouse babysitting my sister," he said, bobbing his head.

Running out the door to the waiting truck, I wasn't very confident that Sam would bring Rose to the schoolhouse. But while he'd been giving me a hard time about his sister, I had decided that this weekend I'd talk to my dad about Rose. I'd finally tell them whom I'd chosen to be with—then wait for the ax to fall.

11

Rose
The Art of Sneaking

LYING ON A COMFY MATTRESS FLIPPING THROUGH a *People* magazine wasn't a horrible way to spend a Friday night, I tried to convince myself, rubbing Hope's belly as she cuddled against me. After all, I'd spent quite a few weekends this same way. It never bothered me before. But that was pre-Noah. Now that I actually had a boyfriend, I'd rather be out doing something with him.

If he were English, we could go to the movies or just hang out together here and snuggle on the couch while we watched something on the satellite. I breathed an irritated sigh and stared at the dancing Georges wallpaper. Maybe I wouldn't mind spending time in my room if I didn't have to look at *that,* I growled to myself.

The clock radio was turned up loud and my favorite song came on. Still lying on the mattress, I swayed to the music, throwing my head back and forth to the refrain. I just couldn't imagine living without music, and I wondered if Noah would mind if I played the radio if we lived together. I was confident I could talk him into it. I could barely suppress a grin from creeping to my lips thinking about the tactics I'd use, until I heard the knock at the door, immediately souring my mood.

"Who is it?" I asked harshly.

"Sam—I have to talk to you."

"Come in," I grumbled.

He lazily moved through the room, sitting at the edge of the mattress. He stole the magazine from me, browsing idly through it. The jerk totally ignored my dropped jaw.

"What do you want, Sam?" Why was he invading my self-induced purgatory?

"Your boyfriend wants me to bring you to some school-house benefit tomorrow night," he said nonchalantly.

Hearing what he said, I bounced up into a sitting position and smacked him on the shoulder playfully. "No way!"

"Unfortunately, I'm not making this stuff up," he said, staring at a photo of Angelina Jolie and not paying much attention to me at all.

"Why do you sound so bummed out, Sam?" I asked suspiciously.

"The catch is that you can't be there alone. You'll need a chaperone or at least someone to give the impression of keeping an eye on you. That means, since Dad will be at the hospital, I have to spend part of my Saturday evening in Amish land." He glanced up, sighing dramatically.

"You'll do it, right? Sam, *please?*" I drew out the *please* and made my cutest little-sister face. I almost thought it was working until the bozo shook his head.

"I'll take you, Rose...on one condition."

Uh-oh, this could be bad. I replied, "Sure, anything."

"Really—anything?" Sam's mouth pinched together obnoxiously, making me very nervous.

"Well, within reason. What do you want?" I hissed, losing patience with him.

"It's nothing bad, Rose. I just think that you need to meet

some normal people here. We'll be going to a new high school in about a month, and it would be nice if you had a couple of friends by then," he said pleasantly.

"So what does that have to do with going to the Amish schoolhouse?" I asked with growing annoyance. What the heck was I missing?

"One of the guys I got to know from football camp this week invited me to a party he's going to. It's tomorrow night."

"Sooo...?" I still wasn't making the connection.

"The deal is that I'll stay with you at the thing tomorrow so you can see your earthy boyfriend, if you'll come to the party with me afterward," he said slyly, turning the page.

"Why do you care if I go to a dumb party with you, Sam? Do you need backup or something?" I was beginning to think he was losing it, when he got right to the point.

"I think you're spending too much time with these people, Rose. It's not healthy for you. You know that this thing with Noah can't go anywhere," he said, sounding very sure of himself.

"Maybe he'll convert," I volunteered wistfully.

"I talked to him about that today, and I don't think there's a chance in hell he'll do it. He's hoping you'll turn Amish, I think." Sam tossed the magazine on the floor and looked me square in the eyes, waiting for my reaction. *Uh-oh.*

"What exactly did he say?" The idea that Noah and Sam were talking about me was unnerving.

"Something about if he stayed Amish, his folks would give him some land, and his community would build his house, and he'd have a job." He took a breath and continued, "It makes sense for him, I guess—as long as he marries an Amish girl and not my sister."

I couldn't help it. I grabbed the nearest pillow and whacked him with it. "Gee, Sam, I didn't know you cared so much."

Smiling, Sam asked, "Do we have a deal, then?"

"Yeah, fine, I'll go to the party with you." I sighed, hating to lose an argument with him.

He seemed happy with himself and finally left me alone. But I suddenly felt that agreeing to go to the party with him might not have been a good idea after all.

This time I didn't worry too much about what I wore. I felt fairly confident that Noah would like me in anything. I picked out a pale blue stretch shirt and faded jeans. I was careful to choose jeans without holes in them, but since I was going out afterward with *normal* people, I put on a little makeup: some mascara, shiny bronze eye shadow and a tad of blush. I didn't think Noah would even notice, I applied it so lightly. I took extra time brushing my teeth, hoping that I might get a chance to sneak a kiss in sometime that night.

The school was less than a mile away, and when we arrived, I was surprised. It didn't look much like the cute little schoolhouse I had been anticipating. Actually, it more resembled a giant garage than a school. It was just a rectangular white building situated a little ways off the road in a grassy field, with some large windows on one end and two big sliding doors on the other. The open doorway was where all the action was. There was a bunch of people there meandering about. Most of them were Amish, but quite a few English people were also mingling in the crowd.

There were so many long-bearded men that I suddenly felt a little awkward with my hair down, thinking about the whole "cover the hair" conversation I'd had with Noah. Self-consciously, I smoothed my hair down the best I could with my hands to make it less noticeable as I got out of the truck, but Mother Nature had been generous to me in that department. I don't think my attempt helped much.

Walking into the building with Sam and Justin, I quickly scanned the room for Noah. He wasn't anywhere to be seen and I sighed in disappointment. All the girls from the youth service were there, though. They were serving food from behind a long counter overflowing with pots and casserole dishes. The inside of the building was larger than I expected, and the same torture benches were set up in rows facing a raised deck where all the items to be auctioned off were on display.

My eyes wandered briefly over the beautiful quilts in a rainbow of colors hanging on the walls. They were the bright spot in the otherwise boring interior. There were also crates full of jarred preserves, wooden furniture of all kinds and even a few cages that appeared to contain doves.

I searched the room for Noah again. No luck. But Sarah saw me this time. With a big smile, she waved across the room. I waved back at her, and then at Suzanna when she spotted me, from a little farther down the work line.

I noticed that men and women were mixed into the line together. What was that about? Maybe since this wasn't a purely Amish event, they let up a bit on the rules. They were trying to raise money for their school after all.

My stomach was hungry as usual, and my heart skipped a beat in sheer joy that I wouldn't have to wait for all the manly people to get their food first. Grabbing Sam's arm, I pulled him through the crowd to the beginning of the line, happy as a duck on a rainy day. Seeing the donation barrel, I poked Sam's arm and made the money sign with my fingers, pointing at it. He rolled his eyes but stuck a twenty-dollar bill into it anyway.

I thought I was in heaven. Everything was breakfast food. Eggs, biscuits, pancakes, sausage and the same cinnamon rolls that Noah's mom had sent over. This was my favorite kind of meal. And I let the world know it when the girls filled my doubled plastic plate with as much food as could fit onto it while I worked my way down the line. I was surprised at the warm greetings from everyone. Suzanna even said she'd come join me when the line thinned out.

Well, everyone except Ella, who glared at me the same way she did the last time I'd had the misfortune of seeing her. She was dishing out the sausage patties, and I couldn't resist holding my plate out for extra helpings just to bug her. It worked pretty well if the huffing sound she made was any indication.

Just as I started to slide down the table away from Ella, I heard her mumble something under her breath that sounded like "Hure." I just *knew* that wasn't a compliment. When I faced her again, her eyes were squinted at me and her mouth held a smug smile. If I'd been a nicer person, I probably would have felt sorry for her. After all, she had it as bad for Noah as I did. The difference was that he wanted me and not her. Even though it tickled my insides, I took the high road and walked away, suppressing the wicked urge to stick my tongue out at her.

I followed Sam and Justin through the mass of long beards, dresses and caps. We worked our way around all the little groups gathered and conversing, until we finally broke free, entering the big canopy set up outside the school. It was filled from end to end with tables and benches—most of which were already taken. I continued to look around for Noah, and as my eyes roamed the tent, I got the uncomfortable feeling of being watched. Once the feeling stuck, it only took an instant to find the source.

A redheaded boy with black eyes was staring rudely at me. And I knew he was being rude because when my eyes found him, he didn't look away, instead eyeing me up and down as if I was a pole dancer. I didn't like the looks of him at all. I gave him my meanest face before I sat down next to Sam. Justin abandoned us to go sit with the little rebel boys, which suited me just fine. It was nice that he'd made friends.

I was tripping a little bit from the encounter with the red-headed guy, though. There was something disturbing about the way he had looked at me. And it wasn't just that he was checking me out either. His smile had been sinister. I shuddered, remembering it while I poured maple syrup over my pancakes from the jug on the table.

"This food is awesome. Amish women do know how to cook. Hey, Rose, maybe if you went Amish it wouldn't be so bad after all," Sam joked, winking at me. *Creep.*

The food was delicious, but I was having a difficult time enjoying it. Where the heck was Noah? After all, he's the one who invited me, and now he's nowhere to be seen. I sat tensely, just picking at my food while I peered around the tent for him.

As if I had summoned him by sheer will, he suddenly appeared on the other side of the table, sitting down across from Sam. The boy who hit the volleyball into my chest sat on the other side of him. Noah didn't even glance in my direction, but still my belly was abruptly full of the familiar little flutters. My heart sped up, beating erratically. I did my best to ignore him and swirled the food around on my plate, occasionally taking a bite. I was gloomily in my own little world, hardly even aware of all the activity around me, when Sam jabbed me in the ribs.

"Sorry again about the ball." I wouldn't even have known the boy was talking to me, except for Sam's well-placed elbow.

After a little yelp from the pain in my side, I looked up to see the boy had the same apologetic expression he'd worn the last time he'd been begging for my forgiveness. I didn't even know his name.

"Really, it wasn't a big deal at all. I'm great." When my eyes met his, he quickly glanced away, proving that my theory about the carrottop creep was accurate. He was being rude not only by English standards, but by Amish standards, too.

Before I returned my attention to my food, I caught a glimpse of Noah's face, and he looked upset about something. His eyes had lingered on me just long enough for me to see them scrunched in frustration. What was with him? Okay, I was becoming ticked off. What really sucked was that I wouldn't even get a chance to ask him.

Sam broke the strained silence, asking Noah, "Is there going to be some kind of auction tonight?"

"Yes, there are hundreds of different items consigned. It'll go late into the night." I detected a roughness to Noah's voice that I doubted Sam would pick up on.

"I saw the nets set up out behind the school. Will you guys be playing volleyball later?" Sam continued the conversation. I wasn't sure if he was really interested or just making small talk. With him, it was hard to tell.

"Yeah, do you want to play?" volleyball boy responded.

"Sure, for a while. We need to leave here around nine-thirty to go to a party," Sam said, checking the time on his phone, completely unaware of what he had just said.

Even though I wasn't looking directly at him, I couldn't miss the fast swivel of Noah's head in my direction. His eyes had narrowed, and they were piercing into me. His mouth wasn't smiling.

Okay, Sam's big mouth strikes again. I couldn't even chew him out—at least not here in front of the crowd. I decided to focus on playing with my food, trying to calm myself. I attempted to remind myself that my brother couldn't help being so stupid with a brain the size of a walnut. Or maybe he wasn't that stupid at all. Maybe he'd said it on purpose to cause trouble. I certainly wouldn't put it past the mop-headed schemer.

Meanwhile, after a couple of minutes of trying to ignore Noah's frowning looks, I decided he really was annoying me; enough that I got up and left the table. Dropping the plastic plate with my uneaten food into a trash can, I made my way back to the serving line. The Amish women were starting to cover some of the dishes of food on the counter, and there were only a few people left in line. Suzanna met me cheerfully, moving around the counter to join me. She had three pancakes stacked neatly on her plate.

"Do you want to sit with me?" she asked brightly.

"Sure." We went back out to the tent.

Luckily, she sat at the nearest table, which was a few down from the one I had vacated. I couldn't help catching a glimpse of Noah still sitting there with Sam and volleyball boy.

Noah was facing me. Even with the limited vision between everyone's heads, he saw me sit down with Suzanna, and our eyes met briefly. Great, he still wore a scowl on his handsome face. I fidgeted with my hands under the table, letting my hair fall over my face in an attempt to avoid his unhappy stare. What was wrong with him anyway? I certainly wasn't a stranger to anger being directed at me, usually from my brothers, but I always knew what I'd done to provoke them. This was just plain weird.

A minute later, Sarah and Maretta joined us with their dinners.

"Did you get enough to eat, Rose?" Sarah asked.

"Yeah," I lied.

The other girls talked quietly, mostly about playing ball after they ate. I wasn't really paying attention, trying to figure out in my head why Noah seemed upset before he even knew I was going to a party. My thoughts were a jumbled mess, until I heard Noah's name. I popped my head up, suddenly attentive.

"Do you really think Noah's going to ask her?" Suzanna asked with round eyes.

First, glancing around to make sure the coast was clear, Sarah whispered, "Well, my parents want him to. I haven't seen him show interest in any of the other girls."

"I wish he'd ask me." Maretta sighed dreamily.

Sarah ignored Maretta's comment entirely and said, "I heard Mother and Father talking about sending him to go live with my grandparents in Pennsylvania for a little while if he doesn't pick someone soon."

"Why would they do that?" I nearly shrieked.

Sarah smiled at my ignorance. "So he can meet someone he likes there." She went on to explain, "Sometimes a young man just can't find the right person to marry in his own community. Then he'll go to live with relatives in another community to meet new girls, and hopefully his future wife."

"But what if he just doesn't want to marry at all? Would he be forced to?" I inquired with extreme agitation. I was too mad at the moment to worry about what the girls might think of my concern over Noah's romantic life.

"Oh—no, we aren't forced to marry, but most everyone

wants to get married at some time. Don't you think so?" Sarah turned the tables on me.

Without thinking, I said, "I think marriage is overrated."

Seeing the girls' shocked faces, I instantly regretted saying it. I was just in a sour mood and being negative. "I'm just kidding," I said, nervously twirling the end of my hair around my finger.

I decided to change the subject. "Sarah, I don't know if I'm saying this correctly, but what does the word *hure* mean?"

Like lightning, she grabbed my hands, pulling me closer to her, nearly in her lap. "Hushhhh, Rose." She nervously glanced around to see if anyone else heard, then turned her attention back to me with a slight frown on her face. Suzanna was giggling into her napkin and Maretta stared at her sausage patty.

"Where did you hear such a word?" Sarah asked as sternly as she could manage in a whisper.

Quickly I came to the conclusion that the less Sarah knew about Ella not liking me—and the reason *why*—the better.

"Aw, I think it was, hmm, a German movie I saw on the... the foreign station the other night." *Phew*. I handled that okay. I guess.

Sarah exhaled and, looking me straight in the eyes, said, "It's not a nice word, Rose. Just don't say it again. Okay?"

I nodded vigorously.

"It looks like ball time," Maretta said, shooting into a standing position.

All the Amish teens were charging away from the tables in separate squadrons of guys and girls. I continued to sit, and Sarah looked questioningly at me. "You're coming, aren't you?"

"I'll probably just watch you guys play tonight. I'm not really in the right frame of mind for it," I informed her, standing up much slower than they had.

"Darn it, you're so good, though. Maybe you'll change your mind later," Suzanna said hopefully.

"Maybe" was all I could muster as I absently ran my hand through my hair, searching for Noah with my shifting eyes; I tried not to be obvious about it.

Before I got too far from the table, Sam sneaked up behind me, giving me a little fright when his finger poked me in the back. I had hoped it would be Noah and when I saw it was only Sam, I huffed and put my hands on my hips. I was about to "quietly" give him a piece of my mind, but before I could, he leaned forward as if to whisper in my ear.

I felt him stuff something crinkly into my hand. He held his finger to his lips to shush me and grinned, walking away with a group of guys, minus Noah. The girls had already left me. I glanced around to see if anyone had noticed Sam's bizarre behavior. When I was convinced that no one was paying any attention to me at all, I smoothed out the small piece of paper. Quickly I scanned the note.

Rose—Please meet me in my buggy. It's the last one parked behind the school—look for Rumor.
Don't let anyone see you! Noah

My breath caught in my throat, and my heart pounded so wildly I thought I'd have a heart attack as I read it. Sticking the note into my pocket, I made my way through the school, heading to the back door. Unfortunately, the door was guarded by a group of old, scary-looking Amish men who stood rigidly, with not the hint of a smile on any of their tight, lined lips.

The rattle of the auctioneer's fast-moving and unintelligible words began, and I paused for a minute to watch as hands shot up to purchase a blue-and-burgundy quilt. The material was beautiful, but that's not really what stalled me. Instead, I needed time to work up the nerve to walk through the throng of long beards ahead of me. The auctioneer was a middle-aged man with a chestnut beard. He was a cheery-looking man, and he was speaking English. Yeah, I wished the group of men at the doorway looked as friendly.

The bidding was still going on for the quilt when I started to move again, determined to get through the bearded obstacles to reach the door. Before I got far, though, I was stunned when Noah's mom appeared at my side and gently touched my arm. She was a little shorter than me and had dark hair and eyes, like Noah. I could definitely see the resemblance between the two. She was an attractive woman, except that her forest-green frumpy dress made her look older than I figured she actually was. She also had a nervous twitter about her, reminding me of a rabbit.

"Rose, isn't your father here with you tonight?" she asked kindly, with the words rolling out of her mouth slowly, almost as if she was translating in her head before speaking.

"No, he's working a shift at the hospital," I replied timidly, wanting desperately for her to like me but terrified of her at the same time.

"I worry that you're all alone there in that big house, and without a mother to care for you. Are you doing all right, dear?" she said.

As I gazed up into her dark eyes that looked so much like Noah's, I saw that they were glistening with moisture. She pitied me. The realization that Mrs. Miller wasn't the judgmental woman I'd first thought her to be rolled over me in a wave of understanding.

"I'm doing okay" was all I could get out of my mouth before a stupid teardrop formed in my right eye; I rushed to wipe it away before she saw it.

"Oh, I'm sorry, child. Have I upset you?" she asked, putting her arm around me.

I knew I had to get out of there before I started crying in front of the entire community. The mother-hen behavior coming from Mrs. Miller was too much for me to handle right then. I think I liked her better when she was scaring the crap out of me.

"No, I'm just an emotional kind of person. Thanks for your concern, though. Really, I'm fine. I was just going out to play volleyball with the girls, so I'll see you later," I said, starting to pull away from her, but before I could escape, she pulled me into a tight embrace, really freaking me out.

"If you ever need anything, please call me. And do watch out for the ball this time." She smiled, letting go of me.

"I'll be careful," I mumbled, embarrassed, as I ducked away from her into the crowd.

Putting the strange encounter out of my mind, I focused on my goal. After a bunch of "excuse me's," I finally dodged all the old men and reached the prized door. Once through it, I stopped to investigate the long line of black buggies parked neatly beside the board fence. Squinting, I could just make out the last one. Sure enough, Rumor was tied to the fence next to it. My heart beating loudly in my chest, I headed in that direction, thankful for the parked cars that shielded me from anyone's prying eyes.

It was kind of exciting sneaking away to meet Noah in his buggy. I was feeling more upbeat playing James Bond as I lurked between SUVs and pickup trucks before finally arriving at my destination. Hearing the 007 music in my head,

I quickly glanced around and crept to the fence side of the buggy. Once there, I squeezed in near the door, which popped open unexpectedly. Cautiously, I peeked in. Noah was lounging on a bright blue velvet seat that seemed out of place in the drab, funeral-style buggy.

Even more surprising was the big grin on his face when he saw me. With relief, I grasped his extended hand and let him pull me into the buggy. The windows were opened only a crack, probably for secrecy. With the warm, late-afternoon summer sun beating down on it, the interior of the buggy was hot and humid, making me feel as if I'd just stepped into a hotel sauna.

With unbelievable swiftness, Noah pulled me into a tight embrace, smashing me into his body. I relaxed for the first time since we sat together at the table earlier. With the hot air around us, I melted into him, staying very still, with my face resting against his chest. He stroked my hair, softly rubbing his hand up my arm.

Right then and there I knew where I belonged, in Noah's arms like that forever. The thought that his family could rip us apart and send him off to some faraway community terrified me to the bone. I suddenly felt despair at the impossibility of the situation. Although I desperately squeezed my eyes tightly shut, the tears sneaked through onto his blue starchy shirt. My loud sniff indicated to him that I was having an emotional breakdown and he pulled back, supporting me with his hands, lightly gripping my shoulders. Furrowing his brow and with eyes holding extreme concern, he asked in a gentle voice, "What's wrong, Rose?"

After a few more seconds of sniffing and swallowing, I murmured, "I thought you were angry with me."

My words caused an unexpected response from Noah when

he brought his lips to mine in a near-desperate kiss that took the breath from me. My face was still wet from the crying, but he didn't seem to care as his mouth moved over my cheeks and nose and eventually my eyes.

Sighing deeply, I delighted in the feel of his lips on my skin and the scent of the slightly damp sweat beneath his shirt. I tried to impart it all to memory, fearing that someday he might be embracing a pretty Amish girl in this same way, and I might be somewhere else, far, far away.

This time when he moved back a little, just enough to look at me, he continued to hold my face in his hands, stroking my cheeks with his callused thumbs. His eyes were dark with emotion. They were penetrating so deeply into me that I feared he could see into my soul. Then he'd know how much I really needed him…and wanted him.

Suddenly his eyes became even more intense, sweeping over my face. He asked tightly, "Rose, why are you wearing makeup?"

The question threw me off balance; I wasn't expecting it. I told him without hesitation, my voice rising, "Sometimes I wear makeup, Noah. It's no big deal."

"Is it because you're going to a party tonight?" he asked with a guarded voice, but his eyes continued to wander over my face with the same scrutiny.

Without even considering a lie, I answered honestly, "Yeah, I guess when I go out places I like to wear a little makeup. But really, Noah, I hardly have any on at all. I'm surprised you even noticed."

"Of course I noticed. You have such a naturally beautiful face. You don't ever need to wear any makeup," he said with sureness.

Why is he being so difficult over a little bit of makeup? I'd much rather be snuggling against him again—but his sour face staring at me prompted me to pull away from his hands and lean back on the sapphire seat. "I didn't mean to upset you. It wasn't anything I even thought about," I told him, trying hard not to sound too annoyed.

My statement didn't seem to satisfy him. He moved in closer with a troubled look spreading over his features. Studying my face fixedly, he murmured, "Rose, why are you going to that party anyway?"

Swiftly I defended myself. "Sam wants me to go with him."

"I bet he does," he said with an angry grunt as he leaned back again, peeking out the window. Satisfied that we weren't about to be ambushed, he returned his tormented gaze on me.

The action made me realize with sudden poignancy how dangerous it was that we were meeting here in his buggy—all alone. Just past the window were hundreds of people who certainly wouldn't approve. If we were discovered, Noah wouldn't just get a slap on the wrist about it; he might literally be shipped away. I needed to stop acting as if this was a silly game and start taking it a whole lot more seriously. But still, I couldn't quite shake the stiffness my insides were feeling at the moment over his bizarre reaction to me wearing a little tiny bit of makeup. He was definitely overreacting on this one. He'd better get his butt down off his high horse before he made me really angry.

Was he jealous about me going to the party, and that was why his hackles were up? Didn't he know that I'd much rather be with him than go to a stupid party with Sam? Could he actually be insecure about me? That thought made me feel better, and a teeny bit sorry for him. I asked softly, "What's the problem, Noah?"

With a long sigh and not meeting my gaze, he said, "I get the feeling your brother doesn't approve of our relationship."

"He's just trying to watch out for me, Noah. With Mom gone and Dad busy with his new girlfriend, Sam thinks it's his job to make sure I don't get into trouble or something," I said, sliding closer to him. Gathering my courage, I reached up to touch his cheek lightly with my fingertips.

He responded with another search out the window for spies and then, with his lips turning up into an amused smile, which I could see he was trying to fight off, he promised, "He doesn't have to worry about me getting you into trouble. I'm going to take care of you, Rose. So your brother can get a new job."

"I know you will," I said, hardly hearing what he said. His warm almond eyes were hypnotizing, and my heart was beating like crazy in my chest. I didn't want to talk at the moment. With the pounding in my chest, I crawled up onto him and pressed my lips against his mouth. A deep moan escaped from him and his arms encircled my waist, pulling me even closer.

I don't know how long we were lip-locked like that, our mouths moving playfully together, but it must have been a while, because my left leg began to cramp slightly, forcing me to change positions. That gave Noah the opportunity to be sentry again, and when he turned back to me, he scolded, "Really, Rose, if this buggy starts shaking too much, someone is going to notice."

The stern face he put on for show disappeared when I settled back onto his lap and sighed happily. He shook his head halfheartedly and said in his raspy voice, "I don't know what I'm going to do with you, Rose."

"How 'bout more kissing?" I joked, moving my hand to his wavy dark hair, letting my fingers caress through it, massaging his head. I loved touching him, and I was feeling more comfortable with it. He was my guy now, and that still amazed me. I was astonished by the feelings I was experiencing. They were so powerful. Mountain-moving strength. I wondered if everyone felt this way when they fell in love. Yes, I had thought the *L* word and I knew that it was true. I had fallen in love with this Amish boy, and I couldn't do anything about it. He would forever own my heart.

He brought my face to his again, our mouths just inches apart, his breath coming out in a heated rush. "Rose, I don't want you to go to that party."

Sighing, I tilted my head, watching the anguish play out on his face. I wanted to kiss away his worries, but I could tell he wanted more than that from me. "But it's kind of complicated, Noah. You see, I promised Sam that I'd go to the party with him if he brought me here tonight."

With determination, he said severely, "I don't care what you promised him. Tell him you're sick. I'm sure you can put on a good act and get out of it. This is important to me, Rose."

"Why?" I inquired, feeling a little on the defensive. Every Sunday he got together with all *his* friends for youth church activities without me. I didn't harass him about it.

He touched my face gently, tracing his fingers over my cheekbone, down my nose and along the contours of my lips, which I parted slightly without thought, allowing him to move his finger lightly into the moist interior of my mouth. Just when I thought I was going to pass out from the light-headed sensation his movements were causing me, he trailed the same finger down to the hollow of my neck, settling there briefly, before moving down lower to trace the outline of the formfitting shirt I was wearing. It was crazy what his touch was doing to me, like a million pricks along my skin. Inwardly cussing out the lack of control I had over my body, I swayed into him and closed my eyes. I would agree to anything he wanted at that moment.

"It's just not right for you to be in mixed company without a chaperone, Rose. It's not safe." He said it firmly and the look on his face told me that he wouldn't budge on the subject either. He appeared much older at that moment, unmovable, like a tree that had been rooted in the same place for hundreds of years.

He continued to watch me with growing impatience, waiting for my answer. The frustration was evident on his face. I was torn—really torn. I didn't even want to go to the dumb party, but I didn't want Noah thinking he could tell me what to do either.

"Don't you trust me, Noah?"

He sighed, shaking his head. "It's not about trust. You shouldn't put yourself into the kind of situation that could get you into trouble—or cause the others to think poorly of you."

"Others?" The conversation was traveling into strange territory. I was beginning to worry about the direction Noah was heading.

He stared at me, appearing to think about his words carefully before he spoke. I was glad he was taking his time instead of blurting out something that would really piss me off. Because the last thing I wanted was to be angry with him.

When he finally spoke, his voice was coaxing. "I can't expect you to understand my world, Rose—it's so different from yours. But you have to trust me on this one. If word got out in the community that you were going to parties, it would make you look very bad in the eyes of my people…and then you'd never have a chance at being invited to any of our youth gatherings. I don't want anyone thinking poorly of you. Besides, you never know what might happen at a place where there are a bunch of young people drinking and carrying on without supervision."

"It's not like that, Noah. Even if I wasn't dating you, I wouldn't do anything stupid that would get me hurt or into trouble. I'm not that kind of person…and I thought you knew that." I pulled a little farther away when I said it, feeling for the first time that Noah really was from a different world—or time period.

His arms went around my shoulders, pulling me against him as he buried his head into my hair. He hugged me quietly like that for a minute before he released me and leaned back.

"I'm sorry. I didn't mean to offend you. That wasn't my intention. I just want for us to be together, that's all."

Looking at his worried face, my heart beat out my head, and I said resignedly, "Okay. If it means all that, I won't go. I'll talk my way out of it. But don't think you'll always get your way, Noah."

His face relaxed and a light smile played at the corners of his mouth. Taking my hands between his large ones, he placed them over his heart and said forcefully, "You belong with me, Rose, and I only want what's best for you. We won't have to sneak around like this forever. Things will change soon. I promise."

"But how?" Part of me wanted desperately to believe him. The more rational side needed more convincing.

"I'm going to talk to my parents soon and tell them about you." He paused and then with certainty breathed, "I don't care what they say about it. I'll do whatever it takes to be with you. But I'll know better what we're dealing with after I've discussed it with them. So just hang in there awhile longer."

There were so many what-ifs to consider that it wasn't even

worth harping on all of them. So instead I asked him a question I'd been thinking about for the past few days.

"When will Jacob and Katie get married?"

The question threw him off for a second. His eyebrows rose in surprise, but when he recovered, he replied, "Sometime this autumn, when all the farmwork is done for the year."

His eyes were inspecting me now with such extreme interest that I blushed and glanced away before asking him, "Is that the time of year when all the Amish get married?"

Still directing his burning attention at me, he said with mild amusement, "No—some couples wed in the springtime." Pausing, he then asked carefully, "What's your favorite season?"

His eyes were glittering now. I could tell he liked the direction the conversation had taken.

Without pause, I told him, "I love October—when all the leaves are changing and the cool air is just arriving." I would have said more, but I got a little tongue-tied, and I peeked at him, wondering what he was thinking.

He quickly licked his lips and then spread them into a devilish smile. "October is a fine month for me," he said softly, his eyes searching mine.

I couldn't help that my curiosity was up now. I rambled on, "What are Amish weddings like? I mean, do you do the cake—and does the girl wear a special dress? And do you have a little boy be the ring bearer and...all that stuff?"

He looked thoughtful for a moment before answering. "Well, for one thing, we don't have wedding rings." He held my gaze, waiting for my reaction.

"Why not?" I was shocked, and my voice probably showed it.

"Our women don't wear jewelry of any kind. We don't

need a ring to show our everlasting love," he said slowly with a shrug.

"Oh" was all I could manage, not sure what I thought about never wearing a wedding ring.

He must have sensed my trepidation on the ring issue, because he told me other, more pleasant things about the ceremony.

"The weddings are huge events with hundreds of guests. Everyone from the community and even some from other communities attend. And yes, there are cakes and desserts and a wonderful dinner." Pausing to catch his breath, he continued, "The women in our community wear blue, but the bride can pick out the shade she wants her dress to be—that wouldn't matter for you. You look beautiful in any color. And the girls decorate the wedding area with flowers and wreaths."

I was still on his lap, and the entire time he was talking, he trailed his hand over my arms and down my legs, making me lose any kind of concentration on what he was saying, only catching bits and pieces of information. Then his talking stopped and his mouth was on my neck. I stretched it to give his tongue full access. Closing my eyes and breathing deeply, I realized that the buggy's temperature had dropped now that the sun was almost gone from the sky. Time always went by so swiftly when I was with him.

When his mouth was back on mine, I stopped thinking altogether—until I heard the annoying voice from outside.

"Rose, Rose—are you here?" Sam whispered loudly.

Noah heard it, too, and quickly opened the window a bit wider to softly whistle to Sam. He was beside the buggy peering in the window in a flash.

"Come on, Rose. We've got to get going," Sam grumbled.

Reluctantly, I pulled out of Noah's embrace. Before I got

far, his hands snaked around my waist, pulling my back against his hard chest. He whispered hotly into my ear, "Remember what you promised me, Rose."

I nodded my head and mumbled, "Uh-huh."

Not releasing me, he instructed, "Meet me in the fields on Wednesday at seven o'clock. We're done working on your house for now, so I won't see you until then, but hopefully, I'll have some good news for you."

And then he kissed below my ear, sending a shiver down my neck before he reached over my lap to open the door for me. Sam was standing there, waiting with a look of mild disgust on his face. For some reason I suddenly felt embarrassed having him staring at me, with the thoughts of our birth-control conversation flitting into my brain.

Once I was out of the buggy, the cool evening engulfed me. I breathed in the fresh air, watching the fireflies blink in and out around us. We didn't say goodbye. Noah's eyes just smoldered at me, and I gave him a half smile, disappointed to be leaving him and his warm arms. The moment was broken when Sam jerked my own arm and ordered, "Come on."

Noah was outside the buggy in a heartbeat. With narrowed eyes directed at Sam, he threatened, "Easy there."

Sam stiffened next to me and rose up taller as he glared back at Noah. The two of them stood there not moving, with the sounds of the auctioneer and people talking not far away blending into the dusky evening. I couldn't believe this was happening. Wasn't there enough conflict in our lives already? I just wanted to be with Noah and have our families accept us together. Was that too much to ask?

"It's okay, Noah," I said forcefully, glancing hard at him. Then I whirled away from them both. I stalked through the cars to Sam's truck, parked within sight. I was working hard to hold back the tears that were threatening to drop out of my eyes. Justin was already waiting in the front seat when I tried to climb in. I ordered him into the back. He scrambled over the console out of the path of my hurricane emotions.

I waited, looking straight ahead, praying inwardly that the two testosterone-filled guys didn't come to blows. What was wrong with them anyway? I was running through the scene in my head when a minute later Sam jumped in and started the engine. Anger was emanating from him, but he wasn't bruised or bloody. As he backed out, I warned him to go slow; there were lots of little kids around. Nodding, he exhaled loudly in agreement and drove carefully past the buggies, horses and people until we were finally free of the crowd and out on the road.

Without wasting time, I said in a sickly voice, "I don't feel well, Sam."

"You've got to be kidding me, Rose. You were perfectly fine a minute ago," he accused.

"No, really, I haven't felt well since dinner. Something didn't sit well with me." I doubted I'd win an Oscar, but for good measure, I cupped my hand over my mouth and made a gagging noise that caused Justin to start searching the backseat for a plastic bag.

"You hardly ate a thing. The food didn't make you sick. Your boyfriend doesn't want you to go to the party. Is that it?" He turned a sharp eye on me.

I kept up the act, though, until I felt as though I might really vomit and Sam had slammed on the breaks in front of the house. Justin jumped out and headed for the house, while I weakly opened the door and began to slide out. Before I was free of the truck, Sam grasped my arm again, which was beginning to become an annoying habit of his.

"Look, Rose, I'm not trying to be a jerk about Noah. I just don't want you to get hurt." He said it with seriousness that didn't sound right coming from his mouth.

I nodded and muttered, "I know," before pushing the door closed and walking slowly to the house. I actually got out of going to the party. Yay for me.

Sam backed around and drove back out the driveway. I couldn't help being just a little touched by my big brother's warped concern. But that thought disappeared quickly to be replaced by the desire to see Noah again on Wednesday.

When I'd finally find out what his parents were going to do about their son hooking up with a girl like me.

12

Noah
Discovered

THE DARK CLOUDS THREATENED RAIN, MATCH-
ing my mood. I quickly crossed the barn aisle to the tack room.
Grabbing the saddle roughly from the rack, I hauled it on my
shoulder back to Rumor, who waited patiently for me, not
aware of the storm clouds on the horizon.

I couldn't believe Wednesday was already here, and I hadn't
even had the chance to talk to Father and Mother about Rose.
There were always people around. Either my littler brothers
were shuffling underfoot or the girls were lurking around
the corner. Whenever I even thought about starting up the
discussion with Father, one of the children would pop out of
nowhere, making it impossible. And then there was the un-
fortunate stroke of bad luck when the Bobcat broke down in
the middle of bush-hogging the lower field. Father had been
in such a bad mood the past few days that even if I'd somehow
managed to catch him totally alone for a heart-to-heart about
my future wife, it wouldn't have been great timing.

As I was getting ready to meet Rose, I felt like a coward.
What would she think? I told her that when I saw her next,
I'd have news for her. Now, I had to try to explain that I
never got the opportunity to even mention anything to my

folks. She would probably think I was avoiding the subject on purpose. And then I worried even more that she'd get bored with where we were in our relationship. Maybe she'd begin to think there were better options. After all, she was beautiful and smart. She could have any English guy she wanted. And he'd be able to pick her up in his shiny car and take her to the movies. The only thing I could do at the moment was arrange secret meetings in cornfields and buggies, and even then there were problems.

I still bristled at the way Sam had yanked Rose's arm, pulling her away from me. And that feeling nearly got me into a fight with her brother. I'd seen the look of fear on her face when Sam and I were sizing each other up. The last thing I wanted to do was cause her any pain. For the most part, I liked Sam. He was just trying to protect his little sister. I'd do the same for Sarah or Rachel. I was just so fed up with the entire situation with Rose. I didn't like sneaking around and breaking my parents' and the church's rules, but I wasn't going to give Rose up either. I had overreacted to Sam because of my own frustration with the lack of control I had in my life.

Leading Rumor out of the barn, I decided I'd have to apologize to Sam sometime soon. Rose and I would need all the allies we could gather in the days to come. As I swung into the saddle, I glanced up at the sky to see the clouds stacking ominously on top of each other. The wind was picking up, and it was unseasonably cool for July. I had my black knit hat on and was wearing a simple navy blue coat, so I was quite comfortable even in the stiff breeze.

I hoped Rose dressed appropriately, but I figured I'd probably end up giving her my coat to wear anyway. Hearing the clip-clops of hooves on the road, I slowed Rumor to watch two buggies go by. Arms came out of the open windows, followed by several beeps ringing into the air for me. I waved back. There was a baseball game at the schoolhouse for the youth group tonight. I would have to plan my timing carefully to avoid meeting someone on the road. Once the Yoders were well away, I took Rumor into a slow canter down the driveway, hoping to get to the hidden fields before another buggy came up the road. The community had been buzzing with activity all evening, and for over an hour bicycles and carriages had been zipping by the house, heading toward the schoolhouse.

Inwardly I cringed at having to explain to Jacob and Sarah later that I'd opted to go for a ride alone rather than meet with the others for the game. It would look very suspicious. These events were mandatory, especially now that I was supposed to be looking for a mate.

Sighing deeply, I crossed through the gap in the fence and began searching for Rose. I was a few minutes early, so I wasn't expecting to see her, but there she was, waiting by the hedgerow for me. Surprisingly, she had a warm-looking pink jacket on. Granted, she stuck out like a sore thumb against the green vegetation around her, but at least she wouldn't be cold.

The sudden urge to be with her was too great, causing my legs to bump Rumor's sides, sending him into a gallop. When she saw me coming, not understanding my desire, she let her horse go and galloped up alongside me, challenging for another race. Allowing all my worries to blow away with the pounding wind, I leaned down and pushed Rumor faster. We ran side by side over the tractor path with the horses perfectly in sync. I didn't think either horse was eager to leave the other.

When I glanced sideways at her, Rose had a big grin on her face that made my heart thump hard in my chest. It was crazy how I reacted to her. I'd only known her for a couple of weeks, and I was already in love with her. Seeing Rose happy, even for that brief instant, nearly sucked the breath out of me. We ran like that with total abandon until we came to the curve, where we both stood in our saddles, leaning back to slow the horses.

Rose's face was flushed from the wind, and her hair blew wildly around her. At that moment she was more beautiful than I'd ever seen her. Her face was eager and expectant, but I glanced away, unable to immediately darken the moment.

"Hey, how was the rest of your weekend?" she asked casually enough, but her eyes were unusually bright when I looked back at her.

"Boring—what about you, did you put on a good act for Sam?" I examined her face closely for a possible lie, still worried that she might have gone to the party after all.

She broke out into a wide grin. "Not only did I get out of going to the party, but Justin waited on me hand and foot all evening, thinking I was really sick. It was kind of great," she said with a mischievous twinkle in her eyes.

Well, that made me feel better. I relaxed a little, preparing to tell her about my lack of opportunity to have the important discussion with my parents, when she launched right into it.

"What did your parents say?" she asked under her long eyelashes in a little voice.

Taking her hand, I brought it up to my mouth and kissed her palm, smiling down at her before I said, "I didn't get the chance to talk to them, Rose. Father was never alone. And then he wasn't in a very good mood."

"I guess it would be difficult to have a private conversation in a house with eight kids." She laughed, not seeming to be bothered by what I'd said.

She handled the news better than I expected, worrying me

a tad that she didn't seem to really understand the seriousness of the matter. As much as I'd wanted to get the conversation with Father out of the way, I was also terrified of how he and Mother would react. They would be more than unhappy about it—they'd be devastated. And the fact that Rose didn't fully get it made me realize that even though she looked the part of a young woman ready for courtship, her mind was still childlike.

Her laugh turned into a flirtatious smile, clouding the doubts that had crept up within me. I couldn't resist her. Bending down, I kissed her lips, with the bouncing of the horses moving our mouths for us.

Pulling out of the sweet kiss before I wanted her to, she began thinking hard with her lips pushed out and her brow tight. I wondered what she was thinking, but I humored her, waiting patiently for her next question.

"Why are there so many kids in your family?" she finally blurted out.

Hmm, this will be an interesting one to answer, especially when I was trying to be so restrained around her physically. I took my time considering the different ways I could explain, until she made a sexy growling sound in an attempt to get my attention.

Unable to avoid the suggestive smile I was sure was developing on my face, I answered her truthfully. "We don't use birth control, Rose." Seeing her eyes widen to plate size, I had to control myself from laughing at her.

"You're kidding!" she gasped.

Now I was curious. "Why is that so hard for you to believe?" I was hoping her answer wasn't going to bother me. I hated being frustrated with her during our rare times together.

She let out a loud breath and lightly shook her head. "It's

just that...well...hmm." She stopped talking, and she held her lips tightly together. Her skin turned an appealing shade of bright red.

"What were you going to say, Rose? Come on, tell me," I encouraged her, squeezing her hand and shaking it. "You can talk to me about anything, anything at all," I tried to convince her gently.

When she met my eyes again, she was still red-faced but apparently resolved to speak. She picked her words carefully. "That means that a couple of healthy...and affectionate people would always be pregnant." When I continued to stare at her and not get ruffled by her point, she arched her eyes and went on more forcefully, "The woman would be in a constant state of pregnancy. She'd get all worn-out, tired and old." She wrinkled her cute little nose in disgust at the thought.

"I hadn't really thought about it like that," I said, wondering if maybe she did have a point. Mother did seem tired most of the time.

"I mean, don't get me wrong, I wouldn't mind having a few kids—maybe even four. That's a nice number." Pausing, she peeked at me with confused eyes, and she asked with worry, "You wouldn't want more kids than that, would you?"

Her agitation was amusing, and I couldn't help chuckling about it. Again I brought her hand to my mouth and kissed it. That didn't satisfy me. So I leaned over to her neck and kissed her there, lingering long enough to breathe in her lavender scent.

"You worry too much. We haven't even gotten to the official courting yet, and already you're in a titter about the children." I tried to hide my smile.

Her mouth dropped open and out came a "But—"

Cutting her off, I said, "Really, we aren't supposed to use

birth control, but I'd never want you to have more children than you could handle or wanted. I could live with four—and maybe you'd change your mind later on."

Wanting desperately to know what she was thinking, I intently studied her for signs. Her face was scrunched up and she twisted a wad of her mare's thick mane between her fingers—I took both as signs that she was anxious about the discussion we were having.

"What's wrong?" I asked, very much afraid of what her answer would be. Maybe she was changing her mind about being with me.

She glanced at me and then away, saying, "This is all a lot to process at one time. I wasn't planning to get married and have kids until I was, like, twenty-eight or something. I can hardly believe that we're even talking about this stuff."

The air went out of me, and I suddenly felt very tired. What was I doing with Rose in the first place? Though I wouldn't admit it before, I worried that she would bolt from me at any moment. I couldn't possibly hold on to such an independent girl. She was an outsider and she'd been brought up with a whole different set of rules to live by. How could I expect her to change her entire way of thinking for me?

I couldn't.

"Look, it's just our way, that's all. You don't have to agree with it," I said.

Besides the creaking of our saddles, there was silence for a minute. I was afraid to say anything else on the subject, waiting for her instead, but when the quiet started to become uncomfortable, I opened my mouth to speak. She beat me to it, though.

"Hmm...that's interesting how you can change the rules when you really want to." She grinned up at me.

Her complete change of emotions threw me off and it must have shown on my face, because she quickly followed up, saying, "It's okay, we don't have to figure everything out today."

Relief surged through me, invigorating my senses.

I wasn't taking any chances of the conversation souring, though, so I stayed in what I thought was safe territory.

"Do you have your driver's license?"

She looked mildly surprised by the change of subject. "No, I have my permit. Unfortunately, I don't get to drive much."

"Why not?" I was truly interested now and marveled that a girl her age was allowed to operate a car on the road.

"Well, Sam won't let me drive his truck—says it's too big for me—and Dad's always working, so he doesn't have the time to go with me. I won't be able to drive alone until I'm seventeen." She seemed bothered by all that, but then she added, "Up until now I've been lucky, because all my friends have cars and they've always taxied me around."

I realized right then that I hadn't even gotten a real glimpse of her world, and instantly wanted to know more. "What are your friends like?"

"Amanda and Britney are my best friends. They're both a year older than me, in Sam's grade. But since I've always tagged along with his friends, it was just natural for them to take me in. I'm like their little mascot."

"Do they have boyfriends?"

"Amanda and Heath have been hot and heavy for two years now, and I think they might actually get married someday, but Britney plays the field." She paused, laughing. "I think she's dated just about every cute guy in her class and mine."

"And your friends...do they sleep with their boyfriends?'

She glanced shyly at me before answering. "Yeah, Amanda

and Heath are quite the item. Britney doesn't sleep around or anything like that, but she isn't a virgin either."

The word *virgin* coming out of a girl's mouth so readily heated my face. I took a long minute to think about what she had said while we ambled through the cornfields, her hand curled safely in mine.

"So, what kind of things do you do with your friends, then?" I asked carefully.

"During the summer we go to King's Island and the 'Beach'— that's a big water park. We also go to all the open-air rock concerts, the movies and out to eat at the cheaper restaurants. But sometimes we just hang out at the mall and shop."

"It must be pretty boring for you here in Meadow View," I observed, with fear creeping through my bones that she could ever get used to living a Plain lifestyle.

"I gotta say, it hasn't been at all boring since I've moved here. You've managed to keep me very entertained," she said, clearly working to contain her laughter as tremors touched her mouth.

Unease began pounding away at my mind, forcing my heart to beat faster. This was important and I had to find out more. I asked quietly, "How would you feel if you couldn't do all those things anymore?"

She didn't even hesitate, surprising me. "It would depend on if you could keep me busy," she said in her velvety voice. Her eyes were laughing, and I knew she was teasing me. She was not taking the question as seriously as she should be. A gust of wind traveled through the cornstalks, bending them down deep, erasing our natural cover. The sound of the brushing stalks against each other was a constant scratchy drone now, and Rose's horse began to prance nervously, affected by the cool temperature and the swaying corn around us. The mare looked as if she might bolt, and I let go of Rose's hand to grasp her one rein, holding her horse while she side passed along the narrow path with extra spring to her stride.

I was pleased that Rose let me lead her horse; I had expected an argument from her, but she had relented placidly enough. The horse was a lot to handle, even on a calm day. Today, the mare was close to coming unhinged. I decided if Rose wouldn't let me hold the rein of her frisky horse, I'd ask her to switch horses with me. Since she relented, I didn't have to resort to doing that, thankfully.

Sooner than I wished, we reached the forest. I began to guide the horses around, when Rose asked disappointedly, "Aren't we going in there?"

I held my smile in and sighed, not wanting to disappoint her. Especially since that was exactly where I wanted to take her. "No, Rose, I don't think it would be a good idea for us to go back in there today."

"Why?" she asked like a girl used to getting her way. But I had to be firm with her. I said pointedly, "I find it very difficult to do the right thing when we're alone together in a situation like that. And I don't want to take advantage of your willingness."

"I'm okay with it, though," she offered, trying to convince me with her alluring eyes fluttering like Samson's Delilah.

"But I'm not. You aren't going to be like your English friends. As horribly difficult as it's going to be—I want to wait until we truly belong to each other before we cross that line," I said sternly, trying not to look at her eyes, fearing I'd be turning the horses around and leading her back into the woods myself.

"Can't we at least kiss a little?" she pleaded with an undeniable pout on her honeyed lips. I became frustratingly aware that she could make me do anything she wanted with that look. I was doomed to be her slave for the rest of my life. That thought both bothered me and made me happy at the same time.

"With you, it never seems to be a little," I teased halfheartedly. But unable to resist her any longer, I stopped the horses, and holding the reins in one hand, I put my other hand around her lower back, giving her the kiss she wanted.

Her mouth was soft and willing against mine, and for a few seconds the fields disappeared, and the push of the cold wind against my coat couldn't be felt. It was only me and Rose, alone in the entire world. Nothing else mattered except the feel of her breath against my skin and the tangle of her hair around my face.

There are those moments in your life when you suddenly realize you've made a mistake, and that second of clarity, when it becomes all too clear that something is going to happen, whether it's mildly irritating or downright bad, you brace yourself and accept the inevitabile. That's what happened right then while I was enjoying Rose's warm mouth on my own.

The air-splitting whistle made me separate instantly from her. I swiveled in the saddle to the direction of the sound. How foolishly stupid I'd been. I should have anticipated that some of the Amish kids might cut through the fields to go over to the ball game. And with no time to gallop away or hide in the trees, I saw coming from the forest edge the ghostly face of Levi Zook. A few strides back was his sidekick, Nathaniel Yoder.

By the unrestrained glee shining off Levi, I knew he'd seen me kissing Rose. I released my hold on Lady's rein and consciously moved Rumor in front of Rose, waiting. She was being uncharacteristically quiet behind me, but strangely I could sense her presence, even though she was making no sound at all. It was as if our bodies were connected by an invisible string—a very strong one. In the distance, a threatening rumble of thunder rolled toward us, and an oppressive stillness settled in the cornfield when the wind suddenly died down.

"So what have we got here, Nathaniel—did I just see what I thought I saw? Was Noah Miller, the most popular bachelor in the community, son of the minister Amos Miller, making out with an *English* girl—in a field?" He exaggerated every word, his high-pitched voice thick with malice. I already knew that I wouldn't be able to negotiate with him, but now I realized with sudden clarity that he'd attempt to destroy me with what he'd stumbled upon. A sense of dread washed over me.

"This is none of your concern, Levi," I warned him.

Levi's pale face tilted and he shifted his attention to Rose, stretching to look past me at her with his snake eyes. Those eyes were hungry and he openly appraised her, with a nasty smile forming on his thin lips.

The rage that had been building in me spilled over. "Don't look at her," I demanded, repositioning Rumor again to hide Rose from his evil leer.

He laughed. The sound of it was unnatural in this quiet place that had become a haven for Rose and me.

After glancing over at Nathaniel, who was also openly smirking, Levi fixed his eyes on me and mocked, "Poor Noah, you're going to get into so much trouble for this little incident." He paused with a dramatic sigh, then went on, "But... you know, Nathaniel and I *might* be willing to forget what we saw...if you'll share your little girl with us."

Every fiber within my body screamed out for me to jump from Rumor's back and sprint over to him, drag him off his horse and hurt him with my bare hands. And I calculated the distance to him, on the verge of doing it. But I knew that was what he wanted, an evil deed he could report to the church about Noah Miller. That was, if he survived my attack. And even though Levi was probably sick enough to actually mean what he said, I needed to control myself or I'd make it worse for me and Rose.

"You can go to hell, Levi Zook. And you, too, Nathaniel Yoder," I said in a barely controlled voice.

Watching Levi's expression change from wicked enjoyment to disappointment made me think that maybe he really believed I would offer Rose over to him to avoid getting into trouble. The thought sickened me, and I backed Rumor up right into Lady to be even closer to Rose. To keep her safe from Levi's and Nathaniel's disgusting desire for her.

Upon doing that, Rose reached out and touched my arm. The feel of her hand sent a powerful kick to my senses, suddenly filling the darkening, stormy sky with a warm light.

When Levi saw Rose touch me, his eyes narrowed with unhidden jealousy. He kicked his chestnut horse, galloping right at us, only to swerve before full impact. His horse bumped hard into Rumor's side, catching my leg, too, before he passed by us down the path toward the road. "You're going to regret the day you ever saw that girl, Noah!" he shouted back to me over his shoulder. Nathaniel went with him and within seconds they were out of sight, the sound of their pounding hooves fading away.

At that instant a dazzling claw of lightning streaked across the sky. The trees in the woods seemed to leap forward in the brilliance of the flash. Immediately after the light blinked out came the tearing noise of thunder right above us.

I turned to Rose, seeing her face ashen-white, masked with shocked worry. Every muscle in Lady's body was as taut as a bowstring and she pranced in place, but Rose deftly held her in check. Grabbing Lady's reins, I pulled Rose into my arms. Her breathing was hectic and her heart was pumping so hard I could feel it through her chest. Gently I rubbed her back and hair, holding my face against hers.

Her voice came out in a hoarse whisper. "What will happen now, Noah?"

She sounded terrified, and I kissed the side of her mouth before drawing a long breath and answering honestly, "I don't know, Rose. But at least we'll get it all out in the open."

Her face twisted with emotion when she said, "But I don't want you to get sent far away. I wouldn't survive if I lost you." Her lips quivered. "I can't go through it again, Noah. I can't lose you, too."

Her wet eyes were glinting and I knew she was talking about her mother. I was ready at that moment to run away with her, take her anywhere that we could be together without the prying eyes and rules that were working so hard to keep us apart. But I still held out hope that I could do it the right way and keep my oath to the church. If I left with Rose now, the church would forever shun me, and the English world was foreign and harsh. I'd heard the stories and seen with my own eyes how most of them lived. Besides Mr. Denton, the other drivers talked of getting drunk on the weekends and playing around with many women. The men divorced easily, forgetting their vows to their wives and the responsibility of their children to seek freedom and dishonorable experiences. Even Dr. Cameron had taken up with another woman without the bond of marriage. And then there was the fact that I didn't even have a high-school education. How would I support Rose and our children in her world?

Having her close to my chest evoked the determination

in me to fight for her within the church. It could still work out for us. I couldn't give up on it now, without even trying. Surely Father and Mother would understand if they knew how much I loved Rose. How we were perfect for each other.

I moved my hands to her face, wiping away the tears spilling down her cheeks with my thumbs. I leaned in close enough to feel her warm breaths.

"It's going to be okay, Rose. Really, I'll take care of everything. We may have to lay low for a while, but we'll be together in the end. No matter what happens, trust me, I'll make it work." She sniffed and wiped her face on my shirt, giving me a reason to smile even as the insanity was crashing down upon us.

Then the rain came. It started with a few large splatters attacking us from the sky, as if the trouble we were dealing with on the ground wasn't enough. Within a few breaths, it was a waterfall, causing the world to become fuzzy and indistinct.

Trying to blink the rain out of my eyes, I wondered what God was trying to tell me at that moment. Was the angry deluge because I had fallen in love with an English girl…or possibly was it that I was about to be separated from her?

Letting go of her hand, I urged, "Come on, we need to get out of here before we get struck by lightning!"

She nodded and picked up her reins. Together we took off, cantering over the squishy, water-drenched earth side by side. The rain gave us no mercy and continued to pelt down on us, stinging my face and hands. I glanced anxiously at Rose, who had somehow managed to get her hood up and tight around her head. A few wisps of her hair had escaped and were plastered against her jacket, but otherwise she seemed to be surviving the weather conditions. Her resiliency amazed me.

She looked all dainty and small on the outside, but inside she was tough as nails.

The water was soaking into the farm soil around us, sending an earthy smell of mud and worms into the air. It was a familiar scent and it calmed my nerves, giving me the chance to breathe and think. What would Levi do? Was he going to put the information through the rumor mill? That would give me a little more time, and the chance to talk to Father and Mother about Rose before they heard about her from someone else. That would be the best scenario, and I silently prayed for Levi to follow that course.

But when Father came into view, riding his tall black buggy horse, cantering up the lane toward us, my heart sunk. Levi had gone straight to Father and told him. That would be the only reason in the world that he'd be riding out in the field in the middle of a rainstorm at such a fast clip.

I reached out and took Rose's hand. I decided I wouldn't let go until I absolutely had to. Meeting her eyes, I felt strong and right about my love for her. She saw him, too, and although her eyes looked fearful, she smiled encouragingly at me. I slowed Rumor to a walk when we were almost to Father. Rose followed my lead with Lady. She tried to wiggle her hand free, but I clenched hard, not letting her go.

The fury on Father's face was plain for all the world to see. He didn't bother to hide it from Rose as he narrowed his eyes, staring at our locked hands. He looked at Rose's face briefly; then he settled his gaze on me. We were stopped now and Father's horse, Simeon, was close enough to sniff noses with Rumor.

"Let go of her hand, Noah." I had never heard his voice that fierce before, filled with a deep rage, so contained it splintered the wet air, sending a trickling of fear coursing through me.

I wouldn't release Rose, though, fearing deep within me that if I did, I'd never be able to touch her again.

I met his fiery gaze, defiant and unblinking. "Father, I love Rose and we want to be together. That's why I wouldn't pick one of the other girls, because I had already lost my heart to this girl."

The rain was coming down harder, blurring my vision and changing the world into a hazy picture of brilliant, glistening greens. In the back of my mind I worried about Rose being out in it, but I couldn't hold that thought for too long as I watched what I'd said sink into my father's mind. I thought I saw a flicker of emotion play on his features. Almost a sad understanding as his eyes passed between Rose and me again. The look was there only for a second, and then it disappeared, to be replaced with indignation, but more subdued, as Father spoke again. "Son, release her hand so that she can go home and get out of the rain."

He was a sly one, my father. He knew instinctively I didn't want the girl I loved out here in the cold, driving rain and wind.

I gazed at Rose reassuringly and released her hand. I couldn't tell if she was crying or if the wetness on her face was only the rainwater flooding her features, but she sat straight in her saddle and smiled sadly at me before squeezing her horse, trotting past my father.

I was glad to see her riding away from this emotionally charged scene to the dry house waiting for her. I didn't take my eyes from her until she slipped through the gap in the fence, disappearing from sight. When that happened, a cold, hard loneliness swept through me.

Father and I sat in our saddles for several minutes in the pouring rain, the dead quiet of the field surrounding us. The cold dampness was seeping into my skin and bones, but I welcomed the discomfort. At least it made me feel alive.

Finally Father spoke, his voice rigid. "Go to the house, Noah."

All too happy to escape his wrathful gaze, I squeezed Rumor into a canter, pulling the reins up to keep his hooves collected over the dangerously sloppy ground. When I rode up the driveway, I had to admit that the fear that had gripped my insides when I saw Father appear on the path was nothing compared to the trepidation I felt now, seeing Mother standing on the front porch, her arms crossed in front of her.

After unsaddling and putting Rumor in a stall, I passed Father in the driveway. All he said was "get dry clothes on" as he stalked by me, not slowing down.

Before I reached the house, Jacob came through the door with Peter, Daniel and Isaac. They all passed me quietly, with the little boys staring at the puddles. Jacob shot me a look of genuine concern, but he didn't say a word as he swept by. Sarah and Rachel were the next to appear, with little Naomi in Sarah's arms. Rachel hurried by without a sideways glance, giving me the silent treatment, but Sarah peeked up with a wary smile and whispered, "Good luck."

I knew that I'd need more than luck to get through what was to come—I needed a miracle.

13

Rose
Dealing with the Inevitable

I COULDN'T KEEP THE TEARS FROM POURING out of my eyes as I dodged the sheets of pounding rain, my feet splashing with each stride I took. Gathering speed, I made a mad dash, reaching the back screen door. I flung it open and bounded into the dry kitchen.

I must have been a scary sight the way Sam and Justin popped their heads up from their usual nightly bowls of cereal when I burst into the room. They stared at me with their faces scrunched up in distaste, watching the water drip off my clothes and pool beneath my feet.

"Hey, I told you it was going to rain." Sam snickered.

I guess it wouldn't have mattered what nonsense spilled from his stupid mouth. It was inevitable that I was going to run from the room, bawling my eyes out. And that's what I did. Taking the stairs two steps at a time, I reached my bedroom seconds before the athlete caught up to me. Slamming the door and locking it, I started stripping my wet clothes off, throwing them on the floor.

"What's going on, Rose? Did he hurt you or something?" Sam yelled, clearly upset, while he banged on the door with major force.

"Go away!" I screamed back, not wanting to deal with his I-told-you-so's.

He didn't let up, though. His banging intensified, forcing me to slip on the first jeans and T-shirt that I could get my hands on. Grabbing the door handle, I quickly unlocked it, turning the knob. King Kong came stumbling into the room when the door swung open. Justin walked in with more dignity, heading straight for my mattress and making himself comfortable.

"What happened?" Sam blurted out, resting his hands stiffly on his hips.

"We were caught, Sam!" I said, flinging myself onto the mattress, almost taking Justin out when I landed with a thud next to him.

Sam's voice came out in a choked whisper. "What were you doing?"

I could only shake my head with amazement at how stupid he was. The only good thing to come from his lack of brain cells was that it almost caused me to laugh, and with the horrible drilling pain my heart was experiencing, that would have been a nice release.

"You dope! We were just kissing. A couple of Amish boys saw me and Noah together in a field, and they immediately galloped off to report it to Mr. Miller," I cried out, falling back onto the pillows for dramatic effect.

Sitting on the bottom of the mattress facing me, Sam breathed deep and said, "That was pretty shitty of them."

"Oh, you have no idea. The one kid looks like a member of the Children of the Corn. He's seriously messed up. I saw him at the schoolhouse on Saturday. He gave me the creeps when he stared at me. I think he has some kind of personal vendetta against Noah. Or at least that's what it seemed like,"

I rambled on, glad to have someone to vent to, even if it was just my two imbecile brothers.

"You should have pointed the jerk out to me. I would have taken care of him for you," Sam said confidently.

"Oh, yeah, that's just what I needed, my brother beating up an Amish kid in front of everyone." I sighed irritably.

Sam shrugged. "What did Mr. Miller do when he heard that his perfect son was sneaking around with a dreaded *English* girl?"

I narrowed my eyes at him, feeling the anger swelling inside me. "It isn't a joke, Sam. Mr. Miller was really pissed off. You should have seen the way he looked at me. Like...like... I was evil." Feeling the moistness at the corners of my eyes, I sniffed it back in, burying my face in the nearest pillow.

Silence filled the room for a few minutes, except for the random sniff or groan coming from me. Even Sam, who always had something to say, was speechless. Justin tried to comfort me by awkwardly patting my back as if I was a dog, which made me suddenly think about the puppy.

"Where's Hope?" I said, panicked.

"She's asleep on the couch," Justin mumbled.

"You guys are spoiling her rotten," I accused, leaning back again.

"So, I guess the little romance is over now—*right?*" Sam asked carefully, searching my eyes for a runaway plan.

"Sam, I know this will be hard for you to believe since all you do is go around picking up girls and using them for their bodies, then throwing them aside when you're bored with them, but what's between Noah and me is real. We love each other, and his family isn't going to keep us apart." I said it with utter confidence that I wasn't entirely feeling deep down.

"Oh, come on, Rose, you're only sixteen. What would you

know about love? Noah has to do what his parents want. He doesn't have a choice in the matter. Even if he really did love you the way you think he does, there's nothing either one of you can do about it for a few years. By then, you'll both have moved on to other people, and that'll be that."

The know-it-all way he said it made me want to vomit, and I bolted into a sitting position, shrieking, "You don't know anything, Sam. There are states where I'm perfectly legal to get married. Maybe Noah and I will head down to one of 'em and do just that."

His eyes widened in surprise at my threat, and he shot back at me, "I'll tell Dad before I let you do that, Rose."

"You wouldn't!" I growled, so angry I could barely see him.

Rising up, he shook his head lightly. In a softer voice, he said, "Rose, this is your first breakup, and I know it's a lot weirder than most experiences, but you'll get over it." With that he headed for the exit, hesitating a second in the doorway. He turned around, saying, "When you need to talk—and I'm sure you will—I'm available."

Justin, on the other hand, hung out with me for the rest of the night, playing his DS while we listened to music together. I could deal with his video-game stupor much easier than Sam's alertness and penchant for butting into everyone's business.

Hiding my face in the fattest pillow I could find, I silently cried myself to sleep, not really wanting to think about the complexity of the situation. A dull headache had already developed on the left side of my head, and all I wanted to do was escape it. I was so glad when the darkness finally filled my mind.

14

Noah
The Right Path

I DID AS FATHER INSTRUCTED AND WENT immediately to my room, pulling the soaking-wet clothes from my body and flinging them into a heap on the floor. Putting on the first dry clothes I reached, I paused to look out the window. I watched Jacob's buggy moving quickly through the pelting rain down the driveway with all the children packed inside. They had been sent away to a neighbor's house on my account. Father and Mother didn't want the others to hear all the sordid details about my love affair with an English girl.

Running my hand through my wet hair, I left the room, eager to get the fight over with. As bad as it was going to be, it was a relief to finally have it all out in the open. When I entered the kitchen, I was greeted by the hostile eyes of both Mother and Father. Trying my best to ignore their looks, I walked across the room, sitting on the first chair I reached.

"How long have you been secretly seeing the English girl, Noah?" In the stillness of the kitchen, with the faint scents of dinner still lingering in the room, Father's voice was an unwanted guest. It was loud and menacing, and finding the bravery to look at him, I saw his hands were gripped tightly in a knot, his face skewered in anger.

With my stomach in its own knot, I replied, "Her name is Rose, Father, and I've been in love with her since the first time I met her."

Mother shook her head vigorously, exhaling loudly, her face pained. But she didn't speak, leaving that for Father.

"I think you might be confusing lust with love, son." He said it in a calmer voice, but his features were belying his growing agitation. "The girl is beautiful. I won't argue with that. I can understand the temptation she offers you, but the feelings you think you have only for her you can easily find with another girl."

Shaking my head, I didn't want to listen to his nonsense. "Could you so easily transfer the love you feel for Mother to someone else?" When he only squinted at me soundlessly, I forged on, "Nothing you or Mother say is going to stop me from loving her." In a quieter voice I added, "Someday she'll be my wife."

Mother sucked in a gulp of air loudly, placing her fingers to her neck.

Father barked out a laugh and aimed all his fury at me. "Do you actually believe that is possible? Where will you live? How will you provide for a wife and children without your family and your church?" He caught his breath and threatened, "Because you will lose everything if you go down that road, son."

"I'll still have Rose, and that's all that matters to me."

With an exasperated sigh, Father leaned back in his chair, shaking his head vigorously. After a second, his movements stopped, and with troubled eyes searching my face, he asked, "Have you lain with this girl?"

Mother was holding her breath waiting for my answer. When I said no she visibly relaxed, blowing out a long breath.

"By the grace of God, that's a relief anyway," he said roughly, rubbing the side of his face.

My heart pounded and my stomach tightened as I found my voice of conviction. "I am not planning on leaving the church, Father." Their eyes peered at me, the anger temporarily replaced by cautious curiosity. "I believe Rose will become Amish and join our church."

Father's eyes shot to the sky and he spat, "You are dreaming if you think that girl is going to give up all her material things and her spoiled life to follow our ways. Don't you see what she's done to you? She has corrupted your mind, filling your head with visions of lust and pleasure, blinding you, crippling you from thinking straight."

His voice losing a small amount of its fire, he continued, "Noah, even if she did agree to become one of us, and she joined the church and the two of you were married, after a time, maybe a few months or even a few years, she would become bored and frustrated with our lifestyle. She would leave you. And by that time, you might have children that would suffer for it."

"But, Father, what if she did agree to become Amish, would you consent to our marriage?" I asked desperately, hoping that my voice sounded mature enough that he might actually listen to me.

Father looked toward Mother and with some kind of silent communication that they shared, asked her to leave us alone. She stood swiftly and left the room with only a quick glance at me. Seeing her solemn face and her head nod slightly, I narrowed my eyes, wondering what torment Father had in store for me.

He stared at me for some seconds, his eyes narrowed. When

he finally spoke, his voice sounded resigned, and a little glimmer of hope sprang to life in my gut.

"There is something that I'd like to tell you, son, that I haven't even shared with Jacob." He stopped and breathed, seemingly gathering courage before he spoke again. "There was a short time before I met your mother that I courted another girl."

The news startled me, pushing aside my own problems for the moment. I blurted out, "Who was she?"

Father spread his lips in a playful smile that I rarely saw on his face. "Her name doesn't matter now. She left our community many years ago."

"Why didn't you stay with her?" My head was swimming with images of my father with a woman who was not my mother. Even though he would never lie to me about such a thing, I had a difficult time grasping it in my mind.

Sighing, Father leaned back in the chair and searched out the window toward the pastures with the expression of a man who was far, far away.

"She was very beautiful, Noah. Don't ever tell your mother this, but she was the prettiest girl in the community at the time of my youth. I was fascinated by her even as a young child." He still looked away from me, but even from the side, I could see a smile touch his face. "She was different than the other girls—more rambunctious. She acted like a boy in many ways—able to hit the baseball farther than anyone in the school when we played during recess, running as fast as my brother William in the races and riding the wildest ponies with ease.

"All the boys had crushes on her, but I was the only one that she would favor with a grin or a friendly word now and then. She was mean to the boys and ignored the girls. The teacher was concerned. Her parents and the bishop were constantly meeting to discuss her behavior. And, as she aged, she didn't grow out of her rowdy ways. In truth, the girl was a complete mess, not fitted to the lifestyle of a woman of our Plain ways.

"Still, I couldn't get her out of my mind. She plagued me morning, noon and night with her sparkling eyes and mischievous mind. And, when one afternoon the two of us were unknowingly left alone in her father's mill, I discovered that her curiosity was not limited to the small, dead animals in the roadway that she poked at with sticks."

I was suddenly embarrassed, feeling the heat creep up my neck. I was also becoming annoyed, wondering if Mother knew about this wild girl's relationship with Father.

"Secretly, the two of us carried on, always mindful of being caught, while my feelings for her deepened. But a nagging doubt began to grow within me." Father finally looked me in the eye after a pause. "Why was I being so secretive about my involvement with the girl? We were both of an age that courting would be acceptable in our community and our families got on well—so why was I hesitating?"

I remained silent, unsure of what to say to him. After all, Father was the one who solved all the problems that arose in the family. He knew the answers to most of the questions that came up in day-to-day life, and the thought that he was at one time bewildered and unsure of himself was difficult to grasp.

"And then one day I understood my hesitancy to commit to the girl. It was after a cousin's wedding supper, and the sky had darkened enough to hide the young people from the adults' eyes, when I spotted her. She was behind a shed with several of the other young'uns drinking whiskey from a bottle. The fact that I wasn't surprised to find her doing such a thing made up my mind about her.

"You see, Noah, that particular girl was beautiful and spunky and made my heart skip a beat when she flashed a smile my way, but I knew deep within me that she wouldn't make a good wife for me or mother for my children. She was like a deer—I could capture her and pen her up, but she'd never settle for her confinement. She would leap the fence, possibly hurting herself in the process, to be free. I knew that I would find only heartache with her."

I paused, feeling that the air had become thick with the sadness of Father's memories before I spoke up. "What became of her, Father?"

"She married a man from a neighboring community a year later and gave birth to a daughter nine months following. After a couple of years of being a wife and a mother, she up and left in the middle of a stormy spring night. No one has seen her since."

My mouth almost hit the floor. Things like that just didn't happen within my community. And my own father having been close to the scandal was even more incredible.

"She abandoned her own child?"

Father nodded his head but remained silent.

Speaking out loud, but more to myself than to him, I said, "I guess it was smart that you broke it off with such a girl after all."

Father's eyes closed for a second, almost as if he wanted to stick up for the girl he would not even say the name of, before his face relaxed again. "Yes, you have the right of it. I came near to making the biggest mistake of my life, son. And, even though my heart felt like it was ripped in two, I did find love again with your mother—a more pure, true kind of love. I can't imagine a life without my dear Rebecca now."

"Does Mother know of all this?" I asked, spreading my arms wide for emphasis.

"I spoke to her of it before we wed. There have never been lies or deceit between us." He turned back to me and his face went stern again, when he added, "But she doesn't need to hear speak of the subject again. It would only upset her."

The rain and late hour had diminished the air to a dark gray beyond the window. Father rose and lighted the gas lamps above the table and then seated himself in the same chair. We sat silently, him staring out into the darkness and me looking at the floor but not really seeing it.

My mind was trying to figure how Father's story affected my own situation with Rose. Was he trying to persuade me to leave Rose behind because there was a more wonderful girl around the corner? Rose was nothing like the girl from Father's younger days—and he had no right to make such a comparison. I knew with sureness in my soul that she would never leave her child...or husband. Before I had the opportunity to begin the argument again, Father spoke, and what he said shocked me.

"If Rose were willing to become Amish and follow all our rules and traditions—then I would support a union between the two of you." His words rippled through my mind, sending shivers of excitement through me, but my happiness only lasted a few seconds.

He went on to say, "But, son, I don't know how it would be possible. Her father would have to give her up to be raised by an Amish family, which I doubt he would even consider."

He went on to say in a lighter, almost sympathetic voice, "As difficult as it may be for you to believe, I know and understand all the feelings your body is experiencing around this girl. Because of those feelings, you aren't thinking straight.

What you are hoping will happen with this girl is impossible." His voice picked up in volume and intensity, and it gave no indication that he would waver when he added, "And I'm not going to allow you to ruin your life, because you don't have the same sense to know what's in your best interest as I did."

I stared ahead, not seeing him anymore or caring what came from his mouth. I knew my heart, and he wasn't going to change it with his ranting.

Seeing that I was ignoring him, he fumed again and in a steely voice, he said, "There will be no more discussion on this matter. You will go to live with your grandparents in Pennsylvania in a week's time. You will start over there, and I'm sure that sooner than later your randy thoughts will be directed at a pretty Amish girl, the way they should be. Over the next week you will meet with the bishop and confess your sins before the church. You will ask forgiveness for your disobedience, not only from the church, but also from our heavenly Father. You will not leave this house during that time for any reason. You will stay in your room and take all meals there also. I will not have your siblings learning any details of your relationship with the English girl."

He drew in a long breath, preparing for further attack. I closed my eyes, waiting for the final onslaught.

"Son, you should take the time you have alone this week to think long and hard about your future. Ella Weaver may still be willing to take you, even after this embarrassment. She'd make a fine wife for you—and my own experience that I shared with you should open your eyes to that truth."

He waited for me to say something. Maybe he wanted me to throw myself onto the floor and beg for forgiveness or admit that I was wrong about Rose—and that he knew her better than I did. But those things weren't going to happen.

I avoided his penetrating glare, summoning up a picture of Rose in my head, and straightening my back, I asked, "May I be excused?"

Flicking his hand with annoyance, he said, "You may go to your room."

Once I was lying on my bed, I realized how exhausted I was from all the emotions of the day. I closed my tired eyes. Even in the state I was in, my mind was still working over-time. I had to think about how I could get away with Rose before I was forced to go to Pennsylvania. How would I do it? I had to find a way, but I only came up with more questions and no answers. When the oblivion began to push at me, I welcomed it, gladly slipping into unconsciousness.

15

Rose
Decisions

THE REST OF THE WEEK I WOKE UP AS LATE AS possible, hoping to eat up as much of the day in an unconscious state as I could. The conscious moments were the hardest to bear, and the waiting was driving me crazy. I had no idea what was going on at Noah's house. I couldn't call him on the phone, and he obviously wasn't getting any opportunities to call me either. Was he even still there? Maybe he'd already been boxed up and sent to some far-off community, hidden so well that even if I hired a private investigator I wouldn't be able to track him down.

My mind was going to explode with all the fretting, worrying and questioning I was subjecting myself to. I was about as active as a slug, almost never leaving my room. The only times I ventured out were to give Lady a couple of scoops of grain once a day and take little Hope out to pee every few hours. I kept myself to only muted and minimal conversation with the other inhabitants of the house, which seemed to distress them all immensely.

Sam would pound on my door each day, reciting a few more reasons why my life was so much better off without Noah in it. When I did dare to leave the self-inflicted confinement of my room, Justin would follow me around like a baby chick on its mother until I scared him off with a screaming tirade.

Even Dad, who up until then had been trying to avoid me like the plague, probably feeling the same weirdness that I did about his newly found sexual freedom, came into my room on Friday evening. After an uncomfortable amount of small talk, he had the nerve to offer his girlfriend as a possible psychologist for my boyfriend problems. He probably thought I was verging on insanity when I could only respond with hilarious laughter, pushing him out the door and slamming it behind him.

It was now late Saturday afternoon, and I'd just gotten back from a forced excursion into town that Sam and Justin had quite literally dragged me to. With Sam grabbing me under the arms and Justin holding my feet, they actually carried me down the stairs to the truck and threw me in as if I was a dead body that they were going to bury out in a field somewhere.

I had to give them an A for effort, though. Getting out of the house had made me feel a little bit better. That was until I ran into Maretta at Walmart. I'd been in the shampoo aisle when I looked up and almost bumped smack into her. She mumbled something unintelligible, smiled weakly and hurried away with her sister.

Well, one thing to come out of that painful experience was that I knew the entire Amish community was aware of my relationship with Noah. When I chewed Sam out in the truck for it later, he sheepishly apologized, admitting that we might just have to move to another town to get away from the constant reminders.

Of course, Sam's other solution was that I should start hanging out with his new friends, telling me that they were all pretty cool and I'd like them. I certainly wasn't interested in any social interactions, and ignored him completely whenever he brought the subject up.

Sam also did me the favor of calling Amanda and Britney to notify them of my broken heart. So on top of everything, I had been dealing with their phone calls every hour on the hour. I really didn't want to talk about the situation to anyone. Not until I knew for sure what the heck was going on.

I hated it, the waiting, mixed with fear and tedium that I had to deal with every second of the day. And as I walked to the old barn that nature was trying desperately to reclaim with vines, weeds and bushes, I decided that I truly couldn't take much more. Distractedly shoving the scoop into the feed barrel two times, I filled Lady's bucket. Turning, I started to take it out to her, when a flash of something white caught my attention.

My heart skipped as I moved in slow motion toward the object. It was neatly sitting on the blanket that covered my saddle. My breathing sped up to one hundred miles an hour when I was close enough to see that it was a piece of paper, folded in half, with my name written in bold black letters along the top side. I recognized the handwriting, and I had to stop, close my eyes and take a deep breath. When I opened them, the letter was still there. I breathed out a sigh of relief that I hadn't been dreaming.

Still, I was afraid to see what was written inside. I stood there staring at the note for a very long time until Lady's whinny brought me back to the reality of the barn. Quickly, I ran the bucket out to her and then returned to the letter.

My dearest Rose,
I've missed you so much. We need to talk. Please meet

*me in your barn loft at 2 a.m. tomorrow morning. I'll
be waiting.
Noah*

I read the note over three times before I finally stuffed it
into my jeans pocket. My heart thumped excitedly as if awak-
ened from a deep sleep. Suddenly the whole world seemed
clearer, sharper to my eyes. My other senses were heightened,
too. The lawn that Justin had mowed earlier came to my nostrils fresh and leafy smelling. Even my skin was hypersensi-
tive, feeling the fibers of every piece of clothing I wore, from
my bra to my ankle socks.

I had definitely just woken from a bad dream, and with renewed energy I sprinted to the house and up to my room. The
hardest part would be acting casual the rest of the night. The
last thing I needed was to arouse Sam's suspicions. Justin would
be in his usual video-game haze, so I didn't need to worry
about him. Dad had the night shift at the hospital—no worries there. And stupid Sam was going on a date tonight with
his new girlfriend, which could be a good thing if he arrived
home after I met with Noah, or go bad if he came home early.

It was chilly enough for pj's, and I changed into my Eeyore
ones early. I fixed sandwiches for Justin and me, and we hung
out in the TV room, skipping through a hundred channels for
several hours without finding anything worth watching, until
midnight. I kept peeking out the window, looking for Sam's
big green truck to pull in, but he didn't show up. Going over it
in my head more times than was worth mentioning, I decided
that even if he came home around two o'clock, he would just
go straight to his room and collapse on his bed. He would have
no reason to check on me, but just to be on the safe side, I'd
fix the bed up like a body was in it—just like in the movies.

Shaking Justin, who had fallen asleep on the couch beside me, I ushered his sleepwalking body up the stairs into his bedroom, tucking him in and shutting the door quietly. One bozo brother down, only one to go, I thought as I skipped softly to my room and changed into jeans and a black stretch shirt. I figured I should blend in with the darkness. I even stepped into my black tennis shoes instead of my white ones, taking the camouflage thing to the next level.

Time passed slowly, but there was no fear of me falling asleep. I was so revved up most people would have bet that I was on some kind of drug. Nope, they would have been mistaken. The only chemicals coursing through my body were my own insane hormones. I was both jumping with excitement to see Noah again and nervous to my bones. What if he had bad news for me? Maybe he'd decided to break up with me to court Ella after all? That was hard for even my suffering, insecure brain to believe. Noah really did love me; I was sure of that. And I loved him. But maybe all that love still wasn't enough.

More minutes passed with me struggling on my bed imagining every possible scenario that could happen until it was almost two o'clock. Silently, I crept from my room and down the squeaky stairs as stealthily as I could. Sam still wasn't home, and unfortunately, I could definitely guess what he was doing to keep him out so late. He was such a cad. No wonder he figured I'd be doing the wild thing with Noah, because that's all he ever thought about. I had to admit, him not being asleep in his bed worried the crap out of me. And as I ran lightly across the dew-covered grass toward the barn, I looked over my shoulder several times to see if he'd pulled up in the driveway. At this point, the only thing I could do was pray that he would be physically exhausted from whatever exercise he had gotten with his girlfriend and go right to his room, leaving me the heck alone.

The barn was pitch-black inside. Even if I'd wanted to turn on a light, the electricity had been disconnected for decades. Luckily, the moon was almost full. Its pale light sprinkled through the gaps in the wood siding enough to light the way up the narrow steps to the loft.

Taking a deep breath and swallowing a gulp of air, I climbed the last step into the loft. My eyes took a few blinks to adjust to the darkness. For a fraction of a second I felt disappointment thinking Noah wasn't there, until I heard rustling near the hay bales. Then I only had another instant to prepare for the force of Noah's body slamming into me, pulling me into a tight embrace.

The squeeze of his arms around my back and shoulders, and his face bent down to the side of mine, was the most excruciatingly exquisite feeling I had ever experienced. Nothing in the world mattered as long as he held me like that. I could handle any calamity that was thrown my way with his arms protecting me.

It didn't take long for his mouth to smash into mine. His aggressiveness was a little bit intimidating, but I wanted him just as much as he wanted me. I managed to keep up with his tongue, kissing him back as passionately as I could. His mouth left mine briefly to trail soft kisses over my cheeks, nose and eyes, until he was on my mouth again. Other than the kissing noises, the first sound I made was a little yip when he picked me up, startling me for a second. He carried me into the blackness where the hay was stacked and easily hoisted me up onto the hay. He sat down, still holding me with his back resting against a bale on the top row.

At that point, he simply hugged me while I nestled on his

lap against his chest, his mouth breathing warm air into my hair. It seemed as if he was trying to bring himself under control. I could feel his heart hammering wildly under his shirt, and I pressed my head against his muscled chest, listening to the thumps in wonder. The surge of pleasure I was experiencing was so complete that every portion of my body was being bombarded with sensations, making it almost impossible to think, let alone talk.

I didn't really want to talk about our problems. I just wanted to be happily cuddled up in the hay with him, all alone, while he explored my arms and legs with his hands with such deliberation, almost as if he was imprinting on his memory what I felt like. But then his deep voice broke into the night air, reminding me how much I loved the sound of it, and I was abruptly happy he'd spoken.

"Rose, how've you been, sweetheart?" His voice shook slightly, and I realized how much he'd missed me. He pulled back a little. I could imagine his worried look, but it was too dark to see his face clearly.

"I'm okay...but what about you, what happened with your parents?" I whispered.

I could feel him shake his head slightly and exhale very close to my face. His hot breath sent a tingle through my lips, causing me to sit up straighter and brush my own lips over his softly. I could feel his mouth smiling. I leaned back against his shoulder, waiting for whatever news he had to tell me. Good or bad, I could handle it now.

"Ah...they were pretty upset at first," he said apprehensively.

"What did they say?"

"Well, the thing they were most worried about was whether we were already...making love." He said it seriously, with no hint of humor.

I couldn't help stiffening when he said it. After a second, I said a bit cheerfully, "At least you were able to tell them the truth about that one, right?"

"Yeah, they were pretty relieved. Although they probably would have had fits if they knew all the other stuff we've been doing."

"Really, Noah, I think we've behaved ourselves very admirably. Especially you. I mean, I've practically attacked you, and you managed to keep your pants on."

He laughed hard, hugging me closer still.

"Let's not be talking about that right now. We have more important things to discuss." His voice sounded anxious.

"Like what?" I asked, dreading his answer.

After a long, unhappy sigh, he said, "I've basically been locked in my room like a prisoner since I last saw you. They only let me out to use the bathroom. Yesterday, I had the pleasure of getting reamed out by the bishop and the other ministers for several hours. In the morning, I get to look forward to confessing my sins to the entire congregation."

"Oh, Noah, I'm so sorry. But how'd you get away to leave the note for me—and come tonight?"

"I've been climbing out my window. It's a pretty good drop from the second floor, too, but I've been managing to land without breaking anything so far."

"How do you get back in?" I asked, worried.

"My folks don't lock the basement door and the lock to my room is on the outside, so I just sneaked in last night. They never even knew that I was gone."

"Who puts a lock on the outside of a kid's door?" I questioned, silently fuming.

"My parents."

"Wow, and I thought I had it bad."

"What do you mean?" His potent curiosity came through in his voice.

"When I lock myself in my room to be alone, Sam tries to tear the door down like a raving lunatic."

"Really?" He sounded bothered now.

"Yeah, but luckily my door has been around for a couple hundred years and it's up to the challenge." I giggled.

Quiet had descended in the loft again. He brought his hand to my chest, placing it over my heart, feeling the wild beating. He was so still, I wondered if he was falling asleep.

"I missed you so much. The only thing that's kept me going this week was imagining what it would be like to hold you in my arms again."

"I know. Me, too. I was so afraid that I'd never see you again—that you'd be sent away," I whispered.

With an agonizingly strained voice, he said softly, "But I am going to be sent away. This Friday our driver is hauling me to my grandparents' house in Pennsylvania. I'm to stay there until I settle down and find a wife."

He sounded miserable. I didn't know what to say. I was too young to have any ideas, other than running off to a Southern state to get hitched in some roadside wedding chapel.

Taking his big, callused hands between my own, I said in a fervent whisper, "Noah, we could run away together. I can do some research online about it, but I think that some of the Southern states allow kids to get married when they're sixteen."

"You would do that—run away with me and leave your family…and your life?"

"My life isn't much without you in it. I couldn't deal with you being gone, Noah. I'd have a nervous breakdown or something."

He wrapped his arms securely around me and began kissing my neck. The electric current running through my veins consumed me as his mouth moved on the same small place for a long time. Fleetingly, part of my brain registered that he might be leaving a mark on the spot. Then another part of my brain warned me what I'd have to listen to from Sam if I did wake up with a hickey in the morning. Bringing my hand up, I carefully disengaged his lips from my skin and brought his mouth to my mouth—a perfectly safe place.

He was distracted now and broke the kiss off. Breathing hard, he said, "We can't run off like a couple of stupid English kids. We have to be smart about this. There is an option, though."

The "stupid English kids" statement did not go over well with me. I was experiencing slight irritation, along with all the crazy, out-of-control emotional excitement my body was dealing with.

Curiosity won over irritation, so I inquired, "What option?"

With sudden eagerness, he said, "Father told me he would accept a marriage union between us if..." He stumbled and paused for a second before rushing the words out. "If you become Amish."

The words slammed into me. My brain seemed to cloud over. I wasn't sure what I thought or what I should say. I could feel Noah shifting uneasily beneath me, while his fingers rubbed the skin on my arm nervously, waiting for my answer. I had actually imagined myself dressed like the Amish girls, going to bed with him each night and even carrying his baby around. But now, with the possibility of that reality looming on the horizon—for real—I was suddenly paralyzed with fear.

He must not have been able to wait any longer. "Rose...

please…tell me what you're thinking. Will you do it? Will you become Amish so that we can be together?" Pausing just a second, he went on with enthusiasm, "Just think of it. Every night I could hold you in my arms just like this, and no one would be able to keep us apart."

Even in the thick darkness, I could picture his tortured face as he pleaded with me. But still I was torn.

"Why don't you become English, Noah? Wouldn't that work, too?" I countered.

His voice came out frosty, and I was sure he was grimacing. "No, that wouldn't work for us. I wouldn't have the ability to support you and our family in your world."

"Couldn't you go back to school? You're supersmart—we could even go together. Think about how cool that would be," I suggested.

Dashing my little illusion, he said, "I'm not going to an English school now. I'm too old for that, and besides, I don't need to. My family's business makes very good money and we could live comfortably. What's the problem, Rose? Is it that you don't want to miss out on driving a car or going to your rock concerts? Or maybe you can't stand the thought of never being able to dance for all the English men again."

That did it. The fury billowed up in me, and I couldn't stop my hand from pulling free of his grasp. I smacked him hard on the side of his face. The sound seemed to echo across the loft. I immediately wished I could take it back when I realized that he might have a bigger mark on his face than I'd have on my neck. How would he explain *that* to his father?

Right when I anxiously squeaked, "I'm so sorry, Noah, I didn't—" He grasped the hand that had been the weapon and pinned it down to the hay.

Through gritted teeth, he said, "Maybe what I said struck too close to home for you—is that it?"

Wincing at his words, I tried to move. Failing, I said helplessly, "Why are you being so mean to me, Noah? You're asking me to give up my education, my family and my entire way of life. I'm only sixteen, for goodness' sake. How could I decide that in just the blink of an eye?"

He continued to hold my hand and body uncomfortably tight. Even without seeing his face I could sense that a battle was raging inside him. Then without warning, he released his grip and brought his hands to my face with a softness that erased the memory of the discomfort. He stroked away the tears that had begun trickling down my cheeks, then brought his mouth along each line of wetness and kissed them, tasting the salty water with his tongue.

Mumbling, his face only inches from mine, his voice sounded pained when he said, "I'm sorry, Rose. I deserved your slap—I really did. It's just that I love you so much, and I can't begin to think of my world without you in it. I was so frightened when you didn't immediately agree to become Amish. I just felt that if you really loved me, you'd give up your English life so we could be together."

"I do love you. With all my heart I love you." And I leaned into him, letting my mouth find his. I kissed him deeply, trying to prove that my words were true. My head was spinning out of control, and I was suddenly filled with indecision. With a gasp, I separated from him and tried to pull back, but he held me tight. I struggled with him until the words tumbled out of my mouth.

"Please, Noah—stop, I need some time to think this all out."

He released me then and sighed with resignation. "We

don't have much time. Remember, I'll be in Pennsylvania next week."

Lifting my body and gently setting me on the hay, he climbed down the bales, walking away from me into the spot where the moonlight was shimmering through a window opening. I could finally see him, and I saw torture, anger, frustration and sadness all distorting his beautiful face. I couldn't stop myself from jumping off the hay and running to him. I clung to his waist, burning, hot tears running freely over me and his shirt. He tried to act indifferent for a few seconds, but then his arms encircled me. I felt his warm strength holding me again.

Raising my chin with his finger, he told me in a hoarse voice, "You have to make a decision soon. I can't live this way—not knowing what you really want. You have the power to keep us together. It's all up to you now."

With that, he leaned down and kissed me so softly it felt like a butterfly's wings caressing my lips.

The roar of Sam's truck pulling into the driveway made us both freeze in place, waiting. I heard the truck door open and slam shut and then a few seconds later the house door, as well.

"Boy, he's keeping late hours," Noah muttered.

"Yeah, he has a new girlfriend. I guess he was trying her out tonight."

"You shouldn't talk that way. It's not very ladylike," he reprimanded me.

Feeling slightly miffed, I said, "Well, it's true."

"And your father is okay with him staying out all night with his girlfriend?"

"I think Dad is too busy with his own woman to give Sam's curfew much thought these days," I said matter-of-factly.

"See what I mean about your society, Rose—there are no morals about such things. It's disgusting."

Anger boiled up in me again and I shot back, "Well, at least my dad doesn't lock us up in our rooms and threaten to send us away to other states to get us hooked up with people we aren't even interested in." Life had come full circle in the past few days. Now I was sticking up for Dad.

In the pale moonlight, I could see that my words had stung him. His lips were pressed tight, and I thought I could hear his teeth grinding. I didn't want to part like this, with him hating me, but I was afraid to say anything else to him, fearing he'd rebuff me.

I didn't need to worry, though. He bent down, and after lightly grasping my face in his hands, he kissed my forehead. The next second he was gone, heading down the steps, leaving me alone in the loft.

I hurried after him, just catching his arm in the doorway. "When do you want to meet again?"

His eyes searched the darkness and he took a breath. "Tuesday—same time. And remember, Rose, I need an answer."

He turned, and I watched him make his way through the moonlit hay field, moving slowly toward his prison cell. I didn't move a muscle until he was completely out of sight. A shiver fluttered through me and I didn't want to be standing there alone in the dark barnyard. Suddenly, finding my muscles, I whirled and ran to the house. Going through the doorway as quietly as a mouse, I tiptoed across the unlit kitchen—and smacked into a hard, unmovable object. *Crap.*

Rubbing my nose, I waited for the light to go on. When it did, I was momentarily blinded, having to cover my eyes with my hands for a few seconds before I could start to blink. When I could finally see again, I wasn't surprised to find Sam standing there, a glass of milk in hand. At that moment, I remembered the one factor I forgot to consider in all my hard-thought plans—that Sam would have a snack before he went to bed, even if it was three o'clock in the morning.

"Where the hell were you, sissy?" I actually stepped back, surprised by his words.

Defiantly, and hopefully sounding less intimidated than I actually was at the moment, I retaliated, "What about you, Sam? Where've you been all night?"

"That's none of your business," he shouted.

"Well, it's none of your business where I was either." I bravely stared him down.

With an exasperated sigh, he bellowed, "It's not the same with girls. You're the one who could get knocked up or kidnapped or something horrible like that. I, on the other hand, don't have to worry about any of those things."

Okay, my boyfriend was from the 1800s, but my brother lived in the Dark Ages. There was no talking to him about any of this. He was acting more like my father than my brother, and I didn't like his role-playing one bit. I tried to walk by him, when his arm whipped out. Once again, he had my arm in a tight grip.

"Well, what do we have here?" He poked at my neck with his hard finger. I absently jerked my hand up to cover the spot, silently cursing Noah.

"Leave me alone, Sam," I warned him with the most threatening look I could put on my face.

He wasn't impressed, simply snorting and letting my arm go. Before he let me pass, he said in a steely voice, "You had better not be thinking about sneaking out again to meet Noah—I'll be watching you." He brought his two fingers to his eyes and back at me threateningly.

"Why do you even care, Sam?" I demanded.

"Because, Rose, someone has to keep you from destroying your life. It looks like I've inherited the job since Mom's dead and Dad's going through a midlife crisis."

I pushed at him, and when he finally moved aside, I blasted past him and up to my room. Before I shut the door, I heard him call up the stairs, "It's for your own good."

That made me slam the door hard, and I didn't even bother to change before sliding under the covers. What should I tell Noah on Tuesday? I definitely loved him, I knew that for sure, but was that love strong enough to give up everything for? And if I didn't become Amish to be with Noah, could I live without him? Would I ever meet someone else I wanted to be with as much as him? And then, could I handle the thought of him marrying another woman or even worse, making love to her? Because that's what would happen if I told him no; he'd be forced to pick someone else, maybe even Ella, and I'd have to stand by and watch.

I knew Noah had it tough, but not as tough as me. He'd already made up his mind, and he was just waiting for me now. An hour later, when my eyes finally blacked out, I was no closer to making a decision.

16

Noah
Waiting

THE LATE-AFTERNOON SUN MADE THE ROOM stuffy. But the boredom was the worst part of my confinement. At least if I was working with the crew, I'd have distractions to keep my mind occupied, but I didn't even have that option.

Smacking the Bible onto the bed, I leaned back against the pillow, closing my eyes. Instantly, Rose was with me. Her blue eyes sparkled and her mouth turned up playfully. The imagined look affected me as surely as if she really were there, my groin heating at the seductive smile.

Popping my eyes back open, I sighed irritably. Father thought he was reforming me by keeping the door locked and providing only a Bible for my entertainment. But he'd obviously not considered my thoughts and the daydreams that would plague me every minute—making me even more convinced that I was meant to be with Rose and no other. There wasn't an Amish girl here or in any other state that could take her place in my heart. I loved her.

Father wouldn't hear any of it, though. A dark shadow crept across his face each time I mentioned Rose's name. He'd silence me with squinted eyes and his hand raised high to the ceiling. Then he'd begin reading from the Bible again.

Since the telling of the story about his own wayward romance hadn't changed my mind about Rose, Father became angrier with me, spending what seemed like hours each day reciting passages from Scripture. His voice boomed in the small room, the words mixing together to leave my mind foggy and tired. *Exhausted* was a better way to describe my feelings.

I finally realized that the only way I'd get any peace from the man was to act as if his biblical assault was beginning to work. I began dribbling lies from my mouth to convince Father that I was becoming contrite. It came easy enough. Accepting that within days I might move to Pennsylvania to live with my grandparents and begin a new, less rebellious time in my life was hardly a thought in my mind.

Rose loved me as much as I loved her—I was certain of it. Surely, she would pick a life with me.

The rapping on the door startled me. Glancing at the pocket watch on the dresser confused me even more. Father should still be at work.

Hearing the lock jiggling, I remembered that the knock was just a formality and my mood soured instantly.

The door opened wide, revealing that it was Jacob and not Father. Seeing the frown on my big brother's face made me realize that he wasn't a great alternative to our uptight father for a visit.

My words reflected my surliness. "What do you want?"

Jacob let out a sigh of his own irritation and sat down on the end of the bed. He stared at me for some uncomfortable seconds before he finally spoke in a subdued voice.

"Has your confinement not changed your mind at all about the girl, Noah? Are you really willing to lose everything to chase after something that you can never have?"

I stood up in a flash, and looking down at Jacob's wide eyes, I said, "I can have her. It can work for us—I know it can."

Seeing Jacob softly shake his head stirred my anger even more.

"Oh, you could run away with the girl and enjoy your time together for a while maybe, but Father is right. You will not be able to hold on to her. She is from a different world than us, Noah. And you wouldn't be happy in that world."

I sighed, shaking my head. Why were the people in my family so deaf to my own words? I had already explained to Father and Mother that I believed Rose would join our community and live our ways. I was certain that Jacob knew this—but still, he acted as if that wasn't even an option.

Leaning against the windowsill, I watched the black-and-white colt rear up and strike out at one of the older buggy horses in the pasture. The little rascal was attempting to get the aged horse to join in some play. The colt was unsuccessful, though, when the other horse turned its rump to him, laying its ears flat against its head. Not willing to show his defeat, the colt kicked out his hind legs and lurched into a canter across the field, scattering Rumor and Jacob's new team of Belgians.

I smiled. The colt was another reminder of Rose.

When I turned back to Jacob, I felt calmer. I caught the slight rise of Jacob's eyebrow when I spoke with controlled smoothness of my voice. "It really is no concern of yours, brother. You have your own life to live—so leave me to mine."

"You really do love this girl, don't you?" He ran his hands through his hair and slouched down on the bed in defeat. "I thought that you were just being stubborn, not wanting Father telling you what to do…but the look on your face says differently."

His eyes rose and met mine. "What will you do, Noah,

if she is not willing to convert? Will you leave us to be with her?"

The anxious look in Jacob's eyes and the crack in his voice affected me more than I cared to admit, even to myself. The thought of leaving my family, friends and community was not something that I *wanted* to do. But the difference between leaving all of them was that I would survive it.

I couldn't live without Rose in my life.

"I don't think I'll have to make that decision, Jacob."

He stared at me. The sympathy shining from his eyes told me that he didn't agree.

He rose from the bed and in two strides reached me at the window. Jacob slapped his arms around me awkwardly for a few seconds before he broke away and headed for the door.

"I'll be praying that it works out for you. And if you need to talk, just let me know. I'm here for you, Noah—we all are."

He didn't wait for me to answer; his hand was on the door and he was through. A second later the jiggling of the lock could be heard again.

If he was really on my side, he'd have left the door un-locked, my mind said, but my heart knew better. Jacob was just following orders—the way I probably would have done if the tables were turned.

I settled back onto the bed remembering the expression of sympathy on my brother's face. What if he was right about Rose?

No. She would pick me. She had to.

17

Rose
Family Ties

I PEERED INTO THE FAMILY ROOM TO SEE DAD sitting on his comfy chair with a pile of papers strewn on the floor beside him and his laptop open and resting against his knees. The sound was lowered, but the *pop, pops* of gunshots could still be heard coming from the TV, as Justin sat before it, an Xbox control nimbly between his fingers.

They were both so ridiculously oblivious to the drama in my life that if I weren't so torn apart inside, the scene would have made me laugh. If Sam had been occupying the couch, I would have gone back to my room, but since he was off somewhere with his new buddies, I stepped softly through the doorway, seating myself in the chair in the corner.

Several minutes passed. I stared alternately between Dad and Justin, watching how engrossed each was in their technology, completely unaware of my presence. Agitation pricked at me until the sensation began to feel like needles poking sharply into my skin. I cleared my throat loudly—twice— before Dad's head rose.

The lift of his eyebrows and the patient smile that spread on his lips as he shut his laptop and focused on me completely told me that he was all too happy to accept the obvious flapping of my white flag. *Truce*—the word left a sour taste in my mouth, but it was proving difficult to completely ignore the man who'd fathered me. At some point I'd have to talk to him about something, so why not start now? Besides, it wasn't as if I was forgiving him. I was only trying to make my life a little less difficult.

But as I gazed over at Justin, who never did look up from his game, I wondered exactly what I should say to Dad. He was pretty perceptive and I certainly didn't want him knowing about Noah's request for me to become Amish so that we could be together. It would not be good for him to have any idea that I was even contemplating it. Heck, at this point, I didn't know myself what I was going to do.

Dad's voice spread the fog that had been pressing on my mind. "I'd like to take you and Sam to the high school next week to tour the facility and speak with a guidance counselor about your classes for the fall semester." He added with a more careful tone to his voice, "How does that sound, Rosie?"

Facility? I was sure that word didn't apply to the little country school I'd be attending, and I held in a snort. It wouldn't help the conversation if I was rude. And if I decided to become Amish, I might never even see the inside of the high school anyway.

"Hmm?" The rolling trill coming from Dad's throat lifted my eyes to him.

"I, ah…yeah, that's sounds fine," I stammered out.

"Good. I'll make a call this afternoon and get the ball rolling." The excitement in his voice seemed to bounce off the walls and I suddenly felt guilty—something I wasn't used to.

I shook off the coolness that had swept through me and said, "Dad, why do you think the Amish people live the way they do?"

Dad didn't take much time to think about what probably seemed like a random question, replying, "Well, I believe a part of it is that they truly enjoy a simpler lifestyle. Even I can understand the attraction of not having a cell phone constantly vibrating in your pocket, or being bombarded by the distractions of the TV and computers taking away the little time we have to spend with our loved ones."

I nodded, wanting to get past the obvious. "Yeah, but what's the other part?"

Dad sighed and I leaned in closer, knowing that he was about to get to the heart of the matter.

"It seems to me that if you're raised in such a community with a lack of opportunity for education or meeting people from the outside, you'd be hard-pressed to escape the lifestyle once born into it."

"Escape? You make it sound like it's a terrible thing or something," I retorted, bristling at his words and not really understanding why.

"Knowledge is the most powerful and freeing thing in the world, Rosie. Think about it—if everyone were Old Order Amish, then there wouldn't be any doctors, engineers or scientists. On a very basic level, a person's quality of life would diminish greatly."

Before I had the chance to interrupt, he pressed on with more enthusiasm. "For instance, in the nineteenth century it was common to have large families since there was a strong likelihood that some of the children wouldn't grow to adulthood, and there was so much labor involved in just surviving that it made sense to have ten kids. Now, however, the Amish are still having nine, ten, even a dozen babies, but they're all surviving to adulthood."

"Ah, so—why does that matter?"

"Well, that's one of the reasons that their numbers are growing so rapidly, but the point that I'm trying to make is that even though these people might think that they're living their lives away from the technology that they so adamantly spurn, in actuality, they are benefiting from it on a daily basis. They can't truly escape the modern world."

"But why do you think that they are so strict about everything, having all those rules?" I asked, getting closer to all my worries.

"For control—plain and simple. In order to make the society work, the group of people involved must adhere to a set of rules or the community breaks down. The children are conditioned at a very young age to follow the rules and be obedient to the ideas that the community has agreed to. From what I've heard, if a youngster were to question the authority and become rebellious, the elders would remove him or her from the church by the act of shunning."

Just the sound of the word *shunning* caused my body to tense.

"What exactly does that mean, Dad?" I asked, although I already had a strong notion about it.

"I don't know the particulars, but I surmise that when a person is shunned, he's forbidden from involvement with the church members and his family ever again."

I regretted the rise in my voice but couldn't help it when I blurted out, "His family? A person who's shunned can never see his family?"

"Oh, I don't know how far it goes, but I have the understanding that family members have very limited contact with a shunned person." Dad paused, and as if a lightbulb popped on in his head, his eyes narrowed slightly and he stared at me.

"Why all the interest in the Amish punishment system, Rosie?"

I slowed my breathing and took a small breath. Dad would have to wait until I made my decision. He couldn't find out now about my real curiosity in this culture…not yet. I'd be the one shipped off, probably to Cincinnati, if he discovered what was going on between me and Noah.

When I glanced back at him, my heart skipped a beat. He was focused on me like a bird of prey on a mouse scurrying in the grass. Dad knew something was up.

Frantically, I searched my mind for a believable comeback, when amazingly Justin came out of his gamer haze and saved me.

"Do you have any batteries, Rose? My remote's dry," Justin said with just a slight hint of a smile that Dad couldn't see.

I bounded off the chair. "Yeah, sure—they're up in my room."

Justin joined me at the doorway, but before I got a foot across the threshold, Dad said, "I'd like to continue our discussion later, Rosie."

I slowed just enough to look over my shoulder and say, "Oh…all right. Later, okay?"

Dad sighed. He wouldn't push me too hard. Not so soon after the whole "getting caught with a strange woman in the house" thing.

"That'll be fine."

Justin stayed on my heels until we were safely behind my closed bedroom door. When the latch clicked, I leaned against the heavy wood, blowing the air out in relief.

"Brilliant, Justin. That was perfect timing." I swept a few stray hairs away from my eyes and watched my little brother settle onto the end of my bed. When he looked up, I said softly, "Thanks."

He shrugged. "No problem. Maybe you can pay the favor back sometime?"

"Sure, anytime."

"So, why were you asking Dad all those dumb questions about those people anyway?" Justin tilted his head. At that instant, he looked a whole lot like Sam, and I had to hold in an obnoxious reply, telling myself that he wasn't the nosy brother.

"I didn't think you were even paying attention."

"Hah. You all underestimate me. I'm always paying attention." The left side of his mouth raised and his eyes twinkled.

Hmm, Justin may turn out to be more trouble than Sam someday.

"What, is it some gamer thing to be able to split your attention between things?" I said, crossing the room and dropping down onto the bed beside him.

"Yep, but don't change the subject. You know, I'm not a little kid anymore. You can tell me what's going on."

I studied Justin's face, seeing that what he said was true— he wasn't little anymore. And he'd always been more easygoing about things than Sam was. Maybe I could trust him...

"You can't breathe a word of this to anyone—definitely not Sam. Do I have your word?"

He silently crossed his hand over his heart.

"Okay, then." I stared at the door while I said, "Noah wants me to become Amish so that we can be together. He doesn't think he can make it in our world—that his is a better place for us to be a family."

I glanced at him to see his eyes widen for a second, followed by a snorting sound that was very uncharacteristic of my little brother.

When he recovered, he said, "What are you going to do?"

The tears welled in my eyes and I sniffed them back in,

wiping the wetness away with my hand. The fact that Justin hadn't said a word about how crazy the whole thing was or try to tell me what I should do touched my soul. He would never judge me harshly. Justin would love me no matter what decision I made.

And suddenly that fact made my choice even more difficult. Could I really live without my own family?

"I don't know what to do, Justin. I just don't know." I leaned my head against his shoulder, letting the drops of moisture from my eyes wet his shirt. He patted my knee, but otherwise said nothing at all.

He didn't need to speak. Just being there was enough. I was the one whose life would forever be changed by whatever path I took.

And neither one would be easy.

18

Noah
Expectations

I WATCHED THE BAT FLUTTER IN THE MOON-
light on light wings until it escaped out the window near the
stairway. I was alone again, left with my embittered thoughts
in the darkness of the hayloft. It hadn't been gloomy yesterday
when Rose was here with me. The entire loft seemed to suddenly glow when she appeared. Even though I was planning
to be reserved during the encounter, I couldn't help going to
her and wrapping her in my arms.

And as usual, her warm, sweet body was all too receptive.
Surely we were meant to be together. How could we both
feel such intense emotions toward each other if we weren't
destined to be man and wife?

But now my entire life rested on her shoulders, and the
feeling of helplessness overwhelmed me. What would she decide? Would Father and Mother be right after all? Maybe Rose
wouldn't be willing to leave her cushy existence to be with
me. A part of me could hardly blame her for it, if that's what
she decided. Amish women worked much harder than ordinary English women. She would also go from the freedom of
being able to do just about anything she wanted, to a strict set

of rules to follow and live by. Hell, I didn't even know if Rose could follow rules, even if she was willing to become Amish.

She was so irritatingly stubborn and outspoken. Last night was the first time I'd felt real anger toward her. I wanted to grip her shoulders and shake some sense into her, make her understand that the best thing for both of us would be if she became Amish. But as much as I wanted to do it, I couldn't physically force her to submit to me. And if she wasn't willing to become Amish to be with me, then what good would it do for me to run off and be English with her? In the English world, there would be so many forces at work to make our relationship more difficult. Like her going off places whenever she wanted to or dressing in her tight clothing. I couldn't deal with all that. I didn't want to. I knew, deep down, that leaving my community would be a disaster for the two of us.

Another idea had briefly penetrated my brain—getting her with child. My folks and her dad would be forced to allow us to marry. But Rose probably wasn't ready for a baby yet, and besides, it would have to be a decision that we made together.

Thoughts raced through my mind while I sat on the hay bale waiting for her to show up and tell me what my future was going to be. And damn, it was hard just sitting there waiting. I arrived an hour early, too strung up to lie in bed a minute longer. I was extremely paranoid as I made my way out of the house and through the damp field earlier.

I noticed Sam's truck was in the driveway, but Dr. Cameron's car was missing. What if she couldn't get past Sam to come to the barn? I sighed. I'd just have to go in after her. There was no way I was leaving tonight without an answer. Whether it was good or bad, I needed to know.

The shuffling on the stairway warned me she was coming up, and my heart started to race uncontrollably. I held my breath waiting for her to step into the moonlight. When she did, I was struck with how young and fragile she looked, standing there timid and alone, like a deer who'd picked up the scent of the hunter. She was frozen in fear.

Again, unable to resist her, I leaped from the hay and closed the distance swiftly. Within a second, she was in my arms, where she belonged. I held her like that in a tight embrace for some time before her sniffling told me she was crying again.

She did an awful lot of crying, I reckoned. I wondered if that would change once we were married. The direction my mind had immediately gone made me breathe out suddenly. I smiled at my confidence in her decision now that I had a hold of her. Hearing the noise, she leaned back to look up at me.

Her little face was wet with tears and her hair was a mess. Still, she was the most beautiful girl in the world. Without any thought, I dropped my head and kissed her swollen lips. Her mouth parted and a gasp jumped from my throat as she slid her tongue into my mouth forcefully. We had really caught on to the whole kissing thing quickly. I was always stunned at how her mouth moving on mine made me feel.

I was almost lost to the pleasurable sensations once again, until that little voice in my head started pestering me about her decision. Breaking my mouth from hers, I quickly led her back to the hay, and into the darkness, guiding her up to the place we had sat the night before.

"Did you have any problem getting out of your house tonight?" That wasn't the question I needed to ask, but I was warming up to it slowly.

"It was tricky—Sam is asleep on the couch with the TV on. I had to tiptoe by him, but I don't think he'll wake up." Her voice sounded strange, guarded in a way. "What about you?" she asked in the same polite voice.

"Went like clockwork."

I could feel her head bob up and down next to me. She hadn't made any attempt to get in my lap, the way she usually did. I was feeling greater apprehension when I asked gently, "Rose...what have you decided?"

In a surprising huff she blurted out, "It's not fair that I have to make this kind of choice before I've even entered my junior year of high school."

With an angry sigh, I leaned back against the hay. She sounded as if she was throwing a temper tantrum about something she didn't want to do. How was I going to convince her to do what I wanted when she was behaving like a child?

Struggling to stay patient with her, I said firmly, "You're not a little kid. In a lot of cultures, you'd already be married with a baby in your arms by now."

"Maybe in some primitive tribe in the middle of Africa— but not here in twenty-first-century America!" she contradicted icily.

"You forget, I don't exactly live in the twenty-first century." I laughed cynically into the darkness.

"Oh...yeah," she breathed quietly.

She was really getting to me. I asked harshly, "What's your decision?"

"Um—I'm not really sure yet..." Her voice trailed off.

"That's not an answer," I accused. In desperation, I decided to use all the tricks I had to tempt her into saying what I wanted to hear.

Leaning down, I softly caressed her jaw with my lips, wandering my mouth to the beating pulse of her neck and lingering there for a few seconds before working my way back up to her mouth. My actions were affecting me, too. I let the tingling sensations roll over me at the same time I tried to convince Rose that she belonged with me.

She was all too willing, and before I knew it, I had pushed her down on the hay and was pressing my body into her. I wanted to get closer, much closer. The crazy thought I had earlier flashed into my mind. When she groaned into my mouth, I became suddenly aware that if I didn't stop right then, there'd be no turning back. In an abrupt motion, I pulled away from her and sat up. I smiled when I heard her disappointed murmur, and reaching down, I lifted her up and onto my lap, where she belonged.

"That was nice." She sighed peacefully.

I couldn't stay angry with her for long. She always said the cutest things.

"You know, Rose, that's the way it would be for us every night—if we were married." She was my entire life, and I showed no mercy trying to get her to agree.

"I know. And that would be amazing for sure."

"Then what's the problem? Please tell me," I begged.

"Noah, I don't think my dad will go for it. He expects me to go to college. If I told him that I was converting to Amishhood and getting married at sixteen, he'd probably kill me."

She had a point, but I still plowed on. "We would wait until you were seventeen to get married, giving us a reasonably long courtship. You said yourself that he's preoccupied with his own girlfriend."

"Not that preoccupied!" she chirped.

As a last-ditch effort I went down the road I had vowed not to. In a coarse voice I suggested, "Maybe if your father thought you were pregnant he'd agree."

"My dad's a doctor, Noah. I couldn't fool him about something like that." She stopped speaking abruptly, and comprehension must have dawned on her, because she shrieked, "Are you kidding?"

"No—I mean, they'll have to agree to a wedding, and what's the difference if the baby is born after we're married anyway?" It seemed logical enough when I said it like that, but I could tell she wasn't buying it when she jerked off my lap and sat close—not touching me.

I could feel the tension coming from her. I was confused that she was so upset about my suggestion. Her voice darted out of the darkness, "Noah, I am in no way, shape or form ready to have a baby. So don't even go there."

"But you're the one who's been so eager to go all the way," I accused, my own anger building steadily.

"No, I haven't. I just like kissing. There's a big difference between making out and trying to get pregnant to force our parents to let us be together!" she thundered. Briefly, I worried someone might hear her, but I was too caught up in my own emotions to care much.

"I don't see any other way for us to be together. So if you don't want to try that option, and you don't want to become Amish...then I guess it's over between us." I didn't want to say it, definitely not with the venom that I'd used. But damn it, I wanted to wake her up and scare her.

After an unbearably long moment, she felt for my hand and finding it, pulled it up to her lips. She kissed my palm so softly. My skin hardly felt it at all, but the tiny nerves below did, and they went crazy.

"I love you, Noah... I do, really, but...I can't marry you... not right now. I'm too young and...stupid for that kind of commitment. I'm so sorry." She stuttered the words out, sniffing and wiping tears away the entire time.

Shocked, I watched her scramble away over the hay, across

the loft and down the stairs without looking back. My heart was tight and I had a difficult time drawing in a breath of air as the realization dawned on me that I'd lost Rose forever.

19

Rose
Not Alone

I RAN THROUGH THE HOUSE NOT CARING about any noise I was making. When I reached the bed, I couldn't remember the trip across the yard or up the stairs to my room. The only thing in my mind was Noah—and the look he gave me when I told him that I wouldn't join his world. The memory of the devastation on his face was crushing what was left of my heart. As I cried into my pillow, I kept wishing over and over that Noah was not Amish.

I heard the rap on the door but ignored it. It didn't matter now who knew about me sneaking off in the night—nothing mattered at all.

When Sam's voice spoke close to my head, I wasn't surprised. "Damn it, Rose, what the hell's going on now?"

I turned my face on the wet pillow and breathed out in exhaustion. I felt as if I'd run a mile-long race, and I had to blink several times before Sam's face and bushy hair came into view clearly.

"It's really over." I sniffed, trying desperately to control my voice from cracking. "I told Noah I wouldn't become Amish."

Sam's face was tight with concentration, as if he was angry that I had even considered doing such a thing. But then his face relaxed, and he came off his knees and sat on the bed beside me. When his arms extended toward me, the tears came freely from my eyes again and I rose up, letting him pull me into a hug. Sam patted my back awkwardly and maybe a little too hard, but I didn't care. I was just happy that I wasn't alone.

"I wish Mom were here to handle this. But, I guess, since she's not, I'll have to fill in for her," Sam mumbled near my ear, and I pulled back and looked up at him to see his own eyes glistening in the moonlight from the window.

Somehow, seeing Sam all torn up about Mom pulled me together, and I was able to speak again. "If Mom hadn't died, I'd never even have met Noah. She'd never have allowed Daddy to move us out here."

"Oh, I don't know 'bout that. Mom had an adventurous spirit. And she always wanted to see Dad happy. She might have gone for it. But then again, if she hadn't died, Dad probably would have been content to stay where we were."

The fact that Sam hadn't cracked a joke or said something rude yet made me even more thoughtful. I leaned back against the pillow, finally able to breathe normally again. The threat of tears was still present, but a strange calm came over me.

Sam and I sat in silence for several more minutes, both lost in our own thoughts, when I looked back at him and asked, "Are you happy here, Sam?"

"Oh, it's all right, I guess. I mean, I miss our friends back in Cincinnati, but it's also exciting to meet new people. I'm looking forward to my senior year and playing ball here. I'll be able to help the little school's country team win a few games."

Sam's arrogance made me feel lighter—as if things were the way they should be.

"Do you miss her?" I said, knowing that I didn't need to say her name to him.

He sighed heavily. "Yeah, of course. But I think she'd want us to stick together as a family, Rose. She's probably smiling down right now."

Yes, I believed she was. Even though my heart was broken and I felt as if all the life was leaking out of me, I also could feel the peacefulness creeping in that Mom always created when she was beside me.

I reached over and squeezed Sam's hand. He was right—as long as we stuck together, everything would be all right.

20

Noah
Life without Rose

I SAT IN STUNNED DISBELIEF. THIS CAN'T BE happening, I screamed in my head as I raked my hands through my hair. She had made her decision and there wasn't anything I could do about it. Sadness, disappointment and anger mixed together to create a tidal wave of emotions slamming into me. I couldn't cry or scream. All I could manage was to get up in slow motion and make my way to the stairs and out of the barn into the cool night air. With the moon shining down, I made my way through the hay field, half expecting Rose to run up behind me and say she'd changed her mind. That she'd made a mistake.

But that didn't happen.

Just as I passed the shed, with my head hung low and my thoughts racing, Father stepped out of the shadows. Normally, the sight of him in this kind of situation would have made me tremble with fear, but I was too numb to feel anything. I stopped and met his gaze in the moonlight.

"Where have you been, son?" He voice was barely controlled, a little louder than a whisper.

My throat was suddenly dry, but I managed to choke out, "It's over, Father—between me and Rose. It's done."

Father exhaled, rubbing his fingers through his beard. After a minute, he said almost sympathetically, "Do you want to talk about it?"

I drew a breath and found my voice. "You were right, Father. She didn't want to leave her world for ours."

Father did something very uncharacteristic at that moment, stepping over to grab my shoulders and pulling me into a rough embrace. His bear hug did nothing to make me feel better, but at least he wasn't angry with me anymore.

"Son, how do you feel about going to Pennsylvania now?" he asked solemnly.

Shaking my head, I answered truthfully, "I don't know, Father. I certainly didn't want to go before. But now, maybe it would be good to get away from here for a while."

"It's up to you, Noah—we'll not be sending you there against your will now that the relationship with the English girl is over," he said kindly.

I decided quickly, answering, "I think I'll stay here for a few weeks and think about it some more before I make a decision."

"Fair enough, then, and that will give you some time to reconsider Ella Weaver. You know, we'll be having a picnic dinner here at the house with the Weavers on Thursday. That might give you the opportunity to explore your options." He winked and threw his arm over my shoulders as we walked to the house.

The numbness was beginning to wear off, and a wrenching pain was filling my insides. I could hardly believe that Rose was no longer mine. She had chosen to turn away from me.

Somehow, I'd have to live with it.

The week went by in a strange blur. I could hardly recall anything at all from it. I woke, ate, worked, ate, worked and slept. Of course, by Monday, the entire community had heard the news of the breakup. My family walked around me cautiously, not saying much at all, which was just as well because I didn't feel like socializing anyway.

Mother had given me a big hug and murmured to me in Dutch that everything would be all right. Jacob had patted me on the back a few times, mumbling something I couldn't understand. It didn't seem right that it was already Thursday—and up until this moment, the girls had completely ignored me.

Now, uncomfortably, Sarah had followed me into the barn and was quietly watching me nail a shoe on Rumor's hoof. I pretended she wasn't there for most of the process, but her eyes boring into my back became too much to take. I sighed in frustration, straightening up, and asked, "What do you want, Sarah?"

She shrugged and replied, "I just wondered if you needed to talk to someone."

"Why would I need that?" I narrowed my eyes at her, wishing she'd just go away.

Quietly, she said, "I know how much Rose meant to you."

"And how would you know that?" I questioned in a voice that probably sounded mean to her.

She leaned back against the wall, swirling her bare foot in the shavings on the floor, and said, "I had an inkling something was up between the two of you. I caught you looking at her in a love-struck way a couple of times. Then, when she got hit by the ball, you absolutely gave yourself away."

Hating myself for it, I asked, "Did she ever say anything to you about me?"

She thought a minute and then nodded her head. "The night we were at the schoolhouse dinner, she got very upset when she heard that Mother and Father might send you to Pennsylvania."

"Really?"

That was interesting.

"Yes." She paused, fidgeting with her cap's white ribbon, and asked in a very curious but hushed voice, "But, Noah, did you really think that she'd become one of us?"

I was tired of keeping it all in. Sarah seemed willing to listen, without being judgmental, and that's what I needed at the moment. I decided to trust her and admitted, "Yeah, I believed she would do anything at all to be with me—stupid, huh?"

"No, it wasn't stupid at all. I think she really cares for you, Noah, and she's so beautiful and full of life. I can see why you fell in love with her. But you shouldn't take her decision so personally, I think."

"Why not?" I was beginning to wonder what she might know about Rose that I didn't.

"Well, for one thing, she's so young. I certainly couldn't imagine getting married for a couple more years myself."

"Normally, I wouldn't have wanted to get hitched that quickly either, but it was different with me and Rose. We couldn't have waited for a long courtship."

"Why not?"

She asked with such naive interest, I had to turn away to keep her from seeing my blush. I certainly wasn't going to attempt to explain to her the crazy physical attraction Rose and I had for each other.

"It's not anything I want to discuss with you, Sarah." I stayed turned away from her while I clinched the nails on the hoof.

But then she got my attention again with her next words.

"I don't think you should rush into another relationship

right now, Noah. If you really cared that much for Rose, you should give her some time to change her mind."

All week I'd been trying to forget about Rose. Now my sister was stirring up my feelings again. I wasn't going to have it. I threw her a hard look, and with an angry voice I yelled, "She's not going to change her mind, Sarah. So just stay out of it."

"I didn't mean to upset you, really I didn't," she said and ran out of the barn.

What was with all the women in my life crying so much? Well, Rose wasn't in my life anymore, but what Sarah had said sunk in a little bit, even though I didn't want it to.

Maybe Rose was regretting her decision?

The clip-clops up the driveway pulled me from my wavering thoughts. I peeked around the doorway to see three buggies carrying the Weaver family park at the hitching rail close to the house.

Running my hand through my messy hair, I exhaled in annoyance. I had almost decided to consider Ella for courtship. It would be the easiest thing in the world to do. My parents and her parents were all for it, and she was the prettiest girl around. If Rose wouldn't have me, then I had to move on and make other plans. That was the only way I could get by—the only way that I wouldn't go insane with regret. But I knew that once I announced a courtship with Ella, any chance of getting together with Rose would be gone forever.

It was odd that Sarah would be encouraging me to get back together with an English girl anyway. What was she thinking? I guess she'd been put under Rose's spell, too. But I wasn't fooled by the beautiful girl any longer. When given the choice, Rose picked her comfy, materialistic world over me. And even though it still hurt like hell, I knew what I had to do to get over her.

With my mind made up, I sneaked in the back door, hoping I didn't run into any more family members before I took a shower and washed the horse smell off myself. There was still a heavy weight resting deep inside me, but for the first time in days I felt the stirrings of life under my skin—and I was ready to embrace the feeling.

21

Rose
Consequences

STARING DOWN AT MY CALZONE, I WASN'T hungry at all, but I managed to swallow the piece I had in my mouth without choking. The little Italian restaurant was cute, I had to admit. The green tablecloths were perfectly pressed and the white napkins were folded fancily. The water was in gold-rimmed goblets and the bread sticks sat in an intricately woven basket neatly. The sparkling chandelier above our heads was close to the table, sending off a dim, romantic light.

I couldn't help imagining what it would be like to sit in a nice restaurant like this with Noah—alone. That would never happen now. I'd made sure of that when I refused his marriage proposal, then ran away from him crying into the night. I was the one who made the decision. I dumped him, not the other way around, but why was I in so much pain, then? I couldn't get rid of the twisting knife in my gut. It just kept turning and turning, making it almost impossible to exist. I could hardly eat, sleep or move around. Sometimes I could hardly even breathe. I thought I might just keel over from a heart attack at any moment.

My mind played the scene over and over until my head hurt from the image.

Sometimes panic would take hold of my insides, and I wished that I'd agreed to his pregnancy idea. How bad would it have been? Surely it wouldn't have hurt as much as the pain that I was feeling now.

Today was the first time in the two weeks since the breakup that I'd been out of the house. After Sam had blabbed to Dad about everything, my father had left me alone, keeping his distance. He probably figured that I'd come out of my depressive state on my own in a few days, but when that hadn't happened, he'd finally taken the matter into his own hands, insisting that I come with the family out for dinner. I would have refused, but when Dad had threatened to take me to some shrink friend of his in Cincinnati on Monday, I changed my mind. The thought of telling some stranger all my insane inner thoughts about my ex–Amish boyfriend was not something I wanted to do. The threat finally got me up and moving again.

So here I was, Sam on my right and Justin on my left, squeezed into the couple-size booth across from Dad and… *Her.* She had a name, but not only would I not utter it out loud, I refused to think it also. Glancing up from my calzone, I studied her face for a moment. She was pretty, in a sort of soap-opera way, with her perfectly layered blond hair and her pert little nose. She was being exceptionally nice, too, still in the "I want to show my new man how loving I can be to his adorable children" phase. I wondered how long it would be before she grew a tail and horns.

"You know, Rose, Tina drives to Cincinnati twice a week to visit her mother." I let the fog clear momentarily to glance at my dad. I really hoped he read the "I don't give a damn" look I shot him.

"Oh, really?" I said with forced politeness.

"Yes, and she's offered to take you with her each week so

294 Karen Ann Hopkins

you can start up your dancing again." His face was bright and expectant for my reaction.

Pulling my eyes from him, I looked over at *Her* in concentration. The thought of being stuck in a car with Dad's plaything for hours every week was not appealing in the least. As a matter of fact, jumping into Lake Michigan in the middle of January sounded better. But the dancing part was intriguing. I had turned into a zombie lately, sleeping all day and prowling around the house at night when everyone else was asleep. I never wanted to have a conversation. Even walking seemed to exhaust me.

The thought of putting on my ballet shoes, stretching my body again and gliding along the dance floor to the sound of music on the tips of my toes was inviting. Especially after the nasty things Noah had said about me dancing. That really made me want to go out and do the sexiest routine I could to some pump-and-grind song.

But could I stand to be around *Her?* I deliberated in my mind while I took a large sip of water, peering over the rim.

"Rose, did your father tell you I used to dance? I was even on a dance team in college for two years, until the practice schedule started to interfere with my other classes," she said cheerfully.

She definitely wasn't as pretty as Mom, who had been born with natural, earthy good looks, but I could kind of see why Dad found her attractive. She was one of those people who had a very upbeat personality that made her seem prettier than she actually was. And she did have a dancer's body, even in her middle-aged years. Of course, it was easier to stay slim and trim when you hadn't popped out three babies the way Mom did or eight like Mrs. Miller—poor thing.

With the new information, I loosened up a bit. "No, Dad never mentioned it."

"Well, I want you to know that not only am I willing to drive you to your classes, I would really enjoy watching you. I've missed being in a dance studio," she said in a soft voice. I could tell she really meant it.

My brain must have frozen up or perhaps I was in the middle of a nightmare I'd soon wake up from, because I found myself replying, "Sure, that sounds good."

"Wonderful. I'll call Ms. Lily next week to start the ball rolling," Dad said with uncontrolled excitement.

I, on the other hand, was disgusted by my weak nature. That I could so easily be lured into acting nice to the woman, just because she had been a dancer and was willing to drive me far away from my torturous memories here in Meadow View. The guilty feeling was the worst part. How could I do that to my poor dead mom?

Sometime after my shocking agreement to bum around with Dad's mistress, I had also agreed to go to the movies with Sam and his new friends. Again, either my brain wasn't working at all or I was still dreaming.

After we'd all finished our lemon Italian ice, Dad took Justin with him to drop *Her* off while I rode silently with Sam to the theater. I rationalized that at some point during our weekly drives I'd have to say her name, but until then, I wasn't budging.

When we arrived, I was surprised that the lot was packed, forcing us to park all the way in the back. Watching kids walk by, we waited in the truck like a couple of rednecks until two SUVs and a pickup truck parked nearby and Sam's friends got out.

Sam had been unusually quiet about the Noah thing for

days, hardly bothering me at all. Now I knew why. Jumping nimbly out of one of the cars was a gorgeous blond-haired girl who bounced over to Sam's window and wasted no time in planting a sloppy kiss on his lips. I now knew how grossed out he must have been seeing me kissing Noah. I had to look away before I threw up. Erin had been a much more reserved girlfriend, keeping all their major kissing sessions behind closed doors.

"Rose, I want you to meet Amber," Sam said, a little flustered.

"Great to meet you, Amber." I reached over him and shook the girl's hand, not able to miss her long pink nails with little yellow starburst applications.

"Oh, I know we're going to be good friends, Rose. I can't wait to introduce you to everyone," her melodic voice rang out, and I had to ask myself if this chick was for real. She seemed more like a life-size Barbie doll than a real human being.

Sam had managed to fall in with a large group of good-looking jocks and their girlfriends. Everyone was overly nice to me, making me feel a little bewildered at their automatic acceptance of me into their gang.

My confusion turned to total discomfort, though, when Amber dragged me over to a very tall, attractive guy. Not shocking me, he was the only other person in attendance, other than me, without a date.

"Rose, this is Hunter Braxton." She nearly pushed me into him. I had to stomp the bottom of my tennis shoes into the pavement to keep from skidding into his personal space.

"Hi," I said shyly, glancing up to see that he had dark blond ruffled hair and expressive brown eyes. One glimpse and I knew what he was thinking. I had more experience reading guys now. Noah had looked at me like that all the time.

Blushing, I shifted uncomfortably in front of him, wondering how the heck I was going to get out of having to sit next to him in the movie. In another lifetime I might have been thrilled to have such a cute and *normal* guy eyeing me that way. But now I was an emotional disaster, not interested in ever having another relationship again.

"Hey, it's really nice to meet you." He had a pleasant voice.

He held out his hand to me. I stared at it for a long second, trying to decide whether I should take it or not. Somehow it just didn't seem right to touch this strange guy's hand. Especially the way he was looking at me, openly interested.

In the end, I gave him my hand. I was relieved when his skin didn't cause any fluttering in my stomach or tremors to my heart. Okay, I felt much better knowing I wasn't doomed to fall for another guy. I decided that if Hunter didn't make my belly do flips, then no one else would. Well, except for Noah. So I guess my body would feel pretty bored for the rest of my life.

Even though I begged Hunter not to, he bought me a medium popcorn and Coke, and just as I guessed, he made sure to sit next to me. He wasn't shy about leaning in close to make small talk either. I was forced to sit as far as I could to the side of my chair away from him, pushing into Sam's arm. When Sam saw what I was doing, he just shook his head at me. I would have loved to smack the rotten look off his face, but I still didn't feel quite energetic enough to pull it off.

I couldn't even have told anyone what the dumb movie was about, just the usual action flick with lots of special effects and no story line. I spent the entire time thinking about Noah. I wondered what he was doing at that moment. Had he already gotten over me? Did he miss me even a little bit? Was he courting Ella Weaver? The last question caused a sick feeling to develop in my stomach and halfway through the movie I left for the restroom. I stayed in there for the next hour, leaning against the wall, crying as quietly as I could. Life sucked even more than I ever imagined it could. This breakup with Noah was hauntingly familiar to Mom's death. I knew from experience the numbness, the agonizing pain...and the crying would eventually go away, but right now they were killing me. A knock at the door shot my head up.

"Rose—are you in there?" Sam's voice whispered frantically.

"What are you doing in here, Sam?" I said, completely stunned that the buffoon was in the ladies' room.

"I wouldn't have to be in here if you were watching the movie like any normal person. Now, come on and get out of there." I hid a smile at the fluster in his voice and opened the door to see him nervously glancing toward the entrance door.

Seeing my face, he sighed. "Why are you crying *now?*"

"Oh, I don't know—maybe because I'm miserable, sad and lonely, just to name a few reasons," I challenged, annoyed at his total lack of understanding.

"You know, Hunter told me he really likes you. He wants to ask you out." He said it enthusiastically, as if that was going to change the world for me.

Putting my hands on my hips, I snorted, "Do you think I care? He's just some guy who'd go out with anyone."

Shaking his head vigorously, he countered, "No, Rose, he's a cool guy. You'd like him if you gave him a chance."

"What—are you pimping me out or something? My love life is none of your concern," I said, losing any composure I had left.

"You'd feel a whole lot better if you started dating someone else. It would get your mind off the guy with the suspenders and keep you from spending your entire time at the movies crying in the bathroom," Sam pointed out with the pinched expression of someone who'd tasted something bitter.

We had a stare down for several seconds until Amber pranced in like Bambi and relieved Sam of his caregiving duties. She performed her job very diligently, giving me a super-strong minty piece of gum, drying my face with a paper towel and then brushing some powder over my nose and cheeks to mask the redness.

By the time I walked out of the restroom, I only looked as if I'd been crying for a half an hour instead of a full one. Hunter was waiting in the lobby with Sam. I could have just died when he looked at me with concern.

I was at least thankful that he didn't say anything to me as we all walked out, pushed tightly together in the middle of the exiting crowd. Reaching the truck, I quickly crawled in. I sat staring straight ahead while the new gang hung out in the parking lot. I only halfheartedly listened to all the chattering until I heard my name mentioned. I honed in on what Sam was saying in a flash.

"Yeah, sorry, I'd like to go back to your place, Hunter, but I should get Rose home before she starts leaking again."

"What about the party tomorrow? Do you think your sister will come?" Hunter asked in a much too nosy way.

"Maybe—I'll see what I can do." He paused, and I could tell he was thinking, a foreign activity to him. He went on to say, "You know what would be a good idea? Why don't I pick you and Amber up tomorrow afternoon. I'll bring Rose, and we'll go get supper at that little diner on the corner of Route 48 and Maggie Road."

"Sounds great—call me with the exact time in the morning," Hunter said brightly to Sam. Then turning away from my brother, he stalked over to the passenger-side window like a hungry lion. He rested his arms in the opening and said, "I'm looking forward to seeing you tomorrow, Rose."

"Mmm-hmm," I mumbled, trying to ignore him. Maybe my rudeness would deter him. Grinning at my discomfort, he stared at me for a few seconds, his eyes roaming over my face before turning and hopping into his Blazer. His action signaled the rest of the group to begin dispersing. His self-confidence bugged me. It was as if he expected me to faint at his feet or something absurd like that. Well, I'd show him. He was cute, but he didn't hold a candle to Noah. Besides, he didn't make my body go nuts when he came near me.

I had to sit for another few minutes while Sam rammed his tongue down Amber's throat before she finally left with a few of her girlfriends. He jumped in the truck beside me.

"You're really disgusting, you know that?" I informed him.

"You should talk. You've ruined me forever with the image of you lip-locked with Noah on the bed." He said it with amusement until he saw that I was crying again.

"Goddamn it, Rose. You've got to stop crying every time you hear the guy's name." He sounded worried and angry at the same time.

"I can't help it, Sam—it just hurts so bad. Noah and I were meant to be together and he's the one I want to be dating, not some jock named Hunter," I said, flinging my head onto the seat back with a thud.

"If you two were meant to be together, then you would be." He sighed heavily and continued, trying to be compassionate and failing miserably, "The fact is that the whole thing was screwed up from the beginning. Noah has to marry an

Amish girl, probably before he turns twenty. You, on the other hand, are destined to go to college, have a career and eventually meet the guy of your dreams. You'll get married and have a couple of kids when you're in your thirties. You can't mess with Providence, Rose."

"What are you talking about?"

"Just that your life is still ahead of you and you can't drastically alter it by becoming Amish, marrying when you're a teenager and starting to pop out babies immediately. If you did, you'd be seriously messing with the universe."

"Yeah, I know," I said weakly.

"Well, if you know, why won't you just move on?"

"It's just hard to, that's…all." I hiccuped.

"Well, I'm going to make it a lot easier for you. Tomorrow you're having a very distracting dinner with me, Amber and Hunter. Then you're going to that party with us and having a buttload of fun. Okay?"

"Okay," I agreed weakly, feeling as if I'd just sold Noah out.

22

Noah
Seeing Is Believing

WITH BORED INDIFFERENCE, I SAT IN THE FRONT seat of the work truck, watching the English filling their gas tanks, the same as Mr. Denton was doing now. Lucky for me today, Father had remained home to meet with the mechanic who was supposed to fix up the Bobcat, giving me the opportunity to escape his probing eyes for a while. He'd been extremely supportive since I told him of my breakup with Rose. But aggravating me to no end, the man followed me around closely every minute of each day. I was enjoying the moment of solitude alone in the truck.

It gave me more time to brood about the mess I'd gotten myself into. It had been over a week since my talk with Sarah. Each day that passed, my desire to see Rose again grew to the point of physical pain.

I had it so bad that every time I heard hoofbeats on the pavement in front of the house, I would stop whatever I was doing and anxiously search down the roadway. I'd hold my breath, hoping to see Rose riding Lady in the direction of the gap in the fence and the cornfields. Of course, that never happened. The only other chance I had to possibly see her was when the work truck passed by her house daily. Those times

I would peer out the window, careful not to be noticed, for any sight of her. Again to no avail.

I was determined to see her one more time before I made a decision about Ella. It would haunt me forever if I didn't give Rose a chance to change her mind. But time was running out. Tonight we were once again picnicking with the Weaver family. Only this time it was at their place. I knew the gatherings were purposely being arranged to throw Ella and me together. I sighed in annoyance, running my hand through my hair at the thought.

The air was frustratingly hot, making me wish for the cooler days of autumn. Now that August had arrived, it wouldn't be too long a wait for summer to fade away. The heat reminded me of Rose, and I didn't need anything else helping me with that. As it was, I couldn't eat Mother's cinnamon rolls any longer. Just looking at them brought images of Rose's lips to me.

Shaking the vision from my head, I focused my gaze on the little diner attached to the market. The smells wafting from the restaurant were pleasant enough, but I knew from experience that the food smelled better than it tasted.

A green sliver in the corner of my eye caught my attention. I glanced out the window to see a green dually truck pulling into the lot. Swiveling in the seat to get a better view, I saw that sure enough, it was Sam. He had a blonde girl sitting almost on top of him in the front seat. My eyes followed the truck as it pulled up to the diner and parked.

Finally, my chance had arrived to find out how Rose was doing. Gripping the door handle with anticipation spreading through me, I began to step out but stalled for a second after seeing a guy climbing out of the backseat. Must be one of Sam's football-player friends, I assumed. My thoughts were suddenly rattled by the appearance of a slender bare leg from the doorway of Sam's truck.

The air caught in my throat and my heart beat wildly in my chest while I waited for her to fully exit the truck. Somehow, instinctively, I knew it was Rose. Then she was out, and for the first time in two weeks, I saw her again. I couldn't keep my eyes from roaming intensely over her. Immediately, I noticed that she had lost weight, which was impossible to believe since she'd been tiny before. Her skin was paler than I remembered, her coffee-colored hair striking against the fairness of her face.

The other thing that slammed into my sight and caused a ripple of anger to bubble up inside me were the short jean shorts she wore and the pink sleeveless top that hugged her breasts tightly. Granted, her shorts weren't as skimpy as the blonde girl's, but still, they were incredibly inappropriate. The shirt didn't leave much to the imagination either.

Not moving a muscle, and with a sick churning developing in my stomach, I watched her huddled together with the others by the truck. Her face wasn't smiling and she appeared to be studying the broken pavement at her feet as intensely as I was watching her.

Then, almost in a blur, the group began to move toward the diner. Sam opened the door and his girlfriend slid past him. My body tensed even more. I swallowed down the bile that started to rise in my tight throat when the new guy placed his hand on the center of Rose's little back and ushered her through the doorway a second later.

He had touched her with an air of familiarity, as if he owned her. And she had let him touch her. She had willingly allowed him to guide her though the door. An icy chill abruptly cooled me in the sweltering heat. I gazed at the sky to see dark, ominous clouds building on the horizon.

Yes, Rose had always been willing when it came to touching and kissing. Now I guessed she was doing those things with the guy that just pushed her through the door. The frosty tentacles filling my body invaded my heart. I sat frozen in place, unable to erase the disgusting image from my mind.

Matthew's voice sounded distant when it cracked into my stunned mind. I blinked at him just in time to catch the Mountain Dew he tossed me.

"Hey, Noah, guess who we just saw in the diner."

When I didn't say anything, he continued loudly, "It was the English girl you dumped. She was with this tall guy."

I didn't think he had any idea that what was coming out of his mouth was killing me, but Jacob did. He roughly smacked Matthew on the head open handed and grunted, "Shut up, Matt—you idiot!"

I found my voice, hoping it wouldn't waver when I said, "Don't worry about it, Jacob. I don't care in the least."

Jacob wasn't buying it, though, by the way he sympathetically shook his head and sighed loudly. While I was struggling to keep my composure, Mr. Denton climbed into the truck and revved up the loud diesel engine. Slowly he pulled out of the lot and away from Rose.

I had prayed so hard to get to see her, and God had answered my prayers. Now I knew that Rose had moved on. She was already enjoying someone else's company and there was nothing I could do about it. The sight of that guy's hand on her back had made my decision about Ella easy for me. Tonight I would ask her parents' permission to begin courting her.

And I'd never look back.

★ ★ ★

Sitting at the end of the table with Matthew beside me, I took the last bite of food, not really tasting it. Everything was about appearances. I had to appear happy enough to be enjoying my dinner and that's just what I was going to do. Even if I threw it up later.

"Um, about what I said earlier, Noah. I wasn't really thinking."

Looking over at him and his anxious chubby face, I decided I had no reason to be angry with him. All he did was say the truth. Yeah, I didn't want to hear it at the time, but Matthew hadn't meant anything malicious by it. He'd never been in love. How would he know what it felt like to see the girl who had once been mine with another guy?

"It's all right. I really have gotten over her," I said firmly, convincing myself of my words each time I pictured her kissing that guy.

"I heard you were going to ask to court my sister. Is it true?" he whispered cautiously.

"Yeah, I guess that's the direction I'm heading," I said with quiet resolve.

"That means we'll be officially brothers someday," he said cheerfully.

Seeing how happy he was at the idea, I couldn't stop the slight smile from creeping onto my mouth. "I guess that's true, Matthew."

"Noah?" It was Father's voice. He had walked to the table with Mr. Weaver close beside him. "Will you please go with Ella to the storeroom to bring a watermelon to the table?" His voice would have sounded innocent enough to anyone else, but I wasn't fooled.

As if perfectly rehearsed, Ella appeared next to my chair,

waiting expectantly for me to join her. Not very subtle, Father, I thought, getting up and proceeding to follow her into the house and down the stairs to the basement.

The storeroom was in the far corner and since we'd eaten outside, the room was empty of any people. An uncomfortable feeling gripped me as I realized that this was the first time I'd ever been completely alone with the girl. Crossing the smooth concrete floor slowly behind her, we entered the small space lined with shelves from the ceiling to the ground, where jars of varying sizes were tightly packed onto the boards, filled with a variety of colorful contents.

The proximity to Ella felt strange to me, but she, on the other hand, seemed to be perfectly okay with the situation when she pivoted around quickly. She openly eyed me up and down with a slight smile on her lips.

I'd never really taken the time to look closely at her before. Now I took the opportunity to examine her. She had a pretty face. That, I already knew, but her eyes were the wrong color and her lips weren't full enough. Her nose was a little too turned up and I appraised her body, trying to imagine what she was hiding under her thick dark blue dress. From what I could gather, I decided her breasts weren't full enough, and she was too tall, only a few inches shorter than me. Ella would have been beautiful to any other man, but to me she was just too different from my first love.

I waited for my body to respond to her nearness. Hoping that my heart would beat wildly or that wonderful tingling feeling would begin to surge from my groin. But my insides were quiet, almost…bored.

Bringing my eyes back to hers, she looked at me with a desire that was obvious, and I was suddenly unsure what to do. I never had to think about it when I was with Rose. My body had all the answers with her. It took charge of my brain, making it all so easy and natural.

I hesitated, wondering, when Ella took the initiative, stepping within a few inches of me. She looked up under fluttering eyes. Her eyes were definitely inviting me to kiss her. In a fluid motion of desperation, to see if this girl, or any other girl, for that matter, could make me feel as alive as Rose did, I bent down and placed my mouth on hers.

Her lips parted very little. They felt stiff and unyielding beneath mine. Her scent was all wrong, too. Instead of the warm lavender smell that was burned into my senses, my nostrils were being invaded with a cool, soapy smell that was totally unsatisfying.

I wasn't going to give up so easily, though. I wrapped my arms around her waist and pulled her tighter into my embrace, attempting to press her into me enough that I could feel her body through the heavy dress.

A soft gasp escaped her lips, and her mouth began to move more urgently on mine. I waited for the powerful feelings of anticipation and desire to wash over me, but they were held at bay, with only a dull ache deep within me that was incredibly disappointing.

Everything about her was completely wrong to me: the smell; the touch; even the taste. Maybe in time she'd become familiar to me, and my feelings toward her would change, but I doubted it. And I didn't want to wait for it to happen. Not being able to handle another second of trying to force myself to respond to her, I pulled back suddenly. I would have let go of her completely, but she swayed and I kept my hand on her waist to steady her. The last thing I needed was for her to faint.

"Oh, Noah, I knew you had feelings for me," she exclaimed breathlessly.

At that moment, looking at her flushed face and her bright eyes, I realized she was exhibiting more life than I'd ever seen from her before. Abruptly, I felt like a complete and utter dog. It wasn't her fault that I didn't find her attractive. Most of the boys, if not all of them in the community, would have been turned on by her kiss. With me it was different, though. Rose had ruined me for any other girl.

"I'm sorry about that kiss, Ella," I apologized.

"Oh—it's fine with me, Noah. Will you be talking to my father tonight?" she asked confidently.

What was I to say to that? After all, I had just kissed her, and in our community that usually meant a courtship would follow quickly.

"Not tonight, Ella," I said without meeting her eyes. Glimpsing the watermelons on the bottom shelf, I squeezed past her to pick up the largest one and hurry from the small room. I could hear her footsteps softly behind me. I hoped that she wouldn't blab the kiss to all the other girls, knowing full well that the entire community would know about it by morning.

I managed to avoid her by playing volleyball with the other guys until the sun disappeared, to be replaced by the semi-darkness of a clouded-over sky. Occasionally, a sliver of the moon slipped through. The air was heavy with dampness, and the smell of rain was quickly surrounding me.

When it was too dark to play ball any longer, the older boys started a bonfire behind the house, and everyone gathered around it to roast marshmallows. Without looking in the direction where Ella sat with her sisters beside the flames, I made my way to Father and bent down to whisper in his ear.

"Father, I'm not feeling well. May I leave for home now?"

He scrutinized me with sharp eyes, trying to detect any

rebellion. I must have acted my part well, because I breathed a little easier when he answered, "You may go, son. But I am trusting that you really are sick and don't have any mischief in your heart."

I could only nod in agreement, feeling slightly guilty, but not enough to deter me. I quickly went to the barn and led Rumor out of the tie stall. In little time I had the horse harnessed and hooked up to the buggy. I was just about to step up to the seat when the crackle of pebbles underfoot sounded behind me, causing me to jump slightly before I whirled around to see Ella watching me.

"Why are you leaving before everyone else, Noah?" she asked suspiciously. I remembered instantly why I'd never liked her before.

Without missing a beat, I told her, "I'm not feeling well. We ate at the diner for lunch today. I think I have food poisoning," I lied.

"Will I see you tomorrow?" Her tone was slightly demanding and her face was set in a tight grimace.

Climbing into the buggy, I said distractedly, "We'll see how my stomach is doing." The disbelief was evident in her eyes, and I quickly added, "Let's not rush into anything, Ella—okay?"

Snapping the reins, I rolled away and left her standing in the driveway. I thought things were bad before. Now I was truly going to hell. Forgetting Ella, I pushed Rumor to cover the distance between the Weavers' farm and ours quickly.

When I turned into the driveway, probably ten minutes had passed, but it felt like ten hours. Poor Rumor was lathered with sweat from the hard trotting I had asked of him. Normally, I would have taken him straight to the barn, removing his harness and rubbing him down before I did anything else.

But tonight I had other ideas. With my heart pounding in my chest, I parked the horse and buggy by the shed, setting the brake. Jumping down, I moved around the front of Rumor, pausing to pat him on the neck and promise him that I'd be taking care of him soon.

Then I did what was probably the stupidest thing in my life by walking rapidly to the phone. Without hesitation, I picked the handle up, dialing the number that I had memorized weeks ago. Settling myself on the bale of hay, I covered my face with my hands and waited for her to answer.

23

Rose
Seeing the Light

HIDING IN THE CORNER, I PEERED ACROSS THE misty, smoke-filled room. The crowd of teenagers was so thick that I could barely see between the dancing bodies, especially with many of the bodies mashed together in passionate embraces. Feeling the color flooding my cheeks, I looked away, trying to avoid the R-rated show by listening to the booming music instead. Feeling the rhythm vibrating through me, I swayed to a song I really liked. The beat made my blood feel warm, pumping more surely than it had since I last saw Noah. Closing my eyes, I let the sensation wash over me.

I wasn't at all worried about being bothered by any of the guys at the party, even though every male in the room had checked out pretty much every female that arrived. It appeared that Hunter had placed an invisible force field around my body when he decided to shadow my every move in the house.

Sam, of course, had immediately abandoned me, bounding upstairs with his Barbie doll, leaving me to face the roomful of strangers alone. I wasn't in a social mood, thoroughly disgruntled that I had been tricked into coming to the party. I must have been giving off the "leave me alone and don't talk to me" vibes, because all the other kids did just that, steering clear of me. Except for Hunter, who would occasionally bring me a fresh soda and say a few words. After he'd run a drink errand, he'd retreat to a safe distance of about ten feet away, spending his time broodingly drinking beer and staring at me.

Ignoring his hot eyes, I continued to move to the music. It was weird to be surrounded by all these people yet still feel absolutely alone. Sadness squeezed my insides. I struggled to hold the tears back, when I suddenly felt large hands on my waist and a deep voice in my ear.

"Do you want to get some fresh air, Rose?" Hunter said loudly enough to be heard over the blaring noise.

I could smell the beer on his breath. I thought about saying no, but the cold loneliness that I was experiencing compelled me to answer weakly, "Sure."

Taking the hand he offered me, I let him pull me through the press of bodies in the center of the room, coming uncomfortably close to several couples tongue tied together. That really grossed me out. *Yuck.* I actually began pushing on Hunter's back to get off the makeshift dance floor quicker.

Finally, we broke through all the writhing bodies and moved down a narrow hall to the back door. Leaving the stuffy warmth of the house behind, I breathed the fresh, cooler air in deeply. Letting it fill my lungs to capacity in an attempt to cleanse the disgusting cigarette smoke from the tissues.

If Hunter didn't have a firm grip on my hand as he pulled me across the dark, unfamiliar yard, I probably would have stumbled onto my face. I glanced up at the heavy clouds that were hiding any glimpse of the moon. The atmosphere tingled with the prospect of rain.

I could see his target now. A pretty little gazebo with an intricate railing of swirls and curlicues nestled between a few large pine trees. The white paint made the structure leap out of the blackness. Although I was glad to be able to see something, nervousness suddenly slammed into me, constricting my stomach, the breath catching in my throat.

Hunter's big feet thudded onto the wooden floor, stabbing the night air. Guiding me to the bench, he sat beside me with his legs stretched out, leaning his back against the spindles leisurely. His overly relaxed posture, arms spread out along the railing, his legs crossed over, reminded me of a stuck-up house cat. Even though his face was well hidden in the shadows, I imagined it held the same arrogant confidence his body was exhibiting. The whole picture really bugged the crap out of me.

My irritation wasn't enough to erase the nervousness. I sat rigidly on the edge of the seat, not really wanting to kiss him, but knowing that it was probably inevitable at this point. I couldn't keep from wondering at the same time if his kiss would be similar to Noah's. My heart began to race, more from terror than anticipation while I waited for something to happen.

He wasted no time when a few seconds later his hands closed over my shoulders. Surprising me, instead of kissing, he began pushing his thumbs firmly into my shoulder blades. I definitely wasn't expecting a massage. Wow. It felt pretty good. Although his touch made me want to bolt back to the house at first, his fingers were expertly working to rub the anxiety out of my sore muscles. Even though my mind was screaming in protest, my back relaxed, slumping a little when the tension was released. This wasn't so bad, I decided, losing myself to the pleasurable sensations for a minute. It certainly wasn't the same as when Noah touched me. I wasn't experiencing all the crazy palpitations in my gut or the blood surging below my skin. But it was okay.

"Your muscles are so tight, Rose," he said slowly, speaking in rhythm with his hand movements.

"Yeah, I've been pretty stressed-out lately," I commented almost to myself, letting him continue. Only now his strong fingers had moved up onto my neck and I wondered how he had learned to work his fingers like that. I was about to ask him when he interrupted my musings.

"Were you and that guy pretty serious?" he asked softly, his hands pausing while he waited for my answer.

Not only could I hear the curiosity in his voice, but also the deep sound of physical attraction. I wasn't just an inexperienced girl anymore. Noah had made sure of that. Thoughts of him popping into my head pricked me into awareness and suddenly Hunter's touch, as good as it felt a moment ago, bristled my skin now and queasiness bubbled in my belly.

What the heck was I doing out here in the dark with this pumped-up jock anyway? I wanted Noah touching me, not Hunter. The knowledge flooded my brain, leaving me with the realization that I wouldn't ever want another guy to touch me the way Noah had. I'd probably end up running away to a convent to become a nun.

Sighing, I mumbled, "Yeah, we were close."

I had been feeling fairly certain that he would behave himself, especially since my big brother, his newest and best buddy, wasn't far away in the house. And even though Sam was preoccupied, he still was here somewhere.

So I wasn't prepared when everything went to hell. He said in a raspy voice, "I'm going to help you forget him, Rose."

In a fluid motion that took less time than my eye blinking, he pounced, swiveling me around and crushing his mouth onto mine. I was so startled at first I didn't react at all. I just numbly allowed him to kiss me. But the shock wore off quickly, followed by fury that he assumed he could do whatever he wanted with me. I started pushing on his chest with all the force I could get out of my little body. Hey, I was only five foot four. What could I do to the football star? I did manage to tightly seal my mouth shut, proud to say.

Either he wasn't getting the picture, or he didn't care. Ignoring me, he continued his rampage of my mouth, not giving me a centimeter of space to even attempt a scream. I had ignorantly believed that if I made it clear to him that I didn't want him kissing me, he'd back off. Now, with his hands roaming around on me, and hearing the muddled groan from his lips as they smashed onto mine, real fear started to take hold of my senses. I didn't have the fraction of his strength, and realizing how helpless I really was sent a spasm of near hysteria coursing through my veins.

Crap. He managed to get my mouth open a bit, and then his tongue started probing around. Once the panicked feeling took hold of me, all rational thought left my brain. It was replaced by a primal instinct that I didn't even know I possessed until I bit down hard, immediately tasting the salty-iron taste of his blood in my mouth.

He jerked back, still holding on to my shoulder, and I could hear him sucking at the corner of his mouth in the shadowed darkness. Expecting his wrath, I was preparing to scream my heart out, punch his stuck-up face and sprint to the house.

Again he surprised me when he spoke in a calm voice with what sounded like amusement peppering his words. "Gosh, Rose, you are really wild."

He must've been the masochistic type. Instantly, I came to the horrid conclusion that my little bite job had only caused him to be more turned on to me.

Now that my mouth was free of his, I growled, "I did not invite you to molest me."

"I know, I know. I'm sorry about that—I just couldn't resist you."

"Well, you better back off, or I'll tell Sam about this," I threatened in a low snarl.

"Hey, calm down. I thought you were used to being kissed," he said coyly.

"Oh, I am, but not by you," I snapped back between clenched teeth.

"I didn't mean to frighten you, Rose, really I didn't. I won't try to kiss you again unless you invite me to. I promise." Without seeing his face clearly, I imagined he was smiling, all sure of himself.

"I won't be doing any such thing. You can count on that," I hissed, wrenching free from him and marching toward the house. I instantly felt better now that I was free from his hold. I figured I was getting the upper hand in the situation, but he kept up with me, staying so close on my heel that if I stopped he would have bowled me over.

"Where are you going?" he demanded.

A few more feet and I'd be in the house, safe again.

I retorted without turning back, "To the bathroom—or do you have a problem with that?"

Flinging the door open, I swerved to the left, into the little room. I attempted to slam the door, but his body blocked the way and impatiently, I glared up at him.

"Do you want a soda?" he asked me, a frustrated expression pinching his face.

He must be totally clueless, I decided, shouting back, "No, I don't want a soda!"

My yell caused the side of his mouth he wasn't still sucking on to twitch slightly. I decided at that moment, as I ran my gaze over his tall, athletic frame, that it was probably a good thing that he had a sense of humor. After all, with most of the inhabitants of the house drunk or doing the wild thing, he could easily have forced me to do whatever he wanted and no one would have even noticed. Maybe in another lifetime I would have even fallen for him—maybe.

He was definitely one of those type-A people who didn't like to lose anything he'd set as a goal for his ambitions, so I wasn't shocked when he amicably replied, "I'll get you a Mountain Dew, then." He sauntered away, and for a brief instant, I thought, he *is* persistent, then I slammed and locked the door securely.

Breathing a huge sigh of relief, I leaned back for a moment to clear my head. Then I swung into action.

I mumbled an "Eww" as I stepped over someone's puke that had pooled up on the sea-blue tiled floor. I didn't even know who owned the house, but I bet there was going to be a pair of very upset parents arriving home from vacation in a day or two.

Reaching the sink, I pumped a big gob of liquid soap onto my hand, and running the water as hot as it would get, I vigorously rubbed the suds all over my face and neck to erase any trace of Hunter from my skin. I even dabbed the foam onto my tongue, zapping any evidence that his tongue had been in there.

The chalky taste of the soap made me gag, and along with the smell of the puke, I started to feel sick. Somehow I managed to rinse my face without upchucking. The towel on the floor was just too disgusting to use, so I decided to drip-dry and hopped over the mess. Opening the door a crack to let some of the choking smoke in, which ironically was an improvement from the smell in the bathroom, I peeked out.

The music was still blasting, and I sighed in relief seeing only a couple of girls sitting on the floor in the hallway, looking as if they were about to pass out. The coast was clear for the moment, luckily without any sign of Hunter.

I knew I'd have to move quickly to get away from the house before he came back. Nimbly, I slipped out of the bathroom of horrors. In two long strides I grabbed the door handle, turned it and was back out in the fresh air in a matter of seconds.

Putting my brain back into action, I figured my house was about three miles away. I could walk that easily, I rationalized. Besides, Sam deserved a real good scare when he discovered his little sister was missing. That's what he got for leaving me alone with his jerky friend anyway.

I still wasn't free, though. After my eyes adjusted somewhat to the darkness, I slunk through the yard, dodging between trees as I went. Several kids were hanging out in the driveway among the parked cars, and my heart skipped a beat seeing them as I ducked down behind a bush. Hoping to get away without raising the curiosity of the teens, I made a final gamble that the darkness would shield me and ran for the roadway. I didn't stop when I reached the pavement either, stretching my legs out to put as much distance between me and Party Central as I could.

Finally, when the *boom, boom* of the music faded away, and I was surrounded only by the chirping night sounds of the country, I slowed to a walk. Breathing hard to catch my breath, I decided I was way too out of shape when I felt a cramp shimmer up my left thigh.

Up until then, there hadn't been any traffic on the road, which suited me fine. Now, though, I could hear the low rumble of an engine coming from behind. Briefly I worried that it might be Hunter looking for me. Quickly, I dismissed that idea, though, remembering he'd ridden to the party with us.

Glancing over my shoulder, I saw that it was a small red pickup truck that I didn't recognize. Straightening up, and hoping the vehicle would pass by, I kept on walking, now with a slight limp due to the cramp. No such luck for me, I groaned inwardly when the truck slowed to a crawl alongside me.

"Hey, sweetie—you need a ride?" a man's voice called.

With a sideways shift of my eyes, I judged that there were two middle-aged guys in the truck. I could only see the driver's features, noting that his hair was buzzed and he had dark stubble on his rough ex-military–looking face. Could this night get worse?

I thought I had been terrified when Hunter, a good-looking teenage guy, was trying to make out with me. Now my mutilated naked body being dragged out of a quarry by a couple of cops in the middle of nowhere flashed through my mind. Thinking fast, I clutched my cell phone from my pocket, deciding to make a run for it to the brick rancher I'd just passed if I so much as heard the click of a truck door opening.

Without looking at the truck, I replied in the most unfriendly voice I could spit out. "No, I'm fine." It wasn't easy to manage coherent words with the muscles strangled in my throat, and I guessed my attempt at meanness sounded pretty pathetic.

"Your loss, beautiful," the man said, sounding annoyed. But thankfully the truck sped up, leaving me alone on the side of the road. The tremors started in my heart and spread out with speed to my limbs until I was shaking almost violently.

After a couple of minutes of walking, I began pulling myself together, especially when I realized I was almost to the intersection of the road I needed to take, a much quieter and, hopefully, safer route. Praying that no other cars would pass before I reached it, I willed my legs to move and flew across the pavement, not slowing until the road split where I hung to the right. I would have kept on running, but the burning in my lungs and the cramping in my leg wouldn't let me. I slowed to a fast walk, trying to control my frenzied breathing.

Hearing another car coming, I jumped the wide ditch without thinking and dived into weeds that were taller than my head. Lying on the damp, prickly ground, I held my breath, waiting for the car to pass. When it did, I rose, deciding as difficult as it would be to travel through, the safest place for me was hidden in the tangle of weeds and bushes parallel to the roadway.

Determined to get home alive, I began trudging through the overgrown field in the direction of my house. Maddened, I hacked my way through the giant patches of briars, the skin on my bare arms and legs being constantly snagged by the sharp points until I could feel sticky blood smeared over most of my exposed body.

Following a few minutes of torture, I began moving at a snail's pace, taking the time to try to unhook the thorns before they tore up my skin any further. I could feel the stinging on my face, too. My suspicion that I had a huge scratch there was confirmed when I reached up to feel a long streak of blood welling up on my cheek. Great, now I'm going to be permanently scarred from this fiasco.

As if hiking home through the man-eating field while trying to avoid being kidnapped by lunatics wasn't enough, the clouds decided that was the time to open up and unleash their moisture. Rain fell to the ground in a soft sprinkling mist, touching the scratches and causing a hundred little stings to sizzle across my skin. After a few more minutes of walking in pain, I began to cry quietly.

I thought I had reached my physical and emotional breaking point until I hooked my toe under a root and stumbled forward. Unable to catch myself, I crashed to the ground, my hands breaking the fall somewhat but being pierced by thorns in the process.

Lying there on the sharp, muddy ground, I couldn't keep the tears from gushing out of my eyes, trailing warmly down my face. I pulled my knees up to my chin and braced my head against them, rocking myself back and forth.

I had been rescued from my suffering for most of the summer by Noah. Now he was gone, and my life was worse than ever. I missed him so desperately it chewed at my insides until there was nothing left anymore.

Why had I been so stupid? I said no to him so that I wouldn't lose the life I'd grown accustomed to, but after tonight, I could honestly say that my life sucked anyway. So why was I clinging so hard to it? At least if I'd become Amish, I would be with Noah, and he would be the one hugging and kissing me, instead of some stranger I didn't even like. I wouldn't be sitting here in a briar patch a couple of miles from home in the cold rain, bleeding.

Shifting my weight to escape the sharp poke of a thistle into my hip, I let the grief take me, losing all perception of time, the minutes blurring together. I lay there on the cold, mushy earth, the weeds and stems jabbing into my body for quite a while. I couldn't find the energy to move. I was too exhausted, and as the misty rain settled into the still, dark night, I listened to the nothingness of complete silence.

My phone split the night air unexpectedly with its unwelcome rock tune, nearly stopping my heart. I fumbled awkwardly with my numb fingers trying to answer it quickly. My sheer focus was on making the noise stop. Without seeing the number, I answered, "Hello?"

A pause, and then his voice, *his glorious voice,* came through the phone into my head. I pressed the phone tightly to my ear, not daring to breathe.

"Rose—it's Noah. How are you doing?" he asked softly, almost shyly.

The question was funny under the circumstances. If I weren't in so much discomfort, I probably would have laughed. But hearing his voice also brought on another emotion, *guilt.* My encounter with Hunter came trickling into my mind, bringing the tears again. In a muted whisper, I stuttered, "I'm...okay."

"What's wrong? You don't sound right."

My wall tumbled down at the worry in his voice. I cried in a rush of sloppy words, "I had to leave this party because this guy was bothering me...and everyone was drinking beer... and...it was so awful..." I trailed off with a gulp.

"Where's Sam?" he demanded in an angry voice.

"He's still at the party—up in a bedroom somewhere with his girlfriend," I croaked, trying desperately to keep the crying to a minimum.

"Where are you?" He sounded desperate. I suddenly regretted telling him the truth, but I couldn't take it back now. So I answered honestly, "I'm sitting in a thorny field beside the road."

"Tell me your exact location, and speak clearly."

I had to focus my mind enough to think.

"I'm on Stone House Road, a little ways from the bridge."

"Are you in that overgrown field in the curve of the road?"

"Uh-huh," I said, shaking my head happily that he knew where I was.

"Don't move. I'll be there as quickly as I can manage."

Suddenly panic shot through me. "No! You'll get into trouble," I nearly shouted into the phone.

An unnerving laugh came through the phone to me. "I don't care about that. I'm coming to get you, and that's the end of it."

"How will you get away?" I asked.

He said impatiently, "My family is at the Weavers'." Pause. "Rumor is already hitched up—so I'll be there soon. Just don't go anywhere…and, Rose?"

"Yes?"

"I love you," he said softly.

"I love you, too," I told him. Then his voice was gone, and the tingle of foreboding nagged at me as I stared into the shadowy grass. He was coming to get me, and I would see him again. Maybe even kiss him. Hugging my arms around myself, I sighed wistfully, thinking that I'd finally get to ride in that buggy of his.

All was right with the world again.

24

Noah
Priorities

HANGING UP, I WASTED NO TIME, SPRINTING through the shed in a few long strides and stepping into the seat of the buggy. Steam was still rising off Rumor, blending into the misty rain that dropped from the sky, and I regretted for an instant that he had to go out on the pavement again. I dismissed the thought quickly, promising that I'd give him a good rubdown when we returned. He was a tough horse and could handle the extra work. What really mattered at the moment was Rose and getting her safely home.

Flicking the reins with force, I asked Rumor to stretch out into a road trot and guided him down the driveway and onto the roadway. Within seconds, a car came up behind the buggy, only to whip out around us. The driver was obviously too impatient to maintain the slower speed for any amount of time.

Once the car was out of sight, the night became dark and still again, with only the occasional whip-poor-will's call piercing the quiet of the countryside. Thankfully, the mist had turned into the occasional soft drop of rain, and I reckoned that if Rose was dressed appropriately, she'd be all right waiting in the field until I arrived.

My heart was beating furiously at the thought of seeing

her again. We'd be alone for a little while, giving me the opportunity to hold her in my arms and kiss her. A small part of me was angry with her for getting herself into such a fix—and maybe a bit hurt that she hadn't called me for help on her own, but all that wasn't really important. Rose needed me and I'd never let her down. The way my body had reacted to hearing her voice—the pounding of my heart, the sweat that rose on my skin and my inability to breathe normally—said it all. I still loved Rose. And nothing in the world would change that fact.

Somehow we'd make it work. Even if it meant that I'd have to turn away from the Amish. I would rather be with Rose and live the English way than be without her, living a lie with another woman.

My mind made up, I was more anxious than ever to reach her and I snapped the reins again, asking Rumor for still more speed. We were fairly close now to the place I guessed she was hiding, the metal joists of the bridge just coming into view. Very soon, Rose would be with me—and I'd never let her go again.

25

Rose
The End of the World

WAITING IN THE COLD WET GRASS SEEMED LIKE forever, but checking my phone, only ten minutes had passed before I heard the first clip-clopping in the distance.

Stiffly, I stood and carefully began retracing the vague path I had made through the overgrown plants, futilely attempting to avoid more cuts. I was soaked through and even my tennis shoes were squishing beneath me. I didn't care, though; my only thought was the desire to see Noah again and feel his arms around me. After hearing his voice and the worry in it, I knew that I had to do whatever it would take to be with him—even if that meant becoming Amish.

When I'd met Noah, it was as if I'd woken from a long, sickly sleep. He had brought to me the feeling of being truly alive and I now understood that I would never get that wonderful bubbling sensation from anyone else. Noah was the only person in the world who would protect me and keep me safe. My dad had his own life to live and was too preoccupied with his job and new girlfriend to care much about what I needed. Sam had proven to be totally self-centered when it came right down to it, only caring about his own good time.

And Mom was gone.

Noah would love and take care of me, cherishing me for the rest of my life, until we were old and gray and sitting on a front porch swing. But could I really handle being Amish? Even with my resolve to be with Noah, I still wondered at that. It would be difficult for sure, maybe impossible, but I would give it my all to be with the man I loved more than anyone else in the world...and to escape the cold, lonely world that I now lived in.

The hoofbeats were closing in, and I searched in the direction of the noise, catching sight of the blinking red buggy lights. Relief washed over me. I picked up my pace with renewed energy, knowing that he was close to me now.

I struggled to engage my chilled muscles and crawl up the other side of the bank, pushing the coarse grass aside with my hands while I moved up and forward.

Noah is going to freak out when he sees the state I'm in. I slowed for an instant to catch my breath. The clip-clops were close enough now that if I yelled loudly I was sure Noah would hear me. And that knowledge gave me the incentive to push myself harder.

That's when I heard the loud rumble, the sound's intensity growing so quick that it shook the air around me. My mind dimmed and time sped up. On my knees, finally free of the vegetation, with my hands resting on the hard, abrasive surface of the asphalt, I saw it. The source of the roaring noise.

The huge white semitruck's horn blasted, rupturing the misty air like an explosion to my ears. Time moved even faster and my heart stopped, followed by my lungs. Then my worn-out muscles locked, freezing me into place. I was forced to watch helplessly in mounting horror as the truck came barreling down the narrow road.

One blink and I could see Noah's carriage clearly enough

that for the briefest instant his face came into view. His eyes were wide and his mouth open. Then the picture was gone, snapped away as if deleted from a camera, replaced by the white blur of the truck skidding by me.

The screeching sound of the tires seared into my head as the giant machine frantically tried to stop. Its brakes locked into place, the monster groaned and cracked with the effort. Each sound sliced through my body like a knife.

The battle was lost as the trailer flipped sideways, covering the road with its enormous body, still surging forward with unrelenting speed and force, unable to be stopped by man or nature.

I felt faint from the spinning in my head. What was left of my brain screamed for me to shut my eyes, but I couldn't do it. They were held open by invisible pins.

Another second passed.

I couldn't see anything except the white mass of metal careening down the road, blocking out the sky and obliterating everything. The sound of Rumor's scream mixed with the crunching and racking of metal and ripped across the world.

Time abruptly stopped when at last, the mechanical beast fell silent.

Somehow in the haze of the cataclysm, my legs came to life, and I surged onto the road, running over the scarred and torn-up pavement. With the grayness of shock pushing into my mind, I managed to pull the phone out and, still running, dialed 911. Only a second, and the clinical voice on the other end said, "Nine-one-one—what's your emergency?"

I found my voice. "Accident…tractor trailer and buggy… Stone House Road…near bridge."

"Could you repeat that, ma'am?"

I was at the belly of the behemoth, the smell of rubber and friction poisoning the air, and I couldn't believe the size of it.

The stranger's voice sliced into my shocked head. "Did you say Stone House Road?"

I was able to give one more reply before the adrenaline took hold of my body. "Yes, Stone House Road, come fast. *Please*." My voice cracked, the sound not real, not my own.

My body worked of its own accord, stumbling and half running around the left side of the truck. The cab hung off the road, leading me once again down a steep embankment in an effort to get around the demolished machine.

Finding strength from somewhere deep inside, I scrambled up the other side. The scene that met my eyes caused me to hesitate a second before I ran straight into hell.

My eyes were locked on Rumor; lying on his side, the buggy nearly unrecognizable, crumpled like a piece of black paper that had been wadded up into a ball against his body. His loud grunting filled my ears and my stomach rolled violently when I saw his front legs snapped at the cannon bones. The pearly knobs jutted out, bright red blood gushing over them.

In the horse's terror and pain, he began flopping, trying desperately to get up onto mangled legs that would never support his body again. The muffled pounding of what was left of his legs mashing into the pavement lightened my head and without any control, acidy bile rose up in my throat and out my mouth.

Brushing my wet lips with the back of my hand, I recovered enough to take the six or so strides needed to reach the poor horse. I hesitated at Rumor's bleeding and broken head, glancing at the wreckage of the buggy…where Noah was.

He must be dead. No one could survive such a thing. I couldn't breathe and the tears dripped from my eyes in a constant stream that I didn't even try to wipe away.

Rumor's pained whinny and his attempt to rise again caused me to look back at the horse and waver; the desire to go to Noah pulled at my gut. But I couldn't leave his beloved friend—I couldn't just step over his body, ignoring the large brown eyes rimmed in white from fear.

Grabbing the check piece of Rumor's bridle, I dropped to the pavement and pulled his head down to my lap, murmuring soothing words of encouragement. Seeming to understand me, he stopped struggling and rolled over to his side, breathing rapidly. As he quieted, I placed my hands over his eyes and whispered softly, "Shh, it's okay, boy. Just close your eyes and sleep now."

I was too numb with agony and shock to shed a tear for the dying horse—the ones that flowed from my eyes were for Noah. I could only keep the soft words flowing out of my mouth so that he knew he wasn't alone.

A great spasm raked Rumor's body, almost throwing me away from him, but I clung to his bloody face, until, with a shuddering breath, his life slipped away into the darkness of the night. He was still. Horribly still.

Sucking in the sob that threatened to erupt from within me, and with a bizarre disconnection from what I was experiencing, I rose and squeezed around the horse's warm body, only to slip in the blood that was pooled around him. I pulled myself back up, gripping the harness for support.

I needed to find Noah. I knew he was dead already and the devastation to my soul was complete. I felt no pain. There wasn't anything left inside me that could feel at all. But still I had to find him to say goodbye, and I crawled along Rumor's body until I could see him.

He was wedged between the horse and the buggy. In the dim light spreading out from the truck's headlights, I saw his eyes were closed. He looked peaceful in a way; certainly not as brutalized outwardly as his poor horse. Reaching his booted feet first, I felt my way up his legs, stopping when my hand touched the warm wetness. I brought my fingers to my face and realized that it was Noah's blood. His leg was cut up badly. I blocked the vision of his destroyed limb out of my mind and continued to crawl under the splintered shaft, until I squeezed in next to his body.

Softly, I began to probe his upper body with my fingers in the muted light. Movement jolted my senses. I was sure I felt his chest rise. As if to answer an unspoken prayer, the clouds divided, allowing a slice of moonlight to shine down on the carnage.

I could see his face clearly in the spray of light. His mouth was working, trying to form words that wouldn't come. Dropping my face to his, I felt his breath stirring the air ever so slightly, and my hand that rested over his heart was lifted up and down softly with his weak breathing.

My heart began to pound madly—*he's alive.*

"I'm here, Noah—it's okay. You're going to be all right."

I hardly believed it myself, but the little speck of hope gave me the strength to bring the phone out. Quickly, I hit the saved number. Now that there was the possibility that he would be okay, my body came alive again as if waking from unconsciousness, and I began to cry and gulp for air.

"Where are you, Rose?" Sam's voice registered in the far reaches of my mind. He sounded incredibly relieved.

"A semitruck hit Noah's buggy. He's still alive, Sam. Come now—*I need you,*" I blurted out in near hysteria.

He didn't question what I said, only saying, "Holy shit. Where the hell are you?"

Thankfully, he didn't sound drunk, and I pushed the words out of my quivering mouth. "I'm near the bridge on Stone House Road. Hurry, Sam—please, hurry!"

"Are you hurt, Rose?" I could hear his truck door slam and the engine start up through the phone.

"I'm fine," I mumbled, dropping the phone and lying down alongside Noah's body. I wasn't really listening to Sam anymore. Noah's mouth had stopped moving, and he was so still. *Still like Rumor.* My hand couldn't detect any breath from his nose or mouth and the rising and falling from his chest stalled.

Pressing my head to his heart, I listened hard, straining to hear any gurgle or murmur of life. Hearing nothing, I felt the shock settle into my mind, slowing it down and then turning it off.

I didn't know what to do. The fear of jostling his body or attempting CPR wrapped around me like a cocoon—I was a doctor's daughter, but I had no emergency training myself. *I couldn't help him.*

"Don't leave me, Noah. Please, don't go," I whispered into the darkness as the light spray of rain touched my face.

If only I could turn back time.

I would tell him yes.

26

Noah
Darkness

THE COLD BLACKNESS WAS PRESSING IN ON ME, chilling me to the bone. With my hands stretched out, I frantically tried to move forward, searching for her—feeling for her in the darkness.

Where was she?

She had been beside me. Her warm, soft body heating my side, and her voice, gentle against my ear. Where did she go? Why did she leave me?

My worried mind screamed her name over and over. *Rose.*

27

Rose
The Long Wait

THE WONDERFUL PEACE OF DREAMLESS SLEEP was broken by Sam's voice. Why wouldn't he just go away? I couldn't make out all his words, only hearing the distress in his voice as he screamed my name over and over.

The wail of the sirens was what finally crumbled the darkness from my mind. I remembered now. Noah was next to me, dead.

Agony exploded in my head, and I tried to call to my brother, the words coming out dry and weak. "Here, I'm here, Sam… here."

I feared that the sound wasn't loud enough, but a couple of blinks later, Sam called out, closer now, "Rose? Rose?"

With an effort that pained my throat, I tried again. "Sam."

I could hear him cussing as he climbed through the wreckage, and then he was next to me, touching my face frantically.

Other voices were now jumping through the air around us, unrecognizable, but kind and strong sounding. The sirens kept coming and the sky was suddenly bright with flashing lights, making me squeeze my eyes shut.

"Rose, are you hurt, too?" Sam's voice was solid, dragging me further into the sickening reality.

"No, no, I'm fine. It's Noah. Sam, he's dead."

Before Sam answered me, I felt other hands poking me urgently, and then a second later I was being slid out from under the shaft and wrapped in a heavy, scratchy wool blanket.

A fireman carried me a little ways from the wreck and gently placed me on the side of the road.

"Please let me stay with him," I begged, my voice still weak and not working right.

Ignoring me, the man asked anxiously, "Were you in the accident? Where's this blood coming from that's all over you?"

"No, not me…it's Rumor's blood," I stammered.

"That's the horse," I heard Sam say as he hovered over me.

When the man was convinced that I wasn't injured, he hurried back to what was left of the buggy.

Sam's arms hugged me tightly. Even though I had a vague impression of being angry with him, my memories were jumbled. I couldn't remember, so I leaned my head into his chest instead.

We sat in silence watching the six firefighters and two paramedics extract Noah from the wreckage, carefully lifting Rumor away from him. They cut away the shafts and harness with a combination of bolt cutters and a small handsaw. The sound of the tools sent shivers through my insides, but outwardly I didn't move a muscle.

From the corner of my eye, I was aware of another group of yellow-coated men pulling the driver from the truck. I didn't care about him, though, and I looked away without compassion.

Studying the scene in detached observation, I followed every move the emergency workers made, until mere minutes later they had Noah on the gurney.

Feeling that Sam had relaxed his grip on me, I pulled away

from him and bolted to my feet with every intention of going with Noah in the ambulance.

"No, Rose, you can't go with him." Sam's voice cracked like a whip while his arms folded around my waist, holding me back.

Even in my brain-dead state, I knew I could never get away from him, but still I struggled, desperate to not be separated from Noah. The sirens were so loud, penetrating the air, and the sobs that I had been holding in finally broke free. Closing my eyes, I let Sam catch me as my legs gave way and I slipped into the nothingness of utter despair.

Oh, God, why?

Why was I being punished for my decision? My beautiful, strong Noah was broken and ruined—maybe dying—all because of me. The knowledge was chewing away at my insides, leaving a raw, hollow space behind. The fog had faded from my mind by the time we reached the hospital. Now my head throbbed with a pain so deep and sharp that I felt as though I was dying.

My face was a sloppy mess of tears, mixed with dirt and blood—Noah's and Rumor's blood. The stuff was all over me and I didn't care in the least. I didn't care about anything but Noah right now. He was the only thing in the world that mattered to me. I couldn't live without him. *I wouldn't.* My mind screamed, if only this were just a dream—a devastating nightmare that I'd soon wake up from—as the hot tears slipped from my eyes, following the well-worn tracks down my cheeks.

A police officer walked over while I was standing on tiptoe trying to see into the emergency room where Dad and the nurses were frantically working to save Noah's life; I couldn't see much of anything. The windows were small and there were so many hospital personnel in the room blocking my view. The light was terribly bright, piercing my swollen eyes, making it difficult to focus clearly on any one spot.

"Miss, I understand that you were the one who called about the accident with the buggy?" He said it kindly, and I'd been doing an okay job of holding myself together up to that point, but hearing it out loud made me gulp for air and crumple to the floor like a rag doll. I couldn't talk about; it was just too awful. I squeezed my drowning eyes shut, trying desperately to erase the horrendous images that sprang into my mind.

Sam was suddenly there on the ground with me, pulling me up. "Hey, listen, she knew the guy that was in the buggy. They were real close," I vaguely heard him say as he held my weak, quivering body up. I was sure that if he let go, I'd be on the ground again.

"And you are...?" I risked a glance at the officer who was freakishly tall. Meeting my eyes for an instant, he looked back at Sam. His voice was strangely gentle for such a big guy.

Sam cleared his voice. "I'm Sam Cameron and this is my little sister, Rose."

Just when he said it, I felt the air stir, and the cool breeze pushing in from the open doors sent a shiver through me. I felt their eyes on me before I actually saw them, that weird sixth sense telling me they were there. And when I looked up, they were there, Noah's parents, standing in the entranceway of the hospital, accusing eyes directed at me.

Before I had a chance to go to them and beg for their forgiveness, a nurse ran by into Noah's room, shouting, "Life Star is here...!"

A minute later, the door flung open. Noah was on a hospital gurney, being pushed out of the room in a frenzy of activity. I only got a glimpse of his ruffled hair.

I tried to go to him, struggling against Sam's firm hold. I needed to tell him I'd made a mistake and that I loved him, loved him more than anything in the world. But no matter how I twisted and strained, Sam wouldn't release me. He held me back, probably thinking it was for my own good. But instead, he was killing me, forcing me to watch helplessly while Noah's parents rushed to his side and out the building with him to the waiting helicopter.

More tears welled up in my sore eyes and the air hardly reached my lungs as I stared at the glass door. There went my whole life out that door—and maybe it would be the last time I'd ever see him.

My tired mind felt the thought come trickling in on butterfly wings. Yes, I had already made the decision when I was lying in the tangle of brush beside the roadway—I knew what I had to do now.

Right when the decision was cemented into my brain, Dad appeared and engulfed me in his strong arms, picking me off the ground as if I was a little girl again. Any anger I had been carrying toward him for the past few weeks was instantly erased. I clung to him tighter than I did even when Mom died.

He smoothed my hair down my back for a brief time. Then leaning away from me, he lifted my chin, meeting my eyes.

"Rose, calm down and listen to me. Noah has a good chance of survival. I stabilized him and now he's being airlifted to Cincinnati's Good Samaritan."

I stuttered out between breaths, "Is he paralyzed?"

Seeing his shaking head before even hearing his words filled me with glowing relief. "No, Rose, he's not paralyzed, but he has internal bleeding, a serious head wound and a fractured leg."

"Do you really think he'll live?" I pleaded more than asked him.

"All his injuries appear to be manageable, especially once he arrives at Samaritan. They're larger and have a more equipped trauma unit." He paused to catch his breath, obviously still pumped up from the rush to save Noah's life. Then he asked me, looking into my eyes with a doctor's searching gaze, "Can you understand me, Rose?"

Nodding my head, I murmured, "Uh-huh."

"Amos and Rebecca Miller are not going to be allowed to ride in the helicopter with Noah. Even if they could, I doubt their traditions would allow it. So I'm going to offer to drive them to Cincinnati tonight. I want you to go home with Sam and get some rest. I'll call you when I know anything for sure."

"Can't I come with you, Dad?" I begged, choking back a sob.

Sighing, he took a handkerchief from his pocket and began wiping my face softly while he answered, "No, Rosie, that wouldn't be appropriate under the circumstances. I don't want to do anything that might upset Noah's parents more than they already are."

I bobbed my head once in acknowledgment, hating his words but knowing they were true.

Dad then turned his attention to Sam. "I want you to take her home and make sure she has a shower to get this blood and grime washed off. Then I want you to put antiseptic lotion on these cuts and put her to bed. Do you have all that, Sam?"

"Yeah, sure thing, Dad," he said in an unusually subdued voice.

Dad let go of me, and while he was moving toward the entrance, he glanced back at me, promising, "I'll call you when I have any news."

Then he was gone, and the agonizing wait began.

28

Noah
The Light at the End of the Tunnel

FROM SOMEWHERE FAR AWAY CAME A VOICE, and I strained to listen. It was Father. He sounded desperate. Then, as my mind cleared, leaving the dream behind, I felt hands on my face, and abruptly the voice was loud in my ears.

"Son—son, wake now. Rose is fine. You're having an ill dream."

Hearing her name out loud, I snapped my eyes open. The world was fuzzy at first. I could tell where Father's face was, but I couldn't make out any of his features. I tried to blink away the vagueness, and after several attempts, my sight began to slowly return.

I could see his worry now, and then I noticed Mother on the other side of the bed. She was gently holding my hand, rubbing it with her fingers. I breathed in deep with relief that I could feel her hand at all. Several things hit me at once: first, the crisp, cool sheets against my skin…second, the stark, bright whiteness of the room…and third, probably the most profound, the aches that immediately seemed to invade my senses from every part of my body.

But where was Rose? Why wasn't she here with me? My mind was still blurred with confusion. In an attempt to look around the room I shifted in the bed, directing my limbs to move. They responded somewhat, but sluggishly. In frustration, I began to struggle and, for the first time, felt the sharp tugging of the tubes poking into my arm and stuck up my nose.

"Where's...Rose?" I sputtered in a weak voice that sounded strange to me.

Father's hands were instantly on me, holding me down. His voice said gently, "She's at her home, Noah, and she's perfectly all right. Now, calm yourself, and we'll talk."

"The truck—it didn't hit her?" I asked, panic still gripping my heart.

"No, no. She wasn't in the accident. But she was there, Noah. She saw it happen," Father said with a twinge of something in his voice I couldn't quite understand in my frazzled state.

"Why isn't she here?" When neither of my parents answered, I shifted my head to Mother and said forcefully, "I want her here with me."

She sighed deeply, and without letting go of my hand, she sat down on the chair near the bed and cleared her throat. When she spoke, she sounded so tired, and I realized how difficult this ordeal must be for her.

"Noah, why were you out on that road with your buggy?" she asked softly, squeezing my hand tighter as she said the words.

The memories were cloudy, and I had to think for a minute. I remembered talking to Rose on the phone, and her wavering, upset voice. I remembered that she had left a party because some guy had bothered her, and she was alone in a field. I remembered she needed me, and I went to get her. To rescue her from whatever mess she'd gotten herself into.

And I was almost to her, when the lights of the truck appeared, and the blaring sound of the horn thundered through the night air. Those were the last things I could pull from my mind. Straining, I tried to recall the impact…but I couldn't. My mind had blocked that memory from me. The last thing I could recollect was the fear that had stabbed me when I thought that Rose had been run over by the truck, and then the peaceful relief that had come over me when she appeared beside me, and I felt her lying there, near me.

After everything that had happened, I no longer feared my parents. Seeing the exhausted worry on their faces, I believed they would support me in any decision I made.

Finding my raspy voice, I said, "I called Rose to talk to her…see how she was doing. She told me she had left a party on foot because a guy had been harassing her." Pausing, I watched for their reactions, which appeared to be rapt curiosity, so I continued, "She was stranded in a field, all alone, and I couldn't leave her like that. She didn't want me to come, though. She didn't want me to get into trouble."

"Yet, you went anyway," Father finished with a heavy sigh.

Looking into his eyes, I quietly said, "I love Rose, Father. I can't erase the feelings I have for her just because you want me to."

Grimly he said, "You are very blessed, Noah, that you weren't killed in that accident. You need to focus your energies on recovering, not on the English girl."

Anger flared in me at his words. "I need Rose in order to recover, Father. It's not just about my body. It's about my heart."

"The doctors tell us that you have a small fracture on your skull, bruised ribs, a fractured leg and a punctured lung, among other injuries. All will heal in time, but your body is definitely in worse shape than your heart at this point," Father pointed out gruffly, sarcasm creeping into his words.

"I need to see her, Father. I need to talk to her about something," I pleaded in a low voice, figuring if he wouldn't grant my request following a near-death experience, he never would.

I watched him glance at Mother, who nodded her head. Then he turned back to me, saying, "I know what you want to talk to her about, son." After a long pause he went on, "All right, I'll see if she can come."

"Thank you, Father."

For the next hour or so, I was poked and prodded by a number of doctors and nurses. My eyes were tired of the flashes of light, and I was thoroughly sick of repeating my birth date, address and the names of all my siblings over and over to prove to them that I didn't have significant brain damage. One younger doctor had joked that if I could remember all those names, I must be in good shape.

Just as the last nurse left the room, leaving me alone with Father and Mother, Dr. Cameron walked in. He sat down in the corner with my parents for several minutes explaining as best he could exactly about my injuries. I was sure they didn't understand half of what they were being told. I sure didn't, but the man was trying pretty hard and they were doing the best they could to listen.

When Dr. Cameron finished talking, he rose up fluidly and crossed the room to me, placing his warm hand on the inside of my wrist while he studied my eyes.

"You're a very lucky young man, Noah," he said in a friendly tone, going on to say, "Within a few months you'll be back building houses and riding horses."

Without thinking about the rudeness of it, I said, "I want to see Rose."

His eyes widened for a second, but he regained his composure quickly and glanced at my parents questioningly.

Father cleared his throat, and rubbing his beard uncomfortably, he said, "David, I would understand if you didn't allow this…but, Noah really wants to talk to your daughter. I think it would relieve the anxiety he's feeling if she was here with him."

Dr. Cameron looked from Father to me, and sighing, he pulled the phone from his pocket as he left the room.

The couple of minutes he took to return seemed like an hour. But when he did stroll back into the room, he nodded his head, saying, "Sam's going to bring her. They're on their way."

"Thank you," I said, feeling instantly better as I settled back into the bed, letting the tension go that I hadn't even realized I was holding in.

Turning back to my parents, he said, "I have to get back to the hospital in Meadow View now, but I'll be in contact with the doctors here, and when Noah is ready to be released, I'd be happy to make arrangements for you all to be driven home."

Father stepped forward and grasped Dr. Cameron's hand tightly, and with an emotional voice, he said, "Thank you so much for all that you did for our son and for taking your time to bring us here. We will always be indebted to you for your kindness at such a dark moment."

"I was just happy to help in any way I could…and I believe that your son had a guardian angel watching over him last night." He stared at me for a few seconds before going on to say, "I appreciate what you did, Noah—going out with your buggy to get Rose and bring her home." There was an awkward pause, as if Dr. Cameron had more to say but wasn't sure if he should, before he turned back to Father and said, "If you or Rebecca would like a ride back to your farm later today, I'm sure Sam could drive you when he heads home. Just let him know. I estimate that Noah will be kept here for six or seven more days."

"Yes, thank you for the offer. We've contacted our driver and are working out the details," Father informed him politely.

"Well, I'll see you all soon," Dr. Cameron said, sweeping out of the room, in a hurry to move on to other emergencies, I imagined.

Closing my eyes, I decided to try to sleep a little bit before Rose arrived. My head was filling with shadows again from all the drugs the nurses were pumping into me through the tubes. I hoped to be more alert when I finally got to talk to her. Once my eyelids blocked out the bright light, my mind slipped away into the darkness.

The soft lips that were pressing against my forehead and the warm flowers filling my nostrils told me she was finally here, gently pulling me from unconsciousness.

Happiness teased me as I opened my eyes, turning quickly to shock when I saw her face. Dark circles beneath her eyes sharply contrasted with the blue of the eyes themselves. Even more alarming was a long, jagged scratch sliced across her cheek.

Reaching up with the hand that was free of needles, I softly trailed my finger across the cut. Worry filling me, I asked, "Are you okay, Rose?"

She threw back her head and laughed heartily. The sound was music to my ears. When she straightened out and could speak, a grin touched her mouth. "Aren't I supposed to be asking you that, Noah?"

"I'm better now that you're here," I said flirtatiously, dismissing the fact that Mother and Father were only a few feet away watching me. I was feeling pretty bold right then.

It felt good.

She leaned in closer, and I could smell her wonderful scent again while she studied my face.

In a near whisper, she exclaimed, "You look terrible, Noah. Like a raccoon."

Now I was the one laughing, and it really hurt, so I breathed in sharply to cut off my amusement quickly. I had forgotten all about my black eyes and the stunned look on her pretty face would have brought the laughter back, if she hadn't placed her fingertips over my eyes, softly caressing them. At that point I just relaxed, shutting my eyes to let her touch work its magic.

The sound of two throats clearing burst through the room, and for the first time I noticed Sam standing at the end of one side of the bed. Then my gaze was drawn to Father, who held a slight frown on his mouth while he stood on the other. Rose either didn't notice the others' discomfort or didn't care, because she continued to move her fingers softly over my face, ignoring her brother and my parents completely.

Inwardly, I smiled about that. While I was dealing with the pleasant little tingles her fingers left behind, and the jabbing pain in my ribs, I said, "Thanks, Sam, for bringing Rose to the city."

"Oh, no problem, bro, just glad you're still alive," he said as he made his way to the chair by the window, flopping down in it.

I really wanted to talk to Rose alone, but Sam looked settled in for a while, causing me to sigh in irritation.

"Sam, my boy, why don't you join the missus and me for dinner in the cafeteria. It'll be my treat. I've been told the food isn't too bad," Father said in a friendly yet determined voice.

Breathing deeply in exaggerated annoyance, Sam rose from the chair. "Yeah, I get the idea. The lovebirds want to be alone."

After my parents were through the door, Sam smirked back and before disappearing, he said smugly, "I guess I don't really have to worry about you getting carried away with my sister—not in your condition anyway."

The guy really irked me. I decided that he would be a very difficult brother-in-law to have as I focused my attention back on Rose, who, seeing that we were now alone, brought her lips ever so softly to mine.

Even in my near-dead state, the feeling was still amazing. But it didn't last long enough, when she pulled back, staring at me with a faraway, glazed look in her eyes.

"I thought you were dead, Noah," she said, a single tear appearing at the corner of her eye.

If I had been in better shape, I would have yanked her into a snug embrace, but at the moment all I could do was caress her hands with my one usable one.

"But I'm alive and healable, so why are you crying? You should be incredibly happy," I teased.

"Oh, I am happy. That's why I'm crying again," she mumbled wetly, wiping her face on the sheet like a little girl with a cold.

"You cry too much, Rose. I can hardly keep up with your tears." I said it jokingly, but secretly, I kind of meant it.

"Why do our lives have to be so...complicated...and difficult?"

I thought for a while before answering. "Maybe God's throwing all our troubles at us now, when we're young and strong enough to deal with them. Which means someday our lives will be incredibly boring."

She rested her chin on the bed railing, pursing her lips, and considering my statement, she muttered, "I just want life to be boring now. Not when we're old and gray."

I longed to comfort her, make her forget all her troubles, but there were still so many obstacles standing in the way of our happiness. I tried anyway, saying, "Everything is going to be okay, Rose. We're together right now and we're both alive. That's all that matters."

I said it hoping that the words would cheer her up, but utterly confusing me, they had the opposite effect and she began crying again. Moving my hand to her cheek, I wiped the tears with my fingers and begged, "What's wrong now, sweetheart?"

In between gasps for breath she stuttered, "I'm so sorry about Rumor… I was with him when…he died. It was awful."

Interestingly enough, I hadn't asked anyone about my horse. Somehow I knew he was dead, and I had pushed it to the back of my mind. I didn't really even want to think about it. Now looking at Rose's stricken face, the horror of what had happened to my poor horse hit me full force.

Her tears flowed freely and she leaned over to press her wet face against mine. I kept my own tears bottled inside. But the water from her eyes was enough for both of us, soaking my cheeks as if I were crying also.

"I'm sorry you had to see that, but in a way I'm glad you were with him. That he wasn't alone," I whispered hoarsely into her ear.

Her body rocked with the tremors of her sobs. She sucked in with a gulp before saying feebly but with more control to her voice now, "He died with his head in my lap. He just went to sleep. He didn't suffer long."

"Rumor was the best horse in the world. He was always

willing to do whatever task I asked of him—and he was smart, too, for a horse." I paused, collecting my emotions before going on, "I'll never have another horse like him, I'm afraid," I said, sadly wistful.

She jerked back then, so abruptly it startled me.

Her eyes suddenly shinning, she said, "But you have little Rebel—he'll be a good horse for you."

Her enthusiasm was sweet, but that little colt was an obnoxious headache. Biting and kicking all the other horses, even though he was half their size. And then there was the irritating fact that I could barely catch the little demon in the field.

"Where did this name Rebel come from anyway?" I asked, frowning. I couldn't remember ever having named the beast.

Coyly, she shrugged. Doing the flirty thing with her eyes, she said, "Oh, I named him that the night you bought him at the sale. It just seemed to fit him." Suddenly appearing unsure of herself, she added, "But, Noah, you can call him anything you want."

"Well, that name actually suits him fairly well—so Rebel it is, then."

For some strange reason, whenever Rose was truly happy about something, and she smiled that big smile at me, my heart loosened, and I felt weak all over, weaker even than my broken body was now.

"I'm so glad you like the name," she breathed excitedly, her face beaming.

I wondered if she'd still be happy when I told her of my decision. I stared into her eyes, searching for her thoughts, and just when I was about to say that I would leave the Amish to be with her, she blurted out in a rush of words, "Oh, Noah, I've changed my mind about becoming Amish! I'll do anything it takes to be with you—anything."

The breath caught in my throat, and I swallowed. Rose was willing to abandon her world and become Amish after all? My mind rationalized very quickly that the two of us raising a family in the Amish community was much better than me going English. But still, knowing that I had been so close to making the sacrifice, I felt a stab of guilt that I'd let her go ahead and do it and that my horrific accident had propelled her to make the decision. But my selfish mind didn't really care what changed her mind—as long as she had. Everything would be okay now. We could begin courting and be married by next year this time. I only wished that I could give her a real hug, but I guessed that would be something I could look forward to in the near future.

"Are you sure about this, Rose?" I needed her to say it again to convince me I wasn't still dreaming.

"Yes, Noah. I am absolutely, completely certain about it. I'll become Amish…and be your wife," she said, sounding cheerfully determined.

Plans were already running through my mind, and I forged ahead. "We'll need to tell my parents so they can make arrangements for you to stay with another Amish family in the community—are you going to be okay living with strangers?" I started to have doubts trickling in and worrying me.

"I'll be fine with it, Noah. It's my dad who's going to be the problem." After a pause where she scrunched up her face in thought, she whispered, color flooding her pale skin, "I'd even go through with the—you know—baby idea you had, if you think it would help."

I couldn't keep from chuckling even though it killed my sides. She was so willing at the moment that I believed I could get her to agree to anything. That thought was very intriguing, but I was good and said, "I don't think we'll need to take such drastic measures as that now. If worse comes to worst, you'll be eighteen in a year and a few months and then you'll be able to do whatever you want." Suddenly realizing I didn't want to wait that long to be with her, I quickly added, "But maybe my parents can talk your father into it."

"We'll have to wait and see, I guess." She yawned big.

"Were you up all night?"

"Mmm-hmm…" She yawned again.

"Why don't you come up here and lie beside me," I said, trying to keep the suggestive grin from my mouth, but unsuccessfully.

Frowning, she replied, "I couldn't do that, Noah. You're all banged up, and I might hurt you."

"My right leg is the broken one. But see—" I motioned to the ten inches available on my left side "—there's more than enough room for you over here."

"Won't your doctors get mad?"

"Oh, who cares what they think. After last night, don't you think we deserve some time together?" I said encouragingly, hoping she'd agree.

My own eyes were getting droopy again and the prospect of falling asleep with her by my side was very appealing.

Glancing toward the door, she grinned and said, "Okay."

After slipping off her tennis shoes, very slowly and extremely cautiously, she crawled up from the bottom of the bed, squeezing in between the railing and my side. She was overly careful not to touch my body, keeping her arms pressed up to her chest.

Once her head touched the pillow, she murmured, "I am sleepy."

Within a minute, I could hear her soft, deep breaths and I

knew she was sound asleep. Just when I was going to join her in dreamland, a nurse walked into the room, her eyes bugging out when she saw Rose next to me.

"Young man, I don't think any of the doctors on your chart would approve of your...friend being in the bed with you," she said, tilting her head, with a deep frown.

Thinking fast, I played on her womanly sympathies. "I probably shouldn't be telling you all this, ma'am, but you see, Rose is English and I'm Amish, which means we can't be together. And we're very much in love. That's why I'm lying here in this hospital bed right now, because our families wouldn't let us be together. I had to sneak off to meet her in the middle of the night. This might be the last time we're allowed near each other." I paused for dramatic effect. "So if the doctors don't know, it won't hurt them—and it would mean so much to me if she stayed."

Her face continued to soften while I spoke and by the time I was finished, I could have sworn her eyes were wet.

Wiping her eyes absently, she said, "Oh, all right."

She moved quietly around me, trying not to wake Rose as she took my blood pressure, temperature and pulse. She also removed the oxygen tubes from my nostrils, deeming me able to breathe on my own, to my great relief. When she finally completed all her tasks, she headed for the doorway. Turning, she smiled sadly at me before walking out.

Just when the relief that she was gone filled me, Father, Mother and Sam returned. All three pairs of eyes widened at the sight of Rose sleeping beside me. Before any of them could say a thing, I put my finger to my lips to silence them and whispered, "Father, Mother, I need to talk to you both alone."

"You've got to be kidding me," Sam barked.

"Shh," I warned him.

"Oh, don't worry about her, Noah. Once she's asleep, it's near impossible to wake her," he said smartly, knowing it would bother me that he knew something about Rose that I didn't.

Father surprised me then, saying to Sam, "Why don't you go on home, Sam, before it gets dark. Rose can stay the night with us, and our driver will take her and the missus home in the morning."

What he said was reasonable enough, and he had spoken convincingly, but seeing Sam's narrowed eyes looking at his sister, I wondered if he'd agree.

"I don't think that's a good idea."

"Oh, but leaving her alone with one of your drunken buddies was?" I was angry that he had the nerve to think he knew what was best for Rose.

My words cut him, I knew, seeing the conflict settle onto his face.

"Fine. If Dad has a problem with it, he can come get her. I have things to do," he said, turning on his heel and marching out of the room.

"Was that really necessary, Noah? After all, his father saved your life," Father said.

"Actually, it was, because if he had taken better care of Rose, she wouldn't have been out walking the road in the middle of the night."

Father nodded in understanding and Mother approached the bed, timidly, brushing Rose's hair out of her face with her fingertips.

"She is such a lovely girl, even with that nasty scratch on her cheek," Mother commented, lightly touching the cut before retreating to the lounge chair in the corner of the room.

"Father, Rose has decided to become Amish," I told him,

suddenly feeling very much awake as I stared into his face, watching the astonished look develop.

"Are you sure, son, that she understands exactly what she is agreeing to?" he said as he placed his hands on the bed rails, looking down at Rose and studying her face for the first time.

"Yes, I've explained most of the details to her."

"Noah, you must know that your accident probably had bearing on her decision," he pointed out in a level voice, still staring at Rose.

"Maybe it does, but that doesn't matter to me, Father. We love each other, and I know that we're meant to spend our lives together. Can't you just be happy for me that she's agreed?"

"I only worry that in time, when the fear of almost losing you wears off, she'll regret her decision, and you or possibly your children will be affected. Noah, your mother and I don't want you to be hurt—but if you remain in the church and follow the Ordnung with this young woman by your side, we will be happy for you."

"Thank you, Father." And I glanced over at Mother, who seemed to be tolerating the conversation extremely well.

"But what about her family, Noah? Will they actually allow us to take her from them?" he asked with a raised brow.

Looking down at her beautiful dark head nestled against my shoulder, I felt confident saying, "It doesn't matter what they think, Father. Rose will be my wife someday—and no one is going to stop that from happening."

29

Rose
A New Beginning

IT SEEMED AS IF ALL I DID ANYMORE WAS WAIT. I lay draped across the mattress in my comfy cotton shorts and sleep shirt, with the warm afternoon sun spilling onto me from the window. The music coming from the clock radio was low, and I couldn't help yawning sleepily.

The only plus to Noah being in the hospital was the telephone beside his bed. He had definitely worn the thing out the past couple of weeks. The hospital stay had grown from the expected weeklong event into a three-week ordeal, after the doctors realized that their Amish patient would not be able to rest and recover on the busy farm as easily as he could in the city.

I grinned to myself wondering if his parents had any idea that their son was spending his nights talking to me on the phone for hours until the sun started to rise in the sky each day. The phone calls were the only things that kept me sane over the past few days since Dad had ordered me home from the hospital. But that didn't matter now, because today, Noah was coming home.

I could barely control my happiness, especially since the Millers had invited us over for dinner tonight. Not that dinner interested me that much. I hadn't really had an appetite since the accident. It was that I'd get to see Noah again, and we were taking the first step toward being officially together. Noah had told me that tonight his parents were planning to discuss my whole conversion with Dad. That thought made me feel sick, causing my heart to pound unnaturally hard and the breath to catch in my throat.

Would Dad actually go for it? I highly doubted it, but as Noah said, in a little over a year I'd be old enough to do it without his approval anyway. I didn't want to wait, though. All I wanted to do was get on with my life with Noah, and the prospect of waiting all that time would be difficult.

Yeah, I was definitely intimidated by the whole Amish thing—for sure. I'd be wearing a dress and covering my head with one of those uncomfortable caps for the rest of my life. But after almost losing Noah, feeling the earth-shattering pain of that experience, I knew what I had to do and where I belonged. It was completely bizarre how Mr. and Mrs. Miller were treating me now, as though I was already part of their family. The day I came home from the hospital, Mrs. Miller had insisted I stop by their house first so she could gently apply a soothing home-remedy ointment on all my cuts. She was acting very motherly. I felt as if I was a five-year-old again, being fixed up by soft, maternal hands.

She even took the opportunity to measure me for a new dress she said she'd make for me, telling me I could have one of Sarah's extra caps. She also informed me that pretty much any simple black shoes would do. I secretly hoped that included the cool black Nikes I bought last spring.

All in all, our time alone together, while the other girls were out working in the garden, was pleasant enough. She wasn't the scary woman I'd originally thought she was. But I had to admit that all her questions about my mother's pregnancies were mildly disconcerting. She would definitely be the type of mother-in-law who would hound me about grandkids. I guess if that's the worst I had to deal with, I could handle it.

Glancing at the clock, I could see it was almost five. Noah should be home any minute now, and he was under direct orders to call me right when he arrived. Stretching, and with one more big yawn, I rolled off the mattress and proceeded to pull on the same brown dress I'd worn to the church service that seemed so long ago now. I figured even though it wasn't an Amish dress, at least it was a dress and I should start playing the part. I also pulled my heavy hair up into a bun, using several clips to hold it in place.

They didn't work well. Almost instantly, wisps of hair were escaping, curving around my face. Maybe my hair would be too thick to stay in one of those little white caps? But then again, I groaned, figuring the other women probably had some supertorture pins that would hold anyone's hair up.

Hearing a car's engine, I drifted to the window and peeked out to see *Her* getting out of her car. I wasn't too happy at first that Dad had invited his girlfriend to go with us to the Millers', but then the idea occurred to me that maybe she'd be the perfect distraction for Dad when the Millers talked to him. She had been Dad's constant companion lately, and I hardly ever saw him without her by his side. They were obviously smitten with each other, and I finally had to admit to myself that the woman was probably going to be a permanent fixture in our lives now.

Hiding behind the curtains, I spread them just enough with my fingers to observe her walking to the house. She wore tan dress pants and a pretty, white button-up blouse. The outfit would have been perfectly appropriate for any usual dinner date, but going to an Amish household, I looked at her with more scrutinizing eyes and decided her blouse showed too much cleavage and her pants clung to her legs, revealing their shapeliness.

The phone ringing made me lose interest in the woman, and I jumped on the bed, answering it in one fluid motion.

"Hello?"

"Hey there, sweetheart." His voice sounded strong, with a hint of amusement.

"Are you home?" I squealed.

"Yep, I just pulled into the driveway. Mother wanted to settle me in on the couch immediately, but I insisted on calling you first," he informed me.

"How are you feeling today?" I was still plagued with worry about his injuries. Now that he was home, I was sure he'd overdo it, wearing himself out.

"Pretty good. I didn't take any of the pain meds last night— they make me so loopy. So today I'm feeling the soreness more, but at least my head is clear."

"Are you using the crutches?"

"Yeah, walking on them bothers my ribs a bit. Still, I'm able to get around by myself, which is worth the pain."

"I'm so sorry, Noah," I told him quietly, still feeling tremendously guilty that all his pain was directly due to my irrational behavior leaving the dumb party.

"Don't you start crying again, Rose, do you hear me?" he said forcefully.

"Yes, I'm fine. No more crying, I promise." I hoped I could keep it.

"When are you and your family coming over?" he asked.

"Pretty soon, and guess what?"

"What?" He sounded worried all of a sudden, and I had to smile at that.

With extra drama I said, "*She's* coming with us."

"Who?" More confusion permeated the word.

"You know—Dad's girlfriend," I muttered fiercely, thinking some of the painkillers must still be affecting his mind.

"Oh, her. Well, perhaps she'll keep your father's attention off you becoming Amish," he volunteered in an even tone, echoing my thoughts exactly.

"That would be a miracle, Noah. Really, I think he'll flip out when he hears," I said, nibbling on my pinkie nail.

There was a few seconds of silence before he said softly, "Don't worry, Rose, I'll be with you—and my parents are fully supporting us now. So you're not alone in this."

"I know."

"Listen, my mother is striding toward the shed right now to take on her job as nursemaid. I'll see you in a little while."

"Okay. See you soon, Noah."

"Rose?"

"Yes?"

"I love you, sweetheart," he said soothingly, almost making me forget what we were up against.

"I love you, too." I ended the call staring at my hideous wallpaper for a few minutes, totally wrapped up in an enormous amount of worry. Worry about how my dad would react to the news, worry about becoming Amish, worry that if the whole thing fell through I'd be heading off to a new school in a few days, and I definitely was in no shape for that kind of mental challenge. The queasy feeling spread through me, and I willed myself not to throw up as I smothered my head in the pillow.

The knock at the door, and Dad's voice saying it was time

to go, pulled me back together somewhat. I stood and caught a glimpse of myself in the mirror before leaving the room.

And I had to admit, I looked about as sick as I felt.

Sitting around the Millers' table was as awkward now as it was the last time. I already gave Dad's girlfriend the heads-up on the drive over about the whole Amish tradition of the men getting their food first. She seemed curiously excited about the idea, as if it was a fun adventure for her.

So now I found myself sitting between Sarah and *Her* and directly across from Noah again. Although, this meal was extremely different than the last, in that Noah hardly took his eyes off me at all. I was surprised he didn't miss his mouth with the fork the way his penetrating gaze never abandoned me. I was slightly bewildered. He didn't seem to be worried about what his parents thought anymore.

Trying to be the good, future Amish girl, I worked hard not to stare much at him. But it was difficult. The glistening colors around his eyes had actually spread out farther on his face, creating an incredibly fascinating montage of blacks, blues, purples and, around the very edge, pinks. I found my eyes drawn to his unnatural skin tones in morbid curiosity. Besides my sick obsession with his bruises, when my eyes would meet his, the fluttering in my stomach would start up, along with my thumping heart. It was interesting that his face was hardly recognizable, but his hot gazes still gave me goose bumps.

Dinner flew by under Noah's watchful eyes, and I was stunned to have *Her* working alongside me to clean up the dishes. Surprisingly, she seemed to know her way around a kitchen, and she and Mrs. Miller were in a constant state of chattering, obviously enjoying each other's company. It was just weird, I thought as I stacked the last of the dishes, how two people so completely different could be getting on so well.

"Are you very nervous about what your father will say?" Sarah murmured softly near my ear.

She hadn't said much to me throughout dinner, and up until then, I didn't realize that she had any idea about what was going down after the meal.

Searching her eyes for support, and finding it, I replied in a hushed tone, "Totally freaked out, to be exact."

She grinned big at my choice of words and rubbed my back reassuringly. I was beginning to discover that Noah wasn't the only one in the Miller family with a touchy-feely personality. It seemed whenever Mrs. Miller got the chance, she was squeezing or patting me. As if perfectly orchestrated, Sarah left me and ushered Rachel and the younger children out the door, saying it would be a nice evening for some fishing in the pond at the back of the farm. Justin rushed to join them, but Sam stayed rooted to his chair at the table. Jacob then excused himself abruptly to drive Katie home, leaving just the pertinent parties in the room, plus nosy Sam.

I glanced over at Dad, who seemed to be expecting something when he sat down close beside his girlfriend with a resigned look on his face. Mr. and Mrs. Miller took the seats across from them, beside Noah, and I, after sizing up the family dynamics in front of me, took the seat next to *Her.* I caught Sam from the corner of my eye roll his eyes as he leaned back in his chair with an obnoxious look on his face. He was ready for the show. Deciding that I wasn't going to let Sam bother me, I stared ahead, at Noah, for emotional support.

He smiled confidently back at me, not really improving my anxiety. Actually, the rolling in my stomach had returned, and I swallowed down the hot juices, praying silently that I wouldn't be sick in front of everyone.

The tension in the room multiplied during the silence, and I couldn't help bringing my finger to the corner of my lips to absently chew on the already short nail. A muffled cough came from Dad. I glanced at him and saw it written on his face that he wasn't looking forward to this conversation. His girlfriend was feeding off the tension now, fidgeting with her hands on the table, in stark contrast to Mrs. Miller, who, as expected, sat calmly, not even a twitch.

Finally, Mr. Miller spoke with a deep and sure voice. "David, it seems we have reached a time when we need to discuss our children's relationship."

Noah was studying my dad now with a look of anticipation.

"Yes, that would probably be appropriate under the circumstances." Dad's voice was guarded, and I couldn't read anything into his words.

"Rebecca and I have agreed to allow Noah to court your daughter," Mr. Miller said, with the more important issue of turning Amish still hidden from Dad.

Dad seemed to suddenly relax. Exhaling in relief, he said, "Oh, Amos, is that what you wanted to talk to me about?" He paused, smiling around the table. "Well, I'm perfectly fine with Rose dating your son."

Even the girlfriend seemed to breathe easier. In the far reaches of my mind, I wondered, why the heck would she care so much?

Mr. Miller frowned slightly, looking from Noah to me and back again, before turning toward Dad and saying, "David, I don't think you understand what I'm saying to you." After a heavy breath, he continued, "We have only agreed to allow

Noah to court your daughter because she has made the decision to...become Amish."

The words hung in the air like clothes on a wash line, just
glaringly out there in the open. I risked a peek at Dad's face
to witness it go from shock to fury. Dad was usually a pretty
coolheaded guy, but when he was mad about something—
watch out. The poor Miller family didn't know what they
were in for, and I braced in the seat, closing my eyes tight.

Dad's uncomfortable laugh snapped my eyes back open,
when he scoffed, "You're kidding, right?"

Calm as a cucumber, Mr. Miller countered, "No, I'm perfectly serious. Our children have fallen in love, and I tried to
stop it from happening, without success. Then I attempted
to keep them apart, with tragic consequences. After praying
to the Lord about the matter, I found peace that these young
people should be together."

"Look, Amos, I'm fine with them dating, but there is no
way on this earth we live on that I will allow Rose to become
Amish," he said with angry certainty.

Mr. Miller was more determined than I ever imagined
when he continued to hammer away at Dad, saying, "I understand that you wouldn't want your child to walk a different path than that which you chose for yourself, but you must
consider her desires in the matter."

Oh, great. Now Dad's head swiveled sharply to me and
with squinting eyes, he demanded, "What is going on, Rose?
Did you actually tell these people you were going to join
their cult?"

Cult was a harsh word, I thought, but seeing Noah's reas-
suring gaze on me, I found the strength to stand up to Dad
and inform him in a slightly quivering voice, "Dad, I love

Noah with all my heart. We're meant to be together. Can't you see that?"

"But what does this have to do with you becoming Amish?"

"It's just the way it has to be, sir," Noah interrupted. Now Dad's wrath was directed at him.

"If you think I'm going to let my daughter drop out of school to live in your antifeminist world, you're delusional," he said scathingly.

Mr. Miller said in a louder voice, still in pretty good control of his emotions, though, "I anticipated your feelings about the education part of this issue, and I talked to our bishop and the other ministers about this matter. We all agreed that Rose would be allowed to continue studying her learning materials in the home of the Amish family she lives with during the courtship."

A loud snort from Sam reminded me that the big lug was still in the room, and I shot the meanest look I could manage at him. I was disappointed when he just snickered at me.

The conversation was over when Dad abruptly stood, grabbing my arm and hoisting me out of the chair, as if I was a garbage bag, half-full. I caught Noah's enraged expression as he gripped the arms of the chair ready to bolt his still-broken body up, until his dad's hand caught his shoulder, holding him down.

Tears began spilling out of my eyes uncontrollably, and the wet gasp that erupted from my mouth caused Dad to loosen his hold on me slightly. Simultaneously, the girlfriend was beside me, with her arm tightly around my waist. I didn't want to lean on her, but my stupid body felt all weak with the realization that Noah and I were still being kept apart. I pushed my face into her embrace against my better judgment just before I saw Sam's eyes widen as he rose from his chair. "This conversation is over, Amos. I'm sorry, but I think it's best if these kids take a break from each other for a while." He didn't sound remorseful in the least as he pushed his girlfriend, still supporting me, toward the door.

I heard Noah say frantically, "Do something, Father."

"There'll be no talking to him right now, son. It's better to leave him be for a while."

Dad stopped at the doorway, while his girlfriend continued to hustle me toward the car, still gripping me tightly. I glanced over my shoulder to see him go back in the house, causing my heart to stumble at the thought of what he was doing. Even at the growing distance, his voice was loud and clear as he said, "Don't go convincing yourselves that I'll change my mind on this issue either, because I won't. Just forget about her, Noah—find yourself an Amish girl and leave Rose the hell alone. And if you don't stop pursuing her, damn it, she's still a minor and I'll get the law involved."

The warm August evening air folded around me as we reached the car, and I thought to myself how perfect the night could have been if Dad had seen reason. Somehow he caught up with us and I found myself being shoved into the car like a criminal, before he jumped in and revved the engine. With a spray of gravel, Dad backed up and peeled forward down the driveway. The ride home was like a wispy cloud to my battered mind. Although I vaguely noticed Sam sitting quietly beside me, I made no effort to make eye contact with him.

Locking myself in my room, I cried myself out. Lying in the dusky light on my bed, after all my emotional noises were spent, I heard raised voices downstairs. Curiosity pushed some of my grief aside, and I tiptoed into the hallway and down the stairs.

To my dismay, Sam was sitting on the bottom step already

listening to the voices coming from the family room around the corner. With only mild hesitation, and without looking in his direction, I joined him. He ignored me with the same conviction I had used on him earlier, thankfully.

"That's insane, Tina. I can't believe you'd even suggest such a thing!"

"Just listen to me, David. Love is the most powerful emotion in the world, and if these kids feel that strongly for each other, they'll find a way to be together. If you aren't careful about this, they'll just run off some night, and you won't hear from your daughter for years—if ever." Her voice was emotionally charged.

"I think you're being a little dramatic about it," he mocked, a strange tone coming from his usual friendly voice.

"I minored in psychology, and one of my interests was adolescent behavior. I would bet money that if those two don't run off, then she'll get pregnant—is that what you want?" she asked bluntly. I was surprised that this woman, whom I had despised for weeks, was now my number-one advocate.

"Of course I don't want that to happen to her. But I can control her at this point." He seemed to be wavering a little bit.

"Oh, don't fool yourself about that. Now that she has another man in her life that she thinks can take care of her, you've already lost your hold." She spoke softer, and I strained to hear.

"God, if we hadn't made this damn move, none of this would have happened. She would still be focused on doing her dancing and going to vet school."

"Some things are just meant to be."

"Why the hell did she have to grow up so fast? I feel like I've already lost her." His voice was drained of emotion, empty.

"You haven't been listening to me. You haven't lost her, *yet*.

I think if you go ahead and let her spend a few weeks with this Amish family, wearing those horrid dresses and bonnets and following all their rules, she'll be begging you to come home. Then it will be her decision, so she won't be automatically rebelling against your authority."

"But what if she doesn't? What if I go through with this craziness, and she likes being Amish. Then what?" His words were full of turmoil.

Silence filled the air and when Tina did speak again her voice was so low I had to quickly creep to the doorway to hear her. Sam followed me, and holding his breath, he leaned over my head to listen.

"I guess there is the chance that could happen, but I highly doubt it. And just think about it, these Amish people would take good physical care of her. And they are so strict she'd probably get in less trouble with them than she would here, being in this big house without adult supervision while you're at the hospital."

"Do you really think I should let her do this, Tina?" he asked, sounding pained.

"I don't think you have a lot of choices. Either you put her on lockdown and hire a security guard for her, or you let her experience this lifestyle and make up her own mind to walk away from it. Remember, no matter what you do, she'll be eighteen in no time at all. If she's kept away from him until then, she'll probably rush right into marriage with the guy right when her birthday arrives, which I'm sure you don't want either."

For what seemed like a few minutes, there was dead silence, then Dad spoke. "Okay, then. I'll take the biggest gamble of my life with my daughter's future, and we'll wait and see where the chips fall."

Then there was the muffled sound of kissing, and I stepped back from the door, jogging lightly up the stairs. Before I got the door shut, Sam appeared, not surprising me in the least.

"You know, Rose, if you do this you're making a huge mistake," he said.

But I was too happy to let him bring me down.

"Why don't you focus on your relationship with the Barbie doll and leave me alone, Sam. I appreciate all your concern, really I do, but you're wrong this time."

Amazingly, he let me shut the door.

I waited patiently for Dad and Tina to come to my room and tell me the news. Yes, she had a name now, and I was beginning to feel as if she was my best friend in the world after what she'd done for me.

It was a bit awkward, because I had to act surprised. I figured I did a pretty good job, but I'll probably never know if they realized I'd been eavesdropping. I hugged them both—Tina harder—and an hour later when they finally felt they'd covered every possible point of the discussion, they left me alone.

The door hardly had time to click shut before I was on the phone.

"Hello?"

It was Noah. I wondered briefly if he'd been out there in the shed with his still-damaged body, lying on some hay bale, waiting for me to call him.

"Noah, it's me."

"Are you okay, sweetheart?" he asked tensely.

"I'm good, Noah—real good, actually," I teased him.

"Why, what's going on?" His voice was clipped.

"Tina managed to talk Dad into letting me become Amish," I squeaked happily into the phone.

"Are you sure, Rose? Your father was so against it earlier."

"Well, there is a little catch," I said quietly.

"What catch?" Now he sounded tired.

"Dad and Tina think that I won't like being Amish and that I'll want to come home after a little while. That's why Dad's letting me do it—kind of reverse psychology or something."

Silence followed for an unbearably long time, and I was about to ask what he was thinking, when he said, "Do you think that will happen, Rose?"

Sighing into the phone for effect, I said with surety, "Of course not, Noah. By the time Dad realizes that I'm really going to convert, I'll be eighteen and then he won't be able to say a thing."

"I don't know if your father will give up that easily, but it's definitely a start for us." He still sounded doubtful.

"I love you, Noah." I tempted him into loosening up.

"I love you, too…. So when is this all going to take place?"

I worked hard to control my excitement when I said softly, "Tomorrow."

"What! Are you kidding me?" His voice was suddenly so animated, it was like talking to a different person.

"Dad thinks the sooner I start, the quicker I'll be running back, I guess," I said gently, hoping not to bug him again with the concept.

"All right, then, I'll go tell Father and Mother right now. They'll have to make the arrangements with the Hershbergers. And Mother has to finish your dress—but she's close to done with it, so it shouldn't be a problem," he said, excitement rising in his voice.

I was feeling a little more apprehensive when I asked, "What are the Hershbergers like?"

Noah rattled off, "Oh, you'll like them a lot, Rose. They're an older couple, and all their children are grown. Mother told me that Ruth was especially happy at the thought of having a new daughter around the house. They only live a mile away on Maple Ridge Road."

"Okay."

With trepidation he asked quietly, "You aren't having second thoughts, are you?"

"Absolutely not," I confirmed, still feeling the nausea in my belly.

"Good. I'll come by tomorrow at noon with Mother. Remember, for the most part, we won't be able to be alone together without an adult chaperone—except on Sunday nights."

A little worried, I asked, "Are you driving a buggy?"

I could imagine him rolling his eyes when he answered, "Of course, that's how we Amish usually get around." He must have sensed my confusion, because he went on to say, "I'll borrow Jacob's horse and buggy for now, but when we get closer to getting married, Father and Mother will buy us a new harness horse and a proper family buggy."

He said it so proudly that I had to smile. I was finally going to get to ride in a buggy after all this time, and that buggy would be rolling me into my new life and away from everything I'd ever known. I wished I could feel as confident about it on the inside as I displayed for everyone on the outside.

"Good night, Noah." I sighed into the phone.

"Good night, sweetheart—I'll see you tomorrow," he said in that sexy voice that made my knees weak.

Pulling the covers over my head, I tried not to let my brain dwell on Sam's words about me ruining my life, but still they prowled around in there, making sleep almost impossible.

How could I be ruining my life, when Noah was my whole life?

⋆ ⋆ ⋆

After a fitful night of tossing and turning, I figured I'd probably sleep until noon and not even be awake when Noah and his mom arrived. But my body shocked me, waking at seven in the morning to my utter distress.

I felt too tired to get up, but my nerves kept me from going back to sleep either, so pulling myself from bed, I took a long, hot shower before slipping into some comfortable sweatpants. I would really miss pants—especially jeans. I lamented about my favorite clothes while I moved around my room in a daze. I was unsure of what to pack, so I stuck to the basics: pajamas, a lot of panties, socks and a few bras.

After a while, I grew bored in my room and decided to venture out, risking contact with the other humans in the house.

Dad was already in the kitchen eating a bowl of cereal when I sneaked in, trying to keep a low profile.

It didn't work, though, when he said with a very awake and alert voice, "How'd you sleep, honey?"

"Okay."

"You know, Rose, no one is holding a gun to your head to do this. You can back out anytime," he said innocently, and I wondered about his doctor's sense of perception about people. He certainly seemed to be aware of my apprehension.

His choice of words weren't convincing, though. I wasn't the type of person to back out of something once I made a decision. I believed that when I got used to the whole being-Amish thing, and I was with Noah, I'd be perfectly fine—and my stomach would finally settle down.

"I'm going through with it, Dad. So don't go trying to change my mind," I said stubbornly.

"Oh, I wouldn't dream of it, honey. You're old enough to decide on your own."

He continued to flip through the newspaper, only partially paying any attention to me at all. His blasé attitude was starting to bug me, when he went on to say, "I went online last night and ordered your course books for this year. I'll have to come by your new house several times a week to collect your papers to grade." Offhandedly he added, "It sure would be easier if you could do the work on your laptop—any chance of that happening?"

I hadn't really thought about my computer but doubted it would be allowed. "I don't think that's feasible, Dad," I said, disappointed myself.

He rose up quickly, and after setting his bowl in the sink he caught me off guard by giving me a rib-crushing hug.

"If you need anything at all, Rosie, you call me or your brothers." He lifted my chin and his blue eyes bore into mine. "You understand that you're welcome back anytime of the day or night?"

I sniffed back the tears that were threatening to escape and nodded. "Mmm-hmm."

"I love you," he said, hugging me again even harder.

"I love you, too, Dad—and it's not like I'm going to be far away, just right up the road." I tried to convince him and myself.

"I know…. This is all just difficult for your old dad." Releasing me suddenly, he straightened. He said, "I have an early day at the hospital, so I need to get going. Call me tonight when you're settled, okay?"

"Sure thing." I still felt the tears rippling behind my eyes, but they didn't actually start falling until after he drove away, thank goodness.

If I was lucky, Sam and Justin would sleep until one o'clock, and I'd be long gone. I didn't want to endure another scene like that. Of course, I certainly wouldn't shed any tears for Sam, but I'd miss Justin a little bit.

The minutes crept along through the morning as I attempted to busy myself folding the laundry, emptying the dishwasher and even sweeping the floor. I felt bad that I was abandoning Dad and the barbarians, and I wondered if they'd be able to survive without a woman around the house, even one as domestically inept as me. But then I remembered that Tina and Dad would probably get hitched before Noah and I did, and then she could take over the "womanly duties." Even though I was eternally grateful to her for what she had done for me, I still felt a twang of jealousy toward her that curdled my belly even more than I was already experiencing.

Finally, at about eleven-thirty, I heard the clopping of hooves on the driveway and I pulled the curtain aside to watch Noah park the buggy by the walkway. His mother was the only one to get out, while the faint impression of his body remained in the driver's seat.

I ran down the stairs full blast and swung the door open at about the same time she made it to the porch.

Her smile was genuine, and she said cheerfully, "Rose, the color in your face is much brighter today."

"Really?" I didn't know what the heck she was talking about.

"Oh, yes, the last few times I've seen you, you were very pale looking." She stated it as if I was silly for not noticing.

It was then that I saw the sharp royal-blue cloth in her hands. Seeing me gazing at it curiously, she opened it up and held it out in front of her. "I hope you like it, Rose. I thought this shade of blue would match your eyes perfectly."

Cautiously taking the dress from her, I inspected it closely, and suddenly, overwhelmed by her kindness, my eyes flooded again. "Thank you so much, Mrs. Miller. It's beautiful," I croaked.

"Oh, dear child, I didn't mean to bring your tears again," she said, stepping forward and embracing me firmly. I sniffed, peering past her shoulder, out the door, hoping Noah didn't see me crying again. I had promised, after all, that I would dry it up.

Thankfully, Mrs. Miller shuffled me up the stairs and away from the doorway. Once in my room, she helped me change into the dress, and I felt extremely self-conscious in my panties and bra in front of her, but she took it in stride. She did have a couple of teenage daughters already, so nothing about me was sure to shock her.

Well, except maybe my underwear. I noticed her going through the things I had thrown into the duffel bag. Her eyebrows lifted several times at the Victoria's Secret clearance buys. Oh, well, I was sure that someday Noah would appreciate them. I had to turn away to hide the heat spreading on my face.

The dress fit as perfectly as a frumpy, polyester material-style garment could. Poly pebble is what she called it. Geez, I never knew there were different kinds of polyester. I sure had a lot to learn. But at least she was right. The color did look good on me. Then came the annoying part—getting all my hair up in the little cap. I sat down at the vanity and she began her work. Amazingly, it only took her a matter of a minute to pull it up, twist it and pin it to my head.

"My word, you have wonderful hair," she commented, adding more of the pokey pins.

"Ouch…thanks," I muttered, getting thoroughly irked by the poking.

I had to admit, she did finish quickly, though. A few sec-

onds later the pristine white cap was stuck to my head like
Velcro with an actual pin stuck through the top of the cap and
into my bun to keep it from blowing off my head. Mrs. Miller
directed my fingers to it to feel where it was located, warning me to remember that it was there and to be careful not to
try to jerk the cap from my head without removing the pin.

Gazing at myself in the mirror, I thought, *Holy crap—I look
like one of them.* It was amazing what a cap and a dress could
do for a girl's appearance. Immediately, fear gripped me that
Noah wouldn't find me attractive anymore. After all, now I
looked like all the other girls he found so boring.

I continued to worry about it while Mrs. Miller led me
down the stairs. That was until we ran into Sam and Justin
coming out of the TV room, and all thoughts vanished from
my mind when I saw the look of shock on Justin's face. The
poor kid wasn't expecting to see his big sister looking as if she
had stepped out of one of the John Wayne movies he loved
so much. Sam, on the other hand, reacted just as I expected,
by laughing so hard he had to brace himself against the wall
for support.

Mrs. Miller looked at him disapprovingly. I felt like telling
her not to bother, my brother was completely shameless, but
instead I focused my attention on poor Justin and went over,
pulling him into my arms and giving him a big hug.

"Are you really doing this, Rose?" he asked with wide eyes.

Trying to ignore Sam's snorting noises, I told him gently,
"Yeah. I made my mind up—I'll do whatever it takes to be
with Noah. Dad will explain it all to you tonight, Justin. Don't
worry, I'll come back and visit you every week. I promise."

Knowing that I'd be sobbing in no time if I had to keep
looking at my little brother's stricken face, I swept through

the door, but not before I stuck my tongue out at Sam, hoping that Mrs. Miller hadn't seen.

For some reason the sound of the door closing behind me was significant, and my stomach tightened at the thud. I was brave, though, and I didn't look back. I couldn't look back or I'd probably lose my nerve and run to the house.

So, straightening my back, I walked to the buggy, again wondering what Noah would think seeing me dressed like this. I didn't have to wait long, because he leaned out the buggy door to get a better look as I approached.

His raccoon eyes raked up and down quickly several times, causing that pleasant fluttering to replace the icky feeling I'd been harboring for two days. Then a broad grin erupted on his lips.

"I don't know how it's possible to make an Amish dress look beautiful, but you can sure do it." He said it right in front of his mom, to my horror.

"Mind your tongue, Noah, or you'll be having a talk with your father," Mrs. Miller reprimanded him.

I was heading to the backseat of the buggy, but Noah quickly motioned me to sit next to him with his hand patting the seat beside him.

Nervously, I glanced at his mother, relieved that she smiled with controlled amusement. She said, "That's fine, Rose. You may sit beside each other. I'll ride in the back."

This was all too weird. I grasped the hand Noah offered and climbed carefully in beside him, trying not to jostle his metal brace. For all the strangeness of sitting in the buggy with the funny dress and cap on, when I gazed up at Noah, all those feelings disappeared.

With him beside me, everything felt right—perfect, to be exact.

Not letting go of my hand, he bent forward and whispered in my ear, "I love you so much, Rose. Everything's going to be fine now." His smile filled me with confidence and hope. The squeeze of his hand gave me strength.

Nodding my head softly, I murmured, "I know. I believe you, Noah."

"Wait, Rose. Wait!" It was Justin. He was running from the house with little Hope bouncing in his arms. I held back another urge to cry, thinking how I'd miss the furry little booger. When my brother reached the buggy, he did something totally unexpected and wonderful, by holding the ball of fluff up to me.

"She's your puppy. You should take her with you to keep you company." His voice sounded more self-assured than I'd ever heard from him, and his face was set with conviction.

"Are you sure, Justin?" My heart hammered in my chest, hopeful.

"Yeah, you can bring her when you visit. And, Rose?"

Taking Hope from his grasp and settling her into the extra folds of my dress, I looked down at him with fondness. "Yes?"

"Can I come see you?" he asked worriedly, glancing down at the gravel.

"Of course you can, Justin. Anytime at all."

He looked up then with a relieved smile. "Okay, I'll see you later."

And with a last big grin for me he whipped around, jogging back to the house. Sam was waiting for him at the door with a sour face, and I promptly looked straight ahead, breathing in deep. Noah's hand squeezed mine, reminding me he was there with me, and I wasn't alone. But I couldn't help swallowing hard, struggling to keep the tears in.

As if he was afraid I was about to change my mind, he let

go of my hand and taking up the long reins, suddenly flicked them. The buggy lurched forward, sending me back against the cushioned seat with a jolt. Making a wide turn, we passed Lady, who had stopped her grazing to prance along the fence as we went by. Jacob was coming back for my mare later that day. Noah had promised me the Hershbergers had a nice field and barn for her. With my horse and puppy with me, I wouldn't be alone at the Amish house after all, and that made me feel more confident still.

Turning onto the road, I was amazed at how fast we were going. I worriedly glanced around for cars or—trucks. Noah saw what I was doing, and he smiled reassuringly, placing the reins into one hand. He took my hand into his free one and for the first time in a while, he did the swirly thing with his thumb. Once again, all was right in the world.

Yeah, I still had a nagging feeling, way deep down, that I was not doing the right thing, but I rationalized to myself that nothing is set in stone. I could still go back home if things didn't work out. And maybe this sojourn would give me the time to change Noah's mind about becoming English. There was no way I was saying anything to him about my backup plan, though. I was just going to have to keep my thoughts to myself for the time being. Perhaps I'd like being Amish. I certainly wouldn't know till I gave it a try.

That's what I was going to do—*try*.

Seeing the bright sun shining down on the passing hay fields, and feeling the warm air whip through the open buggy windows, I convinced myself I could do this. As long as Noah was beside me, I could do anything.

And I was determined to be with him, no matter which world we ended up living in.

★ ★ ★ ★ ★

Is love enough to keep Rose and Noah together?
Turn the page for a sneak peek
at the next novel in
the TEMPTATION *series*

Sam

DAMN. IT REALLY SUCKED PLAYING THE SPY FOR Dad. I tried to keep my eyes locked on the red minivan as I maneuvered through traffic on the increasingly slippery road. The blue pickup that passed in front of me momentarily broke my eye contact with the van. *Shit.* I couldn't lose it now. I sped up and managed to get enough speed to inch past the car. Not really enough room for my dually to politely get back in front of it in the heavy traffic, but hell, I was on a mission.

Gunning the engine, I made it back into a spot where I could see the white bonnets bobbing around in the van. Good. I was still with 'em. The rain mix that had been falling all day had picked now to turn to snow, and the large puffy shapes were dotting the windshield in ever-increasing intensity.

It was just dumb luck that I'd spotted the minivan filled with Amish women drive by as I was pulling out of the school parking lot. A little Mario Andretti driving and I managed to catch up to 'em. I knew the chances of one of those goofy caps being on my sister's head were pretty slim, but I'd take the gamble. It was worth it. I guess.

The minivan got into the right turning lane and I backed off a bit, not wanting to be noticed by Rose if she was in the vehicle. I followed it into the Walmart parking lot.

"What are you doing, Sam? We're supposed to be at Jason's house in about twenty minutes," Hunter asked with an edge to his voice.

I glanced over at him briefly. Even though it had been several months, I was still pissed off about his overly aggressive moves on Rose. Hell, if he'd been a little more charming, I wouldn't be here stalking my little sister like a maniac.

"Quiet. I'm trying to think," I shot back at him, ignoring his aggravated grunt.

From what I could see, the lady driving the minivan was, oh, probably in her forties with short reddish hair. I'd seen the woman driving the Amish around town in her van but hadn't taken much notice of her before now. She didn't work too hard for a parking spot close to the store, instead pulling the van into the first space she came to at the back of the lot. I found a space in the next row, about four cars away. I positioned my truck facing the back of the van, but not in an obvious location where I'd be seen. Hey, I'm pretty good at this secret-agent crap, I decided as I cut the engine and waited for the occupants of the van to file out.

No. The first two weren't her. But it was damn near impossible to tell with them all dressed the same. And now they were all sporting larger black caps that seemed to be fitted over the white ones, which made seeing their faces even more difficult. The only difference I could register in my head were the varying shades of blue skirts the girls wore, whipping out in the wind below their black coats. That was it. I still couldn't believe that Rose would be dressing like that—and all for a guy.

I couldn't help chuckling when I got a good look at the last girl slipping out of the van. It was Rose—must be my lucky day. I patiently waited, watching the small group head for the store's entrance. Funny, she actually moved differently than the other three girls and two older women she was with. Rose had a more confident stride, her back straight, looking around the parking lot as if she was purposely searching for someone. Hmm, maybe this chance encounter was serendipitous after all.

"Are you following Rose?" Hunter asked quietly, as if it was a big secret.

When I swiveled around, I could see that he was doing the same thing as me; staring at the Amish women as they made their way to the store.

"Yeah, got a problem with it?"

"Heck, no, I've been dying to see her again," Hunter said, still stalking my sister with his eyes.

I could only breathe out my disgust and ignore his comment. After all, who was I to detour the guy from liking a pretty girl. And there was still a chance that he could woo Rose away from Mr. Suspenders.

"Look, I've got to talk to my sister, but we have to be careful about this. I don't want to freak her out or anything." Then as an afterthought, I added, "Or get her into trouble with those Amish people."

"Hey, maybe if they got mad at her, they'd kick her out of their club. Then she'd have to come back to the real world and get on with her life," Hunter suggested.

He had a point. Sometimes I forgot that Hunter was a pretty smart guy. He took all the same accelerated classes I took and got mostly A's. The dumb-jock thing with him was just a facade. He actually had a brain in that pro-athlete body.

As I grasped the door handle, I said, "Yeah, and you'll be waiting for her in the real world, right?"

"Maybe" was all Hunter said as he jumped out of the truck and met me on my side, waiting.

I didn't like the nervous feeling spreading through my body like a grass fire. I was going to talk to my sister, not face a firing squad, I reasoned to myself. The flakes of snow were changing back to rain again, splashing my face and head as they came down with more force. What a miserable day. The weather had definitely soured my mood, and having to deal with Rose's bizarre act of rebellion was putting a hard edge on my emotions as I walked through the automated doors alongside Hunter. I tried to soften my face a bit so I wouldn't scare the old lady greeting the customers in the doorway. When she looked my way, I rewarded her with a big smile. The way she smiled back, warmly, like a proud grandma, I knew I'd won her over.

Now on to business, I hesitated only a second before heading toward the grocery aisles. Hunter slunk along beside me silently. Maybe he was nervous about the encounter, too? He hadn't been around Rose since the night of the wreck. Serve him right if he had nails rolling around in his stomach.

Glancing down the rows from left to right, I spotted a few of the Amish women pushing a cart down the bread aisle. Nope. Rose wasn't with 'em. I continued my search, hoping I'd catch her alone.

After several minutes and exhausting the grocery section, Hunter and I headed over to the beauty stuff. Hunter suggested it, and it was a good bet she'd be there. When I finally found her, she was staring at some bottles of lotion, looking pretty bored, too. The Amish girl standing with her looked like Noah's sister. Couldn't remember her name, but I think she was the older one.

"Hey, sis, did they allow you out of the house today?" From the look on her face, it was probably not the best thing to have said to her straight off. Her eyes threw daggers at me.

She breathed in deep and when she exhaled, a growling sound came with it.

"I see you're still a jerk, huh, Sam?" Her voice was colder than the weather outside.

Hunter almost laughed but swallowed the sound, a little too late, because now Rose's icy glare was directed at him.

Clearing his throat, Hunter said, "Hey, Rose. It's good to see you."

"Sorry, I can't say the same," she replied rudely.

Man, she was in a fouler mood than I was. Before it got into a shouting match, I altered my voice and said as nicely as I could manage, "I just want to talk to you, Rose, just for minute."

The Amish girl then piped up, "Rose, I think we better get going."

Now Rose shot her friend an irritated look, and after chewing on her lip for a few seconds, she glanced from me back to the Amish chick.

"Sarah, I want to talk to Sam alone. Okay?" Her voice was amicable to an untrained ear. But to me, I knew what she was really saying was *You better get the heck out of my way and let me do what I want.*

Sarah stepped closer to Rose and whispered just loud enough that I could hear, "Are you sure?"

"Yep, I'll catch up with you at the van," Rose said smoothly, with no room for an argument.

Sarah sighed but did what Rose said, walking away; smart girl.

Rose then glanced around with nervous energy. "We need to go somewhere more private, Sam."

Her voice carried a kind of vulnerable twang to it. A sound I hadn't heard coming from her mouth since she was ten.

Shucks. That brotherly protectiveness began invading my senses.

"Let's go to my truck," I suggested.

She shook her head. "No. I can't do that." After another birdlike look around, she said, "Just follow me."

Before Hunter had the chance to shift his weight, Rose held her hand out, narrowing her eyes at him. "Not you."

It was hard to believe, but for a brief second, a look of hurt flickered across Hunter's face. I almost felt sorry for the guy.

"Go on to the truck, Hunter. I'll be there in a few," I told him.

Hunter started to turn, hesitated and moved toward Rose in a blur. He got pretty damn close to her, and even though I could tell she wanted to step back, she held her ground, only swaying her upper body back a bit.

"Look, Rose, I'm really sorry about everything that happened that night." He paused, with a deeply drawn breath. "I hope whenever your life gets straightened out, we can be friends." Hunter waited for her to respond, but when it was obvious she wasn't going to saying anything, he left us, moving briskly away.

"That was kind of harsh."

"Why? I didn't say any of the things I was thinking," she mumbled as she headed toward the back of the store.

She was just clueless. "Sometimes not saying anything is even worse than chewing someone out," I informed her.

"Oh, are you a relationship counselor now?" she asked sarcastically, turning right past the shoes and then left along the aisle at the back of the store. I had to hustle to keep up with her feverish stride. She finally stopped by an end cap filled with green bags of cat food. Dozens of faces of smiling tabbies stared at me.

She turned to face me after another quick search around her. "What do you want, Sam?"

Okay, now what do I say? I'd had my little speech memorized in my head for weeks, but now, seeing my sister in the flesh, dressed in the ridiculous clothes, I could only laugh at her. That didn't go over well. *Wham.* She smacked me across the chest.

"I don't have time for your comedy show, Sam." She looked behind her and then over my shoulder, before saying in a frustrated hiss, "I don't have much time at all, so if you have something to say, out with it already."

I got myself under control, but damn, it was going to be difficult to have a serious conversation with her dressed like that. "Okay. Okay. I'm sorry. You've got to understand, you just look strange to me." Rose folded her arms across her chest, popping one hip up while she waited for me to continue. She was still not happy with me. And she didn't seem to understand at all.

"You know, Dad and Justin, Aunt Debbie, they were all really upset that you didn't come see us for your birthday." That was the number-one thing off my chest.

She sniffed. Avoiding my eyes, she said, "Yeah, I'm sure they were."

"Well, what about it? Aren't you allowed to be around your family anymore?"

Rose shifted uneasily, not answering me. Her being without words told me something was definitely up.

"Come on, Rose. What's going on in your little Amish world?" Seeing her lips tighten, I surged on with my interrogation. "Are you happy with all the rules? Are you enjoying the fact that you have no freedom at all?" Still there was no response from her. "Is Noah really worth it?"

That got her. She locked her blue eyes on me and whispered, "Yes, he's worth it." She sighed, then leaned back against the cat food and blew out hard, angrily. "But it's been more difficult than I ever imagined."

"Have they been mean to you?"

She shook her head. "No…not really, they are just *very* controlling. You wouldn't believe the half of it." She stopped to check the vicinity again, then she rolled on, "I can't even wear my lace-up boots when I ride." She said it as if it was the worst thing in the world.

I shrugged. "Why not?"

She said fiercely, "Because the elders think they're too flashy. Can you imagine, my old, dingy brown boots *flashy?* And that's just the beginning of it, Sam. I can't even wear a watch!" she nearly shrieked, although quietly.

"Then why don't you get out of there?"

"I love Noah, that's why."

"So you're going to live this way, miserable, for the rest of your life?"

"Well, it's not all bad. The Millers and the Hershbergers are so nice to me. And I've made friends."

"You didn't answer my question. Are you going to continue with this craziness, or what?" I was becoming irritated with her, and it probably showed in my voice, although I was really trying to sound amicable.

She pushed away from the bags and invaded my personal space. When she was close enough that she must have felt that no one sneaking up on her would hear, she breathed out, "I think Noah might go English."

I couldn't help feeling exasperated with her. "Oh, come on, Rose, we've been through this before." When I saw her hopeful eyes, I asked, "Why, has something changed with him?"

"No, not exactly, but I think he might be coming around to my side." She said it a little sheepishly, and I suddenly felt sorry for nature boy.

"So, your plans all along were to convert Noah—and not really stay Amish yourself? Is that it?"

"No, Sam. I'll stay Amish if that's what it takes to be with Noah." She looked dramatically horrified at my question.

"You're not convincing me. And besides, how much time are you going to waste on this endeavor? The holidays are in a couple of weeks. Are you planning to shun your family for Christmas?" Number-two thing was now off my chest. I leveled a hard look at her, but I thought that I was being pretty mild. She needed some sense shaken into her.

"Oh, I don't know. I really want to see you all for the holidays, but Ruth and James have so much family to visit. And there is *so* much work that needs to be done."

Then she rambled on for a few minutes, something about Mrs. Hershberger's daughter having twins and having to do her laundry for her, scrubbing a fence by hand and making two hundred Whoopee Pies for some event. I tuned it all out. None of it mattered in the least. Really, my sis was losing her freak'n mind.

I interrupted her. "Look, Dad wants to see you for Christmas, and that's the end of it. So you better work it out."

"Yeah, I'll do the best I can," she murmured, staring off into space like a zombie.

"We're all going to Cincinnati to stay at Aunt Debbie's for the holidays. Just think about it, Rose—you can hang out with Amanda and Britney, and go shopping at the mall with

Aunt Debbie for the last-minute sales. You'd have a blast, and it would be really good for you."

"Oh, I don't think I'll be allowed to go away for that long."

"Why don't you just bring Noah with you."

I thought it was the perfect solution, but when she rolled her eyes and spat, "No way will they let him do that. He'd have to have an Amish adult chaperone along, and that would be just terrible—as if his folks would even let him leave town during Christmastime anyway," she said, pouting.

Before I had a chance to respond, a couple of Amish women appeared at the end of the aisle. At that moment, they reminded me of a pair of harpies that just found lunch.

"Rose. Come with us now. We must go," the older, gray-haired lady said. I figured she was the infamous Mrs. Hershberger. She was a little chubby, still managing to be sharp-faced. Other than that, there wasn't anything really distinguishable about her.

"Coming." Rose gave me a fake smile, before whirling and darting over to join the women. When she met up with them, both women put a hand on either of her shoulders and guided her out of my sight.

Shoot. What a mess Rose was in. It was obvious she wasn't enjoying being Amish, and it was just a matter of time before her house of cards collapsed. But I still had the nagging feeling that the fool girl might do something insane, like marry Noah, before she got her head on straight.

Well, if I had anything to do with it, that wasn't going to happen. I'd tell Dad about my encounter with Rose when I got home, and I'd encourage him to go ahead with the family crisis intervention plan he'd been talking about. That's what he called it, but what Dad really meant to do was to kidnap Rose from the Amish and force her to live in Cincinnati with Aunt Debbie and Uncle Will. This charade had gone on long enough. We'd all figured she'd only last a few weeks at most with the strict disciplinary lifestyle of these people. But to all our amazement, especially Tina's, she'd proven she had a pretty tough constitution. Four months was enough, though.

A discussion I'd had with Summer weeks ago materialized in my mind, and after a few seconds of digesting the information, a plan began to sprout. Someday Rose would thank me for it. But I figured there'd be a whole lot of squalling first.

I slowly walked through the store, not paying any attention to the people passing by me. I was too absorbed in thought. Yeah, Dad needed to take action—the sooner the better.

Acknowledgments

I CERTAINLY WOULD NEVER HAVE SEEN MY characters bound forever in the pages of a real book without the love, encouragement and help of too many people to count, and I'm grateful to each and every one of them!

None of this would be possible if Christina Hogrebe of the Jane Rotrosen Agency hadn't seen the glorious possibilities of Rose and Noah's love story, opening that first door for me. Not only has she turned out to be the best partner in the publishing world I could have, but also an excellent therapist when needed and I owe her many thanks on both accounts.

The Harlequin Teen editorial team did a fine job taking care of me throughout the intimidating process of polishing a book for publication, and I want to give a shout of thanks to Adam Wilson for guiding me into my first revision with expertise, understanding and a curiosity for the Amish world, which gave me much fodder to work with and a few laughs besides. Also, big thanks to Natashya Wilson and T.S. Ferguson; their insights and enthusiasm helped refine the story to its very best and have laid the groundwork for the series to prosper.

Special thanks to: my children, Luke, Cole, Lily, Owen and Cora, for putting up with everything—I love you all too much to explain in words; my mother, Marilyn, an avid reader of anything worth reading, who not only encouraged me to follow my dreams, but read all that I wrote, sometimes repeatedly, and gave me her honest opinion every time. I can't thank you enough for all the time you've invested in my blossoming career—I love you; the men in my life, my father, Anthony, my brother, Tony, and my nephew, Jamey, who not only guided me with advice and wisdom when I needed it most, but also helped me with the basics of survival—many hugs to each of you.

Only the friendship and affection of many close friends and family kept my head above water and my focus aimed straight during the making of this novel. The following are some of those people, whom I thank from the bottom of my heart for listening, talking, showing generosity and just plain being there: Devin, Kendra, Kelsey, Grace, Jay, Helen, Carey, Opal, Marian, Tyler, Ange G., Erin, Lane, Matthias, Larry, Tammy, the Dean family and all my friends at Kroger, Maysville.

I would be remiss not to mention the wonderful people of the May's Lick Amish community who inspired me to write this book in the first place. I am humbled by the kindness shown to me and my children since our arrival in Kentucky, and I still delight in seeing the buggies whisking down the road.

"Success is sweeter and sweeter if long delayed and gotten through many struggles and defeats."

~Amos Bronson Alcott